I0631706

Levi Samuel was born in 1986 in Elk City Oklahoma, though he was raised in Springfield Missouri. While in high school, he discovered the game, Dungeons and Dragons, as well as a Live Action Role Playing group, where he truly discovered who he was. Graduating high school, he joined the Army, but quickly realized that wasn't the life for him. He returned home and went to work in manual labor jobs. Being a quick study, he became a skilled tradesman in a number of fields, but the quest for happiness and purpose evaded him. In 2008 he became a father and has raised his daughter by himself ever since. In 2009, he decided to write a book, which was the start to a lifelong and rewarding career. His first book was published in 2013 under a penname. He's since established a laundry list of qualifications and achievements. Levi lives with his daughter and their cat, Alona. Though they moved in November 2018 to take care of his grandfather.
Please subscribe to my newsletter for first access to all new content.
http://eepurl.com/dxRUvL

In many ways this was my first book. I've learned a lot from it since I wrote the initial draft so long ago. And now that I'm able to experience the finished product, I very much enjoyed reading it. I hope you will too. I would ask a small favor of you, dear reader. Whether you enjoy this book or not, please leave a review at your preferred online retailer. Reviews tell me how I can improve my craft. But they also help other readers to decide if they're willing to take a chance or not.

Thank you,
Levi Samuel

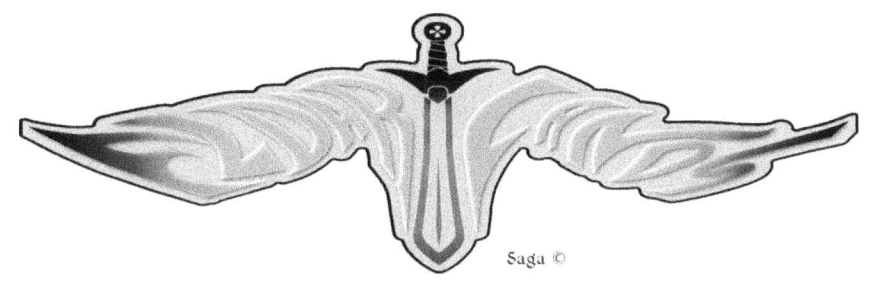

Saga ©

Nightking Duology
Volume One

RISE
OF THE
NIGHTKINGS

Levi Samuel

PUBLISHING

ELDARLANDS©
Nightking Duology – Volume One

RISE OF THE NIGHTKINGS
Eldarlands Publishing
Copyright © 2015-2019

The story, cover art, and illustrations by Levi Samuel.

Genre: Fantasy / Series

ISBN: 1-950541-00-2
ISBN-13: 978-1-950541-00-3

Find all the author's projects at http://www.LeviSamuel.com

In memory of Kevin Edmonds
1964-2018
I didn't have the chance to know you as your family did. But you raised a
strong daughter, who has been a good friend to me. Without her, I
wouldn't have been able to write this book as I have. You will be missed.

Tredensil Kingdom

Contents

Prologue
For Whom the Bell Tolls

A thundering quake echoed through the foundation of Icefall Citadel. There was little doubt the ramparts had fallen. Tremors grew closer, more frequent. That could only mean one thing. The resistance reached the keep.

Stuffing the final components into the pocket of her quiver, Inyalia slung it over her shoulder and quickly strode from her quarters. Her mind raced with excitement and enthusiasm. Who could have guessed they'd turn their attention toward her? The young nightking, so taken by his thirst for power since the defeat of Rezerik, had formed an alliance with the resistance. It was no surprise really. They sought to use him before the corruption became too strong. Before he'd become as dark and twisted as his predecessor. Inyalia recalled a similar station when she ascended the throne herself. But time for recollection would have to wait. She needed to flee, to fall back before the castle was overrun.

Rounding the corner, sounds of battle echoed off the stone walls, ringing out sword on sword in the distance. They'd breeched the courtyard. Inyalia calmly made her way toward the commotion, keeping an eye to the distance. The last thing she wanted was attention. Finding her query, a thick tapestry dangling from a suspended iron rod, she lifted the heavy fabric depicting a white stag skull set in a field of deep blue. A wooden door rested subtly behind it, out of sight for ages. The grain was rough and petrified, having hung in place for so long. She slowly twisted the iron latch and pressed the door inward. The rusted hinges creaked eerily, revealing a long and dark passage into the castle's underbelly.

The cool temperature held the rancid stench at bay, but it was growing stronger in her descent. Her elevated senses didn't help. Though it was also a blessing in times such as these. She could detect the slightest change at a moment's notice. Sure, when faced with the lingering stench of rotting feces and discarded waste, it was a bit of a nuisance. But had her senses not been so keen, she never would have known she wasn't alone. That knowledge was likely to see her safely from this place.

Following her internal compass, Inyalia turned east, approaching a rusted and broken grate. The stone had washed away, weakening the iron bars over time. Grabbing the metal lattice, she yanked as hard as she could. The corroded stone crumbled and the embedded bars tore free. As quiet as possible, Inyalia laid it beside the hole and crawled through.

The walls and floor were made of the same brick, packed tightly together. Though a few had fallen from their mortar here and there. The curved surface was moist and slick. It felt more like the inside of a tube than a corridor. Moss grew along the brick, tracing the grout lines where the shaped stones met. It was thick and patchy. She'd have to watch her step. A fall could potentially alert others to her presence, but that was minute compared to the dangers before her. She was familiar with this moss. The very poisons she carried had been made from it. The slightest touch could release the deadly spores, ending her escape plan long before she reached the outside world. Selecting her path, Inyalia stepped over a large patch and worked her way to the gathered water in the center. She counted her blessings. Were it not for the tunnel's tubular shape, she'd be walking in fetid and stagnant waste. And while the incline was less than ideal, it provided a decent walking path. A mild breeze traveled through the musty tunnel, guiding her escape.

Inyalia traveled the maze of corridors, turning left, then right, following not only the breeze but her memory of this place. It'd taken nearly two-hundred human years to memorize every twist and turn the labyrinth had to offer. Time well spent for one of her position. Her life wasn't one of luxury. Precautions had become a second nature.

The crisp outside air rushed through the tunnel, freezing the hair inside her nose. The sticky fibers thawed with each breath. Paying close attention to the scent, Inyalia knew the trespassers weren't far behind her. A wicked smirk formed upon her lips. If they were foolish enough to pursue her, their choice had already been made. Stepping near the glossy bricks, Inyalia waited for her target to present itself. As expected, footsteps echoed around the bend. She could see the flicker of torchlight growing closer. It betrayed them. Had she not caught their scent, the open flame would have certainly given them away. Fortunately, she didn't require such crutches. Her eyes could perceive even the smallest light, making sight possible in everything but complete darkness. Standing perfectly still, Inyalia prepared herself, awaiting the slightest movement. Finally, a warmth caressed her. Though it wasn't just any warmth. This was body heat, felt nearly thirty yards away. She could feel the torch too, but that was brazen. This was subtle, minute in comparison. And there were multiple sources.

Without hesitation, Inyalia kicked against the wall, sprinting along its curved slope. It was her speed that carried her. Nearing her target, she locked her fingers around the unstrung bow resting in her quiver.

Two men exited a side passage, pausing at the intersection. They were dressed for battle, and on the hunt. Their eyes widened, adjusting to the woman shrouded in darkness at the edge of their torchlight and rapidly growing closer. Unprepared, they reached for weapons.

Denying time, Inyalia was upon them. Swinging her arm as if cracking a whip, her bow came free whistling as the solid shaft impacted the closest man's head. He toppled and dropped the torch. Landing in the muck, it sizzled and went out. Inyalia spun opposite her swing, feeling the wood flex from impact. With trained precision, she released the string and looped it around the polished notch. Her other hand drew an arrow, nocking it before the string went taut.

A solid thud impacted the man's chest. He staggered backward, staring shocked at the thick wooden shaft protruding from him. Pain registered and he fell to his knees.

Inyalia watched the trespasser collapse. He was dead before he hit the ground. If not from her masterfully aimed shot, then from the moss's poison coating her arrowheads. She heard more footsteps down the tunnel. Another torch came into view.

"There she is. Get her!" Two of the newcomers stepped into view, firing crossbows. Another three charged around them, swords drawn.

Inyalia spun, throwing her back against the moist wall. Bolts plinked off the stone behind her. Another arrow nocked and aimed, Inyalia felt the torque as it twisted off the string, impacting its target almost instantly.

One of the swordsmen staggered and fell face first. His weight carried him several feet, sloshing muddy waste about the place.

Nocking two arrows at once, Inyalia spaced the shafts with her finger. Cocking the bow sideways, providing a steady platform, she selected her targets. The charging swordsmen were a growing threat, but the crossbowmen were nearly ready to fire again. They were the largest threat, as they could catch her off-guard. Taking aim, Inyalia released. Both arrows found their marks. The crossbowmen, one elf, the other human, were dead before they finished loading. Slinging her bow around her torso, Inyalia drew her sword. She raised it just in time to deflect a deadly slice. Rolling her wrist, the sharpened steel cut through flesh and bone, severing the hand of her attacker.

The man screamed, grabbing his bloody nub. His sword hit the bricked floor, still clenched in his weakening grip.

Refusing mercy, Inyalia brought her sword around, severing the man's head and silencing his screams. Twisting at the last moment, avoiding a potentially deadly blow, she felt the impact in her side. She crashed to the floor, her assailant atop her. Narrowly able to keep grip on her weapon, she bucked, throwing the man overhead. It freed her, but she was now open for attack.

The prone swordsmen scurried to find his feet. He had a small window before she'd regain the advantage.

Cautiously, the third swordsman approached the prone nightking. Sword at the ready, he stabbed, hoping to run her through before she could recover.

Inyalia rolled, swinging blindly. She needed to get back to her feet. But doing so while flanked was dangerous. Feeling her sword impact, she stole a glance. The tip had buried itself in the standing man's ribs. She'd gotten lucky. He'd lunged at the wrong time, impaling himself upon her blade. Retracting her sword, blood and intestine fell from the wound. He'd soon be dead. But until then he was still a threat. Weighing her options, Inyalia launched her sword at the disemboweled man, releasing at the apex of her swing. She knew it was a foolish decision, but the long blade was next to useless in her current position. And getting to her feet would be difficult, if not impossible, while flanked.

The sharpened steel pierced the man's throat, lodging itself mid-blade. Instinctively, he grabbed his neck. The sudden movement opened him wider, spilling his bowels further. Uncontrollable wheezing escaped as he suffocated and drowned at the same time. His skin turned pale with loss of blood. Staggering, he stumbled and fell forward, landing beside the prone nightking.

Inyalia stole a glance at the one who'd charged her. He was nearly on his feet, and she was unarmed. But there were still a few moments remaining. Seizing the opportunity, Inyalia grabbed hold of his dead companion. Using his weight, she rolled and launched the corpse.

The body hit the wall with a thud, rolling down the curved surface and into the remaining man's legs. Unprepared for the sudden impact, he landed atop the body and rolled with it to the tunnel's center.

Wasting no time, Inyalia brought her armored leg around, kicking as hard as she could. The thick heeled boot caught the man in the mouth.

A sickening pop echoed in the narrow corridor. Eyes rolling, the man collapsed, his slack face disappearing beneath the putrid sludge.

Inyalia got to her feet and approached the unconscious man. Grabbing his chainmail sleeve, she pulled him from the muck, rolling him to his back. It was one thing to kill a man in battle, but to let him drown seemed almost cruel. She looked upon him with pity. His tongue had gotten caught between his teeth and her boot. Only a sliver of useless meat kept it attached. Between that and the damage she'd inflicted, he was unlikely to ever speak again. That meant he couldn't report her presence, provided she let him live. But life in his current state seemed almost cruel. It'd be kinder to end his misery.

An inkling of remorse coursed through her, disappearing almost as quick. She recalled a memory of a time when dealing death wasn't so familiar. Taking a deep breath, she made her decision. Inyalia withdrew her sword from his companion. It desperately needed to be cleaned. But now was not the time. Positioning the tip, she closed her eyes, thrusting the blade quickly and keenly. It slid easily into his spine, offering only minor resistance. His body twitched as the sharpened edge destroyed everything that was left of him. A final gasp escaped, and he fell still.

Inyalia removed her sword, wiping the excess blood and grime onto one of the other bodies. She'd done enough to this one already. Smearing the single tear upon her cheek, she inspected the wet area clinging to her glove. That was all she would shed for these men, but it was more than most received. She didn't particularly like killing, especially when they were no longer trying to kill her. But when she had to, it was best to make it as painless as possible.

Taking a deep breath, Inyalia allowed the frozen air to surround her. She liked the cold. It reminded her of what she had to do. Stealing herself, Inyalia glanced at the bodies. She couldn't leave them like this, not so close to her exit. Any half decent tracker would be able to follow this trail straight to her. She had to cover things up a bit. Only then would she be able to leave undetected.

Inyalia drug the bodies to the last intersection. Strategically positioning them to remove any sign of direction or destination, while adding it elsewhere, she made the scene so confusing that anyone who stumbled upon this massacre would have no idea which direction to follow. That was all she could hope for. Covering tracks was little more than a shell game. If she had to leave a trail, leaving overwhelming options was the only way to go. And once she was through, they wouldn't even have the breeze to follow.

The moonlight glowed bright, illuminating the labyrinth's only escape. This was the only place in all of Irayth where the clouds didn't completely block out the sky. That was part of why she'd claimed it. But even with the partial clearing, it wouldn't have been so bright if not for the thick layer of powdery substance covering the ground. The northern lands had been frozen for centuries, creating an inhospitable terrain that only the strongest dared travel. It was also where the shadow had the strongest hold. But here, the mixture of ash and snow, reflected the light. It was minimal, but it seemed to keep the shadow at bey. In a world covered by a perpetual blanket of black rolling clouds under a red sky, minimal was often enough.

The night seemed almost tranquil. If not for the battle echoing in the distance, Inyalia could have enjoyed its serenity. The frozen winds brushed against her pale skin, carrying strands of dark hair about her face. Tucking it behind her pointed ears, she stepped from the sewer opening and onto the icy ledge. Turning, she grabbed hold of the iron handle protruding from the wall. It was stiff, but she'd expected as much. Giving a firm tug, the hidden gears began to clank, and a solid iron barrier began to slide into place. Within moments it completely covered the tunnel, blocking both light and air from entering. It would also mean flooding for anyone unfortunate enough to remain inside. Locking the iris into place, Inyalia turned her attention to the column of ice. Over time, the trickle of drainage had formed into a thick pillar, connecting the sewage tunnel to the frozen ground beneath.

Carefully, Inyalia climbed onto the massive sickle and slid to its base, faster than desired. She landed hard, her leather boots unable to keep traction against the frozen slab. She collapsed into a heap, hearing the violent pop inside her legs. It didn't hurt. It happened too fast for that. Glancing down, she knew both legs were broken.

Rolling away from the pillar, Inyalia untangled herself and sat up. Grabbing the armor of her left leg, she twisted, forcing her foot to face the correct direction. Whatever pain had eluded her initially, hit tenfold. She fell backward into the loose powder. Lying there, a part of her wanted to die. It was so intense. Hissing through her teeth, spitting every curse that came to mind, Inyalia summoned the will to pull herself upright.

Practicing short, rapid breaths, keeping her body under control, Inyalia ensured her legs were aligned. She'd have to break them again if they weren't. It took everything she had to stay conscious. Methodically, she slipped her hand into the pocket of her quiver, drawing out a slim glass vial. Silver flakes were suspended within the transparent liquid. Bringing it to her mouth, she bit the cork stopper, breaking it between her teeth. Spitting the fragmented chunks, the liquid began to swirl, turning a deep purple. Closing her eyes, Inyalia tipped it back and swallowed.

A coppery taste filled her mouth, but it was the chalky texture that she noticed first. Suddenly, every muscle and bone in her body began to move. She collapsed into the acidic mixture of ash and snow. With no choice but to give it voice, her tormented screams echoed into the mountain peaks. Her body was being torn apart, only to be forced back together. Biting her hand, she felt the skin break. Blood soaked into the leather. But even that wound was already healing. The pain intensified, bringing rage. She wanted to cause pain to anything and everything. But there was nothing for her to hurt. A thick layer of sweat clung to her brow, though she trembled in the cold. She could feel her heart racing within her chest. The thump began to slow, falling quiet. And the pain finally subsided.

Calming herself, Inyalia sat up. She couldn't recall thrashing about, yet the gray and white powder clung to every inch of her. Slowly, she got to her feet, testing her freshly healed legs. They functioned as intended, though the muscles were intensely sore. They were going to hurt for a while, but it was better than the alternative.

Drawing her sword, Inyalia laid a series of deep gashes into the icy pillar. Each swing was hard and precise. White fractures spiderwebbed through the transparent green formation, and the pillar began to groan under the weight.

Inyalia sheathed her sword and turned to make her way from the ravine. Chunks of ice began to break and fall to the ground. What began as a few pieces at a time quickly became a downpour as the pillar broke free of the tunnel and toppled to the earth, shattering into thousands of pieces upon impact.

Halfway up the hill, Inyalia corrected north and continued toward her destination. Denholme was less than a mile away. Anyone attempting to follow would suffer far worse than a few broken legs.

Staying near the mountain range, Inyalia located the icy pass that led into the small town. She paused just off the path, considering her options. Denholme was under her protection. It was the one place she'd denied the others access. It was a sanctuary away from the corruption of life. It wouldn't take much to guess this her destination. Most of her officers knew her fondness of the place. If any of them spoke, an assault was nearly assured. Was it selfish to endanger its occupancy with her presence? On the other hand, would her presence make a difference? They'd come whether she was present or not.

Decided, Inyalia stepped onto the pass and made for the gates of the secluded town. Denholme wasn't just some random settlement. It was a grove protected by mountains. And its only pass was protected by her. In all the frozen north, it was the last place that remained green, reminiscent of her homeland, before everything changed. If she was to escape, this could be the perfect opportunity. Could a dethroned nightking simply disappear? Was escape even possible? She'd asked the questions before, but she'd never been in the position to make them a reality. Unlike the others, she had no desire to bend knee to Izaryle. But the calling was undeniable. She'd resisted it far longer than most. Sooner or later they all had to answer. The trick was in retaining one's identity while doing so. That was something this new nightking was going to have to learn.

The gate was unguarded. That didn't set well. The other nightkings didn't dare invade her territory. And few others knew of the grove's existence, let alone were powerful enough to enter by force. But if the gates were unmanned, that meant her resort had fallen.

Prepared for the worst, Inyalia marched through the pass, keeping watch for the slightest sign of trouble. She followed the road around the natural rock formations. It opened into a wide clearing. The howling wind ceased, unable to find its way through the pass. And without the wind, the snow thawed and melted, leaving the ground constantly saturated and muddy.

Searching the soft ground, Inyalia saw no sign of tracks, new or old. Wherever the guards went, it wasn't this way. That was unnerving. Where had they gone, if not fallen back? Stepping off the road, Inyalia took what joy she could from the grass under foot. It had been a while since she'd last felt the soft cushion. Climbing the hill to her right, she made for the overlook cave. It wasn't deep, but it made the perfect place to send an evening or two. And with its elevation, it was the best place to scout the town. If it had fallen, she'd know from there.

Reaching the top of the hill, the dark opening sat in wait. Though it wasn't as she'd expected. Just outside the entrance, a fire burned within a ring of stone. Fresh logs were stacked neatly, their bark recently blackened from flame. At the far side of the pit a man sat upon a large stone, studying her approach. She'd never seen this man before, though introductions were unnecessary. She knew exactly who he was.

Sighing, Inyalia approached the fire. "And so ends my reign."

ELDARLANDS - Nightking – Rise of the Nightkings

Levi Samuel

Chapter 1
Growing Pains

Strands of golden-brown hair shrouded the elven woman's face, whipping in the light breeze. She leaned through the side door of the two-story cabin, bracing herself against the wooden frame. "Baal, gather your sisters. It's time to eat!" Pulling herself back inside, she closed the door.

It was mid-day in the forests of Trendensil. Though that name encompassed the entirety of the elven lands. This was the eastern edge of Highlor, in the Ashamere barony. Spring had arrived a week past, and already little creatures ran wild, unafraid to show themselves.

Inyalia sat near the top of a massive beechwood tree, overlooking her beloved homeland. Though her sight was not locked on the small city to her back. She knew it intimately, and therefore, had become complacent with its many buildings and streets. It held no surprises for her anymore. Instead, her eyes were fixed to the northeast. By horse, it was nearly a week's travel to the elven capital. But at this time of day, from the tallest trees, and in just the right light, she could just barely make out the faintest outline of the skyward towers and pillaring turrets.

Inyalia had visited Camruun City a few times, when her father had been called away for an extended period. It was bright and beautiful in every way the promise of adventures untold could be. Though there was much about the city she didn't understand.

Inyalia enjoyed spending time in the massive settlement. There was always something happening, always something to do. People rushed about, day and night. And the shops displayed thousands of wonderful treasures she'd never seen before. And while she desired its many secrets, it was the forest that truly called to her. She was most comfortable surrounded by trees. No matter how grand the city was, it could never compare to the beauty found outside its walls.

Inyalia's favorite pastime was pretending to be a member of the Ranger Corps. She was by far a better archer than most children her age, prompting a show of skill anytime the opportunity arose. Though it had gotten her in trouble on more than one occasion. Inyalia took a bite from her juicy golden apple, recalling the scolding she'd received the day prior, for shooting one off her sister's head.

Hearing footsteps below, Inyalia stole a glance from the high branches. Through the outstretched limbs and thick leaves, she saw her brother. His soft steps were nearly soundless as he approached. It was their sister who'd given him away. Vera was clumsy. And she had a habit of ruining any surprise no matter how small.

Reaching the base of Inyalia's favorite tree, Baal searched the peak, spotting her almost instantly. "Inyalia, mom said food's ready. Climb down and let's go home."

Quickly scaling the branches, Inyalia jumped the final few feet, bending her knees to absorb the impact. "Did she say what we're having?"

The siblings were close, but none so close as Baal and Inyalia. The two did nearly everything together. Usually at the expense of Vera, whom they knew would tattle if they got into too much mischief.

"Does it matter? You know as well as I, she's gonna make us eat whether we like it or not."

"Doesn't mean we have to rush home if it's something nasty. What if it's bird soup?" Inyalia wrinkled her nose in disgust.

Baal laughed. "She'll beat our butts if we take too long. She'll think we were past the border. That won't bode well for any of us."

"Fine!" Inyalia surrendered, marching south.

Baal was a cycle her elder, and remarkably wise for his age. He was always able to think of other perspectives, giving him an edge in any contest. It had saved the both of them from trouble many times over.

Reaching the forest's edge, they paused, overlooking the vast ocean extending further than the eye could see. Highlor had been so named because it rested atop the massive cliff shadowing the bay. The port city of Largar'Thor, and a few smaller villages, could be seen on the lower land mass, but there was no way to reach them from here. All travel to and from the lower earldom happened either by ship, or the northern road that bridged to the rest of Trendensil.

Following the cliff, they raced home, singing their favorite hymn. In no time, they reached the northern corner of the small city. Smoke rose from a number of the vast stone chimneys. In all of Highlor's thirty plus structures, their home was the second largest residence, surpassed only by the Baron's manor on the opposite edge of town. Approaching the split-log cabin, they could see their mother through the kitchen window. The filtered sunlight cast a warm glow about her peach skin. She stood radiant, mindlessly focused on her work. Both Inyalia and Vera matched their mother's appearance in nearly every way. Though Inyalia's hair was a few shades darker. Baal on the other hand, while having his mother's hair, resembled their father in likeness.

Rushing through the door, their mother's honied voice echoed from the other room.

"Wash up and get the table set. Your father will be home tonight."

It took but a short time to strip from their soiled clothes and wipe away the day's grime. One by one, they filtered into the kitchen and began their nightly routine.

Inyalia dispersed the wooden cutlery, laying a fork beside each of the seven plates. She found it silly to waste the additional tableware. They were never used, yet they were washed each night, and set out again the following day. Taking her seat, she waited patiently, looking from Baal to Vera, and back again.

They were each equally impatient to dig in, but they knew better. Prematurely reaching for anything was the fastest way to feel the sting of their mother's favorite spoon across the back of their hand.

Just as the sun faded through the kitchen window, the front door creaked open. Footsteps echoed along the wood planked floor, drawing closer. A moment later, their father appeared in the entryway. Elegant armor covered him from knee to neck. The leather breastplate was embossed with the sigil of Trendensil and had been inlaid with gold. Removing his cloak, he tossed it over the banister at the base of the stairs and stepped into the kitchen. A warm smile settled, drinking in the sight of his family. Making his way to the table's head, he ruffed up Baal and Inyalia's hair as he passed. He would have done the same to Vera, but she was seated on the other side. Settling into his chair, Kalen stretched across the table and grabbed a golden roll from the bowl at the center.

Melaena turned just in time to see his hand wrap around the flaky crust. On instinct, she swung the spoon, making contact. A resounding pop echoed in the large dining area. A flirtatious smirk greeted her husband. "You're no different than the kids. Go wash up. You can have as many rolls as you'd like afterward."

"Yes, dear." Kalen stood, pulling his wife into his arms. Holding her for a moment, he kissed her forehead. He'd been away for nearly two weeks. It was two weeks too long. Desire sated for the moment, he turned and made his way toward the wash room.

Melaena laid another bowl on the table, just as Kalen returned. Absent his armor and sword, a dark-green gambeson covered his fine silken clothes. The material was thick and quilted, designed to withstand a single blow in the event of an unexpected attack. Though there was little need for it here. Returning to his seat, Kalen hesitantly reached for the roll once again. He paused, ensuring he was clear of the vicious spoon.

Melaena nodded her approval and fell into her own chair.

Snagging the warm bread, Kalen tore it in half. Looking up from the steaming center, he found the waiting eyes of his children. "What are you all waiting for? Dig in."

Chaos ensued. Hands shot to the variety of platters, bowls, and dishes, displaying everything from roasted ham to jellied fruit.

Loading her plate, Inyalia stabbed the three-pronged fork into a thick slab of meat. Raising it in its entirety, she took a hefty bite, ripping the chunk free. The savory flavor of glazed honey and salt filled her mouth. It was delicious. And it wasn't bird soup. She didn't much care for soups of any kind. They were always so watery. In fact, adding dried and crushed bread seemed to be the only way to make it bearable. But that took longer than her mother cared to wait. Usually, she ate just enough to be excused. From there it was easier to sneak something better. But never bird soup. Nothing was capable of making it tolerable!

The meal progressed, and plates began to empty.

Kalen leaned against the back of his chair, rubbing his bloated belly with one hand. The other was busy picking bits of food from between his teeth. "Dinner was delicious." He stated out of habit more than anything else. Changing the subject, he addressed his children. "What kinds of trouble did you three find today?"

They responded at once, creating an indecipherable mass of volume.

Chuckling to himself, Kalen laid the silver pick beside his empty plate and leaned forward. "Let's try this again. One at a time, perhaps? Baal since you're the oldest, we'll start with you."

"We played hide and seek in the forest for a while. It didn't go so well. Inyalia kept winning because Vera kept giving me away."

"I didn't mean to. I was only trying to find a good spot myself!" Vera insisted. "Besides, it's not like you were hiding in good spots anyway."

"It's my turn to talk, Vera!" Baal demanded, continuing his story before anyone else could interject. "After that, I went for a walk. I was almost back when mom called us home."

"Inyalia, what about you?"

"I practiced my ranger skills so I can grow up to be just like you, Daddy!"

"Butt kiss!" Baal taunted under his breath.

A hearty laugh escaped Kalen. His kids could always make him smile. "You'll make a fine ranger, Inyalia." He had no doubt she'd do well. They all would. But of the lot, she was the only one who frequently expressed interest in following his path. Though she had to come of age first. She had a few cycles to go before she could undertake the trials. As General of Trendensil's Ranger Corps, Kalen needed every ranger he could get. And best of all, the lands had been at peace for as long as he could remember. That was unlikely to change in his lifetime. If his children became rangers, there was little worry they'd have to fight. That in itself put his mind at ease. Turning his attention to Vera, he raised an eyebrow in question to her activities. Of all his children, Vera was the quietest. She was shy and innocently honest, which often raised conflict with her siblings. But she'd grow out of it.

"After Baal got mad at me, I found a fuzzy white rabbit with brown spots. It was so cute and fluffy. I tried to catch it, but it was too fast. But then—." Her eyes filled with tears. Sniffing, she continued through the growing sobs, her trauma renewed. "Then, Inyalia shot it!" Vera buried her face in her hands, crying her pain away.

Kalen gently rubbed her back, comforting her. Directing his attention to Inyalia, he raised a stern eyebrow. "Inyalia, what have I told you about shooting things you don't plan to eat?"

She lowered her head in defeat, wishing to avoid his lingering gaze. "Don't."

"That's right. If you're going to hunt, you'd best not be wasteful."

"Yes, Daddy."

Shaking his head, Kalen sighed, looking around the table at the empty chairs. He missed his other two sons. And while a place was always set for them, they hadn't ben home in quite some time.

Taerel was the oldest. He'd moved away shortly after Baal's birth, and he hadn't returned home since.

Wyrlan, on the other hand, paid a visit about twice a cycle. Magic was extremely rare in Irayth. Estimated reports showed less than three hundred natural born magicians existed among the elven population alone. Considering their race was just shy of ninety-thousand in total, about a third of a percent possessed the arcane arts. Wyrlan was one of those extreme few. He'd left home just under six cycles ago to seek training in Camruun City. But his abilities quickly surpassed those of his instructors. From there, he traveled to the college at Risolde, where he graduated with a specialty in enchantment, though Kalen had no idea what that meant. Unlike his own father, he'd never cared to explore the things he couldn't explain. Since then, Wyrlan was reportedly living in Hailsort, though he never spoke of his dealings when he visited.

After dinner, the children got ready for bed.

Inyalia stared out her window. She could see the pyre of Largar'Thor's lighthouse, guiding ships into the harbor. Lost in thought, her eyes closed and she began to drift into an adventure that would carry her to sleep. She wanted nothing more than to become a ranger. In doing so she could protect the lands she loved so much. Her skills were sharp. She knew that. But she was too young to apply to the corps. Imagining herself running through the trees, bow drawn and at the ready, sleep claimed her.

The scent of elven spice bread and fried eggs wafted through the air. Inyalia's eyes shot open. Jumping up, she threw her clothes into place and ran down the stairs. Turning the corner at the last minute, she lost her footing and crashed into the wall.

Baal's laughter echoed from the kitchen table.

"Inyalia, slow down before you hurt yourself!" Melaena's tone was firm but comforting.

Picking herself up, Inyalia entered the kitchen and took the seat beside Baal.

Melaena gave a loving smile, watching Inyalia climb into her chair. Turning to the stove, she removed the last of the food and sat it on a quilted pad at the center of the table. Taking her own seat, she gestured to the kids, granting permission to fill their plates. Melaena sat quietly, watching them dig in as if they hadn't eaten in weeks.

Vera groggily strode into the kitchen, rubbing the sleep from her eyes. She was still wearing her night clothes. Unlike the others, she had difficulty climbing the stairs. For that reason alone, she was allowed to sleep in their parent's bedroom.

Getting to her feet, Melaena scooped her youngest daughter into her arms and gently sat her in the previously occupied chair. She wasn't quite able to climb into it by herself. Quickly fixing a plate, Melaena sat it in front of Vera and pulled another chair for herself. "I need you to try to stay clean today. Your father will be home early with a wagon."

"Ooh, can we go to the theater?" Baal asked between bites.

"What makes you think we're going to Cammrun?" Fixing her own plate, Melaena surveyed the remaining food. There wasn't much left, but that had been by design. Experience had taught her the formula to feeding them without excess waste. Cooked food didn't keep long, and it wasn't as if she could simply store it for another meal.

"The only time dad brings the wagon home is when we're going to the city." Inyalia offered, scooping the mashed over-easy eggs onto the toasted bread.

"I'm glad your powers of perception are so keen. Perhaps you should employ them during your chores." Melaena smiled, seeing the distasteful glare upon her daughter's face. "Yes, we're going to Cammrun. And if we have time, I'll see what we can do about attending the theater. But that's a big if. Your father has important business to discuss with the king's council."

"Yay!" Baal exclaimed, stuffing his mouth. His father's business never lasted long, and even when it did, they were never expected to wait for him. That meant they'd have plenty of time to see a show.

Rapidly finishing her breakfast, Inyalia rushed out the door before any objections could be heard. She knew she wouldn't have much time to explore the forest today, especially with her father returning home so early.

On the nights he spent home, he was always gone before sunrise the following morning. It was a three-hour horse ride to the Dragon Sanctum, and he would usually return right at nightfall. Calculating the time, she had maybe four hours to explore before he'd be back.

Inyalia had never been to the sanctum, but the stories made it sound marvelous. Trendensil was supposedly protected by a huge white dragon, which was honored in the form of a grand statue erected atop the outpost. The stories fascinated her, though many seemed too farfetched to be real. Dragon Sanctum was headquarters for the second battalion of the Rangers Corps, and it served as the first line of defense against an inland invasion, though no such thing had ever happened. The elves were too powerful. Nobody would risk such devastation.

Inyalia had once asked her father why he left so early. Even with the long ride, he was always the first to arrive. He'd explained that it set a good example for those under his command. Leading by example made them respect him. And that meant he could trust them. She still didn't understand, but he'd assured her that it would make sense one day.

Returning her focus to the path, Inyalia spotted a strange set of tracks in the dirt. They looked like the paws of a dog, but they were much wider. Larger even than those of a wolf. And stranger still, they were grouped in sets of two instead of four. This was an opportunity to practice her tracking skills. Altering course, Inyalia followed the tracks. It took only a moment to realize she was headed back into Highlor.

Just beyond the first row of buildings, Inyalia paused, searching the ground. It was more compact here, but just enough loose dirt remained to be impressionable. She was barely able to make out the imprints. Had she not seen a full print already, she had no doubt she would have lost the trail. Approaching the butcher's shop, the scent of meat filled her nostrils. The tracks circled the meat house several times, seeming to linger around the door. She even found scratches in the dirt on one side, as if whatever she was following had tried to dig its way in.

"Hey, Inyalia, what are you doing?" Baal asked, approaching his sister.

"Following some tracks. They came here, and they go back that way." She said, pointing south. "They seem pretty fresh. Probably made just before daybreak. Come on. If we run, we might be able to see what they belong to." Without another word, Inyalia was sprinting through the trees. She made very little noise considering how fast she was moving.

Behind her, Baal ran just as fast, trying to keep pace. "I don't think this is a good idea." He panted through labored breaths.

Ignoring his objections, Inyalia raced on. She had a mission. She desperately wanted to see it to completion, with or without his aid. Running as fast as she could, she flew past an old fence post that had nearly rotted away. This was the boundary. They weren't allowed beyond this point. But she couldn't stop now. She'd come so far. And she couldn't continue alone. Baal would tell on her. She needed a challenge. If she could taunt him into following, he wouldn't dare tell. "Bet you can't beat me!" Jumping one of the fallen runs, Inyalia charged on, abandoning all grace.

"Inyalia!" Baal cried, slowing to a stop. He didn't want to follow, but he couldn't let her go alone. They'd both be in trouble if they got caught, but it'd be worse if something happened and he didn't report it. Sighing, he climbed over the fence and charged after her, giving it everything he had. His gut told him to stand down, but he couldn't deny the pleasure such a race provided. Inyalia disappeared over the hill. He was gaining. Just a bit further and he'd catch her.

Unable to see the tracks anymore, Inyalia slowed, trying to find the trail. She'd allowed herself to be distracted by the race. They had to be around here somewhere. Hearing Baal approach, she turned just as he came into view. He was out of breath, and a layer of sweat beaded on his forehead. "I told you, you couldn't beat me!" She taunted.

"I would have if you hadn't cheated at the beginning. I wasn't ready! Besides, you didn't set a finish line. Without that how can either of us win?"

"Oh yeah? Let's go again. I'll beat you fair and square. Unless you're scared—." Inyalia froze mid-sentence.

Noticing the expression on his sister's face, Baal turned to see what she so enamored with.

They were standing just a few yards from the mouth of a large cavern. He hadn't noticed it until now, but the cool subterranean air lingered around them. Some of the other kids had spread rumors about a few caves in the area but they hadn't seen one for themselves until now. It was much bigger than he imagined.

Inyalia pulled the crudely crafted short bow from her quiver. She'd made it herself last cycle, and while it did everything she'd asked, there were a few things she'd wished she'd done differently. For starters, a removable string would have been nice. Constantly being under pressure made it difficult to store, and the wooden arms were weakening with each shot. Drawing an arrow, she nocked it to the string and slowly approached the cave. Reaching the moist clay at the entrance, the strange tracks reappeared. This had to be the place.

"I don't think we should go in there." Baal's voice echoed into the darkness.

"It'll be fine. I just want to check it out. You're welcome to join me. Unless you're too scared." Inyalia quickly added.

He didn't want to follow, but he also didn't want her to go in alone. Taking a deep breath, Baal stepped forward and entered the cave. Maybe, if by some miracle, he could talk some reason into her before they got too far. "Remember what mom said. We have to be home early. And without getting dirty."

It was useless. Inyalia kept walking. She was always confident no matter what situation she found herself in.

Baal on the other hand preferred a more careful approach. He usually had a plan in mind before jumping into action. But those plans often forgot to account for Inyalia's impulsive nature.

Once inside, the cavern seemed much larger. It was nearly forty feet from wall to wall, the ceiling was well beyond that. The outside light shined just past the entrance, leaving the deep hole wreathed in darkness. But they were elves. So long as minor light was available, they'd be able to see. It was when they reached total darkness that their vision would fade.

Tearing the old hem line of his tunic, Baal searched for anything to wrap it around. Their clothes had been made long and hemmed over, allowing them room to grow. This particular tunic was nearing the end of its lifespan, having been hemmed three times before. With the removed section, it was just barely long enough to cover his stomach. Light was fading rapidly, and Inyalia didn't show any signs of stopping. He needed to ensure they at least had a torch. If he could find a large stick, or even better, a decent section of bone, they'd be set. It wouldn't last as long as an oiled or waxed torch, but it would grant them sight for a while longer.

Inyalia stopped, noticing her brother had fallen back. It became obvious what he was looking for. If it meant he was staying, she'd aid in the search.

Little more than rocks and dirt littered the cavern floor. There were a few small pieces of wood, broken from various crates, or end pieces of firewood that hadn't burned. But nothing suitable to their desires was present.

Coming up empty handed, Inyalia sighed. "If we're going to find anything, it'll be a matter of luck. Let's keep going. Maybe we'll find something a little deeper."

"Or we could turn back." Baal added, hoping she'd see reason.

Half an hour passed and nothing useable presented itself. It didn't take long for their sight to completely fail.

With no other alternative, Baal scraped a piece of flint against his dagger and lit the cloth. It took a few tries, but he got a small flame going. Though mostly, the fabric just wanted to smolder. He held it out to the side, letting the strand dangle near his knee. The speed of their pace created just enough airflow to keep the embers working their way up. It wasn't much, but it provided just enough light to see their immediate surroundings. Unfortunately, with the constant movement to keep it going, the cloth was burning fast. Feeling the heat upon his hand, Baal dropped the rag. The smoldering embers disappeared no sooner than it hit the ground. Once again, light faded, leaving them in total darkness.

Inyalia slowed to half pace. Keeping her arms extended, she felt for the wall. So long as she stayed in contact, she could remember the way out. The last thing she wanted was to get lost. Unfortunately, she feared it was already too late for that. They hadn't passed that many turns, but she'd forgotten to account for the ones they'd passed when she could see. Doing so from memory had messed up the count.

Trailing behind, Baal crashed into the back of his sister. Unprepared for the sudden impact, he stumbled and fell on his butt. "Hey! Let me know when you do that."

Inyalia caught herself against the wall. The stone was rough and cold. And the slight dampness that coated everything was making her cold. "Do what? I didn't do anything?"

"Stop. I can't see you." Picking himself up, Baal inched forward, placing his hand on her shoulder. By staying connected, he couldn't lose her. "Okay. I'm good now."

They proceeded deeper into the cavern. The lack of sight made it feel like hours had passed. Though, in truth, there was no telling how much time had passed.

"Come on, Inyalia. We need to turn back. Mom's going to tan our hides."

She didn't want to admit it to herself, let alone her brother, but she'd already tried turning back. Her fears were now a reality. But it did no good to panic. It wouldn't change anything. Wherever this cavern went, it was much deeper than she'd realized.

"Come on. We're already going to be in trouble!" Baal nagged, knowing that was the only way to get her to concede.

Inyalia let loose her emotions. Spinning to face her brother, despite not being able to see him, her mouth opened, spilling thoughts before she could stop herself. "Quit griping at me! I'm trying to turn back! I lost count of the tunnels a while back and now we're lost!" Out of nowhere her sight returned. For an instant she thought they'd found the exit, but that thought passed, realizing they weren't moving. "Um, can you see?"

"Yes." Baal searched the walls, looking for the source of light. There was a faint glow off to the side of a smaller tunnel, but it hadn't been there before. "As much as I'm glad to see, we need to go the other way."

"I agree."

An overbearing odor drifted toward them, smelling of wet dog and urine. It grew stronger, as did the light. Shadows began to dance on the wall. Yapping echoes carried, like overgrown puppies excited for attention. They didn't have to see the beings to know they didn't want to meet them. A low growl echoed at their backs.

Slowly, the siblings turned to see a dog-like creature standing on its hind legs. It stood six inches taller than Baal and was thrice as broad. Fur-covered paws shot out, slamming their heads together. A sharp pain erupted, and their vision went black.

Chapter II
The Great Escape

The stench of feces and mold lingered in the air, rousing Inyalia's senses. The pounding in her head made her want to go back to sleep, but it was too late for that. Slowly, she opened her eyes, letting them adjust to the orange firelight dancing across the walls. Groggily, she picked herself up, impacting the top of the iron cage. The rusted strips rung out, but they were too tight to create much noise. Rubbing the crown of her head, flashes of memory fell into place. Inyalia recalled the creature in the cave. On alert, she ducked low, searching for the beast.

A fire burned at the center of the cavern chamber. Several of the dog-creatures sat around it, speaking their racial language. To Inyalia it sounded like a series of chirps and barks. It would have amused her if she weren't in such a predicament. They were disgusting. They walked upright like elves, but their bodies were more beast than anything else. Shaggy matted fur covered them completely, and they wore scraps of crude hide as clothing. She watched them closely. They were little more than wild dogs. Though the fact they'd caged her suggested some level of intelligence.

A painful cramp erupted in Inyalia's stomach. She doubled over, hoping it would pass. It was one thing to miss a single meal. That caused little more than the annoyance of stomach growls and gurgles. It didn't even hurt. But this, this was unlike any hunger she'd ever experienced. It felt as if her midsection was angrily trying to eat the rest of her body. How many meals had she missed to cause this? Holding herself, the hunger pains finally passed. Inyalia unfurled, taking a few moments just to breathe. How long had they been gone?

They? The word reminded her that she wasn't alone. Baal had been with her. Where was he now?

Frantically searching, Inyalia's fears settled, seeing her brother laying in a cage not far from her. He was covered in mud, and a thin stream of dried blood ran down his face, but his chest moved. That meant he was alive. That in itself was a relief. She would never forgive herself if anything had happened to him. Now, she just had to find a way to get them out.

Searching their surroundings for anything of use, Inyalia's eyes locked onto her bow and quiver, lying atop a pile of garbage not far from their cages. Sadly, it'd have to wait. The iron lattice was too small to get her arm through, not that her bow was close enough to reach as it was. She'd be lucky if her hand alone could fit through the square openings. Sudden movement near the fire drew Inyalia's attention. Throwing herself to the floor, she hid behind the heap of refuse and pretended to be asleep.

One of the creatures stood, shouting a mixture of growls and barks over the fire. Immediately, it pulled a crude tomahawk that was closer to a sharpened rock tied to a stick. Swinging at one of the others, the wild swipe missed.

The intended target jumped from the rock it'd been using as a seat. Bringing a piece of driftwood, doubling as a club, to bear, it brought the wood down atop the other's head. Its own growls were louder and deeper than the first, demanding submission.

A solid thud echoed, and the first creature whimpered in defeat. Avoiding eye contact, it released a passive howl and returned to its seat.

The others chirped and barked, pointing and criticizing the defeated one.

Inyalia watched through her fingers, refusing to move. She was curious as to what they were saying. Why were they fighting? And how did it end so quickly? Among these questions, she realized the end result needed no explanation. It seemed social bullying was the same regardless of species or intelligence. Realizing the excitement was over for the moment, she returned to her plan. It would work, so long as they didn't know she was awake. She hoped as much anyway.

Baal rolled to his back, his eyes slowly opening.

Seeing her brother move, Inyalia concealed herself as best she could. She needed to get his attention before he made too much commotion. Remaining out of thought was crucial to her plan. Subtly waving, Inyalia whispered a series of short, fluctuating buzzes. It was something they'd tried a few cycles prior as a means of communicating without words. It'd served its purpose, keeping Vera out of their business, but had ultimately proved to be a waste of time. Not only did Vera tell on them anyway, which ruined their plan, but there was no way to rapidly distinguish the various sounds needed for complete conversation. And spacious pauses only went so far.

Hearing the noise, Baal's eyes shot open. He sat up, looking around. Seeing Inyalia, it took a moment to register what she was attempting. Between the broken language they'd created and her gestures, he believed he understood. Crouching low, he pressed his head against the side of the cage, waiting to hear what Inyalia's plan was.

Doing likewise, Inyalia spoke just over a whisper, frequently looking to ensure they weren't noticed. If these creatures were capable of hearing as well as elves, there was little chance. But they hadn't noticed her yet. She suspected it was safe. "I've counted eight so far, my bow is right over there." She gestured to the pile between them. "I don't know what they're planning, but they've shown some aggression between one another. I think we can use that to our advantage. If we can get them to fight, it may provide the distraction we need to escape."

"I'm so hungry, Inyalia. How long have we been here?" Baal didn't look so good. He was weak and sweating profusely.

"I don't know. I've been awake for about twenty minutes. I don't know how long we were out. But it you can keep it together long enough for us to get out, I promise I'll give you whatever you want. Now, do you have any ideas on how we can start a fight?"

Baal paused, considering her question. "I'll do my best. But I don't think there's anything you can give me that I don't already have. Maybe, if you wanted to do my chores for a week?"

Inyalia smiled. If they got out of here, she'd gladly do whatever chores she could. For a short time anyway. They were chores after all. "Done."

A weak smile came to Baal's lips. Why was he so shaky? He hadn't been this bad since the time they snuck into the millhouse to swim in the grain silo. Between the heat and excitement, not to mention being chased away by the miller himself, he'd nearly collapsed from exhaustion. Fortunately, the shakes went away after his mother gave him a peach. If only he had one now. Returning to the present, Baal considered the creatures. If they were aggressive toward each other, starting a fight shouldn't be that hard. They simply had to direct resentment. A plan coming to mind, he compiled a list of resources. There wasn't much they could reach, but there were plenty of small rocks lying around. They wouldn't do much damage, short of hitting one in the eye, but they were perfect for his purposes. "Okay, so—." Baal quickly ran through the plan, ensuring she understood every detail. The hard part was going to be opening their cages without notice, but that was where he came in.

Inyalia gathered a handful of pebbles, varying in size and shape. She was a better aim, and in their current predicament, she was also stronger. Lining them in order, Inyalia turned her attention to Baal. She'd fulfilled her part of this step. It was up to him now.

Keeping watch on their captors, Baal twisted his fingers through the small opening, reaching his destination. A part of him wished the cages had actual locks. It would have made escape much easier. As it were, it was just a spring-loaded latch that held them shut. These were likely used for trapping animals, if he had to guess. Pressing his hand into the metal, he strained against the release rod. The edge of the lattice was cutting into his hand but he couldn't give up. Not yet. He was almost there. Getting his fingers around the release, he pushed. The handle raised and his cage door came open. Sighing his relief, he held it closed. Now was the hard part.

Inyalia held her breath, watching Baal slowly open his cage. She desperately hoped the hinges didn't squeak. On edge, waiting at the base of her tiny cell, her attention jumped from the dog-men to her brother. They didn't seem to pay any mind to the cages or their prisoners. That was a good thing.

Baal opened the door just enough to squeeze out. Grabbing Inyalia's bow and quiver, he slid it beside her cage and went to work on the door. Now that he had full use of his hands, it came open with ease.

Inyalia took hold of the door, keeping it from latching again. She waited for Baal to return to his cell and lay down. It was all happening so fast. And with any luck, the rest would flow just the same. Seeing Baal in position, their captors still unaware, Inyalia grabbed the first of her lineup and slowly pushed the door open. She set the rock in its path so it could close without latching. Grabbing the second rock, she took aim and released.

The small missile sailed across the cavern, disappearing through the flickering flames. Out the other side, it struck the alienated creature in the top of its head. It roared, grabbing its tomahawk and jumping up.

The others chirped in acknowledgment. It seemed they were finding humor in its actions. Seeing no threat, they returned their attention to the larger one that seemed to be their leader.

Inyalia watched through the mostly closed door, her head resting on her arm. She waited for it to finish its search and return to its seat.

The creature paced back and forth, rubbing the fresh knot. Unable to find where the rock had come from, it sat down, returning its attention to the roasted animal charring within the flame.

Cautiously, Inyalia sat up, securing another rock. It was a little smaller than the last, but that was okay. The purpose was not to kill, or even to wound for that matter. At least not yet. This was all intended to escalate their aggressions toward one another. But it all depended on subtlety. Opening the door, Inyalia cast the second stone. It hit the same creature, this time in the snout. The force knocked it from its seat and it fell backward, triggering excitement from the others.

Inyalia had to suppress a giggle. It was funny to watch, especially since they didn't know what was happening.

The dog-man rolled to its paws, searching its surroundings. The chides of the others were suspiciously suspect. Roaring its anger, barking at its tormentors, it picked up the rock and showed it to them. This did little more than instigate them further. Clearly infuriated, and unable to challenge the pack, it circled the fire and took position in another spot. A spot where it could see the lot of them.

That was what Inyalia was waiting for. Baal had planned it out perfectly, especially after she'd recounted the previous interaction she'd witnessed. Stifling a laugh, she grabbed the last rock. This one was bigger than the others, but it fit perfectly in the palm of her hand. Carefully, she pressed through the door and took aim.

The rock flew forth, striking its target in the back of the head. That was crucial. She'd instigated the runt of the pack. Now it was time to start the fight.

The larger creature, the one with the driftwood club, roar in pain and grabbed the back of its head. Looking around, it found its target, sitting by itself on the near side of the firepit. Bulking its mass, it charged, bringing the weapon down. It struck the weaker creature in the side, sending it toppling over.

In turn, it picked itself up, the makeshift tomahawk in hand and ready to go.

Inyalia watched the creatures circle around one another, the fight ensuing. She grabbed her last rock, chucking it at one of the spectators.

It barked and joined the mix. Within moments, the entire pack was engaged in a brawl.

Now was their chance. Inyalia squeezed out of her cage, slinging her quiver. Only half of her arrows remained, but with luck, that was enough. "Come on, Baal."

Rolling to his knees, he crawled out and took position beside his sister. Everything had gone according to plan. All that was left was the escape. Making his way around Inyalia, Baal led the way. Crossing behind the various piles of junk, he found an old walking stick. It wasn't good for much else, but he needed all the support he could get. Moving as quick as his body would allow, he approached the exit.

Inyalia followed close behind her brother. He was moving slower than usual. Keeping watch on the fight, a pair of dark, featureless eyes fell upon them. Inyalia knew they'd been seen. Before it could alert the others, she released her arrow. It struck the creature in the snout, exiting the back of its head. It fell into the pile of scrapping beasts and disappeared. "We have to move now!" Inyalia warned as loud as she dared.

Baal and Inyalia ran as fast as they could. The light was fading, their vision with it. A howling roar echoed behind them. One became two. And a moment later, the individual cries became a single mass. Whether it was rage, confusion, or pain, they couldn't tell. Either way, it meant their escape had been discovered. Afraid to stop, they continued into the black.

"Baal, do you still have that stick?" Inyalia asked, panting through labored breaths.

"Yes."

"Do we have time to make a torch?"

"Not yet. I'm feeling for the wall. Let's go a while further. We'll listen for movement. If we don't hear anything, we'll try then."

"Okay."

Baal drug the bottom of the stick against the wall as a guide. He could hear Inyalia behind him. They ran for what felt like hours, though in truth it was maybe twenty minutes. Slowing his already exhausted pace, he tried to listen past the beating of his heart and ragged combination of breaths.

Hearing the change in footfalls, Inyalia came to a stop. She was out of breath, trying to listen. It was difficult to hear anything, but she was fairly certain they were alone. If the creatures were still pursuing, they were doing so quietly.

"I think we're alone. My shirt is too muddy to burn, plus I already tore as much as I can without making it too short. Yours didn't look so bad." Baal suggested, preparing his stick for the cloth.

Nodding her agreement, Inyalia took the head of her arrow and started sawing the hem of her tunic. It tore more than cut, but she had a decent section of linen in a fairly short time. Handing the torn cloth to Baal, she waited for the sparks to ignite.

Baal made several passes around his crude staff and tied the ribbon off. He was glad the creatures hadn't searched him. He still had his dagger in the waist of his breeches, and his flint remained in his pocket. Striking it, the sparks danced across the lapping cloth. The clinging dirt made it hard to light, but finally, with the help of his breath, a small flame came into existence. Slowly, it spread across the surface, engulfing the entire cloth. As It grew, more of their surroundings came into view.

"Now that we can see where were going, maybe we can get out of here. Dad will want to know about these things." Inyalia searched the floor, keeping watch for any tracks that could belong to them. If she could pick up that trail, they could follow it back to the surface.

The pair traveled at a brisk pace, following a set of footprints that could have been theirs. Another hour passed before a gust of fresh air hit them, threatening to extinguish the nearly burnt-out torch. Finally, they found the surface. It was dark. Only a partial moon provided any kind of light. But that was enough. Looking around the opening, this wasn't where they'd entered.

Inyalia glanced around, gathering her bearings. "If that way is west, we'll eventually hit the cliffs. From there we should be able to tell if we need to go north or south."

Baal staggered against his stick. Only a few embers remained where the cloth had burned away. He wasn't sure how much longer he could go.

He was so hungry, so weak. Swaying against the breeze, he stared blankly at his sister. "Do what you need." Even the act of talking exhausted him.

Seeing the hazy glaze in her brother's eyes, Inyalia threw his arm over her shoulder and guided him up the steep incline, to level ground. She was hungry and in desperate need of water, but he seemed to need it more. Orienting herself, she led him west.

They walked for nearly a mile before the first sign of civilization presented itself. A dirt road cut through the land, separating the sea of grass and trees.

Inyalia recognized it instantly. In fact, she knew this patch of road. They were less than a quarter mile from the boundary fence they'd jumped what seemed like a lifetime ago. They finally made it. They were almost home.

The snap of a twig drew Inyalia's attention to the right. A wall of trees blocked out all sight beyond the dark threshold. Releasing her brother, she drew an arrow and took aim on the forest's edge. Whatever foul creature sought to prevent their return this night was going to learn a lesson in pain. She was Inyalia Highlor, daughter of Kalen Highlor, Ranger-General of Trendensil, and she was not to be trifled with!

A familiar voice broke the silence. "Baal, Inyalia, where the hell have you two been? Your mother and I have been worried sick!" Kalen rushed from the shadows, stepping into the moonlight. Dropping to his knees at the edge of the road, he wrapped his arms around the pair and pulled them tight. "I've had the entire corps searching for you!"

Inyalia was nearly in tears. She tried to explain what had happened, but the sobs distorted her words beyond recognition.

Baal was too exhausted to speak. He simply slouched in his father's embrace.

Wrapping his arms around his children, Kalen pulled them close. "It's okay. Calm yourselves and tell me what happened."

Managing to steel herself, Inyalia wiped her nose on the muck covered sleeve of her tunic. "We got lost in a cave. Then some dog creatures found us. They locked us in a cage." Her tears were beginning to return. Sniffing once again, she continued. "We managed to trick them and escape."

Kalen held them tight. "It's okay. I'm here now. Let's get you home and fed. I'll take care of it in the morning." Lifting the both of them, he carried his children toward their home.

Chapter III
A Ranger's Call

Crickets chirped in the distance, playing their song for all the world to hear. Exhaling softly, Inyalia pulled the thick blanket around her. She rolled to face the window, snuggling into the soft quilt. It provided just enough warmth in the cool autumn air to keep her comfortable throughout the night. Her eyes fell upon the full glowing moon, glistening just over the horizon. Its soft glow filled her bedroom. How she longed for the calm it usually bestowed upon her. Unfortunately, this night was different. The serenity would not come. This was the end of her childhood, the last of her thirteenth cycle. Tomorrow promised the future. It was the day she'd longed to reach. And she wasn't at all ready for it.

Fueled by excitement and fear, she was too anxious to sleep. Entering her fourteenth cycle meant a great many things. She could engage in politics. She could marry if so desired. She could establish residence in any realm. But most of all, it meant she was finally able to join the Rangers Corps. Inyalia was still a youngling by elven standard, but by law she was now an adult. All those cycles of fantasy and adventure were about to come to fruition. Provided she passed her trials.

A cycle prior, Baal had joined the corps. Inyalia missed seeing him every day, but such was the life of a ranger. He'd been assigned to the Eighty-Fifth Company, a division of the Second Battalion. His days were filled with patrolling Evergrove, one of the smaller baronies east of Ashamere. With his new duties, he returned home about once a month. Inyalia was always so excited to see him. But it wasn't until his last visit that she truly started pressing for answers. She'd begged him to give her the slightest details of the trials, but he'd remained tight-lipped. His only commentary was, it was something she'd never forget.

The trials couldn't be that hard, she assured herself. Though she wasn't sure she believed it. Baal had been gone for almost three months during his. How much of that had been the trials, she couldn't say. Inyalia had spent cycles preparing for this moment. And now that it was finally upon her, she didn't know if she was ready. But Baal, and every ranger before him, had made it through. With such odds, how could she fail?

Inyalia closed her eyes, thinking of the future. They opened a short moment later with morning's first light upon her face. Sighing heavily, she sat up and threw the blanket away from her. She hadn't slept a wink. There was too much on her mind.

Getting to her feet, Inyalia knocked the wrinkles out of her clothes and grabbed her pack. She'd made certain everything was ready to go the night before. Slinging her quiver, along with the improved bow she'd made, over her shoulder, Inyalia headed for the door. Dragon Sanctum was half a day's travel by horse. By foot, she'd reach it just before nightfall. With any luck, her nerves would settle by then. And if they didn't, things were going to be fairly interesting for the foreseeable future.

Inyalia stepped into the hall that ran the width of the upper floor. Vera's room rested between hers and the stairs. The now vacant bedrooms of her brothers were beyond that. Turning, Inyalia raced down the wooden staircase, skipping the steps two at a time. Miscalculating the final few, she crashed into the wall at their base for what had to have been the thousandth time. She didn't have to hear the words to know what her mother said. It was always the same, or some variant thereof.

Turning the corner to enter the kitchen, Inyalia found her mother standing over the stove. She was casually stirring a pot, humming to herself. An empty plate rested before the chair Inyalia had deemed as hers. As it stood, each of her family had a preferred seat, though the majority of the chairs remained empty these days. Hers was likely to join the ranks once she stepped out the door.

Inyalia approached her chair and took a seat. Looking over the full meal spread before her, she knew she was going to miss her mother. But not just for her cooking. Melaena had always been there for her. Even when they were arguing, or when Inyalia was in trouble for any number of infractions, she knew her mother would always love her. And in turn, she loved her mother.

A reassuring smile settled on Melaena's lips. Studying her daughter, she knew they were thinking the same thing. There was no need to pollute it with words. Catching the scent of nearly burnt bacon, Melaena broke her gaze and grabbed the skillet off the wood stove. Laying it gently upon a quilted potholder, she scooped the meat out with precision, allowing the grease to drain away. Doing a quick count, she removed the steaming pot, and ensured all the food was present. There was toast, bacon, eggs, oats, a jar of mixed berry jam, roasted potatoes, and a platter of freshly churned butter. If the table was missing something, it clearly wasn't needed. At least not today.

"It smells good." Scanning the abundance of food, there was no way she'd be able to make a dent in any of it. She had a long journey ahead of her, and there was no time to delay. But the wrath of her mother was an entirely different beast. One that would undoubtedly refuse to let her walk without eating. Pulling the wooden plate toward her, Inyalia gathered a couple pieces of toast. Layering the bacon, eggs, and potatoes atop a single piece, she pressed the other onto the pile, locking everything inside. That seemed to be the best option for loading up on food, while eating it quick enough to get going. "Thanks for breakfast, mom." Inyalia tried to rise, sandwich in hand, only to find her mother guarding the exit.

"Stop, sit, and eat!" Melaena smiled, demanding obedience.

Exhaling sharply, Inyalia plopped down. "But mom—."

"Hush up and eat. There's no telling when you'll have another decent meal. And I'm not letting you leave until I'm certain you're full." Melaena shook her legendary spoon, threatening further dispute. "And when you're done, you're taking some for the road."

Trying, and failing not to smile, Inyalia took a massive bite, filling her mouth. It took some time to chew and swallow, but when she did, she couldn't help but feel for her mother. Inyalia had been witness to Baal's last breakfast. And while she couldn't say whether it was the memory of the actual event, or a story that'd been told so often it felt like memory, but there had been a similar ceremony when Wyrlan had left. She knew the pain and fear her mother was feeling. But the strong woman before her always managed to keep a smile on her face and reassurance in her voice. That alone offered strength when all possibilities seemed so frightening. Swallowing the last bit of her sandwich, Inyalia slid her plate away and cleared her throat. "I love you, mom!"

Melaena paused her busy work. She didn't know whether to hug her daughter or cry. Perhaps both. But she wouldn't do either. This was Inyalia's time to venture out. Finding her resolve, Melaena turned to face her daughter. Extending a small sack that had been loaded with dried food, she offered a reassuring smile. "I love you, too. Now get out there and show em what you're made of."

～～

The beat within her chest kept her moving at a steady pace. Though to her, it sounded more like a war drum urging her onto the plank of uncertainty. Each beat was a step closer to the rest of her life. What if she failed? What if she wasn't good enough? How could she handle being the first of her bloodline to be denied entry? The thoughts filled her with doubt, too numerous to focus on any single one.

The sun was cresting the treetops when Inyalia reached the edge of Highlor. Turning east onto the road, she spotted a caravan just ahead. If she could barter a ride, it'd shave hours off her trip. Increasing her pace, Inyalia approached the rear wagon. The rails jingled and clanked from the multiple traps dangling down the sides. They certainly weren't trying to be quiet. It was piled high with a mixture of dark brown and black furs. From the size and color, she guessed them to be bear hides. There wasn't an abundance of wild bear in this part of Trendensil. But further south, near Ryse, they were a growing menace. Inyalia had overheard her father discussing the problem on many occasions. It seemed the small farming town there was always requesting assistance.

Now that she could see the caravan as a whole, Inyalia realized each of the wagons was loaded to capacity. And with that many hides, Ryse had to be their point of origin. But it did little to suggest their destination. Bear pelt was valuable pretty much everywhere. If they were exporting to another kingdom, they could either go through the Icefall Pass, or travel the north road near Camruun City to Largar'Thor Harbor. One would take her straight to Dragon Sanctum, the other would get her about halfway there. But both were dependent on the generosity of the wagon masters.

Making her way beside the rear wagon, careful to avoid blind spots, Inyalia hailed the coachman. "Excuse me, but is there any chance I can barter a ride to Dragon Sanctum, or as close as you're willing to take me? I don't have any coin to spare, but I'm a decent archer. I'd be happy to hunt for your lunch or help guard your wares while I'm here."

The man pulled the reins, bringing his horse to a stop. He surveyed the young elf for a moment. She didn't look old enough to be out on her own, but it was difficult to tell with elves. They aged differently than humans. Inspecting the unstrung bow upon her back, her claim appeared legitimate. Were they anywhere else, he would have considered the threat of bandits, but the rangers kept the roads around here fairly safe, especially this close to the sanctum. "We're riding straight through to Icefall Citadel. But an extra pair of eyes wouldn't hurt." Extending a hand, he pulled her onto the seat beside him. "The name's Willam."

Inyalia took his hand and climbed up. She rocked against the spring mounted seat as the wagon lurched forward and began moving again. "Thank you, Willam. I'm Inyalia." She studied the human, trying to make sense of him. She'd met a few here and there, but never really spoken to them. Most of Somuer and Noier, the two southern most baronies, were populated with a mixture of human and elf, but she'd never been allowed to explore farther than the southern road. And most humans seemed afraid to travel north.

Willam's skin was worn with age, though she didn't know how to identify which phase of his lifespan he was in. Humans used years, whereas elves used cycles. The two were extremely different things. Though an elf and a human at birth were nearly the same in every regard. The difference came with time. Humans typically reached the end of their lifespan around an elf's thirtieth cycle. Judging from the short, choppy gray hair atop his head, Inyalia gathered he was probably somewhere around his seventeenth cycle. That meant he wasn't that much older than her. But the difference was severely noticeable. Turning her attention to his dress, she couldn't help but notice the dull yellow tunic was slightly stretched at the midsection and frayed around the hems. It stood in stark contrast to the brown leather breeches he wore. They were thin at the knees, suggesting heavy use. This man had had an active life. Far more adventurous than hers it seemed, and with such similar time. A woodcutter's axe rested beside his leg, wedged between the floorboards and the seat. And a heavy crossbow sat behind him, loaded and ready to fire. "You coming from Ryse?" Inyalia asked, not sure what else to say. She'd never been one for small talk.

"Yep. Plenty of coin to be had for those willing to work for it. This is my third trip this month. Damn bears are breeding faster than we can clear em out. But I guess that ain't such a bad thing in my line of work." He kept his eyes on the road, catching up to the wagon ahead of them.

"I guess not." Inyalia watched the world around her. She was, as he'd said, another set of eyes. She stared intimately at the beauty of the world around her. The leaves were turning orange and beginning their descent to the forest floor. The evergreens held fast, standing out among the ocean of browns and golds. For the moment, she was at peace. Her worries and fears forgotten in her renewed love of the land.

"What's in Dragon Sanctum if you don't mind me asking?"

"I'm headed there to join the Rangers Corps."

Willam nodded. "Met a few rangers in my travels. Decent sort if you ask me. Good to have around in a fight too. I once knew one who could knock an acorn from a tree, absent its shell." A hearty laugh bellowed from him, recalling the memory. "Won quite a bit of coin from me on that bet."

Inyalia smiled, wondering if she could do the same. She'd never tried an acorn, but once, she shot an angry wasp out of the air. If that wasn't close enough, she didn't know what was.

The sun was just reaching its apex when Dragon Sanctum appeared in the distance. From the hill top, it stood out like a beacon, spreading hope across the countryside. The round building was open on four sides, though only two could be seen from her vantage point. Atop the towering domed roof, a huge statue of a white dragon was perched. Its leathery wings were outstretched, casting shadow across the ground for what had to have been miles. The recessed webs of the massive wings showed every bulging muscle and vein. Two sets of coal black, ridged horns, matching color of the teeth, spines, and talons, protruded from its skull. One set swept out and back like that of a gazelle. The other protruded and curved around like a ram, framing the sides of its gargantuan head. Inyalia stared in stunned silence, drawing closer to the magnificent structure. The maw was open and aimed at the sky, silently roaring its might. Of the hundreds of sharp teeth, the smallest of them was larger than her entire body. In all her cycles, never could she have imagined such a wonderful and frightening creature. The stories she'd heard could never do it justice.

Willam smiled, seeing her awe. "First time, huh?"

Finding her words, Inyalia broke away from its enchanting majesty. "Is it that obvious?"

"Just a little. When we pass the stable, I'll stop and let you climb down. It was a pleasure meeting you, Inyalia. I look forward to hearing your tales when next we meet."

Thank you, Willam. It was a pleasure meeting you as well."

The coach came to a stop and Inyalia climbed down. She was finally here. Her stomach churned. She felt sick. All the fear that had vacated during Willam's company suddenly returned. But she was too close to turn back now. Releasing a deep breath, she watched the caravan pull away. Willam waved goodbye and disappeared in the distance. This was really it. She'd arrived. Now all she had to do was prove herself.

Turning away from the stables, Inyalia approached one of the wooden ramps that provided access to the grand structure. There were a total of eight of them, two sprouting from each corner. Upon first glance it seemed a bit odd, but now she realized the sections between ramps served as fortified walls for the stable, forge, smokehouse, and a few other commodities. In one of the alcoves, an elf worked diligently, hammering a wooden device together. Beside him, several others rested. Hides of various shades and thicknesses were stretched over the wooden frames, displaying every mark, mar, and scar the creature received during its life. Some of the cured hides retained their fur, while others were stripped and draped over one of many horizontal posts. She suddenly knew this was where they got the leather for their armors. And soon, if all went according to plan, she'd have her own.

A sweet smoke lingered in the air. It billowed from a port at the top of a large iron box. The attending elf slid a small window open at its base, revealing a pile of glowing embers. Closing the window, he opened the door. Scooping a handful of wood from the barrel beside him, liquid dripped between his fingers. It sizzled as he tossed it into the smoker and closed the door.

Hearing an arrow strike its target, Inyalia turned to find another section, not far from the sanctum. Several dummies stood erect, holding wooden swords and shields. Beyond them, an archer's lane rested. It had both stationary and moving targets set at various heights and distances.

Two rangers stood behind one of the many markers, trading shots. It took every ounce of will she had not to fire one of her arrows between theirs. Their shots were sloppy, nearly three inches out. Even from here, she had no doubt she could hit a perfect bullseye. But that was bound to draw unwanted attention. That was the last things she desired at the moment.

Following the curved ramp around, Inyalia reached the northwest corner. Somewhere on the other side of the building, she heard the ring of a smith's hammer. Elves scurried about, both inside and out, performing a number of tasks, though the population wasn't nearly as dense as she'd expected. This was the headquarters of the Second Battalion. She'd anticipated hundreds of elves, most of them rangers, all crowding for space. But that seemed to be far from the case. Though as an afterthought, it made sense. Why would an entire battalion waste their days here when they could be exploring the forests?

Inyalia approached the nearest opening. It happened to be the one above the ramp she'd ascended, though from the corner where it dumped her, she could have chosen either.

Stepping through the large opening, she paused to inspect the wonders inside. It was as grand as she could have hoped for, though it lacked the over-the-top exuberance she'd seen outside. The interior walls were made of a glossy wood that ran vertical from floor to ceiling. Various shades and sizes of stone were locked into an intricate puzzle, sealing the floor. Overhead, exposed rafters left the vaulted ceiling open and inviting. A large chandelier, made from stag antlers, hung in the center, providing light to the layer below. Inyalia inspected the balcony that wrapped the upper level. It connected to a number of closed doors around the outer ring, though she had no ideas as to what it contained.

Her attention returned to the excitement around her. She felt a wave of heat to the right. The stone floor extended up, creating a half circle where a large fireplace protruded from the wall. Flame licked the air from the pile of burning logs within. It was positioned dead center of the two entryways on this half of the structure. Another just like it, rested on the other side. To her left, a wall blocked much of her sight. It stretched nearly to the center of the sanctum before rounding off. She couldn't tell from the wall beside her, but its twin, mirrored on the opposing side, separated nearly a quarter of the sanctum from view. It was then she realized it had been divided into quarters, each one nearly identical to its opposite.

The opening between the two dividing walls held a large round table at the neck of the hourglass-shaped room. An elf stood over it, dressed in officer's armor, similar to her father's. In fact, there was but one difference. The sigil upon his breastplate was inlaid in silver. Her father's armor was gold. Inyalia marched toward the elf, recognizing his as she neared.

Ranger- Lord Traevon Duskwillow was one of her father's closest friends. He'd joined them for dinner on many occasions when her father was home. In addition, he was also Lord of Dragon Sanctum, and commander of the Second Battalion. If anyone knew who she was supposed to talk to, it would be him.

Levi Samuel

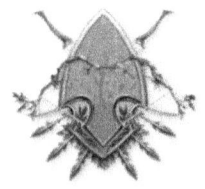

Chapter IV
A Road Less Traveled

Traevon looked up from his reports, seeing the young elf approach. His lips shifted from a content rest to the makings of a smile. "Inyalia Highlor, I wondered when I'd be seeing you. Your father told me you'd be arriving today, but I didn't expect you until later." He leaned over to whisper. "Just between you and me, he suggested I give you the special treatment. But I fear you'd never forgive me."

"Thank you?" Inyalia wasn't sure what the special treatment was, but with a statement like that, it was probably best not to ask. "I'm just happy doing what everyone else does, if that's okay?"

Nodding to himself, Traevon released something resembling a chuckle. It passed nearly as quick and his posture became rigid and formal. "Unfortunately, that's really not up to me. All of our recruits are paired with a senior ranger during their trials. Most of what you'll face will be at their behest. Though I'll warn you, you're petitioning to become part of an elite force, sworn to protect your homeland at all cost, your life included. Personal safety cannot be assured at any time from now until forever. However, any ranger, near or far, young or old, will do everything within their ability to ensure you never come to harm. If you're willing to accept these terms, I'll point you in the right direction."

"My safety cannot be assured whether I become a ranger or not. I think I'd rather face the same odds by being a part of the greatest fighting force known to elven kind."

This elicited a full smile from the commander. "You always had a way with flattery. Though, be careful who you make such claims around. Members of both the army and navy have been known to pass through here. I wouldn't want you to have to defend those words on your first day."

"Noted, sir!"

"And enough with that *Sir* crap. I may be an officer, but I work for a living!"

"Yes, Si— What am I supposed to call you?"

"Traevon in social settings, Commander for formal affairs."

"Yes, Commander."

"Now that we have the formalities out of the way. You desire admittance into the Rangers Corps, by means of the trials. Am I correct in this assessment?"

"Yes, Commander. Unless there's another way. If so, I'll take that." Inyalia didn't think there was another way, but if so, it would mean all of her fears were for nothing.

"None that you would approve of. We used to take a red-hot poker and brand the sigil into each elf's chest. Those who didn't scream were admitted. I think you'll find the trials a preferred alternative."

Inyalia's face dropped. Suddenly the trials didn't seem so bad.

"I'm kidding." Traevon drew a folded piece of vellum from his pocket. "This is an encrypted note, providing any details your mentor may need to know about you. I don't know who it is. Your father made those arrangements, which means they probably already know everything mentioned in the missive and more. But you'll want it for verification anyway." Reaching into a drawer hidden beneath the large table, Traevon removed a tiny glass vial. Holding it up to the firelight, he inspected the clear liquid within and handed both it, and the missive to her. "The vial is quite a bit more serious. You'll have to drink it before leaving here. The contents will affect you in ways I cannot say, though it is not fatally poisonous, at least not in this dosage. Your mentor will have the antidote. You simply have to reach him. The affects have never lasted longer than three days, so if you fail to meet your mentor and receive the antidote, you won't die. But you may as well return home. Every ranger in the corps, your father and myself included, have been subject to this serum. Do you have any questions?"

Inyalia thought long and hard, but nothing came to mind. She had a feeling all of her questions would be answered in time. And if they weren't, she could always ask later. She shook her head.

"Very well. If you're hungry, we'll grab a quick bite to eat. After that, we'll get you outfitted and ready to go."

The next few hours passed relatively quickly. Inyalia had explored most of the lower level. The walled areas housed a number of private bedrooms, though she didn't explore much of the living quarters. She was surprised to learn that there was a complete set of barracks in the upper level, which made sense. Several people lived here full time. They had to have a place to sleep. The sanctum was also equipped with two full kitchens, a dining hall, a recreations lounge, and a library. After the tour, Traevon led her to the armory.

The quartermaster worked with a skill Inyalia had never seen. With a single look, she'd fitted her for every piece of her new armor. And now that it covered her from neck to ankle, Inyalia couldn't dispute that it fit near perfect. Once the stiff leather was broken in, it would fit even better. At least that's what the quartermaster told her.

Running her hands down the sleek leather, accenting her slender frame, Inyalia smiled wide. It was just recruit's armor, displaying no special insignia or markings of any kind, but she felt amazing. If they went to war tomorrow, she knew she could singlehandedly destroy the enemy. Though she hoped that didn't happen. War was a heavy price for looking good.

"Would you like a helm?" The quartermaster asked, lifting the leather item. It was simple in design, contoured to provide maximum movement, while offering the highest protection. It would cover the sides and back of her head, allowing a small gap where her facial features could be seen.

Inyalia thought about it, but most of the other rangers didn't use them. Even her father complained they were bulky and difficult to maintain. It limited both sight and sound, the most valuable tools at a ranger's disposal. "No, thank you."

"Are you sure?" Traevon countered. "It may not seem very useful at the moment, but if you ever find yourself in battle, you're going to want it."

Inyalia sighed. He wasn't wrong. Tools weren't important until you didn't have the right one. "I'll take it, but it's staying in the bag until it's needed."

The quartermaster laughed, handing it over.

Inyalia put it atop her head, feeling it snap into place. All things considered, it wasn't unpleasant. And the loss of senses wasn't as severe as she'd imagined, but it wasn't something she planned to use often. Removing it, she laid it on the table with her newly issued bedroll, rucksack, waterskin, and laundry list of other supplies.

"How about a bow?"

"I have my own." Inyalia offered.

"May I see it?" Traevon asked, extending his hand.

Inyalia removed it from the supplies she'd brought with her and handed it over.

Thoroughly inspecting the wood, Traevon gave it a subtle flex. Stringing it with lightning fast speed, he brought it to a full draw and stared down the sight channel above his grip. Slowly, he let off the draw, unstrung, and handed it back to her. "Not a bad instrument. It has plenty of strength, and the grain is flowing the correct direction. I can tell it's not your first bow, but it won't be your last. When you fire, it hits what, half an inch left?"

"How can you know that without firing it yourself?" Inyalia was stunned by his accuracy.

Traevon smiled. "It's my job to know such things. But give it time. You'll learn to notice them as well." Turning to the quartermaster, he continued. "Her bow is fine but get her some arrows and a quiver. That ratty thing she's been carrying around will dump the lot the first time she has to hit the dirt."

The quartermaster nodded and disappeared into the back room. She returned a moment later with the items in tow.

Inyalia inspected the new quiver. It was about half the size of her old one, but there were several pockets molded inside and out. She could already see how it separated different batches of arrows. But the biggest difference was how it mounted. Her old quiver had a single strap that crossed her torso. This one was similar in design, but there were two adjustable buckles, one near the top and another at the base.

Traevon took the quiver, holding it for her to see. "If you find yourself in a position where you have to drop your gear quickly, pull this tail. It's the same for your pack as well." He gave a firm yank and the strap fell free at the buckle. "You'll also notice it rides a bit different than you're used to. Turn around."

Inyalia spun, feeling the quiver attach to her. He wasn't wrong. She'd always had to reach overhead to draw an arrow. With this, it removed almost half of the action, letting her not only decide which arrow to grab, but do so in a fraction of the time.

"The buckles snap to your armor the same way the overlapping plates do. It works with or without the pauldrons, and the entire design was built to be there when you need it, and to remove easily when you don't."

Inyalia was surprised by how methodical they'd been in its design. It minimized the need for excessive buckles, while keeping it light and slim. "You guys have thought of everything!" Inyalia exclaimed in excitement.

Ignoring her outburst, Traevon removed the quiver, prompting her to turn and face him. "As for the arrows themselves, you see the dividers. It'll take some getting used to, but once you're familiar with it, you can draw any arrow you desire without looking. I tell you this because, for the duration of your trials, you will not be permitted to use your personal arrows." He removed one of the red fletched arrows, holding it up so she could see the tip.

Like a traditional arrow, the wooden shaft was capped by a metal head. But this arrow was not sharp. In fact, it didn't even have a point. Where the head began, it tapered out like an inverted funnel, leaving a shallow dish where it would impact.

Reaching into the pocket of the quiver, he pulled out a linen sack that was drawn with a piece of leather twine. Loosening it, he retrieved a tiny leather pouch that had been dyed green. It was just barely large enough to place a single finger inside. Carefully, he inserted the dished arrowhead into the pouch and pulled the drawstring. It sucked tight, showing definition of the head, and the string broke off in his hand. "You'll be using these. We call them blunt tips, but eventually, you'll have access to other pouches. In the off chance you come across an arrow with any other colored pouch, do not use it without express permission. I can't stress that enough."

"I have a question now."

"What are the other colors?" Traevon answered instinctively. "Not all situations call for deadly force. And you can't always get up close and personal. As a result, we made five variants. The green, as I've explained, are blunt tips. The blue ones have a knockout powder. Shoot someone in the face and they fall unconscious almost immediately. But if you don't want to kill them, make sure they have something soft to land on. Or at the very least, make sure it's not a long drop. The yellow ones deliver a stronger dose of the liquid in that vial I gave you earlier. Those are good for making distractions when your target is unwilling. Let's see—." He trailed off, recalling the others. "We call the red ones boom buttons. They explode on impact, destroying everything within a five foot radius. And last, but certainly not least, the black ones are called poison caps. Even with an antidote in hand, if you get hit by one, you're dead before you can bring it to your lips."

An uncomfortable silence filled the room. Finally, Inyalia found a word to describe what she'd just heard. "Wow!"

"Yeah." Traevon added. "So, like I said, don't shoot anyone without permission, especially with any other head but green."

Nodding her profuse agreement, Inyalia took the blunt tip and returned it to the quiver. "Got it."

Night was just beginning to fall when they left the armory. Inyalia was dressed in her new armor, though the helm was tucked away safely in her rucksack. Her quiver was mounted and filled with blunt tip arrows, aside from the five she'd been allowed to load from her own stash. Traevon didn't want her to be completely defenseless after all. Every piece of equipment she could think of was sorted and organized to the best of her ability, with some minor influence from the commander.

Approaching the north exit, Traevon stole a glance outside, inspecting the last rays of sunlight over the trees. "You sure you want to head out tonight? It's a long walk to Thayer. I'd hate for you to get lost along the way."

"Yeah, I'm sure. I just want to get this over with." Inyalia held up the vial, uncertain what was going to happen when she drank it.

"If you're certain. I wouldn't want to experience that again, especially at night, alone, on a forest road where any number of monsters could be hiding in the shadows." His calm demeanor faded, replaced by joyful laughter. "I'm sorry. I couldn't help myself. You'll be fine." His laughter trailed away.

Taking a deep breath, Inyalia popped the cork and raised it high. "Bottoms up." She tipped it back and swallowed. It went down with ease. There was no flavor, just a warm tingle as it hit her stomach. "How long do I have before it hits?"

"Hard to say. Some have made it nearly an hour. Others don't make it ten steps. Just remember to stay to the road."

Nodding, Inyalia turned and made her way down the ramp. This was it. This was the moment she'd been both dreading and anticipating. Her trials were officially underway. All she had to do now was make sure she passed them.

Within minutes Inyalia was upon the east road and heading north. Traveling at a quick, but steady pace, she repeated what Traevon had last said. "Stay on the road." There was no telling what awaited her, but if she stayed on the road, she'd be just fine. "Stay on the road." She repeated. The words sounded funny. They were deep, but light at the same time. She could nearly see their outline, bubbly and floating overhead. If it weren't so dark, she was certain she could. That was an interesting notion. Where was the moon? It had been there a moment ago. But now she was all alone, walking a forest road at night, with any number of monsters hiding in the shadows.

Inyalia shivered. She was cold. And there was definitely something following her, many somethings. But she couldn't see them. They moved only in the dark, in the places she wasn't looking. Her heart raced. The sounds of nature disappeared, leaving nothing but her thoughts. She was alone and cold, traveling a forest road in the dark, with any number of monsters hiding in the shadows.

Fear grew inside her. She wanted to run. But she couldn't see the road. If she ran, she could lose it. And then the monsters would certainly have her. A twig snapped off in the distance. She jumped, spinning its direction. "What was that?" Her breath hastened. She could see the steam escaping with each rapid breath. That wasn't good. If it left her, she'd never get it back.

Inyalia reached to catch her breath. It was no use. The steam passed right through her grip. Panic grew. She was going to suffocate. The faster she breathed, the quicker her air would be gone. "No!" Inyalia demanded. She had to stop it. Holding her breath, the steam stopped spilling from her. She was safe now. At least for the moment.

Her lungs burned. She couldn't hold it any longer. Releasing, she was pleased to see that she could breathe. The steam still escaped her, even faster now that she was panting. But now, it went back inside when she inhaled. So long as it continued to do that, she was going to be okay.

Looking around, she wasn't sure which way to go. The road was hidden, and she was fairly certain she'd turned. But which way was she headed? And from where was she coming? She was all alone. All alone with nothing but the lingering presence behind her. She was haunted, tormented by its watchful, yet elusive gaze. Was she helpless to its shrouding grip, closing around her like a candle's flame being snuffed out?

A strong breeze blew across the nearby leaves, clinging to their skeletal branches. Inyalia could hear it, but she could not feel it. Shadows danced at the edge of her sight. But no matter how many times she looked, nothing was there.

Swallowing hard, Inyalia wiped the clinging sweat from her forehead. She tried to force the fear into the pit of her stomach. There was no reason to be alarmed. The rangers protected these roads. She was becoming one of them. Soon, she would be a protector herself. And as it stood, she'd seen no threats as of yet. Why should she fear? How long had she walked? The outpost couldn't be that much further. Or had she just begun? She couldn't remember. It could have been minutes, or it could have been days. There was no way to tell. And since the moon was gone, that could only mean the sun was gone too. She was trapped in perpetual darkness, never to see the light again. But that was no reason to fear. She was never one to fear shadows. Most days she was never one to fear the things she should.

Exhaling sharply, forcing her resolve, Inyalia trekked on. She'd never been to Thayer, but its location was well known. And so long as she stayed to the road, she'd run straight into it. She just had to follow the mountains north. That was it. That was her sense of direction. Finding the towering peaks, blocking out the lightless sky, she oriented herself, placing them to her right. So long as they stayed there, she'd be headed north.

She walked toward her destination, burying the fear growing inside her. It was all she could do. The was no sound. No wind. No light. She was alone, surrounded by monsters. Suddenly, her fear escaped. She stopped dead in her tracks, unable to take another step. The things she thought she knew were wrong. She could hear the wind. She could hear the footsteps encircling her. The sound of cloth rubbing against itself rang out like a trumpet. Constricted breaths echoed in the dark. Despite the lack of light, dark shapes filled her vision.

The beat of a drum increased in both pace and volume. It blocked the other sound, banging inside her head. It was so loud, threatening to destroy her ears. It echoed into the mountains, drowning her in noise. More noise than she'd ever heard. She squeezed her eyes shut, hoping to somehow block it all out. If not the noise, then the creeping shadows. She breathed deeply through her nose, sucking in and out. She could feel hands upon her skin. They were touching her all over, tormenting her, begging her to open her eyes. If she did, they would claw them out. Unable to take any more, Inyalia screamed. She had to hear something, anything over the banging drum. "Stop!"

The drum stopped. The wheezing breaths vanished. Even the scratching fibers of twill were gone. The only sound that remained was the fading echo of her own voice. Slowly, carefully, Inyalia peeked from beneath her eyelids, hoping the shadows were gone. They weren't touching her anymore. That was an improvement.

She couldn't see movement, but that didn't mean anything. They'd hidden from her before. There was only one option and it was a dangerous one. But she had no other choice. Dropping her ruck, Inyalia removed one of the torches she'd been given and struck her flint. She was pleased to see the sparks. That meant the torch would at least work. With the absence of the sun and moon, she wasn't sure she'd have that much. Raking the stone over the torch head, the sparks jumped into the wax coating. They melted down, releasing the scent of oil, but it did not light. She struck again, much to the same effect. The third time, a flame appeared. It grew wider, melting away the wax. She held it aloft for a moment, letting the flame engulf the entire head, disposing of any excess wax. With everything else going on, she didn't want to add burning herself to the mix.

Inyalia raised the torch, expanding its glow. Even with its assistance, she was surprised by how little she could see. Her vision had never been so poor. Heaving the pack once again, she started along the path. With any luck, she'd reach the outpost before the flaming target betrayed her. She was free at last. Free of the fear. Free of the shadows. And free of the monsters.

A heavy gust surrounded her, threatening to extinguish the flame. It blew fallen leaves in all directions, rattling those still clinging to their trees. Branches clapped together, cracking and popping. The swirling vortex of wind made her eyes water. And in the lowlight, when her torch was little more than a glow, Inyalia could see the faces. The silhouettes moved in the darkness, just beyond reach. They surrounded the dim glow, refusing to step within its radius. She could see them. They weren't figments of her imagination. No tricks of light, playing her a fool. No! They were real. And they were waiting for her.

Inyalia shivered, frozen within the wind. She couldn't move. The faces were waiting. They smiled, knowing she was theirs. They licked their lips, anticipating the taste of blood. Seeing one swoop toward her, daring the protective barrier of light, Inyalia swung the torch. The flame swooshed, nearly disappearing from the burning wick. Faster than she could react the shadows closed in. They swarmed like a school of hungry fish fighting over a worm, retreating only when the flame grew. So long as it burned, they couldn't get her. But what if it went out? How would she escape? Another charged, revealing ashen skin and needle-like teeth. She swung again, batting it away.

Another gust blew in, this time more violent. And another. The wind was battering her unlike any she'd felt before. And, despite her best efforts, the torch went out.

Thousands of pin-pricks punctured Inyalia's hands and face. It burned her exposed skin. Crushing pressure constricted her entire body. She couldn't move. She was trapped. Trapped between vicious shadows and growing fear. She could feel them, whatever they were. They were cold, malicious, hungry. Whispers filled her mind, undecipherable voices burrowing into her soul. Inyalia collapsed to the frozen earth, her arms wrapped around her knees. She was going to die here. There was no doubt of that. And to make matters worse, she hadn't even completed her first trial yet.

A soft glow formed around her. The shadows shrieked in retreat, trying desperately to avoid the burning light. Tear-filled eyes searched the fleeing darkness, looking for the source of her salvation. A heavy thump shook the ground. Inyalia felt it in her body. She stared into the blue glow, uncertain if she was safe. It stopped the shadows from ripping her to pieces, but what towered over her was much more frightening.

Pearl-white scales shimmered from the calm deep breaths of the massive reptile. Each time its chest fell, the iridescent plating flexed revealing an icy-blue glow. The thick onyx talons churned the dirt where the weight had embedded them. The leathery white wings were folded neatly behind its wide torso, though they were too large to pass out of sight.

Inyalia trailed the glowing form from its beating chest, up the slender spiny neck, and finally to its horned head. The brilliant blue eyes stared compassionately at her, pupils narrow and tall, larger than her entire body. This was the dragon that rested atop the sanctum. Only somehow bigger.

"Do not be afraid child. I mean you no harm."

Inyalia heard the words in her mind as much as she felt them in her backside. They were strong yet forgiving. But what surprised her most, they were feminine. "Who—Who are you?" The question hung on her lips. A dragon telling her not to be afraid was like telling someone not to look. Nature enforced the exact opposite.

"My name is Alonandrensal. But you may call me Alona. Tell me, child, what are you doing out here? Are you not aware the dangers these mountains represent?"

Inyalia picked herself up. She was terrified, but that would remain whether she was lying on her back or standing on her feet. Staring intently at the great beast, she realized her sweating had stopped. Her heart was no longer racing. And, somehow, the moon had returned to the sky. But with the lingering perspiration, the cold was causing her to shiver. That and the crippling fear. The fear certainly had something to do with it. "I'm headed to Thayer Outpost. The rangers sent me to deliver a message. It's part of my trials."

Alona shook her head in an almost human manner. Releasing a sigh, the dragon tucked her legs beneath her, reminiscent of a giant cat, and plopped down. "Elves! Always testing one another. I once saw a father toss his child into a lake in an attempt to teach it to swim. The child did, but there was a moment I thought otherwise." Reaching to her chin, one of the massive talons extended and gently scratched between the dense scales.

"Forgive me for asking, and believe me when I say I'm grateful you got rid of those things, but what— I'm sorry, why are you here?" Her fear was lessening. There was something about the mammoth beast that reassured her safety. Yet the sheer size of it was worthy of terror.

"Those *things*, as you called them, are trapped souls. This realm is unique from the others I've seen. There is no natural order here. We, The Seven Keys, were brought here to fill that void in an artificial capacity. But, as with all things, when one neglects their duties the machine ceases to function properly."

"I don't understand what you're talking about."

"One day, sooner than you realize, my words will make sense. But until then, just know that I offer my apologies. I should have trapped those souls long ago. It was my fault they attacked you. As repentance, please allow me to offer you a gift. May it lead your way when all seems lost." The glow beneath Alona's pearl scales grew vibrant, near blinding in the dark night. It expanded, wrapping around the young elf.

Inyalia felt the cold leave her. A calm replaced her fear, drowning the lingering doubts inside her. For the first time in a long time, she was truly at peace. And suddenly, as quick as the glow had enveloped her, Inyalia was standing alone on the eastern pass. There were no shadows to be repelled by the faint glow emanating from her. The soft rays of moonlight lit the way, better than any torch could. In the distance, Inyalia heard the flap of large leathery wings.

The remainder of the journey didn't take any time at all now that she could see where she was going. Along the mountain pass, she could see the glow of civilization. Thayer Outpost was settled in an alcove between two of the mountain's roots. It was of fair size, larger than a village, but smaller than a city, and still not quite a town. Sharpened posts comprised the outer wall, blocking out all sight with the exception of a few thatch roofs. There were two however that stood much taller, suggesting a second floor.

Inyalia approached the sealed gate, looking up at the elf on watch. His eyes locked onto her and he signal below.

"Welcome Ranger. Will you be staying long?"

Inyalia was caught off-guard by the title. She hadn't prepared for it yet. And now that it was thrown upon her, all she could do was smile.

The watchman cleared his throat and spoke again. "Will you be staying long?"

Pulled from her glee by the vocal grumblings, Inyalia replied. "I'm uncertain to the length of my stay. I'm here to deliver word from Dragon Sanctum. Are there any rangers inside I might speak with?"

The gate began to groan as it opened. "Only one to my knowledge. You'll find him at the inn. Last table to the right. Follow this road. It's the first two-story building you'll come across."

"Thank you." Inyalia stepped inside and marched toward her destination. She heard the gate close behind her. The security of this place seemed odd. There was no real threat as far as she knew. Why did they bother closing the gate? But then again, she'd literally just been attacked not an hour prior. Perhaps they were more justified than she knew.

Reaching the inn, Inyalia heard several voices before she neared the door. For such a small settlement, it seemed quite chaotic. Everyone in town had to be here. Approaching the wooden barrier, she grabbed hold of the bronze handle and pulled. The stale odor of pipe smoke and ale rolled out the door, assaulting her nostrils. Flickering light illuminated her face, and the numerous conversations quieted to see who was entering. Though it didn't last long. They resumed almost immediately, realizing it was no one of importance.

Inyalia stepped inside, taking in the full visage of the tavern before her. She'd never been in one, but it was about how she'd imagined it. Lots of people talking and having a merry time. Tables filled with people playing cards. Subtle music lingering in the background, and a long bar, topped in granite, that ran the entire length of the wall. Though this bar was topped in wood.

Inyalia noticed a half-elf behind the bar, wiping the counter with a rag. She didn't see many of his kind, though it was more frequent than seeing a human. Half-elves were often shunned by certain noble families. It wasn't right as far as she was concerned, but there wasn't much she could do about it.

Glancing around the room, Inyalia took note of a narrow hall that extended past the bar. At its entrance, where the row of staggered circular tables ended, there was a set of stairs that rounded the corner and disappeared into shadow.

Turning her attention toward the people, she was surprised by how many could fit in here. It wasn't crowded but it remained the largest collection she'd seen in months. The majority of the population was made of elves. There was no surprise there. But there were also about half a dozen half-elves, including the barkeep. And shockingly, three humans engaged in a card game. Finding the last table to the right, Inyalia spotted the elf she sought. And he apparently knew who she was, as his gaze was locked intently upon her.

She studied his armor as she cut through the crowd. It wasn't as fancy as many of the others. In fact, it was relatively simple. There were no flashy additions or really anything out of the ordinary. The browns were dulled from use, and the hardened material appeared broken down and worn near the joints. The only real way to describe it was rough and neglected, but still functional, much like the elf wearing it. Despite his less than enthusiastic appearance, Inyalia still knew what she was looking at. There was no mistaking the sigil displayed across his left collar guard. This elf was a lieutenant. And given he was the only one in town, he was her lieutenant. Though there was one part of his insignia she did not expect.

Making her way across the room, Inyalia approached the elf. Without word, she extended her hand bearing the encrypted missive.

The elf took it, keeping his eyes locked on hers. Unfolding the thin vellum, he broke his gaze and quickly scanned the words. "I see. Well done, recruit. Take a seat." As if the chair beside him obeyed the command, it shot out from beneath the table, its wooden legs sliding gently across the wax planked floor.

Inyalia unwrapped her cloak and sat, allowing it to rest comfortably beneath her. She stared in silence, awaiting word. She had no idea what she was supposed to do now. Moreover, why had her father sent her to a wild elf?

A slight smirk formed on his otherwise stern face. He pulled a glass vial from the leather pouch resting along his belt. Laying it on the table in front of her, he studied her face, seeming to read what she was thinking. "It doesn't appear you need this, but it's better to be safe. Drink up."

Inyalia popped the cork and swallowed the contents.

"As I'm sure you know by now, the first vial you drank is known to cause a number of effects, including hallucinations, paranoia, and occasional memory loss. In fact, most people never remember drinking it to begin with. So, I have to ask. How did you do it?"

"Do what?"

"I hadn't expected you until tomorrow evening at minimum. Even then, you would still be showing signs of influence. Yet here you are, calm and collected. The only way that should be possible is if you've ingested the contents of the antidote I just gave you. My current theories are, you acquired another, or you possibly made your own with an advanced knowledge of herbalism. So, I ask again, how did you do it?"

"I assure you, prior to the one you just gave me, I've had no such potion. It was unnaturally dark. I was terrified. There were all these— things surrounding me. I didn't know how much more I could take. And that's when the dragon showed up."

The elf leaned against the back of his chair. He glanced around the room, making sure no one was listening. "A dragon?" A soft chuckle escaped him.

"Yes. She said her name was Alonezara, or something like that."

The elf smiled in disbelief, though there was something in her voice that suggested honesty. "You? You met the white queen?" Shaking his head, he sighed. "I guess that's an explanation. Though I'm surprised. She rarely chooses to interfere with our affairs. A few have reported seeing her high above the mountains on a cloudless day. But, to my knowledge, none have spoken with her since the first elves settled here——." He cut himself off, seemingly lost in thought.

Inyalia waited several moments in silence before speaking. "So, perhaps you can answer a question for me?"

He waved his hand, granting permission.

"Forgive me for being so blunt, but why did my father pick a wild elf?"

His smile grew as he nodded to her question. "Yes. Because wild elves are lesser than all the rest of you highborn nobles."

"I don't mean it like that."

"Sure, you do. You wouldn't care about my status if you didn't. But, to answer your question, your father chose me because I've earned his trust. He knows I'll perform my duties to the best of my ability, and he believes you have the potential to learn from me. But anyways, where are my manners? My name is Tylor Caer'Moor. As I'm sure you've already gathered, I'm a Ranger-Lieutenant. Though my rank will have little impact on our relationship. Using my wild elf status, I serve the corps outside the traditional means. I can go places others cannot, and if things go bad, nobody, including your father, can be held accountable for my actions. While we're together, it will be my job to assess your abilities, and ensure you become the best ranger you can be. Only after my job is complete, will you be formally invited into the ranks and assigned to a unit. Do you have any questions?"

Hanging on each word, committing them to memory, Inyalia nearly missed the prompt. "Um, no?"

"Very well. Eat, drink, and be merry. I'll arrange a room for you tonight. Tomorrow your training officially begins."

Levi Samuel

Chapter V
The Path to Enlightenment

Floorboards creaked just outside Inyalia's door. Her eyes shot open, hearing a soft rap against the wooden barrier. She glanced out the single window, realizing it was still dark. Quickly, she sat up, swinging her legs off the bed. The wood was cold against her bare feet. Grabbing her dagger from the table, Inyalia wrapped her cloak tightly and approached the door. Carefully, she unlatched and pulled it toward her. Lantern light pierced the darkness of her room. She saw Tylor standing just outside, fully dressed and ready to travel.

"Good morning. The sun will rise soon. Gather your things and meet me downstairs. We'll have a quick breakfast before we head out." Without another word, he spun and disappeared toward the stairs.

Inyalia closed the door, latching it behind her. She wasn't used to being up so early. And her previous day's travel had caught up with her. Yawning, she stretched her arms wide and approached the bed. Inyalia disrobed and lifted the shield from the lantern on the end table. The fire sticks rested beside it in a small canister. Grabbing one, she quickly struck it, watching the flame come to life. It released the scent of burning pine and sulfur. Carefully, she lit the wick of the lantern and adjusted it to light the room. Shaking the firestick, it went out with a wisp of smoke. She replaced the shield and laid her dagger on the table. She wasn't ready to start. But that choice was no longer hers.

Exhaling sharply, Inyalia pulled her clothes and armor into place, ensuring they were coupled properly. Positioning her quiver, she wrapped the heavy cloak around her and slung the pack over her shoulder. With a final look around the room, Inyalia grabbed the rest of her effects and twisted the knob on the lamp. The flame shrunk and disappeared. Making her way across the room, Inyalia opened the door and stepped into the lantern lit hallway.

Hurrying down the stairs, she was surprised to find only three people in the large room. An elf stood behind the bar, casually wiping out the previous night's mugs. One by one, he stacked them on a shelf. Another elf was kicked back in a heavy leather-bound chair. She hadn't seen it the night before, but that area was fairly crowded. The elf was staring intently into the fire pit, his back to her. Inyalia could only see the tips of his ears, and what appeared to be a rather thick book opened somewhere near the midpoint, though he clearly wasn't reading it. And lastly, Tylor sat at the table he'd occupied the night before. A wooden platter sat in front of him filled with sliced meat, eggs, and toast. A similar platter rested where Inyalia had been sitting.

Tylor nodded to the young elf descending the bottom steps. He gestured to the chair beside him and slid the undisturbed platter closer to the edge.

Inyalia took a seat and dug in. It was a simple meal, rather bland as far as spice went. She'd grown accustomed to the meals her mother made. Even the food at Dragon Sanctum was pretty good. This was extremely poor by comparison. How anyone could mess up meat and eggs was a mystery, yet somehow they'd managed. Even the toast was burnt completely through. It was like they weren't even trying. But, if she could force it down, it'd sate her for a while. Worst case scenario, she still had about half a bag of the dried meats, fruits, and cheese her mother had given her. And if that failed, the sanctum had supplied her with a week's worth of rations.

Taking a long draw from his tankard, Tylor slammed it down next to his plate. It clapped against the wooden tabletop and echoed through the near empty pub. Belching loudly, he turned and addressed Inyalia, speaking as if no one else mattered. "We have a long journey ahead of us. If all goes accordingly, we'll make camp just before nightfall and set out again at first light."

Nodding her understanding, Inyalia scooped the overcooked eggs onto the burnt toast and blackened meat. That was the only way she could get enough moisture to cut it. Even then it was difficult. Taking as large a bite as she dared, Inyalia suffered through the gritty mixture and swallowed. It clung to the back of her throat. She tipped back her mug in a desperate attempt to wash it down. The sour concoction did little to aid her, but at least it went down. The entire experience was dreadful. But the quicker it was gone, the quicker she could forget about it.

They finished their breakfast in silence and made for the gate. Inyalia recognized it from the night before. She hoped they weren't heading back toward the sanctum. If so, why did she waste the energy to come here? Containing her concern, she looked to the elf standing atop the gate. He was also the same. But that part made sense. After all, she'd only been here a few hours.

"Good morning, Tylor. Heading out?"

"That we are. Would you mind opening the gate?"

"Of course. Terrence, wake up and open the gate!" The watchman shouted from his perch. After a long moment the wooden gate began to creak open. "Damn fool's always sleeping on the job. Ancients forbid we ever have a real need. My apologies for the delay. Any idea when you'll be back?"

Tylor gestured toward the opening. "After you." Returning his attention to the watchman, he started forward. "It's hard to say. Though when I do, I'll be sure to swing by. Always a pleasure seeing your wife and my kids."

"You know, I thought they looked a bit like you." The watchman laughed off the joke and gave an awkward salute. "Be well, my friend."

"You as well." Tylor sauntered through the gate, joining Inyalia on the other side. Reaching into the liner of his cloak, he removed a long-stemmed pipe and a leather pouch. Opening it, a musky scent waft into the air. Tylor grabbed a pinch of the shredded leaf and carefully stuffed it into the bowl. Tucking his supplies away, he scraped a short firestick along the top rim of the pipe. It flared to life. No sooner than the flame erupted, it inverted and shot into the bowl. The crackle of burning leaves echoed in the silent morning. Tylor took a long draw before blowing a thick cloud of smoke overhead. "Shall we?" He gestured to the trail heading south.

Inyalia broke her halt and began down the path. It seemed odd she'd been sent so far north, just to backtrack. It was going to be a long day if she spent it on already traveled dirt. But maybe they'd alter course at some point. Maybe there was a road she missed. She hoped so anyway. Being a ranger meant everything to her. But thus far, none of it lived up to her expectations.

Inyalia walked aimlessly. She had no direction. Her mentor hadn't said a word. His only input came in the form of cherry scented tobacco drifting past her. She was surprised his pipe still burned. It felt like hours had passed, yet he continued to puff.

The sun crested the mountain peaks, showering the area in golden rays of light. Inyalia froze, seeing the road split. There was something about it she couldn't place. She knew she'd never seen it. Prior to the horrors of the previous night, she'd never been here to see it. Yet, somehow, she knew it belonged. Moreover, it called to her.

Glancing around, she couldn't remember anything about this area. None of the landmarks stood out. But then again, her attention was otherwise occupied during her previous trek. Standing at the intersection, Inyalia turned to face Tylor. "South or East?"

"You choose."

"But—I—Aren't you supposed to—I thought you had a place you wanted me to go?" She was already growing tired of these games. And apparently this was just the beginning. Was it the same for everyone? Or was she getting the *special treatment*, Traevon had whispered about? Either way, she was sick of it. But, if they were intent on playing these little games, perhaps she could beat them. She was good at games after all. She just had to learn the rules. And so far, rule number one was do whatever you want. They'll work around it.

"I do. But I'm not the one leading us. You are. Pick a direction. We'll make do with the results." Exhaling another cloud of smoke, Tylor's lips curled into a brief smile, which he quickly suppressed.

Sighing, Inyalia stared down both paths. The rays of light were becoming less intense, spreading to other areas. Somehow, she knew she had to choose quickly. Something told her she'd never have this chance again. A decision made, Inyalia stepped onto the mountain road.

They marched, quietly trailing the subtle incline. What had been mostly dirt was rapidly yielding to stone. Inyalia had no idea where she was going, but she could see the trail. It was faint, winding its way across the bluffs, but it was ever present.

The climb hadn't been difficult, but already they were quite a way up the mountain. Inyalia glanced back, watching Tylor. He seemed content, not a care in the world. For him, it was just another day. How could he be so nonchalant? More importantly, how was this training her for anything? She'd already wasted the better part of a day on this walk, and she'd learned nothing new. At least nothing that would turn her into a ranger. And so far, it'd been simple games rather than tests. She hoped it would become a little more traditional once they reached wherever she was supposed to be leading them. Nothing would be more disappointing than having her dream turn out to be a big game of night watch or guard duty. If she wanted that, she could have joined the city guard, or even the Army. At least they traveled places from time to time. Rangers rarely ventured beyond Trendensil. Homeland defense was their first and last duty.

Hours crept by, unannounced by lingering shadow. What had started as a narrow trail was now a wide road, worn from travel. It was too small for a wagon, but a horse could navigate without much difficulty. Unfortunately, she didn't have one. And even if she did, it's hooves wouldn't last long against the grating surface. Not to mention the weather.

The wind was picking up, the temperature falling with it. Inyalia pulled her cloak around her, clipping it shut. She could feel the cold, but it wasn't bothering her as she'd grown to expect. Still, there was no sense in taking unnecessary risks.

Snowflakes drifted casually to the earth, spreading a thin layer over the hardened surface. The landscape below was losing definition in the foggy haze. It was a beautiful sight to witness, though Inyalia was having trouble enjoying it. Her muscles were beginning to ache. She wanted to rest. And of course, Tylor's continuous lack of input was beginning to wear her patience. Despite her growing exhaustion, she'd decided she would keep moving. At least until he said otherwise. Perhaps that was the point of this game, to see how long she'd go.

Shaking the thoughts from her mind, Inyalia watched the puffy clouds. They seemed just out of reach, though she knew it was a trick of the remaining light. They'd breeched the stratus hours ago. They'd seemed just as far away then as they were now. It was like walking through a fog. It surrounded you, obscuring all vision, but never got close enough to touch.

As if walking through a wall, the misty clouds disappeared in a final solid layer. Heavy snowfall took its place, raining from the endless sky above. Already, a thick accumulation had gathered on the rocky steeps.

Stepping over a mount, Inyalia's boot slipped against the frozen rocks. Pain shot through her left hand, catching a jagged stone. She hissed, digging her heels into a shallow crevice. Cursing beneath her breath, Inyalia climbed to her feet, ensuring they would hold. She dusted the clinging powder from her and looked up, only to find Tylor standing back, patiently waiting. He didn't say a word, nor show the slightest sign of concern. A rage ignited within her. How was he her mentor? He didn't seem to care about anything. And worse, now she'd hurt herself.

Pulling the glove to the side, Inyalia inspected the wound. It was deep, but not so much that it wouldn't heal properly. Would it hinder her draw? She had yet to even fire her bow. But the time would surely come. Certainly these trials would have to test her skills—eventually. But now, poor footing during a seemingly pointless trek had risked her performance. Sighing her frustrations, Inyalia covered the wound. It would need to be cleaned, but not here. Nightfall was a few hours out. Provided they stopped, she could clean it properly then.

The starless sky encased everything that wasn't glowing white from reflected moonlight. The opposite spectrum of colors made it difficult to see anything. Squinting into the distance, Inyalia could faintly make out the outlined peaks extending miles overhead. The road twisted and curved, narrowing rapidly. Approaching a steep canyon between the rocky slopes, it shrank to little more than a goat path.

Continuing forward, the wind ceased suddenly. The frozen tundra became a comfortable chill as the snow-covered path faded to slush. Just as quickly, dry rock returned.

Inyalia searched her surroundings as best she could. She was still half blind, but her eyes were beginning to adjust. It made no sense. They were still in the open. The mountain walls towered around them, but it shouldn't have been enough to block out the cold, let alone the drift. Where was this pocket of warmth coming from? Loosening the clasp of her cloak, Inyalia opened it to allow ventilation. There was no sense in allowing herself to sweat. That would prove dangerous if they entered the cold again.

Tylor's voice boomed through the narrow pass, shaking the walls around them.

The volume made Inyalia jump. She hadn't expected him to speak in the first place, let alone for it to be so loud.

"We'll camp just ahead." Without warning, Tylor skirted around as if she hadn't been there at all. And just as quickly, he disappeared around one of the large rocks.

Searching the narrow canyon, Inyalia couldn't believe he'd vanished like that. Moreover, how did he pass so easily? There was hardly enough room for one person to stand without restriction. Passing her should have been impossible. But the worst part, the part she was kicking herself over. She didn't see how he'd managed it. That was the type of stuff she desperately wanted to learn.

Inyalia paused, studying the cramped passage. There was no room to hide. And the stone Tylor had passed was simply that, a stone. There was no crevice, divot, or passage. And yet, he was nowhere to be seen. Inyalia inched forward, thoroughly exploring every shadow she could find. She had to locate him. It wasn't a matter of survival. It was a matter of pride. If she could find him, if she could prove herself, perhaps he'd drop these silly games and teach her. That's really all this was. The Rangers Corps, masters of fun and games. Hide and seek shouldn't have come as a surprise.

Passing the stone once again, Inyalia noticed a slight change in temperature. It was subtle, little more than a breath upon the back of her neck. But there was no mistaking it. She turned, facing the wall. There was no shadow there. But the slight breeze remained. Gritting her teeth, hoping she wasn't being watched, Inyalia extended her hand and touched the surface of the rock.

To her surprise, her gloved fingers didn't make contact. Instead, they went inside the stone. No! That wasn't right. It was a hole they entered. That's all it could be. Inyalia stood there, watching. She could still see her hand. That meant it wasn't some kind of illusion. But her eyes said there was nothing there. Pressing a little further, she could see her shadow. That answered her questions. There was a tunnel here, set in the face of the rock. But the coloration was so pristine that it was nearly invisible. How did Tylor find it? How did he know it was here?

Stepping into the strange passage, Inyalia smiled at the cleverness of it all. Once inside, her perceptions shifted. She could now see the walls, though they were difficult to observe. Every step was a challenge. She couldn't rely on her eyes. Already, she'd tripped and fallen, having miscalculated the distance to the floor. With difficulty, she reached the end. It turned into another corridor and traveled a short distance. An ancient tarp hung down the wall, covering what appeared to be a carved doorway. Inyalia lifted the flap and stepped through, finding herself in a rather large room.

Tylor knelt beside the firepit, blowing softly into a pile of smoldering tinder. A pillar of white light beamed through the ceiling above him. Curved polished plates caught the light, distributing it to every corner of the chamber. Stone furniture rested throughout the hovel, and a series of smaller rooms connected along the back wall.

Adjusting the kindling, Tylor turned his attention to the young elf. "Glad you could join me. Toss your cloak on one of those hooks. You won't be needing it here." Before she could speak, he'd returned his focus to the pit.

Inyalia glanced around the unnatural room. It had the feel of a cavern, but the straight walls and carved décor delivered an atmosphere only found at home. Inspecting the wall near the door, she was taken back by the expert craftsmanship. She hadn't noticed from a distance, but it was more than a simple hook. A series of pockets were built into the wall, providing the perfect place for armor, weapons, gear, or anything else. And with a cloak in place, it was all hidden from view. Inyalia counted eight hooks, eight rooms, excluding the main chamber, and eight chairs. This had to be some kind of barracks. The question was, who built it? Elves were known for woodwork, nature and art. Discounting the furniture, this clearly qualified. But this was not the work of elves.

Inyalia quickly removed her armor, stashing it away in one of the pockets. She was surprised to find her bow and quiver fit perfectly. Tossing her cloak on the hook, it draped over the gear. She grabbed her pack and turned her attention to Tylor. "What is this place? And why was it so hard to find? Is it magic?"

Tylor chuckled at the barrage of questions. "No, it's not magic. There was once a race called dwarves. I don't know much about them. They were long before my time. But they were once friend to the elves. Masterful stone carvers and miners, they built their home inside the mountain itself. Some claim they built entire empires beneath the rock, impossible to find by anyone who wasn't a dwarf. We are in but one outpost. There are hundreds of them littering this mountain, though you'd never find them unless you knew where to look." Giving a final slow and steady breath to the crackling tinder, a small flame erupted. Tylor carefully fed it, watching the fire spread to the larger pieces. Content it was self-sustaining, he piled some larger logs around the outer edge.

"I've never heard of dwarves. Where are they now?" Inyalia took a seat in one of the chairs, surprised that it was not only light, but comfortable. She carefully removed her gloves, inspecting the wound in her hand. It was purple and swollen. Using her free hand, she dug into her pack, searching for anything to clean the wound.

"I'm not sure. Some say they died of plague. Others claim they went mad and sealed themselves inside the mountain. Even the elders seem clueless as to their fate." Reaching into his pack, Tylor removed two iron rods, a skillet, a pot, and a small leather sack. Placing the rods over the flame, he laid the cookware so it would rest evenly. Pouring his waterskin into the pot, Tylor grabbed the sack and emptied its contents. A few carrots, an onion, and a large potato fell out, followed by a wrapped bundle. Drawing his knife, he chopped the vegetables into pieces. One by one, he raked them into the skillet. They sizzled as they hit the pan. Unwrapping the bundle, two thick cuts of meat soaked the inner layer of cloth.

"Do you need some help?" Inyalia asked, realizing she'd sat there watching him work the whole time. She'd grown accustomed to her mother doing everything. Now that she was in the world, she needed to do things for herself.

"No, I'm okay, thank you. Besides, you need to tend that." Tylor gestured to her hand. "Can't have it getting infected." The water-filled pot was just beginning to boil. He grabbed the handle and swiftly set it on the table beside her. "Use this to clean the wound. Once it's all bandaged up, you can help me breakdown what's left of the firewood. I need a hand-full of shavings. Two fist worth of slivers, nothing thicker than your pinky finger. And the rest I want quartered and halved."

"Where was that concern when we were out in the cold?" Inyalia asked as a half-joke.

"Trying to keep warm." Tylor laughed. "Besides, what would making a fuss about it have done? You kept it covered. That prevented blood loss. And there was no easy way to bandage it then. I knew you were okay when you picked yourself up. Didn't see any reason to coddle you."

Inyalia paused a moment, thinking over his words. He wasn't wrong, though she was still irritated by them. "It's just—It would have been nice to know you cared."

"Why? I'm not your father. I'm not your friend. I'm barely your mentor. It's my duty to teach you how to survive on your own. Aside from that, it shouldn't matter to you what I do or say." Sensing this wasn't going to be the end of it, Tylor turned away from her. Laying the meat into the skillet, among the vegetables, the scent filled the air, promising flavor and a full belly.

Inyalia watched him a long moment, studying his demeanor. There was more she wanted to say. There always was. But he was clearly finished talking. Internalizing her thoughts, Inyalia dipped a rag into the boiling water and began wiping away the crusty blood.

Inspecting the cleaned wound, Inyalia was pleased it wasn't as deep as she'd believed. All things considered, it was relatively minor. The skin had torn at an angle, making it wide, but shallow. That would save her when it came time for nimble fingers. Though it was going to hurt for a few days. Methodically, she wrapped a cloth bandage around her hand. After the third attempt, she tied it off, unhappy with the end result. It didn't seem to matter how thin she tried to keep it, the layered wrap was bulky and cumbersome. Knowing it wouldn't get much better, she put away her things. Reaching into Tylor's pack, she removed the bundle of chopped wood.

"While you're in there, will you hand me the round canister from the side pouch?" Tylor stirred the vegetables with his knife.

Laying the bundle on the table, Inyalia located the pocket he'd referred to. The canister was a tight fit, protruding from the top of the pocket. Carefully, she pulled it free, inspecting its odd shape. It was cylindrical, with one end slightly larger than the other. The smaller end had a spiraling notched carved into it. Uncertain as to its purpose, Inyalia handed it over.

Tylor held it over the skillet and twisted the notched end. It came apart, revealing a similar pattern beneath. Pea sized holes had been drilled into the metal device. Quickly, he turned it to the side and shook gently, sprinkling bits of ground spice onto the food. Content with the even layer he'd distributed, he twisted the cap back into place and handed it to her.

Inyalia took the canister and repeated his actions. She stared into the ported end, sniffing the contents. Exotic flavors filled her nostrils, making her sneeze. Quickly recapping it, she stuffed it back into the pocket.

Tylor chuckled at her reaction. "It's called a shaker. I got it from a trader in Risolde. It keeps my spices from getting damp. Not to mention the time I save by grinding them each time I cook. Though it's easy to use too much spice before you get used to it."

"Interesting." Unsure how to follow, Inyalia returned to her chair. Scooting closer to the table, she drew her dagger and untied the bundle of wood. Grabbing one of the top pieces, she went to work shaving the bark away. This was the kind of thing she'd expected to learn. And as much as she hated to admit it, Tylor had saved her from hardship twice over today. Had she made this trip alone, there was no telling how long she'd go without cooked food, or a warm bed. Her tent could provide shelter, but it could only do so much against the cold. Even now that it didn't bother her as much, a few hours in the snow were still a few hours in the snow. Trees were few and far between this high up, and she didn't know the first thing about hunting wildlife in the mountains. His foresight had ensured them warmth for rest, cleaning, and cooking. And the fact that he'd brought fresh food meant they were going to have a decent meal. That was good. The charcoal they'd consumed for breakfast didn't last long. Inyalia hadn't considered either option when supplies were plentiful. She had the basics, rations and a blanket. But wood and real food had been the last things on her mind. Though that was going to change the first chance she got. Stocking a few nights worth of each was the least she could do.

It didn't take long for dinner to finish. Tylor laid a slab of meat into a wooden bowl and piled vegetables around it. Handing it to Inyalia, he pulled a chair for himself, grabbed his own bowl, and dug in.

Clearing away the wood shavings, Inyalia's attention was locked on the food. She stabbed one of the pieces of potato and took a bite. It was sweet, with a subtle lingering heat. The fat from the steak had soaked into the outer layer, leaving it firm and crispy with a tender core. If every meal he made was as good as this, perhaps this whole training thing wouldn't be so bad after all.

Brilliant light filled the room, burning into Inyalia's closed lids. Shielding her face, she sat up slowly, taking in her surroundings. It took a moment to remember where she was. Her back and legs were stiff from the past two days of heavy walking. That meant it was going to be a rough day, at least until her muscles loosened up. Crawling out of bed, Inyalia pulled her boots on, abandoning the buckles. She glanced into the main chamber, surprised by how quiet it was. Tylor was nowhere to be seen. Quickly running fingers through her long brown hair, Inyalia twisted the tangled mess into a single roll and pinned it in place. It was sloppy, but it would work until she could properly maintain it.

She made her way into the main chamber, stealing a glance into the room Tylor had taken. His bed was empty, save for the thin mattress that had been there when they arrived. Searching the wall where their armor and cloaks were hung, a fear grew inside her. Tylor's gear was missing. Had he abandoned her? Was she all alone at the top of the mountain? How was she supposed to proceed without someone to guide her?

Suddenly, she remembered he hadn't been her guide. But rather, she his. This was another test. If she could find the way on her own, she'd pass. Defiance in her soul, Inyalia quickly dressed and prepared to leave. She slung her pack over her shoulder and marched toward the entrance. It was amazing how much of the sunlight was filtered by the overhanging rocks. No wonder she hadn't seen it the night before. Though the gap in the stone was barely visible even now. And she knew where it was.

Glancing into the sky, squinting against its blinding might, Inyalia felt closer to the heavens than ever before. She wasn't quite to the peak, in fact, she was at the last crevice between a pair of them, but even at this height, the world below seemed so small. There wasn't much to be seen through the cloud cover, but where it remained sprawled hundreds of miles into places she'd never imagined.

It took a moment to gather her bearings. Each stone looked the same, and she hadn't actively studied it the night before. But there were only two possible options. If she chose the wrong direction, surely their tracks would remain from the night before. Picking a direction, she made her way along the stone path. It took only a few minutes to reach the wall of wind. Pulling the cloak around her, Inyalia stepped into the open. Slush and partially melted snow awaited. There were no boot tracks or signs of any kind. Aside from water droplets and the occasional ice crystal, it was relatively undisturbed. She expected as much where the snow fell in full force. But here on the edge, something should have remained. Provided this was the way they'd come. With no signs, this had to be her destination. But where were Tylor's tracks? If he'd come this way, why would he leave no evidence?

"It's a test!" Inyalia stated aloud. Taking a knee, she inspected the snow closer, searching for anything out of the ordinary. She could see where the drift had fallen naturally. It was smooth and wavy, despite the melted portions. Those had turned to ice. But there was another type here as well, impossible to see without close examination. Hundreds of thin bristles had swept the snow over, smoothing out any discrepancies. It reminded her of a broom or horsehair brush. Someone had intentionally covered their tracks here.

Smiling her success, Inyalia stepped into the snow. She followed the trail around the southern peak, staring out over the vast landscape below. The clouds were patchy here, leaving much to be seen. It was one of the most beautiful sights she'd ever beheld. In no time, she came to a set of partially covered tracks. These hadn't been tampered with. Judging by the size and depth, they belonged to an elf about Tylor's size. How many people on the mountain could that description match? Inyalia turned her attention to the wind and snowfall. It wasn't harsh, but it was steady. If she had to guess, he was about two hours ahead of her.

Inyalia made her way along the twisting path, following the contours of the massive range. She wasn't sure if she was on a road any longer. Whatever road had brought her to the peak seemed to end just past the canyon. The sun was nearing midmorning. With no cloud cover, it provided more than enough heat to keep her comfortable, but it was melting the footprints faster than she desired. It'd stopped falling a few minutes prior, and the accumulation was thinning. It wouldn't be long before she'd be out of it completely, Tylor's tracks gone along with it. She wasn't sure how she'd be able to follow them once the path returned to stone. And she didn't think he'd be so careless as to leave anything behind. Unless he wanted her to track him. If so, he'd do exactly that.

The weather was beginning to feel warmer. The bright rays of sun melted what was left of the snow, drying the ground almost as quickly. What had been a brisk hike through winter was rapidly becoming a slow march into spring. Beads of sweat were beginning to form on her brow. Unclasping her cloak and throwing it open, Inyalia brought it up to wipe her forehead, obscuring her sight for the briefest moment. Before the thick canvas could fall to its original position, the young elf noticed a drastic change. She was still on the mountainside, but the stone was now padded by grass and dirt. The rocky pathway planed out, displaying a grove of luscious greens and browns. Thick and wonderful tree trunks sprouted from the earth all around her, though these were not the trees she was familiar with. The straight, tapered trunks of those back home were nowhere to be seen. Instead, these grew wild. Their bark was lighter in tone, almost peach in color. It was smooth, rather than rough and jagged. Each one was curved in a wide variety of ways, as if gravity had little say in their design. It was a peaceful sight, serene even. Birds flew overhead, landing where they desired. A pair of squirrels chased each other around one of the twisted trunks, barking and playing. And there, between two of the blossoming tree tops, Inyalia could see what appeared to be architecture.

She made her way through the grove, absorbing her surroundings. For the first time since leaving home, she felt the joys of her childhood. There was no need to be cautious. No need to be armed. She was safe in this wonderous place. Safe from threat and enemy alike. In a trance-like state, Inyalia sauntered through the garden of perfectly manicured trees. They were beautiful in every way, kempt, yet wild and free. The soft grass grew in thick patches but remained evenly heighted just below the ankle. After the rigidity of stone she'd walked the past few days, it was a welcome reprieve.

The buildings in the distance were unlike any she'd seen before. They were open and inviting, much like Dragon Sanctum. But these were square in shape. Even their roof tops were a series of squares, small at the top, growing wider with each pass. They were shingled in smooth, curved plates, colored like the peach tree bark. Each corner was capped and rounded in the most ornate fashion, preventing wind damage or water build up. The walls themselves were minimal, appearing to serve as wind block and little else. Inyalia couldn't help but feel their thin appearance was misleading. These were constructed in a way she'd never seen, foreign and harmonious. But there was a strength to them as well.

From this height, she was able to see the full extent of the mountain settlement. It felt like a village, but seeing it in its full glory, it was more like a small city that had been split into several smaller sized sections. The mountain had been carved out, leaving numerous shelves staggering below. The city rested upon these shelves, in essence being taller than it was wide. Some of the lower tiers had buildings that protruded two or three shelves above, but those appeared few and far between. Most of them were single story structures that had little ant-sized people trailing in and out. Though there was a single structure that extended from the lowest levels and into the heavens above. From the mountain, a river poured, spilling its essence from one tier to the next. Inyalia knew it was the backbone of the entire settlement.

"Welcome to Caelum." Tylor's voice echoed behind her.

Inyalia spun, glaring her frustrations at the wild elf. "Why'd you leave me? How'd you know I'd find this place on my own? You're the worst trainer ever!"

Tylor chuckled at her outburst. "Calm yourself. I was never further than earshot. Besides, you would have found this place, with or without me. Or you wouldn't have. Not everyone does. But I had a feeling about you. It seems I was correct." He spread his arms wide, as if cradling the mystical city before them. "Caelum is a sanctuary for those in search of enlightenment. That's why you had to find it on your own. I could have spent cycles looking for it and never come close. And once your training is complete, you'll never find it again either." Turning to face the young elf, his tone became stern. "Now to address your assessment of my methods—We'll, you're entitled to that opinion. It matters little to me. Though I will urge you to listen and do as I say. You may not like it. You may not agree. But every decision I make is made for a reason. Eventually, you'll begin to understand why things are done this way."

Levi Samuel

Chapter VI
Birds of Prey

Pain shot through her ribs. Inyalia winced, locking her arm around the connecting weapon. It was a wooden short blade, blunted and capped to prevent breaking skin, but still heavy enough to crush bone. The weapon was nearly identical to its lethal counterpart in every way. It made the transition from training to live-steal nearly unnoticeable. She was just happy she was wearing armor. It didn't do much to prevent bruising, but it dispersed the blows enough to minimize lingering damage.

Twisting her torso to keep the blade locked, Inyalia brought her fist around, catching her attacker in the side of the head.

The elven girl, a few cycles Inyalia's senior, staggered back, holding her ear. Realizing almost instantly that she'd abandoned her sword, she drew a dagger from her waist. Like the sword, it was also wooden and capped. Taking a defensive stance, she waited for Inyalia to approach.

Inyalia wrapped her fist around the leather grip. It was snug, a near perfect fit, but she didn't like it. Inspecting the polished surface, Inyalia questioned if she'd made the right decision. These sparring matches were supposed to be a method of training. But all too often they became a gladiator pit where feuds were settled. To the victor went the bragging rights.

Thus far, prior to today, Inyalia had entered the pit twice. The first time was merely for show. She'd lost the instant she stepped in. A blunted arrow caught her in the side of the head and left her unconscious for nearly a week. The second time had nothing to do with her. Tylor had gotten into an argument with one of the other mentors. To settle the dispute, they set their perspective recruits upon one another. Inyalia was pleased to have won that fight, though not without her fair share of pain.

She'd cracked three ribs and broken a finger. To this day she still wasn't sure it was worth it.

Today was different. Today she was here for her own reasons. Since arriving, her surname had done her no favors. In fact, having the Ranger-General for a father did nothing but put a target on her back. Everyone wanted to test their mettle, or at the very least, knock her to the dirt.

Her combatant was the worst of these people. Lorena would go out of her way to torment her. She'd trip her while they were waiting in line. And while Inyalia had no physical proof, she knew Lorena had been the one responsible for dropping her pants when they left herbalism class. Those were just a few of a laundry list of inconveniences she'd suffered at the bully's amusement. Unfortunately, she had no proof.

Lorena was a mage in training. That meant they didn't even have to be in the same room for strange and mysterious things to happen. But each time misfortune struck, Lorena was always there, giggling with her friends.

That would end today. Inyalia issued a challenge of combat in the pit. It was the simplest solution to what had become a major problem. But she had to win. Things would only get worse if she didn't. And to complicate things further, there were conditions. Their perspective mentors agreed that each had to fight at a disadvantage. For Lorena, that meant no magic. And for Inyalia, no bow.

Inyalia extended the sword she'd stolen away. She'd trained with them, as Tylor had insisted, but it was uncomfortable. With her bow unavailable, she preferred hand to hand. Which was what she'd chosen for this fight. Lorena on the other hand, hadn't been so foolish. She'd chosen a short blade and dagger combination, which had already left a series of whelps along Inyalia's legs, arms, and ribs. But she'd managed to disarm her opponent. That was going to be the cherry on top, provided she won.

Charging, Inyalia feigned left and darted right. She swung the short blade, releasing it just as it reached its full extension. It flew from her hand, straight toward her opponent.

Lorena sliced with the dagger, knocking the loose sword away. She hadn't expected it to flip when the blades connected. Heading toward her face, Lorena ducked, only to find Inyalia ready for her.

Fist balled, Inyalia punched as hard as she could. Her knuckles impacted the mage's left cheek, knocking her back a few steps. Denying time, she rushed to close the gap. She had to disarm the dagger before her opponent remembered to use it. Locking her about the waist, Inyalia pinned the limbs as best she could. The mage was a few inches taller, but her angle should have compensated. Hoping her feet were off the ground, Inyalia twisted and fell.

Lorena slammed into the loose dirt. Her head swam and her arms were pinned. She still hadn't recovered from the last hit. Defenseless, she retreated inside herself, allowing a plan to form.

Straddling the mage, Inyalia sat up. Now was the time to apply what Tylor had taught her. She rolled her shoulder, letting her fists fly. A resounding pop echoed from the solid blow. One, two, three times she connected.

Lorena's eyes rolled to the back of her head, leaving nothing but the white pupils visible. Summoning the power within her, she let loose a blast of energy. The air hardened and exploded out, wrapping around her assailant and launching her back.

Inyalia shielded her face as best she could. She didn't have time for anything else. The dirt, churned as it was, offered little cushion as it caught her. Everything hurt. She wanted to lay there and let it pass, but the fight wasn't over. Grunting her frustrations, she rolled to her stomach and pushed herself to her knees. It took a moment to regain her bearings. She spotted Lorena not far, still on the ground. Inyalia threw her arms into the air. "We said no magic!" Fuming, she searched the crowd of spectators, looking for anyone willing to call foul play.

Nobody said a word. Lorena was guilty of dishonorable combat. And nothing was going to be done about it. The ranger-in-training was on her own.

Gritting her teeth, Inyalia got to her feet and marched toward the mage. She had to be prepared. Lorena had cheated. She'd resorted to magic. And that meant she was willing to use it again.

Exhausted, Lorena rolled, picking herself up. The would-be ranger would be upon her any moment. Raising her hands, she pulled at the energies around her, gathering them into a compact orb. Shaping it to her will, she launched it with a forceful thrust.

Inyalia saw the ball of energy flying toward her with remarkable speed. It was aimed mid-chest. She had to act now or it would be too late. Tumbling, she tucked her head and hit the dirt. The momentum carried, springing her to her feet at a full sprint.

The ranger was nearly upon her. Rushing herself, Lorena summoned another bolt, pulling any energies that would obey. It was risky, but so was letting the ranger too close. Time for games was over. One way or another, it ended here.

Dropping her shoulder, Inyalia put all her weight into the strike. She impacted as the second blast detonated. The energy embraced her, stopping time for the briefest moment. Her weight inverted, unaffected by gravity. She was flying backward, unable to stop herself. Her body tingled. Her hair stood on edge. And before she could make sense of it all, she slammed into the ground. Lying still, hoping to catch her breath, Inyalia struggled to move. She felt sticky. With each movement static popped, echoing in her ears. It was difficult, but Inyalia pulled herself up. Stunned, unsure what had happened, she glanced around.

Chunks of mud and dirt littered the ground. A shallow crater rested where Lorena had been, but the mage was not present. Inyalia spotted her nearly twenty foot from the impact site. Lorena was sprawled out, laying at the edge of the pit. Her feet were elevated, dangling over the grass. Blood flowed from her nose and ears, but her chest moved. She was still alive, though if she were conscious, she'd probably wish she weren't.

One of the elves stepped into the pit, speaking loud enough for all to hear. "Last one standing, and winner by honorable combat is Inyalia Highlor!"

A few of the spectating mages, including her friends, rushed to Lorena. From their expressions, it seemed the spell did more damage to her than it had Inyalia.

Many others flocked around the champion, offering praise and congratulations.

Inyalia had no use for any of it. It was never about the worship. It was these same people who'd singled her out for reasons beyond her control. In her mind, they were no different than Lorena. But perhaps, now that she'd taken a stand, they'd leave her alone and let her get on with her training. Making her way through the crowd, Inyalia found the one face she wanted to see.

Tylor leaned against the same post he always supported when she was in the pit. A prideful smirk rested upon his lips.

A gentle breeze passed through the plump leaves of the unnaturally large tree. Inyalia sat among its twisted branches, buried in the green cover. Studying the road intently, she waited for her target to appear. She'd stalked him most of the day, waiting for the perfect opportunity. He was moving slower than usual, but he also had a designated path he was restricted to. That meant his arrival was imminent.

An unexpected sound drew her attention away from the road. Stealing a glance down the mountain side, the multiple layers of inhabited landscape stretched on for miles. Her initial assessment of Caelum had been wrong. It was so much more than a simple city. The sacred training ground was welcome to any being in search of higher learning. It had a way of calling those who sought its influence. And only those who were called were able to reach it. At least that's how it'd been explained. And very few were called. In fact, according to Tylor, about one in a hundred rangers found their way here. But this place wasn't restricted to just rangers.

The citizens of Caelum followed a variety of paths. Rangers, magi, scholars, even the occasional soldier ended up on the mountain. But only a select few remained beyond their training. Those few were known as the Emerald Circle. They maintained the upkeep of Caelum, and ensured it remained a safe place for those in search of knowledge.

Upon her arrival, Inyalia was introduced to the masters of the circle. It was supposedly tradition for all new recruits to meet them. In that meeting, her curriculum had been decided. Though Inyalia hadn't found it overly intrusive. She had a total of four classes that met once a week. The rest of her time was spent training with Tylor, though it seemed most of his methods revolved around testing her capabilities. He'd push her to her limits, and then take a few steps beyond. She enjoyed their sessions, but she always needed a day or two to recover afterward.

Of all the masters of the circle, only one caught Inyalia's attention. She was an elven girl, much like herself, but about Vera's age. Though her age was misleading. Serena, the master archer, was nearly two thousand cycles old. Inyalia didn't believe it at first. Few elves reached their six-hundredth cycle. But Serena had been more than happy to explain.

The Emerald Circle was more than the masters of their arts. They were the apprentices of The Watcher, the founder of Caelum and establisher of its laws. But he couldn't maintain it himself. In exchange for their assistance, any member of the circle was bestowed near immortality. So long as they remained in Caelum, they would not age. This allowed them the time to become the masters they were, while allowing the opportunity to live a full life upon their retirement.

Inyalia found it an interesting tale, but somewhat farfetched. She'd seen The Watcher. His subtly pointed ears made him look like a half-elf, but he was not. He was something else. She wasn't sure what race he was, though he had a strong elven air about him. Like the circle, he didn't appear overly old, though he was fully grown. Being a mage, she hadn't spent much time around him, but when he was present, she always felt like he was watching her, even when faced away. Inyalia believed that was why they called him The Watcher.

Approaching footsteps pulled her to the task at hand. Carefully, quietly, Inyalia peeked beneath her, watching the figure approach from the south. She'd found her mark.

Tylor walked casually along the road, keeping an eye to his surroundings. He didn't know when she'd strike, or even where. But it was bound to happen sooner or later, though he preferred sooner. Her task was simple. Locate, execute, and escape. The rangers were not assassins. But this particular trial required elements of stealth, scouting, agility, accuracy, and wit. All things an assassin needed. And right now, all things Inyalia needed.

She'd seemed downright giddy when he offered her the chance to shoot him. So much so that he feared she wouldn't wait for the challenge to begin. He wasn't looking forward to being shot. Even though all she had was blunt tips, they still hurt. And it wasn't like she couldn't fail. There were an undetermined number of rangers on the lookout. If she was spotted by anyone before the shot went off, she wouldn't get another chance. But he didn't think that would happen. Inyalia was a competent trainee. She'd proven herself ahead of the curve many times over. But he still had to push her limits. That was the only way she'd reach her full potential. Whistling to himself, Tylor approached a fork in the road and turned east.

Waiting for him to pass, Inyalia dropped to a lower branch. She was exposed, but the fewer leaves allowed quieter movement. Carefully making her way to the thinner limbs, she straddled the small gap and climbed into another tree, keeping pace with her target. She'd been lucky to get ahead of him. It'd taken the better part of the day to memorize his routine and calculate his timing. All she had to do now was finish the assignment. Tylor was headed for the leisure tier ramp. He'd passed through three times since she'd located him. Each time, he stopped at the pub, spent a one-thousand-count inside, and finally exited the side door to continue his path. This was the last time. She was going to end it before he could make it a fourth.

Extending her reach, Inyalia grabbed hold of the lower branches of another tree and jumped. It was a bit of a risk, changing tiers in such a way, but she wouldn't have gained ground had she not. Scaling to the highest branch, Inyalia felt the soft wood flex beneath her weight. It carried her to the next in lineup. She wrapped her arms around the smooth bark, hugging tight as the leafy crown sprung back. It was risky, but it bought her exactly six-hundred and twenty-two counts before Tylor would be beneath her again.

Moving into position, Inyalia watched him approach the Ranger's Lodge. It was but one of the many settlements along the bluff. He'd only stopped there once before, first thing in the morning. It'd taken him nearly an hour to come out that time. She didn't feel like waiting again. Besides, it'd be dark before long and she wasn't fond of tracking him all night. It was now or never. If he got inside there was no telling when he'd come out.

Inyalia huddled into the mass of limbs and leaves, ensuring she was hidden on all sides. Stringing her bow, she nocked one of the blunt tipped arrows, stealing a quick glance at the marking carved in the shaft. Each one held a similar etching, though they were all extremely different. It was her way of identifying one from another. Inyalia wanted to carry one of her real arrows, but Tylor wouldn't allow it. He said he wouldn't risk her killing him by mistake. She understood, but it still stung. She'd nearly master the quick draw technique. In fact, of the last twenty attempts, she'd fired the correct arrow eighteen times. With those numbers, how could he refuse her? Grinning, Inyalia pressed through the leaves, bow drawn and ready to fire. All she had to do was take aim. And when she did, he was going to pay for his transgressions.

Sighting along the thin wooden shaft, Inyalia aligned his center mass, adjusting for the half-inch correction, wind, and elevation. Certain of her shot, she released. The arrow flexed under the sudden pressure. Realizing it had been fired, the force transferred, launching the arrow at breakneck speed toward its target. Inyalia watched the manicured feathers cut through the air as if moving in slow motion. They furled outward, grabbing the wind as it sailed, twisting the shaft like a corkscrew. It flew true, perfectly aligned to its mark.

Tylor stepped to the doorway of the Ranger's Lodge. Before he could pass the threshold, a sudden force hit him between the shoulders, shoving him into the wooden frame. He doubled in pain, knees slamming to the floor. Breath forced from his lungs, it took everything he had to stay calm. Regardless of how prepared he'd believed himself, an arrow to the back proved him wrong. Inhaling through his nose, Tylor pulled himself against the post and glanced around in search of the arrow's source. Trailing its trajectory, he spotted Inyalia near the top of a tree at the far side of the road. Ignoring the growing pain in his chest, he lifted his arm and pointed. "Assassin! Assassin in the trees!" His voice was weak, constricted by lack of breath, but it was enough to signal the alarm.

Horns echoed all around. Panic erupted in Inyalia's stomach. The words were just loud enough to hear, but they triggered a fear deep inside. She was no assassin. Why would he say that? None of this was supposed to be part of the test. At least not a part he'd told her about. But she was beginning to realize there was much he wasn't going to tell her.

Rangers filed from the lodge, bows drawn and arrows ready. Movement echoed in the surrounding trees, flashes of armor between the leaves. Like a well-trained unit, they strategically swarmed the area, forming a perimeter. Within seconds, they were in position and expanding outward, entrapping her.

Inyalia needed to move, and quickly. She hadn't prepared herself for this. And having learned from past experience, she had a pretty good idea being caught would count as a failure. Quickly scanning the approaching rangers, she knew she had less than ten seconds to make a decision. Nocking two arrows at once, Inyalia spaced them with a finger. It was a long and difficult shot, but she'd managed it once before. Taking aim at the ground between the two approaching rangers, Inyalia exhaled and released the string. Both arrows rocketed toward their targets. The first made contact, striking the closest in the chest. The second was a little low. It hit the ground and bounced between his legs. It was a bad shot, but it served its purpose. They both dropped.

Using the opportunity to her advantage, having gained a few seconds before they'd give away her position, Inyalia turned and sprinted across the thick branch. Her leather soled boots were slick against the smooth bark, but the flex allowed her to feel each step a little easier. She reached the end of the run and leapt to the next tree. Catching the branches, Inyalia pulled herself up. Shouts echoed behind her. She'd been located, but there was no time to worry about it.

Wrapping her arms around the trunk, Inyalia slid to a lower branch and skirted around the side. Tree by tree, branch by branch, she worked her way toward the bluff's edge.

Her heart raced within her chest. Seeing the one tree she'd longed to reach, Inyalia released the swinging branch and stepped onto the elevated perch. The rangers were hot on her tail. She could hear them. Arrows planked around her, hitting limbs, narrowly passing her by. As scary as it was, it offered two revelations. The first, they were firing live. And the second, they weren't very good shots. But she was thankful for that.

And arrow lodged into the trunk at her feet. It was closer than she liked. Using it as a step, Inyalia jumped and grabbed hold of a branch she wouldn't have been able to reach otherwise. She had to go now. They were too close to delay any longer. Pulling herself up, Inyalia gained her footing and broke into a sprint. Approaching the end of the limb, she swallowed her fear. She couldn't afford it. It would cause her to slow. The rapidly thinning wood began to flex. Now was her time.

Inyalia jumped, using the flexing tree to her advantage. With the sudden lack of weight, it shot up, giving her the slightest lift. She reached the apex, spreading her arms wide, bow in one hand, hope in the other. If she missed, it'd be a long drop to a sudden stop. And it'd be about as forgiving as the arrows sailing past her.

A barrage of juicy leaves slapped as she passed. She was falling. But at least she'd made the distance. That would provide the space she needed to evade. Branches were flying past. She needed the slow before she hit something solid. Grabbing at anything and everything within reach, Inyalia caught one of the thinner limbs. It ripped through her gloved grip, gathering leaves and bark alike. One of the forks snagged, slowing her. The limb flexed beneath the exaggerated weight. Unable to take anymore, it snapped. It wasn't much, but it allowed her to orient herself.

With feet beneath her, Inyalia continued her descent. She had to stop before she hit the ground. At this height she was going to break her legs, that was if it didn't outright kill her. A large limb came into view. She was headed straight toward it. Bracing herself, Inyalia brought her feet together, angling her toes toward her knees. The impact was going to hurt, much less if she'd angled them down, but she needed the limb to pass in front of her. Heel side wouldn't have done that.

As expected, her feet hit the branch. The slick soles slid against the bark, throwing her to the side. Her calve muscles screamed in protest, but they held. Offset just enough, she passed the branch, seeing her opportunity. Inyalia threw her arms, desperate to lock them around the wood. Between the speed of her fall and the angle, the force broke her hold before it could be established. She could feel the pressure of the bark against her bracers. It made her glad she wasn't bare skinned. It would have shredded her arms, though nowhere near to the extent of the trees back home.

Slipping, straining against her weight, Inyalia clapped her hands to each side of the branch. It worked, but it wouldn't last long. Dangling, her arms trembled to keep pressure. She was growing weaker by the moment, slipping little by little. Inyalia stole a glance beneath her, hoping maybe there was something she could step onto. Maybe something a little safer to grab. Her hopes were dashed. All that remained was the ground, too far away. If she rolled, there was a chance the impact wouldn't cause long term damage, but it was a big risk, too big. Hurting herself was about the stupidest thing she could do right now. Not only would she fail, but she'd have to heal before she could try again. Provided she was allowed a second chance. That had never been discussed. She wondered what would happen if she failed. But now was not the time.

Weighing her options, Inyalia made a decision. She kicked her legs front to back. It made her grip even weaker, but she had to do something. Anything was better than waiting to fall. And at least this way, she could say she tried.

Each kick gave a bit more momentum, but at the cost of her waning stability. Her palms were no longer in contact. All that remained was her finger tips, shakily wedged into the bark. She needed just a little more height. Kicking as hard as she could, Inyalia's hands came free. She was falling. Closing her eyes, expecting pain, she felt her descent cease. Peeking through her clenched eyelids, she was hanging just beneath the branch, her legs wrapped and hooked at the ankle. Relief washed over her, drowning the fear that had grown in her gut. She'd made it. She wasn't going to fall.

Hanging there a moment, enjoying what she'd just accomplished, Inyalia let out a heavy sigh. It was time to move. She'd gained quite a bit of ground with such a stupid stunt, but it wouldn't stop them forever. Bending at the waist, Inyalia threw her arms around the branch. Now that she wasn't falling at terminal velocity, she was able to lock them with little effort. It took some strength to reposition herself, but she managed to climb to the top of her perch. All things considered, it was a nice branch for walking, though she'd spent far too much time on it.

Deciding her next move, Inyalia calculated how much time she had. The rangers wouldn't have to go all the way to the ramp, but they also weren't likely to follow her path. But most of the time she'd made was lost when she decided to save her legs. They would likely be within arrow range within the next three minutes.

An arrow hit the tree beside her. "I was wrong!" Inyalia took shelter behind the trunk. Working her way around, she dropped to the next lowest branch. Keeping the tree between herself and the rangers, she scaled down a branch at a time. Finally, she was low enough to jump without fear of damage. Peeking around the trunk, she located three rangers. They were still on the higher shelf. That explained why they were within range. She hadn't considered that option. But she was glad they decided to wait until she was on her feet. She hoped they didn't really want to kill her after all.

Scouting the ground beneath her, Inyalia dropped into the soft grass. The leaves were thick enough to cover her movement from above, but they did little for anyone on the ground. She had to find somewhere to hide until she could figure out a plan.

Making her way along the bluff's edge, careful to stay beneath the cover of trees, Inyalia came to the large river that cut through the middle of Caelum. It started in the mountains and snaked its way along each shelf, providing water to the entire city. It was a common joke to piss in it at the top and see if anyone below noticed. Though considering the order of the tiers, the mages didn't find much humor in it. And so far, no one would admit to actually doing it.

Inyalia stole a glance behind her. She could see figures in the distance, though they were too far away to offer much detail. If she was fast, she was certain she could slip into the water without being seen. But where could she go? The nearest bridge was too far away, and that was a likely hiding spot. Suddenly, an idea came to her.

Taking a deep breath, Inyalia dove into the freezing water. It was colder than she'd expected. Her body was already stiffening. Allowing herself to be carried by the current, she floated toward the bluff's edge. Straining against instinct, Inyalia locked both hands around her bow. Stabbing as hard as she could, she buried the end in the mossy dirt along the shore. It was a dangerous gambit, one that would result in death if she went over the falls. Even if she did survive, she wasn't sure she'd want to.

Several stones had collected at the crest, slowing the water before it fell to the next level. Struggling against her body, Inyalia wedged her bow between the rocks, creating a barrier. The force of the water sucked her against the wooden device, but it held. Using every ounce of strength she possessed, Inyalia clawed at the stones, working her way out of the current. She found a crevice where one of the stones had washed away. The water swirled there, but it wasn't so strong she couldn't move. Wiggling herself into the gap, Inyalia submerged everything but her face. She was concealed on all sides, save for directly above. And it was unlikely her pursuers would check the edge of the fall. After all, who would be crazy enough to hide there? But she did just dive out of a tree and into another on a lower tier. If that didn't qualify as crazy, she didn't know what would.

Inyalia laid among the rocks for what felt like an eternity. She could barely think, let alone comprehend time. The uncontrollable shivers had ceased, replaced by a comfortable numb. Floating in the rushing water, held stationary only by the gathered stone and her bow, Inyalia closed her eyes. It was the only way she'd be able to stay still long enough to ensure no one saw her.

Slowly peeking through her eyelids, the sun had changed position. It was touching the peaks of the towering mountains. Nightfall would be here in minutes. She remembered thinking about it when she let loose her arrow. How long ago was that? Was it even the same day? There was only one certainty. She couldn't stay here much longer. The water was robbing her strength. She'd risked staying too long already. Forcing her body to move, Inyalia crawled from her refuge. It wasn't so difficult being out of the main current, but her muscles didn't want to cooperate. One hand after another, she pulled herself into the grass, using every bit of strength she had. Her fingers hurt. They were frozen, the sudden flow of warming blood made them itch. Pulling herself completely from the water, Inyalia convulsed. Her shivering returned, burning and itching covering her from head to toe. Weakly, she peeled her cloak and armor away. She needed to shed the wet clothes if she was to correct her temperature. It seemed frozen wind and snow was nothing compared to mountain spring water on a warm day.

Exposing her skin to the fading sun, Inyalia rubbed her arms, keeping her body curled as best she could. She could feel the warmth spread through her body, but it made the itch worse.

Opening her pack, Inyalia was pleased to see the contents were mostly dry. Some of the water had entered through the leather flap, but the wax coating had prevented the majority of it. She pulled her spare clothes from the middle, pleased they were little more than damp. Dressing as quick as her muscles would allow, Inyalia stuffed the wet armor and cloak into the bag.

It took a few minutes for most of the itch to subside, and when it did, she was discovering cuts and bruises that hadn't been there before. Her strength was far from returned but she'd have to make do. After everything she'd been through today, she wasn't giving up just yet.

Slinging the rucksack, Inyalia grabbed her bow and quiver and made for the bridge. Caution would be needed. The exercise wasn't over, and there was no telling who would be waiting for her.

Climbing into the nearest tree, Inyalia took her time approaching the lodge. It was bound to be the most patrolled, most protected area of Caelum at this point. She couldn't risk failing now. Keeping watch on the distance, Inyalia climbed into one of the trees she'd used before. She didn't have her armor to help camouflage her, but if she was careful, she wouldn't need it. Slowly, she moved into position, finding a place where she could see both the lodge and the surrounding area. She squinted through the doorless opening. It was difficult to see into the dark building, but the fading sunlight would help. She just had to wait a few moments longer and hope that Tylor was still there.

Allowing her eyes to adjust, Inyalia saw several people within the lodge. Most were of no concern, but it seemed fortune smiled upon her.

Tylor sat alone at a small table, not a care in the world. His leather-backed chair was lush with padding and his feet were elevated. The pages of a thick book had his full and undivided attention.

Inyalia's nose wrinkled in distaste. After all she'd been through, he was relaxing in a plump, comfortable chair, and she was exhausted and sore. She wanted to shoot him again on principle, but there was no way she could outrun the rangers a second time. All she had to do was get to him and she'd pass. But it wouldn't be that easy. She was still undergoing a test. There was no way she could simply walk in, especially after running for her life. No, there had to be more to it.

The sun had nearly disappeared behind the mountains, providing plentiful shadows. They would aid her, but it also provided cover for everyone else. Birds circled overhead, searching for something.

Inyalia watched them for a long moment. What were they looking for? It was too populated for food. And these birds weren't nocturnal. They should have already returned to their roosts for the evening. Scanning the trees, Inyalia spotted the nests near the top. Nothing appeared wrong with them, and many of the neighboring birds had roosted already. Why hadn't these few?

Staying as still as possible, Inyalia studied the trees with empty nests. Starting at the base, working her way upward, she found what she'd expected. Hidden among the leaves, much the same way she was, she found a ranger. His bow was drawn, eyes searching the road. A smirk came to her lips. She'd guessed right. The birds weren't landing because the rangers were too close. And she'd found them before they found her. That meant she could finish this without another chase. But first—.

Inyalia glanced overhead, making sure there was no empty nest in her tree. She had the advantage. There was no sense in squandering it. Content, she returned to the task at hand.

Working her way to the back side of the trunk, Inyalia opened her pack and pulled a small piece of lambskin from one of the side pockets. It was soggy, but that didn't matter for her intentions. She grabbed a chunk of charcoal from the same pocket. Black grit rubbed off on her hands. Stretching the lambskin as best she could, she scribbled a single word into the soft fabric. Cutting a piece of twine, she wrapped the damp lambskin around the shaft of an arrow and tied it off. Ensuring it would hold, she tucked the arrow into her quiver and quickly scaled the side of the tree, hoping to remain out of sight. Inyalia took position on the far side where she had full cover. From there, she dropped down behind a row of manicured shrubs. She was in position, all she had to do was finish the game.

Inyalia aligned herself with Tylor, ensuring a clean shot through the opening. So long as no one stepped through, the way was clear. She located as many rangers as she could find. Selecting the most likely target, she drew and nocked a generic blunt tip and took aim. Awaiting the perfect moment, Inyalia released. The arrow flew into the darkening sky, up over the tree tops. One of the flying birds crossed into its path. With a squawk, the blunted head struck, and both bird and arrow tumbled down. It was a long wait, but it paid off.

A high-pitched scream echoed across from the lodge. One of the rangers flailed about, tumbling from his perch. He landed hard on the ground, batting and kicking as the stunned bird flopped and fluttered, trying to get away from the floundering elf.

Open laughter echoed from the trees, announcing the location of the other rangers, including a few Inyalia hadn't seen. She didn't care so much about that. The bird had simply been a distraction. Nocking her message, she took aim and fired. The slim, wooden missile passed through the opening and struck the book in Tylor's hands, knocking it into him. The arrow landed in his lap, as the book wrapped around his head.

Inyalia crawled from the shrubs and disappeared into the trees. She didn't have time to wait for Tylor's response.

Approaching Inyalia's sleeping quarters, Tylor knocked on the wooden frame. Very few of the buildings here had doors. The weather never required it, and they'd been designed to offer privacy without confinement. Instead, he waited patiently before proceeding in. That was the polite thing to do after all. Even from here, he could feel the heat radiating from the small hut. The orange flicker dancing on the wall, hinted to the fire's size.

"Come in!" Inyalia's voice demanded from the far side of the room.

Tylor stepped through the opening and rounded the corner. He found himself staring down the shaft of a blunt tip, aimed at his chest. Inyalia was wrapped in a thick blanket. Her armor, clothing, and cloak hung near the central firepit, steam rolling from them. A smile found its way to his lips, though he didn't want to be shot again. "I must say I didn't expect so many surprises today."

"Does this mean I passed the test?" Inyalia kept her bow drawn. She needed to make sure it was over before she let her guard down.

"Today? Yes. Unless you plan to shoot me again? I won't deny I deserve it. But I really don't want to be shot again." Tylor recalled his own trials, he'd had it easy compared to what she'd undergone. But she was the general's daughter. She was going to be held to a higher standard, regardless of fairness.

Lowering her bow, Inyalia removed the arrow and stuffed it into her quiver. "Good. Now go away. I need to sleep!"

Despite his lingering pain, he managed a smile. "I'll see you in the morning." Placing his hand over his chest, Tylor turned and stepped toward the door. Pausing, he glanced over his shoulder. "You did well today."

Chapter VII
Rumor Has It

Morning came quicker than ever. Inyalia rolled, burying her face in the heavy quilted blanket. It was a desperate attempt to hide from the beaming rays of light shining through the open walls, an attempt that proved folly. Her muscles screamed at her, each one tense and throbbing. Unable to escape the day, Inyalia sighed and threw the blanket away from her. Straining, she sat up, placing her feet on the sun-warmed floor. It hurt to move, but the quicker she started doing it the sooner the pain would subside.

Making her way across the small hut, Inyalia pulled her clothes from the iron hooks elevated above the firepit. The pile of wood she'd stacked the night before had burned to cinders. Not so much as a single piece of charcoal remained. Bits of ash clung to her clothes. They were stiff, but dry. Giving a quick few whips to each article, the fibers loosened, returning to their usual flowing state.

Inyalia quickly dressed and went to work gathering her armor. It was stiff as well, but that was desired. In many ways it was better. The armor had been wet molded to her. While it fit well before, it would be even better now. She only hoped it hadn't dried too fast. That would make the leather brittle and more likely to break.

Buckling the molded armor into place, Inyalia took a seat on her bed. Her mind filled with dread. What would Tylor have in store for her today? She wasn't ready for any more tests, though she understood their purpose. It was a way of finding her limits. It would tell her what she was capable of. And considering the elves had never been involved in a war, or really anything more serious than the occasional beast attack, being tested now would prepare her if such a time ever came. The rangers were the first and last line of defense. She had to be prepared, even if her skills were never needed.

Inyalia recalled a statement her father often made. *If being a ranger were easy, everyone would do it.* She'd thought about that line quite a bit. The rangers were the elite. It wasn't supposed to be easy. There was always the army or navy for that. Anyone could join them, surpassing their ranks by the thousands. Though neither branch suited her. The army traveled, which was ideal, but usually only to neighboring kingdoms in need of aid. Rarely did they engage in combat. And the navy protected the coast, while providing escort for the trade ships. Neither path suited her. She wanted to travel, but Trendensil was her home. She couldn't stand the thought of being away for so long.

Inyalia sat quietly, processing her thoughts. No, this was where she wanted to be. This was where she needed to be. Her vow renewed, she picked herself up, grabbed her pack and quiver, and headed out the threshold.

It took no time to reach the Ranger's Lodge, though traveling by road took nearly three times longer than by tree. Inyalia could usually find Tylor inside. They'd created an unofficial tradition, meeting there each morning for breakfast. It provided a short time of revelry before her daily torture began.

She marched through the opening, glancing to the bar along the left wall. The main area of the lodge was mostly open, filled with several leather-bound chairs positioned around half as many tables. The far wall was adorned by a set of twin oaken doors that sealed the officer's lounge from view. Inyalia had seen inside only once, when Tylor had arranged the battle with Lorena. As far as she could tell, there was little more than an oblong table set with several chairs at the center.

On either side of the doors, towering shelves overflowed with books of all thicknesses, colors, and sizes. To the left of the southernmost shelf, a stairwell offered invitation to the basement and second floors. A dividing wall protruded, separating it from the barroom.

Inyalia glanced up the stairs. The second floor served as an inn and bathhouse. She understood the latter, but why anyone would need a bed was beyond her. All newcomers were assigned lodging when they met the circle. Though, her first day of training had answered that question. She'd been so sore she couldn't bare the thought of walking to her hovel. Instead, she spent the evening upstairs, soaking in a hot bath.

As for the basement, her guess was just as good as another. The base of the stairs was sealed by a thick iron door that was always locked. So naturally, many rumors circulated around it. Some believed it protected a vault filled with powerful artifacts. Others said it was the entrance to the catacombs, where those killed in training were buried. And her personal favorite, the entrance to another dimension where strange and wonderful creatures were kept prisoner. Inyalia didn't believe any of it. None of the stories made any form of sense. Even if such outlandish places did exist, they wouldn't be located in the basement of the lodge.

Making her way to the center table, where her and Tylor usually met, Inyalia was surprised to find the place so barren. Typically, there were several ranger's lounging about, enjoying a morning meal. Most of them were recruits, much like herself.

It didn't take long to realize that Inyalia was unique in her training. Very few of the others had a one on one relationship with their mentors. Despite Tylor's assurance to the contrary, she believed it had something to do with her family name.

She'd arrived slightly later than usual, but it wasn't late enough to warrant the place being near empty. Taking her seat, Inyalia gestured to one of the other recruits, an elf named Thurlas. He was talking with a mage from one of the lower tiers. She seemed comfortable with the ranger. Most magi didn't spend any longer from their kind than necessary. Inyalia had seen her a few times, but she'd never caught her name. But that didn't mean much. There were many people Inyalia had met but didn't know. Even Thurlas, she'd spoken to a handful of times. He was nearing the end of his time in Caelum, which meant they were rarely in the same place at the same time. "Hey Thurlas, where is everyone today?"

"You haven't heard?"

Inyalia waited patiently. That was kind of a stupid question. If she'd heard, she wouldn't have asked in the first place.

"Most of the trainers have been recalled to service. And they're rushing those of us who are nearing completion out the door. I got my duty papers this morning. There hasn't been an official announcement, but the rumors say something big is coming." Turning to his companion, Thurlas invited her to join the conversation. "Tell her what you heard."

The mage looked much older than Thurlas. But that was the way with humans. They aged roughly three times faster. Inyalia wondered what life was like for them. Having such a short lifespan had to be torture, simply waiting around to expire.

The human's voice was monotone, reciting the words as if reading a report. Her posture was rigid, her entire body reacting to each movement. "Divination spells are showing dark times ahead, though nobody has been able to discern any more detail than that. They haven't even agreed on a time period as to when this thing is supposed to happen. But things have been growing increasingly odd. Spells are misfiring as if they were cast incorrectly, despite proper handling. Some people are talking about the dead crawling from their graves. Even the weather has been acting up in some areas. A missive from Galmak reported blood raining from the sky. A lot of people are saying it's the end of days."

Inyalia absorbed the story. It was quite a tale. But how could it be true? She hadn't heard anything prior to now. Surely Tylor would have told her if something serious was happening. A smile breeched her lips. "You guys are messing with me, right? Good job. You had me going there for a moment."

"Hey, believe what you want. We're just telling you what we've heard. Speaking of which, it's about time to head out." Thurlas stood and grabbed his pack. "Good luck."

"You as well." Inyalia watched the pair disappear out the nonexistent door. Raising her hand, she signaled the kitchen boy.

"What can I get you today?"

"I'll take some toast with gravy, and a glass of milk, if you please. And while I have you here, have you by chance seen Tylor today? He's usually here before I am."

"I can't say I have, though I'll ask the chef. He was working the counter before I got in."

Nodding her agreement, Inyalia watched the boy rush behind the bar, disappearing between a set of swinging doors. He would have made a good ranger save for the damage to his left hand. He was missing the first two joints of each finger. She guessed that was why he worked the kitchen, rather than drawing a bow. Though she'd seen him wield a knife with a proficiency beyond her own. Given the right motivation, she had no doubt he could hold his own.

A moment later, the kitchen boy returned. A copper tankard rested in his good hand, the loaded plate of food balanced a top it. A sealed piece of parchment was pinched between the nubs of his damaged fingers. Setting the plate and tankard in front of her, he extended the missive.

"Chef says he was here this morning. He requested we deliver this to you."

"Thank you." Inyalia wasted no time breaking the wax. It had been pressed with the sigil of an owl perched upon a broken branch. She knew it as Tylor's personal stamp. Unfolding the missive, a second, smaller piece fell free and floated to the floor. Picking it up, Inyalia studied the elegant curvature of the symbols. It was written in a black ink, though it seemed to pulse between purple and yellow. Were she not in a place where magic was taught, she would have discounted it as a trick of the light. The symbols were foreign to her, but the tone of their intent suggested they were important. Directing her attention to the second, larger sheet, thick blots of smeared ink marred the page. She recognized Tylor's hand at once. It had been hastily written and sealed before dry, leaving smudges along the adjoining side. She silently read the missive, hearing Tylor's voice in her mind.

Inyalia,

I apologize for my absence this morning. New orders have arrived, altering our scheduled itinerary. I've been asked to report your progress and make my recommendations. You'll be pleased to know I've reported favorably. Which brings me to my next point.

Accompanying this missive, I've included a piece of vellum. On it, you'll find an inscription written in a special ink. It's a teleportation spell which, when read, will bring you to my current location, the resting place of the guardians. Consider this the first leg of your final trial.

Tylor Caer'moor

Inyalia studied the scroll more carefully now that she knew what it was. She didn't know the language it was written in, let alone how to pronounce the words. How was she going to read it? Tucking both, the message and scroll into the pocket of her pack, she searched the lodge for any familiar faces. It was clear she was going to need help. But who would be both knowledgeable enough, and willing to help her? If the rumors were true, most everyone was already gone. And the few who remained were likely busy following their own orders. Everyone answered to someone it seemed.

Stealing a look at the food before her, nausea replaced her appetite. How was she to eat when there was so much going on? Taking a deep breath, Inyalia lifted the tankard and tipped it back, swallowing its contents in a single, prolonged draw. She was on her feet before the metal base clanked against the table.

Making her way along the perfectly manicured road, Inyalia was beginning to feel alone. Until now, she hadn't realized how many people resided in Caelum. There was always something going on somewhere, day or night. But with the streets deserted, it held an ominous void she'd never noticed before. There was no ringing of hammers in the background. No clank of training swords in the distance. Even the birds had abandoned her. Only the echo of her boots offered any ambiance.

Inyalia marched on, toward the ramp at the end of the tier. One by one, she descended the levels, searching for someone, anyone who could aid her. Three levels below her own, Inyalia came across the first person she'd seen outside the lodge. She was still in the ranger sector, though this tier was a cusp. Caelum was divided into three major sectors, with several intermediate levels between them. Some enveloped entire tiers, while others overlapped in places. Thus far, Inyalia hadn't strayed much beyond the finesse sector. It was where most of the ranger outposts stood. Some of her training had taken place in the intermediate zones, blending finesse with strength, and even intellect on occasion. The pit was such a place. All three sectors held equal station there, though there was no penalty for leaving your own sector and visiting another. In fact, it was encouraged, provided such activities didn't interfere with training. After all, Caelum was a place of learning. If one wished to learn outside their specialization, no one would stop them. But for the most part, cast remained with their own.

Inyalia approached the young man, seemingly oblivious to her presence. She knew to stay out of range until he acknowledged her. That was one of the first lessons she'd learned the hard way. It'd taken nearly a week for the bruise to fade. She watched him quietly, awaiting an opportunity to speak.

He swung his training sword at the stationary target, dragging the blunted edge across before striking on the back swing. Feigning a parry, he struck again and finished with a stab to the midsection. Having completed the routine, he lowered his sword and returned to a neutral stance, as if aligning to repeat the process again.

Clearing her throat, Inyalia found mild amusement seeing him jump. "Pardon me. I didn't mean to startle you."

Turning to face her, he lowered his sword, which he'd instinctively raised to strike. "No worries. I didn't realize anyone else was around."

"That's precisely why I'm here. Do you know what's going on? Where is everybody?"

"No clue. I woke up and found the place cleared out. I'm guessing it isn't just here?"

"Apparently it's all over. I heard some rumors that most were recalled, but it seems odd everyone would simply leave without making some kind of formal announcement." Inyalia studied the man. He was young. Perhaps younger than her, though she couldn't be certain. "There were a few people at the Ranger's Lodge, three tiers up. You might find some answers there."

"Thanks. I'll give it a try once I finish my count. If this is all a test, I'd rather pass it."

"I understand. Good luck." Inyalia continued down the path hearing his sword strike the wooden target once again. It was obvious he was just as ill-informed as her. If only someone was willing to offer answers.

The drum of footsteps turned into a rhythmic beat, to which Inyalia found herself marching in time. Minutes turned to hours, dragging out for what felt like an eternity. She'd seen a few others in her trek, but they were few and far between, each just as confused as the last. She was beginning to enjoy the solitude. She'd been so busy in the now that she hadn't given herself time to think. That was one unexpected luxury the walk afforded. Her head was swimming with thoughts. Some valuable, others less so. But one in particular kept coming back, intriguing her with each revolution.

Magic was something rare. Only a few possessed it. And even fewer mastered it. The arcane arts ran deep in her family, though she'd never truly understood them. Even Wrylan, her brother after Baal, had been reluctant to discuss his abilities. He treated it like some big secret that everyone was simply supposed to forget. Like their grandfather, Wrylan was naturally gifted. He'd surpassed his instructors within the first cycle of his formal training, granting him invitation to the academy at Risolde. Inyalia on the other hand, had never shown the slightest trace of possessing those secrets. If there was a magic bone in her body, it was buried deep, unlikely to breech the surface any time soon.

That was where her problem lay. She had a magic scroll, which had to be read. But she was incapable of reading it. If only it had passed to her, she'd have the scroll figured out, and be on her way to meet Tylor. But it hadn't. And hope made a poor shield. That was when it hit her. If she was going to read the scroll, she'd need a mage to do it. And the best place to find one was at the heart of the intellect sector, within the massive tower she'd seen upon her first arrival, and every day thereafter.

Inyalia paused, looking upon the massive structure before her. Its peak disappeared into the clouds, and she still couldn't see the base through the fog. She'd once asked Tylor why she hadn't seen it from the mountains. He gave her some confusing and complicated explanation that basically meant it had to do with magic. She still had no idea what any of it meant but decided it best not to push. He'd never admit it, but Inyalia had a feeling he didn't understand it any better than her.

The tower entrance was located on the lowest tier. The trolleys weren't running. And all the horses were gone. On foot, she'd do well to reach it by nightfall. Taking a deep breath, Inyalia turned toward the road that wound its way through the ancient and mysterious settlement. It was a long walk and she needed to reach it as soon as possible.

Towering pillars stood on either side of the road catching the last rays of sunlight. Inyalia pass between them, feeling the subtle power wash over her. She'd passed through others like them, but none as large, or grand. This was also the first set that had been gold. She'd finally reached the lowest tier of Caelum.

The sun had been disappearing for quite some time now. She could no longer see it over the mountains, but its glow was still vibrant. A part of her longed for the routine found closer to the ground. She always knew when things were happening. That was not the case here. Most days she didn't know anything until it had already happened.

Walking the streets, Inyalia was taken back by the architecture. It was nothing like the levels above, though the transitions had been smooth. The finesse levels were mostly wood and clay, with rounded corners and open doors. She was used to that. But when the strength sector began to blend, abrupt edges and stone became more commonplace until it fully overtook. Likewise, intellect slowly blended the two until all that was left was seamless round pillars that sprung from the ground as if grown. Though she'd found no evidence to support that theory.

Inyalia had never gone this deep into the city. Until today, the farthest she'd traveled had been the core of the strength sector. It was both magical and intimidating. A static hung in the air that left her feeling uneasy. Like the levels above, the populace was few and far between, though there seemed to be more people here than anywhere else. That made sense. These people were skilled in magics, including those of travel. They didn't have to spend weeks reaching a destination when they could simply cast a spell and arrive instantly. Provided it worked that way. She wasn't entirely certain.

Following the street, now perfectly organized brick, rather than the grass and dirt of finesse or the rough stone of strength, Inyalia watched a hand full of what she guessed were students. They stood upon intersecting lines that glowed from the earth. Moving in unison, their hands contorted into strange configurations. The glowing rune beneath them became increasingly bright. And then, it disappeared entirely. Inyalia noticed the elf standing before them. His head dropped and he turned to face the others. She couldn't hear what was being said, but the intent seemed to be one of displeasure.

Stepping onto the unnaturally perfect grass, Inyalia approached the group. Perhaps they could read her scroll. Or at the very least, point her to someone who could.

"—times do I have to tell you? Clear your minds! Focusing on anything but the task at hand is the quickest way to ensure your spells fail. And that's provided you're one of the lucky ones. Many a caster has met their end due to an improperly articulated somatic component. Now, reattune yourselves and let's begin again." The mage turned just as Inyalia reached the edge of their gathering.

"Excuse me. I have a teleportation scroll that I'm having trouble reading. Is there any chance you could take a look?"

Impatience passed over the elven mage's face. He was much older than the others, though there was a youthfulness in his eyes that his wrinkling skin didn't reveal. "Very well. Let me see it." He extended his hand as if expecting the scroll to materialize.

Inyalia unslung her pack. Fumbling with the buckle, she reached into the pocket and took hold of both the missive and the scroll. Under the mage's pensive gaze, she felt tiny by comparison. She wanted to deliver the scroll as fast as possible so she could escape his attention. How anyone could impact her so strongly with a simple glare was a mystery. Handing it over, she took a step back, feeling his eyes fall from her and onto the vellum.

He studied the writing for a brief moment, rotating the page as if it would help it fall into context. Returning it to its original orientation, he gently sniffed the page and began rolling it tightly. "I'm afraid not just anyone can read it. The inscriptions are a generic teleportation spell, though the ink is unfamiliar. Such a unique pigment will require more attentive eyes." He handed the scroll back to Inyalia and returned his attention to the students patiently awaiting him.

Tucking it into her pocket, Inyalia raised her hand, risking the wrath of his penetrating gaze once again. "Would you happen to know anyone who might be able to help me?"

The mage took a deep breath and turned to face her a second time. Closing his eyes, he shook his head and exhaled, calming himself. "Most have left to attend to more important matters. Go to the Arcanum. Someone there may be able to give you further insight. Now, if you'll please, I've a class to disappoint me." Ignoring further interruptions, he raised his hands and directed his attention back to the class. The glowing rune burned into existence. "As before!"

Inyalia hesitated. She wanted to offer appreciation. She wasn't rude after all. But he'd made his intentions clear. She didn't want to risk upsetting him further. Turning away from the group, she spotted the tower not far from her. It hadn't seemed so near a moment earlier. Perhaps his advice had something to do with that? She couldn't be sure.

Returning to the road, Inyalia marched intently toward her destination. It was growing dark and she wasn't sure how much longer Tylor would wait, if he'd even waited this long.

As the sun disappeared completely, numerous colored flames sparked into existence, hovering over what Inyalia could only guess were lamp posts. They were unlike any lamps she'd seen before. They were polished and smooth along their tapered poles, splitting into a series of individual fingers that twisted as they spread, only to rejoin in a decorative point. The odd colored flames danced roughly a foot above each one, providing three times as much light as a torch, though they weren't painful to behold.

Stepping into the shadow of the tower, the clinging static became more intense. It crawled on her skin, sparking when she moved. She felt powerless beneath such might, though there was a confidence burning within her chest. She knew nothing could harm her so long as she had a clean shot. Armed with only a bow and wit, she was untouchable.

In answer to her presence, the tower's wall groaned. The seemingly living material shifted and stretched. A small hole appeared, growing wider. And within a minute, an open doorway rested where solid wall had been moments before. Swallowing hard, Inyalia stepped through.

She found herself standing at the center of a rather large room. Despite its majesty, she was somewhat disappointed. The interior was roughly the same dimension as the outside perimeter. Everything had seemed so mystically wonderful and full of mystery up to this point. And while there was still plenty to make her wonder, there was one element that seemed wrong. Why was it not bigger on the inside? Defying the laws of nature should have been an easy feat. After all, what was the purpose of magic if you couldn't alter such things?

Studying her surroundings, Inyalia realized she wasn't alone, though she wasn't in company either. A lingering haze filled the air, transitioning to a dense fog the farther it got. Rows of dark shapes, reminiscent of people, stood on the other side of the fog. Gradually, one would step to the head of their line. They'd stand there a moment. And then they were simply gone, replaced by the next in line. Inyalia tried to listen. The distance was great, but she should have been able to hear something, anything. Unfortunately, the only sounds present belonged to her own little row of fog.

"Name?" A distant voice asked from the far side of the room.

Inyalia glanced around, in search of the booming voice. She couldn't see anyone around her. Only a tall wooden podium at the head of the room. Did she reach the head of her line? She hadn't realized she'd been standing in one. Was it the same for everyone?

"What is your name?" The voice repeated.

Inyalia approached the podium. Its height adjusted the nearer she got, granting sight of the patient, but exhausted face behind it.

A balding middle-aged man stared back at her. He wore deep red robes and a pair of spectacles that rested on the bridge of his nose. Sighing deeply, he spoke again. "I assume this is your first trip to the Arcanum. I need to know your name and destination."

"Oh! My name is Inyalia Highlor. I have a scroll I need read. It's supposedly written in some kind of special ink."

The man's frown shifted into an attempt at comfort, though it settled closer to a creepy smirk. "Now that we're getting somewhere, may I see the scroll?"

Inyalia removed it from her pack. No sooner than it was free, it flew from her grip and floated gently across the chamber, landing on the podium. A part of her wanted to chase after it. She wasn't opposed to its viewing, though the manner in which he'd taken it was a bit rude. But that seemed to be the general commonality of the mages thus far. There was a running rivalry in Caelum. While all three sects trained together on occasion, it was common knowledge that they didn't often see eye to eye.

The man collected the scroll. Unrolling it, he studied the sigil. "Yes, I see. You've been summoned to the Guardians. But this inscription here—" He fingered the page as if Inyalia could see the part he was addressing. "—is unusual in such a simple incantation. And the ink. I see what you mean about it being unique. I've seen this type of scroll work before. We usually reserve it for the more powerful spells. Wouldn't want just anyone opening a portal to the abyss, now would we?" He laid the scroll down and stared expectantly at her, awaiting response.

"Um, no? It doesn't go to the abyss, does it?" Inyalia was feeling suddenly confused.

The mage laughed. For the first time since she'd met him, he seemed rather cheerful. "No, silly girl. Nobody would be so foolish to give a scroll of the abyss to an untrained simpleton."

Inyalia stared at him a moment. She was pretty sure he'd just insulted her. Unfortunately, there was nothing she could do about it. This was apparently the gatekeeper who would eventually decide if she could continue. "So you're saying it's only readable by certain people?"

"You're really out of your element, aren't you?" His smile faded. "The scroll can be read by nearly anyone, provided they've studied the arcane scripture. Its complexity prevents it from being used by anyone but a specific, or group of specific qualified persons. This particular scroll doesn't appear the be either. Though I see the one who crafted it is not able to use it." Scratching at the sigil, his attention fell elsewhere, as if he were witnessing multiple things at once. Speaking to himself, though not so loud for Inyalia to hear, he gestured dismissively.

The scroll flew from the countertop, rolling itself midair and came to a stop in front of Inyalia. She gently secured it and returned it to her bag.

"My dear, you're in luck. All of the conjuration masters have retired elsewhere, but one student remains. I hear she's quite talented in her field of study. She should be able to give you the name for whom this scroll is meant."

Inyalia narrowly had time to brace herself before an orange light surrounded her. She felt weightless for the briefest moment. The orange faded to black, and the ground beneath her disappeared, though she did not fall. A new ground settled under her feet and Inyalia opened her eyes to find herself standing in a new room.

Books were scattered about the place. Several had been piled into towering pillars that nearly touched the ceiling. Others cover table tops, some laid horizontally on their shelves, and a few glided through the air, flapping their pages like the wings of birds. The chamber was dimly lit from the occasional long burning candle. Thick strings of wax dangled from their bases, approaching the floor.

Inyalia searched the room, hoping to find whatever it was she'd been sent for. The stone walls were horrific compared to their exterior counterparts. These were rough and dark. And there were no windows within sight. If there was a hell, Inyalia guess this was it. She was so far from nature. So far from freedom. She felt trapped within this cramped dungeon of books and stone.

"What are you doing here?" A familiar voice cut through the dark.

Inyalia turned to find Lorena standing behind her, arms filled with thick tomes and fingers ink smudged. "You're the conjurer?"

"That's my main focus, though I'm skilled in others. I ask again, what are you doing here?"

"I didn't come to fight. I've spent all day trying to find someone to read this scroll. The guy downstairs sent me here." Inyalia pulled the scroll from her pack and offered it to Lorena.

"Why would I help you? It's not exactly like we're on the best of terms."

"Best of terms? You cheated when we were in the pit. And I still beat you."

"If you'd like a rematch, I'm sure we can arrange that." Lorena tossed the books onto one of the many cluttered tables. They slid against another stack, settling almost expertly. A glowing flame burned in Lorena's hand, pulsing, awaiting command.

"I told you I didn't come here to fight. I just want to get this read so I can be on my way. The sooner you help me, the sooner you can go back to whatever it is you do here." Inyalia stared intently into Lorena's eyes. She could see the pain within them. There was something more happening here. Something she didn't understand. And worse yet, she wasn't sure how long it had been present. This could have been the reason for their strife all along, and she'd never taken the time to notice it.

Lorena squeezed her hand into a fist, drowning the flaming ball. It dissipated into nothing. "Fine! Let me see it." Lorena snatched the scroll from Inyalia's hand, inspecting the markings as so many others had done. Carrying it to one of the tables with an open space, she laid it on the flat surface and grabbed a mortar from one of the many stands. Sprinkling a silver dust over the scroll, sparks of purple skated across the page. Lorena's gaze turned serious. Her head shot toward Inyalia, locked on her rival's position. "Where did you get this?"

"It was wrapped up in a missive I received this morning. I was told it can take me to the Hall of Guardians."

A defeated chuckle escaped Lorena. "Of all places— Do you know what happened to me after our—sparing match?"

Inyalia shook her head, unsure what this had to do with the scroll.

"I spend just over a week in recovery. I suffered what we commonly call backlash. It's what happens when a caster detonates a spell too close to themselves and fails to absorb the excess energy. Think of it as trying to put a fire out with lamp oil. All things considered, I was fortunate. Most people who suffer backlash are never able to cast again. It overpowers them, making it next to impossible to control the smallest spell. Yet somehow, in a manner neither I, nor my superiors can explain, I was able to escape this fate. I had to regulate, as I was completely drained, yet crackling with energy. But it didn't fry me. And now here you are, carrying a spell that is locked specifically to us. How do you think that happened?"

"What do you mean, it's locked to us?" Inyalia wasn't sure what was happening. There was clearly something larger at play. And apparently Lorena was as ill-informed as her.

"I don't have the time, nor the patience to give a full tutorial on spellwork. But, when making a scroll, it takes more than just inscribing the spellwork onto a piece of vellum. In fact, all that does is lay the foundation for the type of spell being performed. It's the ink that determines the specifics. Take this scroll for instance." Lorena gestured to Inyalia's scroll. "The markings are a basic teleportation spell. Anyone can use it, but their destination would be some random place within the scribe's reach. This scroll is to a specific place. A piece of that place, something specific to the destination, was ground into a powder and mixed into the ink. The scribe then went a step further and locked this scroll to us. Somehow a piece of each of us was collected and added to the ink. They then wrote the spellwork, meaning it's utterly useless unless both you and I work it together. Without one, the other is useless."

"That sounds easy enough. If we're all that's needed, let's make it happen." Inyalia stepped forward, ready to continue her quest.

"Just a second." Lorena placed her hand against Inyalia's chest, stopping her. Aren't you the least bit curious as to how they got our essence? I don't know about you, but someone working a spell around me without my knowledge is dangerous territory. Not to mention a violation to the Code of Magi. And to add another element, not that it isn't already deep enough, my final assignment was to find the Hall of Guardians. I've been searching for days and haven't found anything more than basic history. No maps, no coordinates, no landmarks. Among all of these books, the name was only written once, in reference to the first rangers. But nothing tells me where it's located. And then, suddenly, you show up with a scroll that's literally written specifically for you and I to travel there. I mean, I know you're a bit slow. But how can this be anything other than a trap?"

"I hadn't thought about it like that." Inyalia's cheeks flushed red. Lorena had a point. Everything thus far had been a test. Why would this be any different? "We'll, we both have to get to the Halls. And you said the location is unknown, so we can't get there without using the scroll. Is there anything we can do to shift the circumstances into our favor?"

Lorena thought for a moment. Everything was laid out perfectly. It was that perfection that made her question it. There were spells to remove ink from nearly anything. If she used one of those, she could possibly augment the perimeters of the scroll. But if her calculations were off, even slightly, it could mean the death of both of them. "I can't change the destination. Even if we knew where we were going, it's too precise to leave to chance. But I can possibly delay one of our arrival by a few seconds. That would allow the first to scope it out. If things go bad, it would give the second one a chance to react."

Inyalia thought through the possibilities. The delay was a good plan, though they needed something more. "Forgive my ignorance on the matter, but is there any way for us to see what's on the other side before going through? Like, I don't know, invisibility or something?"

"Mixing the magics is too unpredictable. It's already a complicated process. We don't want to lower our chances any more than they already are. But that does give me an idea."

Chapter VIII
Elves and their Tests

Onyx stone protruded through a thick canvas of white. Crystalline sparkles followed the ridges, reflecting the bright moonlight, hung low in the sky. The snow was dense and undisturbed, radiating an eerie sense of solitude even the abandoned streets of Caelum had failed to deliver.

Inyalia walked across the powder's surface, searching her surroundings. Though she knew Lorena was right behind her, she'd never felt more alone than she did right now. The cold lingered on her skin, but she couldn't feel it. Even the wind, forcing its chill through her cloak, did little to affect her.

Inyalia was surprised by how close the mountain peaks were. Not even her journey with Tylor had brought her so close. Given an hour to spare, she could have straddled the highest tip and returned. But that wasn't why she was here. She needed to find Tylor. But where was he? The message said the scroll would deliver her to him. They'd used it as directed. At least in the ways that mattered. But there was nothing here. Just rock and snow.

Recalling the hidden room among the mountains, Inyalia had a thought. Tylor told her the mountain was littered with them. Why would he have done that if not for use at a later time? He was always doing that. He'd say something minor, adding no emphasis, only to throw it at her a few days later to see if she was paying attention. Had that been his plan from the start? Given she was on a mountain peak, it made sense he'd await her arrival in one of the dwarven ruins. The lack of footprints reinforced that theory, especially considering the absence of snowfall.

Lorena's voice broke the silence. "Seeing anything?"

"No. Just snow and rock." Inyalia listened to her echo fade into the distance. Strange that Lorena's words didn't do likewise. "I'm not seeing anything here. Bring me back. Maybe we'll have better luck if we're both searching."

Inyalia's vision twisted and warped around her, drowning out everything she'd witnessed in the moments before. Her stomach knotted, threatening to expel whatever was left of her minute breakfast. Taking a deep breath to calm herself, she found the walls of the tower library staring back at her. Instantly, she wished she was back on the mountain. At least there she didn't feel confined. Wiping a layer of sweat from her forehead, Inyalia focused her eyes in the dimly lit room.

Lorena was standing over a pensive of swirling smoky liquid. Drawing a ladle of the mysterious concoction, she poured it into a tapered vial. It settled to the bottom, condensing in a near-black syrup-like state. A single drop formed on the bottom of the taper and broke free, landing in another dish.

"It's almost ready." Lorena swirled the dish, ensuring the contents mixed equally.

"I'll never get used to magical travel." Inyalia grabbed the wooden bucket Lorena had placed beside her. Her body convulsed, attempting to dislodge the absent contents of her stomach. In many ways it would have been easier if there was something there.

"Give it a few hundred more times. You'll get used to it." Lorena smiled, both in victory and empathy. Conjuration was hard on the body, especially when one was unexperienced with it. In truth, the nausea still plagued her, but she'd grown to expect it. Between that and a little trick she'd picked up, it had almost no effect on her anymore. Though Inyalia had a right to be sick. She hadn't fully teleported. Lorena had drained the original scroll to create two replicas. One would function as intended. That was the one they would be using next. The other, the one Inyalia had experienced, was a blend of conjuration and divination. Rather than sending her through completely, Lorena sent only part of Inyalia through the teleportation spell. She was there in all the ways that mattered, but her physical body remained behind. Such a transformation placed a heavy toll.

Inyalia spit the sticky film clinging to her mouth into the bucket. Drawing her waterskin, she took a swig and swished the liquid in an attempt to wash away the taste of stomach acid. Wiping her mouth, she composed herself and stood. "How much longer?"

"Nearly ready." Lorena tapped the side of the tapered vial, releasing the final drop. Lifting the dish, she gave another swish and poured the blackened contents into an inkwell. Ensuring her quill was perfectly clean of dust or old ink, she carefully dipped the tip into the well. Quickly, delicately, and precisely, Lorena brought the quill to a fresh piece of vellum. In a swift fluid motion, she recreated the sigil of the original scroll. It glowed gold for the briefest moment before turning purple. As the final line rolled into place, a sheen flashed over the vellum and the ink soaked to a near black. "And we're ready." Lorena wiped the remaining ink from her quill and tucked it away. Lifting the new scroll, she gently blew across the fresh sigil, ensuring the ink was dry.

"Let's get this underway. The sooner we find the halls, the sooner we can get back to our lives." Inyalia was beginning to feel tired. It'd been an exhausting day, full of disappointments. And now that she was making progress, she wondered if she had the strength to handle whatever she'd face next. There was a temporary truce between Lorena and herself, but how long would that last. They weren't exactly friends. She had little doubt Lorena would abandon her the first moment she was no longer relevant. But she couldn't wait any longer. She had to see this through to the end. Taking a deep breath, Inyalia extended her hand, awaiting Lorena to take it as she had when they read the first scroll.

"Otkin Adarab Utaalk" Lorena's voice resounded around them, echoing with a power that was both startling and commanding.

The walls faded to black, replaced with a cold unlike any other. The frozen wind whipped across the landscape, cutting to the bone. Inyalia crashed into the snow, scattering the collected flakes around her. Were it not for the initial shock, she had no doubt the dry heaves would have returned. Fortunately, she was too distracted by the intense cold to think about it. How could she have thought this not bad moments earlier? Picking herself up, she looked around in search for Lorena. She couldn't be far, but their hands had separated in the final moments of the twisting.

As if the thought released her, Lorena appeared a few feet above the snow in a flash of orange light. She fell face first, disappearing beneath the surface.

Inyalia rushed forward to help. It was difficult to move. Not only were her joints stiffening, but the snow was at least four feet deep. She had no idea how she didn't sink during her brief visit. "Lorena!" Inyalia reached the mage just as she was crawling from the crater.

Shivering, Lorena rubbed her arms. She wore little more than a set of light blue robes with a spell pouch and leather shoes. "You said there was snow, but I didn't imagine it'd be like this. Why is it so cold?"

"I don't know. I didn't feel it when I was here earlier."

"You wou—wouldn't have. You were lit—little more than a specter." Reaching into her spell pouch, Lorena grabbed a hand full of dust. Rubbing it between her already bluing fingers, she closed her eyes. The powder clinging to her robes began to melt, turning to steam. "That's better. Allow me?" She waited for Inyalia to nod her consent. Waiving her hand over Inyalia, the dust turned to ash and fell away. A heat flowed from her, wrapping itself around the elven ranger. "It'll only last an hour, and I only have enough dust to cast it once more. We need to find the halls before that happens."

"Agreed." Inyalia drew her bow, nocking an arrow in one swift motion. Scanning their surroundings, she searched for whatever it was she'd seen in the corner of her eye.

"What? What'd you see?"

"I don't know. It was there, and then it wasn't." Inyalia pointed to a nearby hill.

Lorena readied a firebolt, taking a defensive stance beside the archer. "Were you able to make out any details?"

"Not really. It was light in color. Like a silver or light gray. It was gone before I could see anything else."

"Are you sure the snow isn't playing tricks on you?" Lorena made her own perimeter check, circling her focus around the pair.

"Yes. I know what I saw. It moved so—There!" Inyalia fired an arrow. It buried itself in one of the mounds near a large stone, absent its target.

"I didn't see anything."

"I hit it. I know I did. It passed right through. We need to retrieve the arrow. The blunted tip isn't good for much, but maybe it'll prove I hit something."

The pair made their way toward the minor disturbance in the snow.

Inyalia had another arrow ready, searching for movement. Reaching the impact site, she stuck her hand into the frozen crystals, watching it melt away. If she could remember, she needed to have Lorena make her a couple scrolls of the heat spell. That would certainly rival keeping a few nights of firewood on hand. Finding the arrow, she pulled it free and inspected the tip. Holding it aloft for Lorena to see, a smile came to her lips. "See?"

The blunt tip was broken. What had been a small piece of leather wrapped tightly around encapsulated sand was now a shredded, useless pocket. The remaining bits of sand poured from the multiple tears, leaving nothing but the ruined leather behind.

"What is that?" Lorena leaned closer to inspect the damaged tip. Reaching into one of the tears, she removed a thin plate. "Ouch!" Blood seeped from her fingers where they'd made contact.

"What is it?" Inyalia inspected the holes for more of the sharp devices. Finding none, she broke the damaged head free and returned the arrow to her quiver, memorizing its location. A headless arrow was next to useless, but it was far better than a blunt tip if lethality was required. Of course, if Tylor had allowed her to carry her real arrows the day before, it wouldn't be necessary.

"It looks like a scale of some kind. It's sharp, I'll tell you that much." Carefully, Lorena grabbed it with her other hand, avoiding the edge. Wiping the blood away from the scale, she inspected the properties. "It's a light blue, almost gray. Not reptilian by design. And not aquatic either." Flexing it between her fingers, she noted its density. "It's almost like a fingernail, but stronger. I don't think I've ever heard of such a creature."

The snow behind them exploded, showering the area in white flakes. Those that came near the pair melted almost instantly.

"We need to find shelter. There's no way we can fight something we can't see coming. Especially when we have no idea what it is." Inyalia slowly made her way through the snow, searching every direction for the creature. If they could reach the cliff face, they could use it to guard their backs.

Lorena stuffed the scale into her pouch and made her way toward Inyalia, attempting to stay in her wake. The snow was loose, caving into the tracks almost instantly. It made following just as difficult as paving the way herself.

Reaching the stone wall, Inyalia sidestepped, allowing Lorena room to take position beside her.

"I told you this was a trap." Lorena chuckled to herself more than anything.

"Noted. Why didn't this thing show itself when I was here before?"

"Hard to say. Some creatures feed on magical energy. It's possible it came when we used the scroll. Or maybe it was waiting for us to let our guard down. Defining the motives of a beast are usually limited to preservation, be it food, defense, or shelter."

"Doesn't matter its reasons, we need to be cau—" Inyalia was silenced. Taken back, she tried to pull away from Lorena's hand covering her mouth.

"Shh!" Lorena gestured to their left.

At the edge of the mound where the arrow had been retrieved, a creature waited, watching them. Slithering in place, it hovered just above the snow. The glossy pale scales shimmered the reflected moonlight. It had a solid mass to its thin eel-like frame, but the movement appeared to pulse between a constant state of existence and something transparent. Whatever it was, it didn't appear completely corporeal.

Slowly leaning in, Lorena whispered as quiet as possible. "It's an ice wyrm. We need to move quietly. They hunt entirely by sound. And there's never just one."

Working free of Lorena's grip, Inyalia matched her volume. "You couldn't tell that from the scale?"

"I've never seen one. They're described in Hogarth's Manual of Vicious Beasts, but there was no picture available."

The creature inched forward, searching for any sign of its prey. Its nostrils flared, revealing fangs that were too large to be contained. A recessed pit rested on each side of its thin head where eye sockets had once been. Now it was stretched tightly, covered by serrated scales.

Slowly, Inyalia drew the string of her bow, stopping when the back side of the blunted tip rested at the edge of her thumb.

"What are you doing? If you shoot it, it'll know where we are." Lorena pleaded as quietly as she could manage.

"I'm not going to shoot it. I'm going to give it something to chase. Do you see that crevice to my right?"

Glancing behind the ranger, Lorena saw only rock and snow. But there was a section where the rocks were more visible than the rest. That had to be where Inyalia meant. "I think so."

"Good. This mountain is riddled with hidden strongholds. When I fire my arrow, I want you to run for that crevice as fast as you can. I'll be right behind you. When you reach it, forget about the shadows. Forget about everything you think you know. Press your way into the crevice and don't look back."

"What the hell does that mean?" Lorena spoke louder than intended. The creature hissed, pausing its casual slithering motion.

Keeping her bow drawn, Inyalia raised a finger, silencing her companion. Lorena had to trust her. That was the only way they were going to get past this thing. She just hoped she was right. She didn't know if the rocks held an entrance. And without inspecting it for herself, there was no way to be sure. But it seemed right. It seemed obviously natural. If that wasn't an indicator, she had nothing else to go on. But everything up to this point had been a test. Why would this be an exception? Waiting for the wyrm to begin its movement again, Inyalia returned her risen finger to the string. "Are you ready?"

"No. Give me a moment." Slowly, Lorena worked her way behind Inyalia. Placing her hand over the quiver, she grabbed a handful of arrows and carefully pulled them free.

"What are you doing?"

"If you're wrong, we're going to have to fight. These arrows won't do anything as they are. If things get ugly, you'll need something that can do some damage." Focusing her will, Lorena's hands began to glow. The radiating light spread through the shafts and surrounded the blunted tips. Encompassing the handful of arrows, it faded from view as if nothing had happened. Lorena returned them to the quiver and got into position. "I'm ready."

Inyalia nodded, giving the signal. She released the string, hearing its pop.

Instantly, the creature launched forward, first toward the pair. The arrow skated across the top of the snow, skimming the surface. Unsure which direction to go, it chose the closer of the two and chased the arrow.

Lorena broke into a sprint, clawing her way toward the collection of rocks. Reaching them, she closed her eyes, hoping there was some merit to what Inyalia had said. Sure enough, she felt an opening. Forcing her way inside, she opened her eyes, unprepared for the horrors that awaited her.

The creature disappeared as quick as Inyalia's arrow had. Keeping watch, the young ranger ran toward Lorena. She was a few feet behind when she heard the screams. Freezing, Inyalia searched the void between the rocks for anything that could deliver answers. Lorena's face appeared in the moonlight, her mouth agape, frozen in terror. Tears flowed down her cheeks, contrast against the pale skin. Inyalia heard a low growl within the crevice. Suddenly, without resistance, Lorena was gone, ripped into the darkness by forces unknown. Her bow aimed, one of the enchanted arrows nocked and ready to fly, Inyalia inched forward. Fear grew inside her. She wanted to turn and flee. But she needed to know what happened. Whether she was alive or dead, she had to find Lorena. She owed her that much.

Reaching the thin opening between the rocks, Inyalia peered inside. Even with the moon as close as it was, her vision couldn't pierce the veil. Swallowing her fear, she squeezed into the gap, searching for whatever evil hid within.

It took only a moment to discover this was not one of the hidden strongholds she'd sought. Instead, it was a small cavern, though due to the lack of breeze, she suspected it was either shallow or collapsed somewhere along the way. There was no light inside whatsoever. Inyalia stole a quick glance behind her, seeing the glowing white outside. Something was keeping it dark in here. That was the only explanation. Slowly, cautiously, Inyalia made her way deeper into the cavern. The hair on her arms and neck stood on end. She felt like she was being watched, but nothing showed itself, not that she could see it if it had. It was certainly being quiet, whatever it was.

Keeping her arrow trained to her line of sight, Inyalia was beginning to make out details in her surroundings. It began as a dim glow in the center of the small chamber. That's what it was. No exit tunnels, no branching veins. Just a small cavity in the rock, narrowly wider than her parent's home.

A silhouette grew in her vision. It was still, in the form of a prone body. Cautiously, she approached, scanning the walls and ceiling. Whatever had grabbed Lorena was still present. Inyalia studied the body. It was wrapped in a cloak, all features hidden from view. Though it appeared larger than the missing mage. Her fear grew. Was this Tylor? Did he fall to the creature? Pressing her booted foot against the shoulder, she gave a firm shove. Maybe she could rouse them. But just in case it was a trap, she kept her bow drawn and aimed.

The figure rocked but made no further action.

Again, she shoved, harder this time. She needed to see who it was. As intended, it rolled to its back. Inyalia's heart leapt. Her breath became short and rapid. Every ounce of will she'd been conserving faded away. "Daddy?" Inyalia lowered her draw and discarded her bow. She fell to her knees, shaking the deceased form of her father. He was covered in blood, though she couldn't see where it was coming from. "Daddy, wake up!" Inyalia sobbed uncontrollably. He was gone. There was nothing she could do. There was so much blood. Rocking back and forth, she held onto her father, unable to stifle her tears.

"Inyalia?" A rasping voice called. It was weak, barely audible.

"Mom?" Inyalia asked, breaking her hold on her father. Standing, she searched for her mother, half blinded by tears. Something hit her legs and she tripped. Inyalia landed face to face with her mother. She was bruised and beaten. Much of her skin had been melted away from heat.

"Inyalia. Run!" There was concern on Melaena's face, what was left of it. She gasped and fell still.

"Mommy, don't leave me!" Inyalia shouted, getting to her knees. In the corner of her eye she saw another figure. Baal had had his throat cut. His lifeless eyes stared at her, cold and uninviting. Vera rested a few steps from him. Her neck was purple and disfigured. Everywhere she looked, she saw bodies. People she knew. People she cared about. Each one dead. And she was powerless to do anything about it. Tylor's body dangled from a pike. Lorena had been shredded to pieces. A cold expression remained on her face. It told Inyalia that this was her fault.

Arms wrapped around her knees, Inyalia sobbed. She was all alone. More alone than she'd ever been. As if the thought triggered something inside her, she saw another figure. But this one wasn't elven. It was a dragon, the dragon, Alona. The warm glow the beast had bestowed upon her came to the surface. Inyalia felt calm. She felt warm. Everything was going to be okay. Taking a deep breath, she pulled herself to her feet. None of this was real. It couldn't be. This was another test. An attempt to break her. "No—I will not break!"

The declaration renewed her will. Inyalia watched the bodies vanish like smoke on the breeze. They were gone, with them, the darkness. She could see.

The cavern was about the size she'd guessed, though it was slightly smaller. But every surface, the floor, walls, and ceiling were covered in thousands of sigils. This was a test. And she passed. How could she not? But where was Lorena?

Wiping the tears from her face, she could feel the heat on her cheeks. They were steaming, and no doubt red. Looking around, Inyalia heard a growl at the entrance. Startled, she saw the ice wyrm in the opening. She'd forgotten all about the creature. And here she was, unarmed and alone. Her bow was laying in the floor, halfway across the chamber. But the beast didn't appear to have found her yet. It was slithering, sniffing, showing all the signs it had when it didn't know where they were. If she was quiet, there was a chance she could reach her weapon before it heard her.

Inyalia made her way forward, moving slowly, hoping to prevent the slightest squeak in her armor. What she hadn't taken into account were the loose stones on the cavern floor. One hit her boot and rolled just enough to resonate.

The wyrm froze, letting out a low growl. It was aimed upon her, its jaw retracted to display hundreds of needle-like teeth, each one longing for the taste of warm blood.

She had to act now. It knew where she was, and she had no doubt it was faster. Charging, Inyalia barely had time to see the creature headed straight for her. She rolled, landing on her right shoulder. But it was close enough to grab her bow. On the follow through, she nocked the arrow and drew, releasing just as the icy breath fell upon her.

Inyalia felt time slow. Everything happened in the blink of an eye, but for her it felt like an eternity. She hadn't reoriented herself yet. She was crouched on one knee, her other leg extended for balance. The feathers of her arrow twisted, slicing through the frozen air around her. She could almost see it. An enlarged mouth was inches from her, those razor-tipped teeth aimed to tear her apart. But it was the arrows trajectory that caught her attention most of all. It was headed straight down the creature's throat. She watched the blunted tip scrape the spine and several ribs on its way down. And when it finally impacted, somewhere near the mid-section, the arrow exploded.

Time resumed. Inyalia felt the force of the blast carrying her backward. Wrapping her arms around her head, she prepared for impact.

The cavern wall was by no means comfortable, but it didn't feel like she'd expected. She also wasn't ready to keep sliding after the impact. Coming to a stop, she glanced around, wondering what had happened.

Tylor sat at the edge of a stone guardrail, watching her with a smirk. "Took you long enough."

.

Chapter IX
A Final Trial

Gaining her bearings, Inyalia leapt to her feet and charged the illusive ranger. She was both furious and relieved. She wanted to hug him and beat him at the same time. Anger won out. Her fists flew of their own accord. She struck him in the side of the head, feeling little remorse. "What the hell? How could you do that to me? Is this some kind of sick joke?" She swung again, stopping just short of her mark.

Tylor held firm, keeping the assault from connecting a second time. "I apologize for what you've experienced. But you should know, we've all experienced it one way or another. It hits some harder than others." His tone became solemn and reserved. "I can only imagine what you've seen. It's not the same for everyone. Most experience the loss of their family, but that's not always the case. Whatever it was, I'm sorry." Releasing her arms, Tylor took a step back, allowing her a moment to regain her composure. "The cave makes you confront your worst fears. It shows you what you're fighting for. But it also tells you what you have to lose. By acknowledging this, you can prepare yourself, should those fears become a reality." Tylor's words drifted off. He approached one of the many basins lining the elevated walkway and held his hands over the flames.

"I'm sorry I hit you." Inyalia watched him. He was retreating, though not from her. There was something in his tone. He'd spoken as if he'd experienced the trauma firsthand. For a moment, she'd seen it in his eyes. It was the same look she'd seen on Lorena minutes before. That reminded her. "Where's Lorena?"

Turning to face the young ranger, Tylor regained his usual demeanor. "She's gone on to finish her own trials. I will say, it was rather cold of you to use her as bait."

"I didn't—I—I was trying—."

"Let me finish." Tylor interrupted. "It was cold. But these are the decisions we are sometimes forced to make. You achieved your objective. You made it here on your own. Lorena did not."

"But—I had to have Lorena's help to get here." Inyalia was feeling confused by all of this. How could he say she'd made it alone, when it was designed to require both of them?

"You needed her help, as she needed yours. You put aside your differences and worked together to reach a mutual destination. And while it had been your plan which ultimately resulted in Lorena's failure, you still went into the cave to rescue her when you had every reason not to. For that, you succeeded. And you managed to do so again against the visions. Your successes belong to no one but yourself. Not me, not Lorena, not some unseen power pulling the strings of fate. You made it. And you should take comfort in that. But enough explanations for now." Tylor extended his arms wide, as if showcasing a prized relic from a time long passed. "Welcome to the Hall of Guardians."

Inyalia glanced around. They were standing under a grand colonnade. A thin layer of snow had settled over the walkway, most of it blocked by the protruded ceiling. The supporting columns were carved, depicting twelve towering statues dressed in ranger's armor. Each one stood against their various bows, ornate and beautiful. A flaming basin rested between each of the statuesque columns, piled high with burning embers. At the end of the long walk, a grand archway guarded the entrance into the mountain. Like the columns, it had been made from the same black quartz Inyalia had seen upon her arrival. "I expected it to be a bit more magnificent."

Tylor was taken back. He hadn't prepared himself for her quirky, quick-witted humor. "Sorry to disappoint. Shall I have the architects resurrected so they can build it to her majesty's specifications?"

Laughter escaped her. It felt good. She couldn't recall the last time she'd laughed. "Only if you can find time between my scheduled torture sessions."

This brought a smile to Tylor's face. "As you wish." He gave a subtle bow. Returning to his full height, he walked beside her toward the archway. "The halls are believed to be the birthplace of the Ranger's Corp. The statues you see here were the first protectors of Trendensil. I know how much you love your trials, but unfortunately, this is the last one. Once you step inside, you'll be on your own. I cannot interfere or help you in any way. Every decision you make will have consequences. But I promise you, when you leave this place, you'll be certain of your path. That said, are you ready to begin?"

A heavy sigh escaped her. His sarcasm aside, she was tired of tests. But this was the path she'd chosen. If she was to follow in her father's footsteps, she'd have to proceed. "Can you give me a clue as to what I'll face in there?" Her gaze lingered deep into the fire-lit halls of the mountain structure. A dark and foreboding presence radiated. She wasn't entirely certain she wanted to go in.

"I cannot say. Though this time it's not for a lack of desire. The truth is, I don't know what you'll face. The only time I've been inside was the day I became a ranger. But the stories suggest it's different for each person."

"So, magic?" Inyalia asked, keeping watch on the distance. There was something in there she didn't like. Something that wanted her to enter.

"I don't think so. This isn't like the cavern. That was designed to show you visions. This is something different. Everything that happens in there—." Tylor gestured to the opening. "—It really happens. The magi have tried to identify it many times, but none have succeeded. Though they all agree, whatever it is, it isn't arcane in nature."

"What did you face when you went in?" His silence drew her attention away from the halls. She could feel the sorrow wash over him. It was strong, lingering. "I'm sorry I asked."

It took a long moment to answer, the events replaying in Tylor's mind. Closing his eyes, he exhaled before speaking. "No, it's okay. I saw what was to come of my life. I didn't know it at the time. I'm pretty sure there's some old saying about hindsight that applies here. But for me, the halls and the cavern were nearly the same. I stepped through the entrance and made my way along the corridors. There were a couple rooms which seemed meaningless to me at the time. When I reached the end, I was greeted by family. One by one, I witnessed their deaths, unable to save them. The halls labeled me a wild elf long before I accepted the title myself. Once I was free, I was sworn to service and given my first assignment. I went home before I was due to report. But when I got there, I learned that they'd been slaughtered." Tylor wiped the tears from his face. "I witnessed their deaths as they'd happened. But I wasn't there to stop it. I wasn't there to protect them." Strengthening his resolve, Tylor corrected his posture and concealed the emotion he'd allowed himself to feel. Sniffing, he continued the tale. "Anyway, I had nothing left but the corps. I accepted my fate and requested reassignment. I was a wild elf. I didn't belong in a unit. And your father granted my request. From that day on, I've served him loyally. But don't let my story frighten you. I assure you, most are nowhere near as dreary as mine. Some claim it was downright enjoyable."

Inyalia stood awestruck at the wild elf's tale. She'd assumed he lived outside society by choice. In many ways, that was probably close to the truth. But to lose his entire family twice over, three times including the cavern, sounded like torture. A sorrow crept into her. She didn't pity him. There was too much respect for that. But she certainly felt for him. Closing her eyes, Inyalia nodded. "Thank you for telling me." Turning, she marched toward whatever hell the halls had in store for her.

Inyalia's footsteps were muffled by the thick rug lining the center of the corridor. Glancing over her shoulder, she saw Tylor standing outside the entrance. Though that wasn't her motive. She felt like she was being followed. But no one was there.

Watching the firelights dance in sequence with the steady breeze from the entrance, Inyalia continued deeper. The reservations she'd had about entering were rapidly fading, but that didn't set her mind at ease. She knew she didn't want to be here. She clung tight to that memory. The comfort the halls provided was little more than a guise, designed to trick her into submission. She was done with that. Never again would she allow magic of any kind to control her. Though it did kind of feel like home. This was a place for people like her. Why should she fear it? Every ranger who'd trained in Caelum had walked these halls. It was a protected piece of history, linking them to the time of their founding. She'd learned from Tylor that her father had taken these same steps, as had Baal. For all she knew, Vera would be the next in her family to do the same. They were with her, though not physically. Not in the way it had seemed for Tylor.

"No—I will not become complacent!" Inyalia demanded, forsaking any comfort the halls provided. She couldn't afford their tricks. Increasing her pace, she came upon her first choice. Recalling what Tylor had said about every decision having a consequence, she paused, carefully examining her options. The path continued left and right. They were identical in appearance, neither holding sign nor indicator above the other. Of course there wouldn't be. Inyalia smirked at the thought. What kind of test would announce, *This way to the finish line!* Scanning both directions, Inyalia turned left. Something inside her said it didn't matter which way she went, she'd reach her destination just the same. All that mattered was finding the path for her.

It took but a moment to reach the first chamber. Inyalia found it odd. She'd just started down this route. Her initial glance appeared to lead on forever. How was she already in a room? Dismissing the question, she decided not to focus on it. This was probably the first of many oddities she was going to encounter in this place. The answer was irrelevant. She simply had to complete her objective, whatever that was supposed to be.

Stepping inside, Inyalia noticed the walls were made of the same dark crystalline rock she'd seen outside. The ceiling was too high to examine, but it held a reflection similar to glass. It was dull and unpolished but reflective, nonetheless. The room was a relatively simple design. It contained two rounded walls connected at the entrance, and again at what she guessed was the exit. Though it was barred by a closed door. There were four sconces mounted just above head level, containing small but powerful flames that lit the entire room. A slim pedestal set in the central floor, marking the only point of interest. Upon it rested a single white feather.

Inyalia approached and inspected the pedestal. Both the base and top were made of stone, though it had been polished smooth. Kneeling, she got a closer look at the feather. There were no markings of any kind. Not even the spine carried a discoloration from where it had once adjoined its owner. Gently, she lifted the flawless plume and inspected the vanes, twisting the shaft between her forefinger and thumb. They shimmered under the orange glow.

The grinding of stone demanded her attention. Inyalia was surprised to find the entrance from which she'd come was sealed much like its opposite. "So much for going back." Glancing to the other door, it now stood open, offering invitation.

Feather in hand, careful to keep from ruffling its perfect configuration, she marched onward. As before, the path came to an end, offering a choice. Versed in how this was going to work, Inyalia turned right, giving little more than a second's thought to the decision.

The crackle of the wood fueled braziers spit sparks along the path, though there was no evidence as to when, or even if the wood had been restocked. Each one was filled to capacity, piled atop a bed of burning coal.

Once again, Inyalia came to an open door. She stepped inside, certain it would close behind her. So certain in fact, she didn't bother to check.

The room matched the previous, with one exception. A ring of stone had been carved from the floor itself. In its center a tree sprouted. It wasn't much larger than a sapling, but the limbs were thick and outstretched, as if reaching for something in the distance.

Inyalia had never seen a tree like this before. The bark was black, much like the stone so frequent in this place. But what made it even more interesting, the leaves were made of crystal, reflecting the light in small concentrated beams.

"What am I supposed to do with a tree?" Inyalia asked aloud, though she didn't expect an answer. Answers seemed to be in short supply when you were training to become a ranger. Though it seemed this time was an exception.

To her surprise, one of the thicker branches snapped. It crashed to the floor, scattering its unique leaves. They shattered, showering the stone in tiny fragments which made it sparkle. Only now did Inyalia realize the floor was covered in the quartz dust of these fallen leaves.

Approaching the downed limb, she stared at it for a long moment. It had broken at a knot, leaving two lengthy, and fairly strait pieces of wood. It wasn't large enough for a bow, but perhaps that, paired with the feather, she could craft a couple arrows. Reaching down, she grabbed the broken limb and inspected it.

The wood was strong, stronger than any she'd handled before. There was no reason it should have broken. Yet it had. And she was here to witness it. Recognizing it for what it was, she silently thanked the tree and placed the broken limb in her quiver. Turning, she searched for the other door, though to her surprise, there wasn't one. Only the door she'd entered remained, open and waiting. Making a mental note, she marched through. It seemed this place was adapting to her. If she thought she had something figured out, it would change.

It took much longer to reach the intersection than she recalled. The feather room rested to her left, its door closed, and likely locked if she was being honest with herself. But now there was another path. This one continued straight across.

Aside from randomly choosing which direction to take in an endless supply of hallways, there hadn't been much in the way of tests. Though she refused to admit that aloud. She was exhausted from her days walk to the arcanum, not to mention everything she'd experienced since. Her stomach was empty, and if truth be told, she was in desperate need of a hot bath. The last thing she wanted right now was a challenge.

The passage ended in another room. As before, a pedestal rested in the center, but this one held a wide basin overflowing with what appeared to be precious gems. Bright beams of every color shot from the basin, decorating the walls and ceiling.

Curious, Inyalia approached to get a closer look at the numerous bobbles awaiting her. It took longer to reach the pedestal than she'd expected, but she began to understand the moment she crossed the threshold.

This room was so much larger than the others she'd seen. Nearly half of Highlor could have fit within these walls. But she couldn't tell that from the door. The proportions made everything seem closer than it was. And now that she was a part of it, she felt small by comparison. Inyalia reached the center. From here, the door was little more than a blip on the horizon, and the towering pedestal was easily twenty foot tall. Standing beneath it, the basin had to be large enough to hold a small pond.

Searching the base, there were no holes or protrusions to climb. But she had to reach the top. Why else would she be here? Her only option was to scale the side. Forming a plan, Inyalia knew she couldn't risk using her grappling hook. If the basin were to fall, it'd crush her in a heartbeat. But there was another way.

Dropping her pack, Inyalia fished out her rope. She'd spent the majority of her younger cycles scaling trees. Not all of them had had rough bark or even low hanging branches to grab hold of. But that hadn't stopped her.

Twisting the rope around itself, she doubled it and secured the loose end. In this configuration, it looked to be just long enough to wrap completely around. She took a few steps back, preparing herself. She'd done this many times over, but never on something so large. Rushing forward, Inyalia twisted at the waist, slinging the thick whip against the smooth surface. It popped, wrapping itself around the polished trunk. An instant later, it reappeared on the left side. Inyalia lunged, catching the folded end as it began to drop. She'd done it. And on the first try no less. Smiling her victory, Inyalia wrapped both ends around her hands and walked the rope as high as she could. Pulling tight, she pressed her feet against the wall and climbed a few steps at a time.

It took some time, but Inyalia finally reached the top. Now that she was here, she was faced with a problem she hadn't considered sooner. How was she going to get around the underside of the bowl? Her rope was in use, and even if it weren't, the grappling hook was still just as dangerous. Though now that she was so close, it seemed unlikely her weight could make much of a difference.

Locking herself into place, Inyalia reached overhead, feeling the underside of the basin. She'd expected it to be smooth, like the pedestal, but she'd been mistaken. Instead, it was ridged and wavy, reinforcing the heavy walls. And conveniently, it'd make climbing a breeze.

Getting a solid grip, Inyalia pulled herself onto the bowl, wedging her feet between the grooves. Carefully, she pulled the rope to her, wrapping it over her shoulder. There was no telling if she was going to need it again.

As ready as she could be, Inyalia extended her legs, pushing herself along the outer wall of the basin. She kept three points of contact, working her way toward the rim. It took no time for her to reach the top, and when she did, she found herself entranced by the sea of gemstones before her. They were so vibrant, so enthralling. There had to be thousands, in a variety of shapes, sizes and colors. They were piled to the top, near overflowing. But she couldn't stay on the edge forever. Eventually, her arms would give out, refusing to hold her weight any longer. Taking a deep breath, Inyalia pulled herself over the edge and fell into the basin.

It wasn't a long drop. In fact, it wasn't much of a drop at all. If anything, it was no different than rolling into a pile of river rock, only without the water. The loose, polished gems were much harder to climb than a wall of rough stone, but she managed to get away from the edge. The last thing she wanted was to be washed over if the pile decided to collapse.

Finding a spot where she could rest, Inyalia laid back, admiring the treasures around her. Some were the size of her fist, while others were larger than her head. Just one of these stones was likely valuable enough to purchase the entirety of Highlor. But wealth was not why she was here.

Shaking its beauty from her mind, Inyalia looked upon the pile once again, only this time, not for its riches. There had to be a reason she was here. Nobody would have left such a treasure lying around. This was simply another test.

Amidst the semitransparent reds, blues, greens, and every other color imaginable, Inyalia now saw other materials. Some were made of coal, some were granite. There even appeared to be a few polished chunks of wood lingering about. She was swimming in a conglomeration of prismatic orbs that made no rhyme or reason. But there had to be a purpose behind it. And she had to find out what it was.

Grabbing one of the gems, Inyalia tossed it over the side. It crashed to the floor and shattered, sending thousands of tiny pieces in all directions. She smiled. Gems wouldn't break like that. Most of these had to be glass. That was the only explanation.

One after another, she tossed the orbs aside, hearing some break, while others bounced harmlessly, landing where they fell. It didn't matter which ones were real and which weren't. There was something here.

Hours passed and Inyalia continued to dig. She was nearly halfway down and in desperate need of food and rest. Unable to turn another stone, she laid against the curve of the basin's wall. Her eyes were heavy, nearly as heavy as her arms. Pulling her pack close, she reached inside and grabbed a piece of dried meat she'd been reserving for a rough day. It seemed no day was rougher than today.

Taking a bite, she rested her head against the retaining wall and stared up at the ceiling. Like the others, it held the reflective surface of glass, but this one was clean. She could see what appeared to be stars on the other side, though they didn't twinkle. Moreover, the moon that had been so bright and so close mere hours before was nowhere to be seen. It made her wonder if it was the actual sky she was seeing, or a simple depiction. It didn't matter either way. Staring into the dark she didn't feel so confined. A part of her was even feeling relaxed. Lost in its eternity,

Inyalia's eyes began to close. And before she could stop herself, she drifted off to sleep.

Inyalia woke with a start. It took a moment to realize where she was, but the uncomfortable gems beneath her brought the memories flooding back. She had no idea how long she was asleep, but it was enough. At least for now.

Returning her attention to the task at hand, she picked up a ruby about the size of her fist, though it was oblong about twice the width. Tossing it over the side, she noticed an off-white opal. It was one of the smaller objects she'd come across, but the first of its kind. Picking it up, Inyalia immediately noticed the change in temperature and density. It weighed next to nothing at all, and, unlike the others, it felt warm to the touch.

Inspecting it closer, she noticed a grain pattern in the surface, but it clearly wasn't wood. Sighing, Inyalia tossed it over the edge. It was interesting, but it still wasn't the right one, not that she'd know it when she saw it.

Second guessing herself, Inyalia got to her feet. She didn't want to risk losing the opal just in case she was mistaken.

Climbing to the edge of the basin, she straddled the brim. Staring down, a realization came to mind. She'd made more progress than she'd realized. Most of the bobbles were scattered across the floor, most of them broken. And the basin itself was maybe a third full, all piled against the side she was currently straddling. That was her mistake.

The basin began to tip. The higher it rose, the more the loose stones rolled to the low edge. In an instant, it was teetering on the bottom lip.

Inyalia knew she was in trouble. She didn't think there was anything beneath her, but just in case, she moved her leg. Feeling the bowl settle to a stop, she was afraid to move. She'd trapped herself. It was her minimal weight, the weight she'd believed inconsequential, that kept the basin stationary. If she moved in any direction, it was going to roll, flip, or tip. Weighing her options, they were few. She could jump, hoping it didn't land on her. But there were too many unknown variables. If the basin didn't hit her, she still had the impact to worry about. And to top it off, she'd littered the floor with shards of broken glass and spheres of death. Jumping was not an option.

Inyalia scanned her surroundings, hoping some stupid, yet equally marvelous plan would come to mind. Seeing her pack buried among the collected stone, the wheels started turning. Inyalia bent at the waist, pulling it free. Her heart raced. If she disturbed the weight distribution too much, nothing but dumb luck would save her. But that was about all she had at the moment anyway. Holding her breath, she watched the gems fill the void. To her relief they settled without too much trouble.

Crouching in an attempt to lower her center of gravity, she pulled the grappling hook from its pocket and quickly secured it to her rope. Finally, it was going to prove useful, provided her idea actually worked and didn't get her killed instead. Racing through the possibilities of her plan once again, she calculated the options. Only one had any chance of success, and it was likely to hurt.

Standing just enough to give clearance, Inyalia swung the hook, letting it gain momentum. This part was key to her plan. If she was off, even a little, the whole thing would come crashing down, literally. Counting down, watching the arc as well as her target, Inyalia released, letting the rope fly. She waited for the perfect moment. Seeing it, she yanked, setting the hook. It caught the top rim of the basin, near center of where she was trapped. It wasn't as close as she would have liked, but it was better than it could have been.

Keeping steady tension without pulling the rope, Inyalia forced several breaths, psyching herself up. She'd made some foolish decisions throughout life, but this was probably one of the stupider ones. Her stomach knotted. She wasn't ready, but she couldn't stay here. Eventually she'd have to move. And when she did, both her and the basin would come tumbling down.

No, she had to act now. This was her best chance. Holding the rope loose in her hand, but with enough tension to keep the hook set, Inyalia jumped.

Weightlessness claimed her for the briefest moment before the rope caught. She watched the basin fall away, only to rise the other direction. This was the tricky part. Timing her descent, Inyalia embraced a freefall, letting the rope slip between her gloves. Rapidly approaching the floor, she squeezed the tether with all her might, stopping inches before the surface. Her hands burned from the friction. She could feel the leather covers hardening around the rope. But she couldn't let go just yet.

The basin rang out like a gong. It flipped and rolled, finally settling on its top.

A sudden jerk lifted Inyalia into the air. Her shoulders screamed against the sudden weight. The ruined leather separating her from the rough fibers became slick and the rope ripped itself from her hold. Inyalia crashed to the floor, collapsing in a heap. Yanking the gloves off in a desperate attempt to cool her hands, she pressed them against the stone floor, hoping it would suck out the heat. Savoring her success, she laid there, breathing deeply. It wasn't the most graceful landing, but she was alive, and relatively uninjured. It was still better than the alternative. She was just glad the basin had dropped straight. If it had rolled even slightly, the rope would have missed the towering pedestal and she would have splattered.

A bright light filled the room, drowning out all lesser light. Inyalia looked up from her pile, unsure what was happening. The basin was misshapen, flat where it had impacted. It laid on the other side of the pedestal. Getting to her feet, Inyalia saw the remanence of her grappling hook. It had gotten crushed, but the bulk of her rope was salvageable. It took a moment to realize, but the floor was clean. The broken shards were nowhere to be seen. The wooden orbs, chunks of coal, smooth marble, even the real gems, all of it was gone. All but one she hadn't seen before.

Lying at the base of the pedestal, a small chunk of blackened ore remained. It wasn't much, but it was ripe for smelting.

Lifting the odd mineral, Inyalia felt something inside it, like a heartbeat. Staring intently, she could see a faint pulse within the subtle veins, ebbing a purple glow.

A wash of motion rolled around the room. The walls faded away, replaced by rough stone. A chill wind wrapped itself around her, extinguishing the sconces. For a brief moment it was pitch black. The shadows of the room shifted and a new light emerged. At the center, a pile of embers burned within a small forge. It provided just enough heat to beat back the cold winds. Moonlight beamed through an overhead ventilation shaft, while reflecting off the snow just outside the entrance. It wasn't much, but for an elf, she could see everything perfectly. A stone workbench rested against the wall on the other side of the forge, and a rack of tools stood beyond that.

Inyalia knew a fletcher's workshop when she saw one. She'd been crafting her own arrows since her third cycle. A wide smile on her face, she approached the workbench, taking inventory of the tools at her disposal. Her father had one like it at home, though this was a masterpiece by its own design. Never before had she seen its equal. She could smelt the ore and pour the molds within seconds of each other. She could hone her arrows to precision, ensuring a perfect shaft each and every time. With this setup, the forge could nearly run itself. It just needed someone to oversee the process.

She suddenly knew what her test was. It had all led up to this moment. And considering the rewards she'd received from each of the rooms, it seemed now she was going to make some arrows.

Laying the ore upon the workbench, Inyalia removed the broken limb from her quiver, and placed the feather on one of the cleaner shelves. And a moment after that, she was forging arrowheads, carving shafts, and shaping fletchings.

The moonlight faded, replaced by the morning sun, but it didn't make much of a difference within the cavern. The blinding snow reflected just the same.

It had to have been at least a few hours, but it felt like minutes. Inyalia fingered the pair of arrows, coddling them like a parent holding their child for the first time. They were perfect in every way. The wood was seamlessly smooth, weighing next to nothing. A diamonded-shaped razor protruded from the business side, cradled for reinforcement by the wooden shaft. Inyalia had found some strips of leather to cut down for the binding, which added just enough weight to increase distance and accuracy. The tail had been tapered to a near point before flaring out to form the nock. About an inch lower, a section of white plume was secured into the split, ensuring perfect balance and proper spin when they were fired. These were the best arrows she'd ever seen, surpassing even those of her father. There was something about them that she couldn't identify, something magical. No, that wasn't right. Magic had nothing to do with it. Mystical was the term she was searching for.

Inspecting the perfect arrow heads, she saw the same glow the raw ore had displayed, ebbing through the sharpened edge. She didn't know when, or how, but these arrows would save her life one day. Carefully, she inserted them into her quiver, ensuring they remained separate from the others. She didn't want to risk grabbing the wrong one by mistake.

Chapter X
The Breaking

A deep roar echoed outside the cavern, shaking the ground. Snow fell loose of the vent hole, sizzling into the burning embers of the forge.

Quickly, Inyalia grabbed her bow and nocked one of the newly constructed arrows. It seemed a shame to use them so quickly, but she had to remind herself this was a test. The arrows had been provided for a reason. Their only purpose was to be fired. Carefully, she made for the entrance.

Inyalia scanned the whitened world around her. Everything outside her focus was a blur. She watched for movement. If her arrow wasn't trained on it, it wasn't worth looking at. The roar hadn't sounded like that of the ice wyrm, but she didn't want to risk encountering another one if she could help it. Regardless of what it was, it had to be close for the ground to shake the way it had.

Another roar resonated, this time right behind her. It was deafening. Unable to withstand its might, Inyalia strained to release her draw. It hurt, but she didn't want to lose one of the few good arrows she had. As soon as she was able, she dropped her bow, throwing her hands over her ears. It did little good, but it was better than nothing.

Massive gusts of wind swirled the loose powder around her, blocking out much of her sight. There was no direction. It blew one way only to be pulled the other, showering her in the flaky substance. Her heart raced, beating violently within her chest. She could barely move from the forceful wind. Shaken to her core, Inyalia dropped to her knees, feeling the slightest reprieve. Fighting her instincts, as well as the elements, she summoned the will to turn.

A pair of leathery white wings spread wide, much wider than her home city was long. It was covered in shimmering white scales, each one peaked in the center and overlapping those beneath. The sheer size of the beast could have easily crushed the entire settlement simply by landing atop it. The body was longer than it was wide, but the muscular width was nothing to dismiss. It had four massive legs, the rear larger than the front, all displaying thick onyx claws that could easily tear her to pieces. Slender but long appendages tapered from both ends of the body, equally decorated by blackened horns and spines, but it was the head that caused her to gasp. She'd remember that draconic face anywhere.

Alona flew overhead, shadowing the mountaintop for a long while, despite the speed in which she moved. If she weren't cowering beneath the wind, Inyalia could have reached up and drug her hand along the scaled underside. She knew she should have felt fear. And she did, but not of the creature. Her fear was of something else. Something in the distance. Whatever it was, she knew in her heart that it was wrong.

The wind receded with the dragon's passing. Watching it disappear over the next peak, a loud crash echoed through the heavens. Inyalia didn't have to see to know what'd happened. Quivering her arrow, Inyalia snatched her bow off the ground and rushed through the collected snow.

After the gusts, it was waist deep in places, but she didn't let it slow her. Elves were naturally light on their feet, but that didn't mean she didn't sink. She simply didn't sink as deep, especially in wet snow. And the morning sun had ensured this was plenty wet. A flurry of powder exploded with each kicking step, but Inyalia made it to the cliff edge. Clinging to the frozen rocks, she stepped into the mountain's shadow. The snow wasn't nearly as deep here, likely shielded from the wind. But the sun did little to melt it either. With the colder temperature, there was greater chance for ice buildup.

Urgency called her. She knew Alona wasn't gone. She could feel the ground shake on occasion. And there was no mistaking the volume of those roars. The question was, what was wrong with her? Inyalia slung her bow and mounted the rocks. It was a slow process, but she scaled the cliff face with minimal trouble.

Reaching the other side, Inyalia could see one of the dragon's wings in the ravine. It thrashed about for a moment before falling still. It reminded her of a downed bird, writhing in pain as it slowly died. The thought troubled her. What would cause such a magnificent creature to react in such a way? Was it the same thing she felt inside herself? Aside from its face, this dragon seemed nothing like the calm, gentle behemoth she'd met a few months prior. This one seemed scared, nearly out of its mind. She only hoped her recognition was correct. She knew of no other dragons, especially white ones, and in these mountains nonetheless. How could it be anyone but Alona?

Cautiously approaching, Inyalia reached the top of the ravine. From here she had full vision of the downed creature, the entire ravine between peaks, and no doubt a great distance beyond were it not for the lingering clouds and kicked up snow.

Large mounds were scattered around the impact site. It appeared as if Alona had hit one of the rocky walls and been forced to the ground. From there, she rolled to the base of the ravine, flattening everything in her path, while throwing the rest into the air.

Inyalia sympathized with the beast. She was clearly in pain, panting when she lacked the strength to thrash. The spines running the length of her back were buried in the rocky surface, leaving her underbelly exposed to the sky. Thick muscular legs hung limp, save for the occasional spasm or attempted reconfiguration. Her wings were outstretched beneath her, contorted at weird angles, but neither appeared broken nor torn. And the last several feet of her thick spiked tail swished back and forth, kicking snow from its path like a cat becoming annoyed.

Inyalia watched the thick scales covering the beast's chest. They rose and fell several feet at a time, in rapid succession. She could occasionally see a blue glow beneath them, though it wasn't nearly as bright as she recalled the last time she met the creature. Tracing the elongated neck, Inyalia finally found the horn-wrapped head, laying exhausted among the rocks. Alona's eyes were closed and her nostrils flared with each ragged breath, expelling huge gouts of steam.

Knowing for certain that this was the dragon that had comforted her in her hour of need, Inyalia charged through the churned snow and leapt onto the steep slope. Her boots slid across the packed surface, but the occasional protruding rock kept her from losing control and tumbling to the dragon's side. Reaching the bottom, she skirted the huge creature. She had no fear of the beast, but she didn't want to be crushed if it decided to pick itself up again. Climbing the rocks where the dragon's head lay, Inyalia spoke softly, as if comforting an old friend. "Alona, are you okay?"

The labored breaths intensified as the dragon moved its head. The eyelid closest to Inyalia cracked, revealing the piercing blue beneath. The large pupil was wide and round but quickly adjusted to little more than a thin slither, focused entirely on the tiny elf. Weakly, the dragon spoke. "Child, you should not be here. I'm not safe for you right now." Alona winced in pain, her body tensed, and her tail slapped the ground, shaking the earth.

Unprepared for the sudden movement, Inyalia fell backward, landing on one of the dense mounds. She rolled off and picked herself up. Waiting for the dragon's contraction to subside, Inyalia stepped onto the flattened snow, close enough to speak without shouting, but far enough to avoid another spasm. "What do you mean? You wouldn't hurt me. What can I do to help?"

Wincing, Alona lifted her head to look upon the girl. "You misunderstand. Willingly, no I would never hurt you." She paused to catch her breath. "Something's coming. Something I cannot fight. I can feel it in my core. You need to run, child. Run as far from me as you can." Alona convulsed again, though this time her entire body contorted. It was is if the bones inside were moving of their own accord, stretching her scaled skin to its capacity. She roared in pain, twisting and thrashing. Her legs caught the ground, leaving deep gouges where her claws dug. Pulling herself up, her wings unfurled, echoing a series of sickening pops as they extended to their full glory. Through gritted fangs, Alona's voice echoed deep and distant, like a plow scraping through gravel. "I can't hold myself much longer. Run!"

Inyalia knew the words, though the voice that delivered them was not Alona. At least not in the way she knew. This was dark and violent. The ferocity behind it shook the world, causing an avalanche on one of the distant peaks. She could hear the roar of the rolling snow, but it was far enough away it wouldn't affect her. Her focus returned to the now standing beast towering over her. The bones continued to move beneath skin, forming several new spines and horns, as black as the others, but these ones bled where they tore through the scales. The blue glow beneath the scales was turning black. Even the scales themselves were no longer shimmering. They'd become dull and discolored. What had been a pristine white was now more of a faded gray. Inyalia wanted to stay and help her friend. But that voice, the warning, the feeling inside her, everything screamed at her to leave. "I'm sorry."

Inyalia backed away. She needed to get up the slope and back to the cavern. She hated leaving Alona in her current condition, but what could she do? She knew nothing about dragons.

An ear-splitting pop echoed through the heavens. The sky turned dark with rolling clouds. Through them, an orange glow burned, but it was too bright to be the sun. For a brief moment, that seemed to last an eternity, the world was still. Alona's heaving movements ceased. The wind stopped. Even the upturned snow hung in the air, refusing to complete its descent. In that moment, the world was forever changed.

Inyalia froze. The terror that had been building inside her came to a boiling point. She had to run. But where could she go? Nowhere was safe. It would find her even in the darkest reaches of oblivion. She watched helpless as the burning sky broke through the clouds. It skated across the heavens, burning everything in its wake. She could feel the heat. The snow around her sizzled. And, as quickly as it appeared, it crashed somewhere far to the south.

Sound returned to the world. Inyalia stood, dumbfounded, searching the distance for any sign of the burning object. She could hear Alona behind her. But more than that, she could feel the evil radiating from her friend. Slowly, she turned, looking upon the gargantuan dragon. Her stomach churned. Bringing her gaze to the creature's, she no longer saw Alona. All that was left was a monster, intent on her destruction.

Frost and steam rolled from the dragon's flaring nostrils. A fire burned in her eyes, dark and devouring. The elf before her didn't have enough meat on her to serve as a light snack, but she possessed something much more filling. Her soul was strong. It would sate her longer than any meat could. Licking her lips, Alona's barbed snout contorted into a wicked smile. She hunched closer to the ground, slowly moving toward the elf.

Recognizing the danger, Inyalia backed away. She had no hope of outrunning the beast. And the slope was too steep to climb, especially with a dragon on her tail. Her only hope was to evade until she could find cover. Focused on the prowling dragon, Inyalia crashed into the snow-covered rocks. Falling backward, she landed in the snow. All hope was lost. She'd trapped herself without even realizing it. Salty tears pooled in her eyes, overflowing into her hair. She could feel it freezing to her skin as she lay there. She was going to die, there was no escaping it now. Helpless, Inyalia watched the horn enwrapped head of the dragon come into view. It towered over her, sealing her fate. Staring into the face of the creature that would be her doom, Inyalia waited for the end. All that was left was a quick snap of the jaws.

Inyalia winced against the frozen air escaping the beast's nostrils. She could feel her skin burning. A thick globules liquid formed at the rim of the dragon's snout, dripping into the snow on either side of her. She could hear it sizzle and crack. Stealing a quick glance, she watched one of the droplets melt the snow, but rather than turning to water, it froze into solid ice, expanding into a solid block. She had no doubt she'd be dead before she knew what happened if one of those globs touched her. But such a fate wouldn't befall her. She read it in Alona's eyes. No, the dragon wanted the satisfaction of hearing her body break between teeth.

It was that realization that triggered something inside her. She didn't want to die. And while she was cornered, trapped on the ground with a dragon towering over her, that was no reason to go out without a fight. If Alona was going to kill her, she was going to give the beast something to remember her by. But how? She couldn't unsling her bow in her current predicament. And she was laying atop her quiver. Even the dagger she kept in the small of her back was stuck. She had one final seed of hope. Reason. Inyalia locked onto it with everything she had. "Alona, you don't want to do this! You're a protector of this realm, not a mindless beast."

Alona's jaw tensed, parting to reveal the pointed onyx teeth. Another glob of the boiling foam spilled, landing to the left of her prey.

"Please, Alona. You helped me once. Don't do this." Using her words as the only distraction she possessed, Inyalia pivoted slightly, sliding her hand under her head. It was uncomfortable, but it was the only option she had. Fingering the shafts of her arrows, she cycled through, locating one of the blackened missiles. Working it free a little at a time, she continued trying to reason with the beast. "Please, Alona. I don't know what's happened to you, but I want to help."

The gaping maw came closer. She was running out of time. Working the arrow free, Inyalia wrapped her hand around the shaft and prepared herself. "Please, let me go. I don't want to hurt you."

What could have been laughter, or possibly the attempted expulsion of a hairball, escaped the dragon's belly. Though it didn't halt its advance.

Inyalia meant her last words. She really didn't want to hurt the beast, if such a thing was even possible. But time for desire was over.

There was only one desire that mattered and that was the desire to live. Squeezing the arrow tight, Inyalia brought her arm around and plunged the arrow into the dragon's jaw.

Alona roared and withdrew. Scraping at her neck, she struggled against the keen needle that had so easily broken through her scales.

Now was her chance. Inyalia scurried to her feet and charged down the ravine. She had no way of getting back to the path she was familiar with, but maybe she could circle around. Either way, she was on limited time. The beast was certain to come for her now. Perhaps, if she could reach the cavern, maybe she could escape the dragon's fury.

Falling backward with a crash, Alona raked her front claws at the shaft. Somehow it had managed to cut through her scales and into the meat beneath. Rage and pain coursed through her, but the arrow held.

Searching for any path that was both shallow enough, and flat enough to climb with haste, Inyalia ran. Seeing no such path, she had to make a decision. She could either continue on her current path and the dragon would catch her, or she could risk the snow and work her way toward more familiar ground. Choosing the latter, Inyalia kicked off one of the mounds of piled rock and jumped. She sank deeper than desired into the undisturbed snow, but it was better than the alternative. Half running, half swimming, she climbed the slope, reaching the top of the ravine. She wanted to glance back. She wanted to know if the dragon was pursuing her yet. Fighting her instinct, she continued on. She was on limited time. Wasting it for a mild assurance was not worth the risk.

Reaching the side of the mountain peak, Inyalia weighed her options. The cliff face she'd scaled was too far away. The only logical choice was to continue around and hope to intersect. Moving as close to the wall as she could, Inyalia avoided the deeper snow. It would hide her tracks, while allowing her to move faster. Following the rocky terrain, she listened for the beast as best she could.

Inyalia came to another cliff edge. From here she could see the cavern that would be her salvation. But she was still far from it. And worse, she'd apparently gained elevation on this side of the peak. It was a good fifty-foot descent to the shelf she needed. But the dragon wasn't upon her yet. Maybe she could make it before it was.

Grabbing hold of the frozen rocks, she realized just how cold her fingers were. But it wasn't just her fingers. Her entire body quivered. She was afraid. Closing her eyes for the briefest moment, hoping to calm herself, Inyalia kicked her legs against the rock, digging her toes into the icy crevices. Carefully, she began her climb.

Alonandrensal slammed into the ice-covered ground. Her claws ripped at the scales around the wound, pulling them free. She dug at the arrow with all her might, attempting to free herself. There was something about this arrow, something unique. Fired at pointblank range, a normal arrow wouldn't have penetrated her beautiful scales. Yet this one did so from the stab of an elfling. More than that, it was robbing her of strength. No, not her strength. Her anger. Her rage. She was still angry. She'd been stabbed, it hurt. Nothing could ease that. But it was lessened enough to free her mind ever so slightly. There was no doubt the arrow was responsible. And while she was still trapped within a body that would no longer obey her command, she was at least awake once again. That was better than nothing. Had it not been for that, she would have crushed the elf before she could run. It had been Alona, the real Alona that threw herself to the ground to give Inyalia the chance to escape. But how much longer would that last? She could feel the arrow coming free. Would the little control she had fade once it was gone?

A bellowing roar shook the wall. Inyalia's hand slipped. Dangling by one arm, her fingers weakening moment by moment, she felt the first chunks of snow rain upon her. Stealing a glance overhead, her fear was renewed. The icy shelf at the top of the cliff was beginning to break free. Already it protruded several feet over the edge, threatening to crash down upon her. The cracks in the underside snaked through the wall of snow, growing more rapid as it went. She had to get off the cliff. Her time was limited. She found a mild humor in the situation. She'd escaped a dragon, only to be killed by an avalanche.

Straining, she twisted her body, getting hold of the rocks once again. Setting her feet, Inyalia worked her way across. Going down was no longer an option. If she could get to the other side, maybe she could avoid the majority of the encroaching avalanche.

Another earthquake hit. The snowy mixture slid a bit further. Some of the larger pieces broke free. Tumbling down the mountain face, they smashed against the protruding rocks, breaking into smaller pieces.

As quick as she could, Inyalia skirted the rocky bluff. Reaching a small shelf, she dove into a pile that had crashed moments before. If she was lucky, the rest would pass her by. She could feel the rumble as the unstable shelf broke apart. Pieces crashed around her, blanketing the area in snow. It was rapidly growing dark. Soon, she wouldn't have room to breathe. That was provided the weight didn't kill her first. But at least if she was buried, Alona wouldn't be able to find her.

The ground beneath her began to slide. Inyalia instantly knew she'd become part of the avalanche. Before she lost her sense of direction, she started digging, hoping to get to the surface before she went over the edge. Fortunately, the snow wasn't overly deep just yet. She broke through the surface, finding herself in a flowing river of powder. It poured from above in a solid wall, breaking against the shelf before continuing down. Climbing to the top, Inyalia ran toward the mountain as fast as she could. If she could grab the rocks, there was a chance it would miss her.

No matter how hard she ran, she couldn't seem to make ground. Instead, she continued toward the edge. Out of nowhere, the strong winds returned. Inyalia didn't need to look to know that the dragon had found her.

Narrowing in on the warm blood coursing through the tiny elf's veins, Alonandrensal flapped her wings vigorously just beyond the falling snow. She had no way to reach her prey until the avalanche stopped. But she deserved death. It would come one way or another. Filling her lungs with air, Alonandrensal prepared to freeze the girl. From there the snow would carry her to the ground where her soul could be collected.

Inyalia felt the change in temperature. All the air had been sucked out of the world. She found it hard to breathe. That could only mean one thing. Alona was going to blow that freezing snot all over her. This was it. She was out of options. She could fall or she could freeze. Either way, her death was imminent.

Suddenly, an idea came to her. She was trapped, again. But her arrow had proven effective last time. And she had one more, and little else to lose. Willing herself, Inyalia kicked off the sliding snow and spun around, grabbing her arrow. Charging toward the beast, she jumped as hard as she could.

Alonandrensal released her breath. It expanded, freezing the moisture in the air. Though the elf's actions caught her completely by surprise.

Inyalia felt the cold. But it didn't freeze her. She was above it, running atop it. The ice froze and expanded so fast that she was able to purchase a few steps more than she'd expected. Though they didn't last long. The ice fell no sooner than her weight changed its trajectory. Reaching the apex of her charge, she saw the massive teeth prepared to snatch her out of the air. Inyalia kicked one final time, pushing herself off the dragon's snout. Overshooting its horns, she stabbed the arrow into the base of its skull and hung on for dear life.

Alonandrensal roared in pain. She clawed at the newly plunged arrow, unable to reach it, or the elf attached to it. She had to land. That was the only way she was going to be done with this pest. More gliding than flying, Alonandrensal fought through the pain in an attempt to land without crashing. Nothing would save the elfling once she reached the ground.

Straining against the constant change in winds and the abrasive scales, Inyalia pulled against the base of the arrow. Her grip was weakening. The dragon's blood was seeping from the wound, making her hand slick, but at least it provided some warmth to her numb fingers. Using the scales to her advantage, Inyalia climbed atop the creature's neck. Now was her chance. Ripping the arrow free, she stabbed repeatedly. This was the only advantage she was going to get. She had little doubt she'd escape if she didn't kill the beast before they reached the ground. Her tenacity was paying off. She could feel the muscles relaxing, though she had to time it just right. If Alona died before they landed, she'd be just as dead.

Alonandrensal crashed into the earth, sending a shower of snow and rock into the air. She slid for quite a way, unable to slow herself. The elf had robbed her of her rage once again. That would possibly save her. Fortunately, the arrow hadn't caused much more than minor wounds, but it would take some time to heal. She only hoped the girl had the sense to run. If she delayed, she wasn't sure how long she could contain herself.

Inyalia covered her face. The impact was harder than she'd intended. But that meant she'd wounded the beast. If she could get a few more stabs, perhaps she could finish the job. Inyalia's thoughts were cut short. The dragon slammed into a rocky outcropping, causing it to stop abruptly. Inyalia was weightless, dislodged from her mount. Flying through the air, she crashed into the snow and rolled. Regaining her bearings, she was closer to the cave entrance than she could have hoped for. But the dragon was rising. Fortunately, the arrow remained locked in her grip. It'd prove useful if it caught her before she could get to the cave.

Inyalia crawled to her knees. Her body ached. Glancing down, her armor was shredded. She could see her own blood in many places, but nothing appeared more serious than a few scrapes and bruises. It seemed the scales had been sharper than she'd anticipated. Getting to her feet, she made for the cavern. She was limping, but at least she was gaining ground.

Feeling the earth shake, Inyalia knew the dragon was behind her. She had to reach the entrance. It was the only thing that could save her. Just a few more steps and she'd be there.

The beating in the ground grew more intense, more rapid. Alona was closing in. Putting everything she had into it, Inyalia dove. She couldn't spare time to look, but she knew the dragon was close. She could see the onyx fangs in her peripherals. She could feel the icy chill of death, that cold breath freezing the air around her. She didn't have to look. She knew she was in the dragon's mouth. A heartbeat longer and its jaws would snap shut.

She hit the floor of the cave, the pointed teeth scraping the sides of her boots as they closed. She'd made it, narrowly. But she wasn't safe yet. She could feel the warmth of the forge. It was nothing against the dragon's icy breath. That was sure to follow. She'd escaped its maw, but she hadn't escaped its reach. Clawing at the floor, Inyalia scrambled to her feet. She had to run and hope the cave would open for her as it had before. If it didn't, nothing would save her.

Trembling from both cold and terror, Inyalia reached the back wall. With no other option, she unslung her bow, grateful it hadn't been damaged more severely than a few fresh nicks in the wood. Nocking the arrow, Inyalia took aim, waiting for one of the massive eyes to present itself.

Chunks of stone tore under the forceful talons, but it was no use. She couldn't dig her way inside. And the cave was too deep to do much but block the entrance. All Alonandrensal had to do was to fill the chamber with her icy breath, but the elfling had wounded her. Such a fate was too quick, too clean. She wanted the pleasure of feeling the elfling's bones break between her teeth, to make her suffer for her insolence. But she had to get to her first.

"Go away, Alona. I don't want to shoot you, but I will!" Inyalia pleaded, waiting for her target. She didn't know if it would kill the great white, and she really didn't want to. But this was a matter of life and death. And she'd fought too hard to die.

Thunder cracked outside the cavern. Inyalia watched the dragon's nostrils flare, sniffing for something. She felt relief flow through her as the dragon's snout retracted. Though it didn't set her at ease. She knew the dragon was still there. And she was still trapped.

The walls shook, filling the room with the gravelly voice she'd heard before. "This isn't over. I'll find you. It may take a lifetime, but one day I'll come for you!"

The wind picked up outside, slinging snow past the entrance. Inyalia heard the wings flap, becoming quiet with the dying gusts. Cautiously, Inyalia approached the opening, keeping her bow at the ready. She couldn't risk it being some kind of trick. Peeking outside, she could see Alona gaining altitude, shrinking into the distance.

Thick droplets began to fall from the sky. Inyalia had first believed it to be rain, but the snow was turning red. Lowering her bow, she extended her hand to collect some of the thick liquid. Sniffing it, she could smell the coppery scent of blood. Something was seriously wrong. She needed to get out of here and find out what. As if the thought were the trigger, the stone faded away.

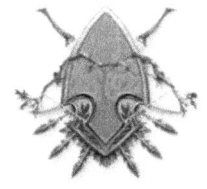

Chapter XI
The Hall of Guardians

Inyalia found herself standing upon a maroon carpet, running the length of a rather long but narrow room. It was remarkably similar to the arcade where she'd last seen Tylor, save for the solid stone walls draped in once elegant, but since deteriorating tapestries.

Slowly, painfully, she limped toward the head of the room, inspecting the numerous statues standing along both sides of the path. These weren't nearly as large as those outside, playing no part in the ceiling's support. Each of the ancient rangers stood proportionate to what she guessed was their likeness in life. They watched her with a stillness found only in stone. But that was the odd thing. Regardless of where she stood, they always faced her.

Uneasy, Inyalia's eyes darted about the room, bow at the ready. She was uncertain as to what she was supposed to do here. Most everything else had been pretty straight forward. Aside from fighting Alona anyway. Well, that and the fire and brimstone falling from the sky. And how could she forget the blood-rain. None of that made any sense to her. But everything else was somewhat simple. She didn't know if the events outside were part of the test or not. If not, the world was in serious trouble. And if so, what was it supposed to teach her?

Deciding her answers would be found near the throne, Inyalia climbed the base step of the dais. The large wooden chair was ornate for something so long neglected and covered in dust. She feared sitting in it, but only because it would likely fall apart. Running her exposed fingers along the armrest, she could feel the deep engravings etched into the wood. The entire chair was covered in ancient elven writing from a time long past. She couldn't understand most of it, dialects and customs having changed many times since the throne was likely built.

A fog began to roll through the room. It was minute at first, lingering about the floor. But as it passed into the firelight from the many basins near the walls, it grew thicker, almost like a solid smoke.

Seeing the smoky substance, Inyalia took a step back. It pooled at the foot of the throne. Catching movement behind her, Inyalia spun, her arrow aimed.

Numerous elves stood in audience along the sides of the ancient chamber. The rangers were still there, but no longer were they stone. Behind them, an army of men, women, and children watched in silence. They were less than solid, spectral if she had to give it a word. Inyalia felt a sense of pride in their gaze. They supported her. Encouraged her. But more than that, they loved her.

There was no explaining it, but somehow, Inyalia knew them. Maybe not their individual names, but she knew their faces. She'd seen them in her dreams. Every time she closed her eyes, imagining what her life as a ranger would be like, it was these people, these ghosts, who smiled at her. She didn't know them in her dreams. They were simply faces among the crowd. It wasn't until now that she knew who they were. Inyalia was standing among her ancestors. And while she hadn't met any of them, their presence made her feel at home.

"Inyalia Highlor, daughter of the Jordnye lineage." The voice was powerful and commanding, but it held no ill intent.

Lowering her bow, Inyalia turned to see a figure sitting upon the throne. She guessed he'd been the pool of smoke she'd seen moments before, materialized. Unlike the others, this man, this Ranger-King, was more solid than ever. Inyalia knew the armor, though no one had held the title since the first age. Her family was highborn, but none of them had taken the throne as far as she knew. If this man was among her ancestors, there was much history missing from the record books. Kneeling out of respect for his station, she awaited his permission to rise.

The Ranger-King gestured and Inyalia rose to her feet.

"Having been tried and tested, you find yourself among the first Rangers of Trendensil. Not in a thousand cycles have we held audience with another. Having borne witness of a change in era, you must prepare yourself."

Inyalia found herself staring at the floor. It felt wrong to make direct eye contact, though she couldn't explain why. "Sir, I don't mean to question, but what makes me so special? Why am I the first you've spoken to in so long?"

His voice lowered, becoming more compassionate, like a father giving lesson to his offspring. "My dear child, each is unique in their own way. Some are destined for great deeds. Others will waste their life pursuing meaningless tasks. It is not us few who decide your worth. That's assigned by you, and you alone. No one is born to fulfil prophecy of any kind. It's the actions one takes. It's your drive, your determination that pushes you. It's that tenacity that saw you through your trials. And now that you've had a glimpse of what is to come, it is we who must warn you."

"Warn me? Warn me about what?" Inyalia was lost in it all. If she was nothing special, why was she standing here surrounded by the ancestors of her people? Why was she in a place no other had been for a thousand cycles? Why did they care enough to warn her? It wasn't like anything could affect them. They'd died thousands of cycles ago.

"Never before have our people faced such a trying time. Our legacy, not just the rangers, but elven kind as a whole, will soon be in its darkest hour. If it is to survive the coming age, it will be because you showed them the way. You find yourself at a crossroad. But at the end, it is you who must choose your path. No other can do it for you." He straightened his posture, returning to his commanding tone. "Inyalia Highlor, will you accept the title of Ranger, devoting your life to the service of your people? Or will you turn from this path, forsaking yourself and your family in the troubles ahead?"

Inyalia knew her answer before he'd finished speaking. She'd spent too long making the decision to turn away from it now. But the way he'd asked made her feel uncomfortable. It felt almost like it was designed to illicit a specific response. A part of her wondered what would happen if she said no. Would life go back to what it had been? Or would this rising threat happen with or without her? It really didn't matter. She had a role to play. She knew she'd be a part of it whether claiming the mantle or not. It wasn't a title that made someone a ranger. It was their actions.

Inyalia smiled to herself. She finally understood. She never had to undergo the trials to become a ranger. She simply had to believe herself one.

"You've made your decision. Please, accept this gift. May it bring you protection in the coming days." The Ranger-King gestured behind her.

Inyalia turned to find a suit of armor proudly displayed in the center of the isle. The leather was similar to what she currently wore, though even at a distance she could see it held the same crystalline fragments as her arrowheads. Approaching, she discovered the blackened plates were rather hundreds of tiny scales, opposed to a single, solid piece. It was nearly half the thickness, and the joints less cumbersome. By design alone, it would greatly aid her movement. Removing it from the stand, Inyalia was surprised by the weight. Her cloth shirt was nearly twice as heavy by itself. Piece by piece, she began replacing her ruined armor, locking the upgrade into place.

The elves began to disappear, returning from whence they'd came. Even the statues that had greeted her were now gone. The mist slowly evaporated, leaving her alone in the chamber. Just before it faded completely, she heard the Ranger-King's voice one final time.

"Be well, Child of Jordnye. We'll see each other again."

Inyalia removed the shredded breastplate, only now discovering how close to death she'd truly come. She winced, pulling the blood-soaked barrier from her wounds. Several gouges lay in her midsection and along her legs. Were it not for the armor, she had no doubt the dragon's teeth would have ripped her to pieces. Carefully, using the unsoiled tatters of her clothing, she wiped away the excess blood, cleaning her wounds as best she could. It wasn't perfect, but it would see her through. Dawning her new breastplate, she adjusted the straps, feeling a comfort unlike any other.

The armor felt like a second skin, holding her tight without hindering movement. But it did something else she didn't expect. The pain faded near instantly. She could still feel the wounds, and she was still sore. But it seemed to lessen drastically.

The large ornate doors opposite the throne creaked open. A breeze rushed through the crack, filling the room with freezing air.

Inyalia approached, seeing the ancient elven writing carved into the surface. She had no idea what it said, but she could feel the power emanating from it. Stepping through the opening, she found herself in the original hallway. In the distance, she could see Tylor huddled over one of the basins. A layer of snow had collected on his shoulders and head. Over a foot of accumulation had in her absence, blowing wildly at an angle. Having never seen it so copious, the only way she knew to describe it was a blizzard. But it wasn't the excessive snow that demanded her attention. It was what was happening at Tylor's back that had her truly concerned.

Clouds of rolling gray spanned the sky as far as the eye could see. Heavy winds seemed the swirl from all directions, carrying the heavy flakes of snow and ice. Among the precipitation, several large chunks of stone broke through the clouds, crushing everything in their path.

Charging toward the entrance, Inyalia could already feel the pressure against her. It was reminiscent of Alona's wing gusts, but this was straight line. Forcing her way through the currents, she reached the opening. "Tylor, look out!"

Inyalia's voice reached him, but he couldn't understand her words. Slowly, he broke his gaze on the dying coals, turning to face her. The temperature had dropped radically, freezing everything around him in mere seconds. He couldn't feel his fingers or toes. In truth, he couldn't feel much of anything. It'd all happened so fast. He'd tried to take shelter when it arrived, but a single step away from the brazier threatened to freeze him solid. Instead, he huddled as close as he could get, absorbing as much heat as possible. It was the only way he could stay alive until Inyalia returned.

A loud crash shook the foundation of the mountain. It didn't take much to glance its direction, but even that was slow. Were it not for the excessive cold, Tylor would have dropped to his knees. Caelum rested in the distance, her beautiful terrain in ruin. Buildings collapsed upon themselves. Trees uprooted and toppled over. Even the tower of arcanum, which had stood longer than most could remember, had fallen. Several pieces were scattered along the many tiers of the grand training ground. Inyalia's voice reached him once again.

"Tylor—What are you waiting—Watch out!" Inyalia pointed helplessly at one of the many falling boulders. Realizing he wasn't going to move, she ran toward him.

It crashed into the side of the mountain, throwing stone, mud, snow, and ice. Cracks spread through the floor and ceiling of the colonnade. Several of the ranger columns collapsed, their broken chunks joining the collection of rubble.

Inyalia knew they couldn't stay here. In a few more seconds, there wouldn't be a *here* anymore. She grabbed Tylor's sleeve, urging him to follow. Hearing the crash, she saw another stone headed straight for them. "Damn it, Tylor. We have to go now!" Seeing little other option, she twisted, locking his arm over her shoulder. Pulling as hard as she could, they began to move.

The stone crashed with a ferocity unmatched by weapons of war. It overturned the protruding platform, destroying the statues and collapsing the ceiling. In the blink of an eye, nothing remained but a jagged edge where it had once rested.

Inyalia pulled herself from the debris. A heavy layer of dust filled the central corridor. Coughing, her senses returned to her. She remembered Tylor. Where was he now? "Tylor!" She searched all around, looking for any sign. He'd been right behind her. She'd pulled him inside. She knew that much. Her eyes fell on the collection of rubble blocking the entrance. It was sealed tight, piled from floor to ceiling. She had no idea how long it would take to dig through, if such a feat was even possible.

Hearing the stone shift, Inyalia caught a glimpse of Tylor's cloak beneath the collapsed stone. Rushing to the site, she dug vigorously, unburying the trapped ranger. "Come on, Tylor. Don't die on me." Removing another stone, she uncovered his face. He was breathing, albeit extremely shallow. But he was alive.

Stone by stone, Inyalia uncovered and pulled him away from the entrance. If it caved in, she didn't want to risk him being crushed again. Or herself for that matter.

Propping his limp form against the wall, Inyalia dug the firewood from her pack. It wouldn't last longer than a night, maybe two if she conserved it, but she had to get the temperature up a bit. Tylor was wounded and cold. He needed warmth.

Raking her dagger, bits of glowing flint landed in the kindling. It smoldered, releasing a dense stream of smoke. Blowing gently, Inyalia struck again, watching a tiny flame come to life. Feeding the flame, it slowly spread to the larger wood and a few moments after that, she had a small fire burning. But that presented another problem. The cave in had blocked all air flow and the smoke was already beginning to linger about the ceiling. She had to find a way to vent it. Otherwise, their two nights at most would end with asphyxiation.

Picking herself up, Inyalia approached the rubble. She carefully climbed to the top and began dislodging chunks of stone and rock. Within a few hours, she'd made a small hole to the outside world. The smoke began to drift out, clearing the air.

Inyalia climbed from the pile and returned to Tylor. She needed to make sure he didn't suffer any serious damage.

Carefully, she removed his armor and tunic. He was bruised in many places, but she couldn't find any broken bones in his arms or chest. Glancing at his legs, she felt her cheeks flush red. She wouldn't be removing his pants if she could help it. Moving into position, Inyalia wrapped her hands around his cloth and leather covered legs, inspecting for damage. Starting at his left thigh, she slowly worked her way to his ankle. Everything seemed okay there. Repeating the process on his right leg, she paused, feeling a large bulge about his knee. It was swollen near twice over and was already developing fever. She couldn't say if it was broken or not, but he certainly wouldn't be walking any time soon, provided he woke.

Elevating his leg, allowing the blood to drain, Inyalia removed his boot and greaves. The leg of his breeches wasn't so simple. It was too swollen. Her only option was to cut the cloth. Grabbing her dagger from beside the fire, she carefully split the seam and uncovered his knee.

Dark bruising showed from ankle to knee. Deep impressions remained from where the jagged stone had crushed, but it didn't break the skin. He likely had his armor to thank for that. But overall, it didn't appear any worse than severe swelling and bruising.

Inyalia wasn't sure what to do. She couldn't pack it with ice. Aside from the tiny vent hole, they were sealed off from the outside world. And with the swelling, she didn't know if she should apply heat. He wasn't bleeding, which was good. But with the swelling, how much more could the skin take? If it tore, how was she going to bandage it? And if she did nothing, would it cause more harm? It was times such as these when she desperately missed her mother. It didn't matter how minor or severe any situation was, her mother always knew what to do.

Inyalia huddled over the dying embers of her fire. Tylor's pack was nowhere to be found, and she'd already exhausted nearly all of her resources. If it could be burned without being missed, it had gone into the fire. A part of her wished she'd never made the vent hole. It was bringing in more cold air than the fire could keep out.

Her stomach growled. She'd allowed herself an eighth ration for the day, which she'd consumed that morning. She wanted more, but there was no telling how long they'd be trapped, and Tylor would need food when he awoke. As horrible as it felt, it was enough to survive provided she didn't push herself too hard. And this way, between the two of them, her rations would last another five days. Thus far, finding a way out had proved pointless. It was now a matter of longevity.

Inyalia had spent the better part of the previous day walking the halls. She'd walked both directions for hours. Not a single room, turn, dead-end, or really anything other than a never-ending hall presented itself. Whatever power was hidden in this place seemed to have disappeared when the entrance collapsed.

Turning her attention to Tylor, Inyalia watched his chest rise and fall several times. His breathing was getting stronger. That was an improvement, but he'd developed a fever the night prior. Sweat clung to his forehead, and his leg had turned a darker shade of blue. Though some of the swelling had gone down.

Inyalia adjusted his cloak to cover him better. She'd donated her bedroll for his comfort. And a section of the food and water had been separated when she inventoried her rations. He was going to be hungry when he awoke. But he was also going to have to take it slow. They were nearly out of supplies, and she had no idea how they were going to get more. Things weren't looking good. And soon, unless she could find something else to burn, they'd freeze to death.

Lost in worry, Inyalia hadn't noticed Tylor's head move. Slowly, he opened his eyes. Everything hurt. He couldn't remember what'd happened, only that the sky had turned dark right before the loud crash. The temperature dropped faster than he'd ever seen. He remembered trying to run for the hall's entrance, but that was it. His memory went blank beyond that. Why did he hurt so much? From where he lay, all he could see was the ceiling and part of a wall. Disoriented, Tylor tried to sit up. Rising slightly, he let out a grunt and fell back to the bedroll. It wasn't much, but it was enough to see Inyalia sitting behind him. Panting, he rotated his head to see her. "Where are we?" His voice was hoarse and dry. It hurt to speak. It hurt to do much of anything.

"You're awake!" Inyalia jumped, abandoning her cloak. Rushing toward him, her arms flew around his chest and she hugged tight. Hearing him wince from pain, she released. "Oh, right. I'm sorry." She backed away and took a seat where he could easily see her. Grabbing her waterskin, she offered it. "You've been out for three days. The ceiling fell in on us. I dug you out, but your leg's in pretty bad shape."

A frail smile came to his lips. "Oh, is that all?" Tylor wiped the sweat on to his forearm, his muscles screaming in protest.

Inyalia matched his grim expression. "No." Grabbing her pack, she pulled a portion of the rations out. "We're almost out of food and water. And I can't find any more wood to burn. At this rate, I'd say we have about three days before we freeze. And about five before we starve." Inyalia's gaze fell to the floor. She was glad he was awake, but to do so only to die seemed cruel. And it wasn't like she could fight her way out of this one.

Forcing through the pain, Tylor pulled himself up and leaned closer to her. He gently placed his fingers against the underside of her chin, lifting her head to meet his gaze. "Hey, chin up. We'll get through this. We're in the halls, right?" He didn't have to ask. Now that his vision had cleared a bit he knew exactly where they were.

"Yeah." Inyalia answered, doing her best to believe him.

"We'll be all right. The halls will provide for us."

"I've already tried. I walked for hours, both directions. I never found so much as a room."

Unable to hold himself any longer, Tylor fell back. Wiggling, he sat up, despite his insides telling him not to. "Do you remember me telling you what happened the last time I was here?"

"Yeah." Inyalia felt some comfort, but she was a long way from feeling comfortable.

"Well, what I didn't tell you is, I knew I would be back here one day. The visions told me I would be trapped. I would be hungry. And just when I felt like I couldn't go on, the halls would open and see me through."

"But—" Inyalia paused, contemplating his words. "—you'll never feel that way. By being told something like that, it virtually ensures that you'll have hope until the end."

Tylor shook his head in refusal. "No. You're overthinking it. Break it into parts. We're trapped. We're hungry. And I can't move my leg. Seems to me like I can't go on."

"That's ridiculous!"

"Oh, really?" Tylor smiled, though it took all of his will to do so. All he really wanted to do was pass out again. But Inyalia needed the encouragement. That was the only way they were both going to make it out of this alive. "Then what is that?" Raising his arm, he weakly pointed to the wall behind her.

Inyalia twisted, seeing what appeared to be a doorway. "But—that—that wasn't there a moment ago!" She declared in desperation.

"I told you, the halls would provide."

Chapter XII
The Lost Stronghold

The rusty hinges creaked as the door swung open. A wash of musty air escaped around her, though Inyalia found it oddly comfortable. It wasn't stale, but it certainly had a strong scent of dirt. Moreover, it wasn't cold. At least not compared to the temperatures in the hallway.

Stepping inside, Inyalia looked around the large room. It was twice as long as it was wide, but plenty spacious for their purposes. A long table ran the length of the room. Behind it, a stone fireplace protruded from the wall. Iron pokers sat on one side and a wood rack rested upon the other. It was a little over half full of chopped and split logs that looked as petrified as the stone tabletop. The right side of the room held several beds, each separated by a shelf sitting against the wall. There didn't appear to be anything upon the shelves other than dust and a few worthless trinkets.

Inyalia walked between the beds and table, searching for anything of use. The general layout reminded her of the guardhouse just outside Camruun City. Her father had taken her there once when they made a trip to the city. This was vaguely reminiscent of the common room, though it was considerably small. Maybe half a dozen soldiers could have been housed here, whereas the one she'd seen was meant for upwards of two hundred elves.

Inspecting the beds, Inyalia noted the simple yet sturdy wooden frames. The mattresses were caked with dust but appeared remarkably well preserved considering how long they'd been here. Some were more plump than others, but that was pretty common with anything stuffed with down feathers. The real trick was going to be beating out the dust without tearing the thin fabric. But once a blanket or cloak was laid down, they'd serve as well as any tavern bed.

Turning her attention to the other half of the room, Inyalia rounded the table, avoiding the fixed benches protruding from either side. She approached the fireplace and crouched to inspect it closer. It showed no sign of having been lit in quite some time. Any ash or charcoal that had remained had long since disappeared. A thick layer of ancient soot covered the inner walls and outer edges. Sticking her head into the hearth, Inyalia twisted to look up. She couldn't see light, but the cold outside air assured her the chimney wasn't clogged. That would have been her luck as of late.

A gentle breeze pulled her attention from the fireplace. It wasn't coming from the door, but rather the back side of the room. If she could find a way out, maybe they'd be able to make their way back to Caelum, provided it hadn't suffered too much damage from the falling rocks.

Reaching the end of the table, Inyalia was now able to see the outline of an opening. It turned, continuing left.

Following it around she came to an intersection. The passage continued straight, but there was a closed door to her right. Wrapping her hand around her dagger, she pulled the bolt and pushed the door open.

Inside was a small, simple chamber. She could have easily touched any of the walls or door from its center. A wooden bench with a fair-sized hole sat against the far wall. Though there was no chamber pot beneath it. She hadn't expected to find an outhouse here, but it made sense. Even soldiers had to relieve themselves from time to time.

Backing from the room, Inyalia bolted the door and continued down the hall. It led into another room with an iron gate on one wall, and an opening on another. Chunks of broken stone spilled from the opening. She could see from here there was no exploring that path. The ceiling had caved in, sealing it off. But she could still feel the breeze. It had to be coming from the other side of the gate.

The bars had rusted some time ago, but they appeared strong. And fortunately, it wasn't latched. Inyalia approached and grabbed hold of the door. Giving a sturdy yank, it groaned, and the rusted hinges popped free. Inyalia pulled it open and stepped into a large square chamber. If she had to guess, it had been an armory at one time. Numerous stands and racks littered the floor. Some remained against the walls, having been bolted in place. Much of the ancient wood had rotted away, but the metal strips were intact just enough to show purpose. Whatever contents the weapon and armor displays once held, had long since vanished out the hole in the wall, the same hole sourcing her breeze.

Pieces of stone were scattered across the floor. Inyalia knew the hole had to have been created from the other side. If it had been this side the debris would have fallen outward, not in. Carefully, she approached and leaned through, bracing herself against the jagged edges. There wasn't enough light making its way to her to see into the opening, but there was no denying that it dropped into a cave. She could hear a large amount of water not far off. With any luck that meant a river. And a river was likely to have fish. Pleased with her findings, Inyalia grabbed one of the broken pieces of wall and dropped it through the hole. Listening intently, she counted, waiting for it to hit the ground. It resounded almost immediately. That was good. It meant it wasn't a far drop to the cavern floor.

"Anything of interest?" Tylor's voice was weak and far off. Had she not been listening there was no doubt she would have missed it.

Retracting herself, Inyalia made her way back toward the main room, closing the gate behind her. The last thing she wanted was for someone to come in behind them without some kind of warning. She reached the main door. Bracing against the stone frame, Inyalia poked her head out. "It's some kind of guardhouse. But the back room has a hole in the wall that leads into the caves. I don't know about food, but I could hear water."

Tylor took a moment to catch his breath before responding. "That's—better than nothing." He attempted to pull himself up but failed.

Seeing his struggle, Inyalia sauntered across the hall and knelt to help him up. "You know, if I weren't such a nice person, I might consider giving you some payback for all the hell you've put me through."

"I guess it's a good thing you're a nice person then." Straining, Tylor took her hand, pulling himself up as best he could. There were no delusions that Inyalia was doing most of the work.

Helping him to his feet, Inyalia took position on his left. She threw his arm over her shoulder, offering him balance as they hobbled toward the door. Inside, she guided him to the closest bed and had him sit. Certain he was stable, Inyalia rushed out the door and grabbed the few supplies they had left, along with her cloak, pack, and bedroll. Returning, she closed the door behind her. "Which bed do you want? I'll get the dust knocked out of it."

"This one is fine."

Holding her breath, Inyalia waited for her target. It was nearly in position. Just a moment longer and she'd have a perfect shot. Seeing her opportunity, she released the string. The blackened arrow sank with precision, its head erupting out the other side. Feeling the string go taut, Inyalia pulled it toward her, wrapping it from hand to elbow. A moment later the arrow broke the surface, pulling the large white fish it had skewered. Inyalia grabbed the wooden shaft, careful to keep the fish from sliding off. It'd only happened once before, but she'd become paranoid since.

Certain she wouldn't lose it, Inyalia drug it from the water and cut the string. Holding the large fish by its gills, she pulled the arrow completely through and laid her catch with the other. Quivering both, her bow and arrow, she tucked the string into the side pocket on the quiver and turned her attention to the fish.

Quickly and precisely, she drew her dagger and made an incision along the belly of each one. Reaching into the mouth, she hooked her fingers and ripped downward, removing the lower jaw and innards in one fell swoop. Inyalia tossed them into the water and rinsed her hands off. Drying them on her tattered breeches, she plucked the torch from the clay at the river's edge and grabbed both fish by the gills.

It took only a few minutes to reach the hole in the wall. Tossing her catch through, Inyalia climbed up and dropped the torch into a bucket. It went out almost instantly.

It was still hard to see. They'd covered the gate with a gutted mattress, ensuring sound and light didn't alert anything in the cavern to their presence. Not that they'd encountered any such creature, but something had to have made the hole.

Inyalia located the dead fish and made for the iron gate. Opening it, she pulled the makeshift tarp aside and stepped through. Quickly navigating the short halls, she found her way into the main quarters and laid dinner on the end of the table. "I'm back. Anything interesting happen while I was gone?"

"Nope. Same shit different day." Tylor massaged his leg. It was regaining color and the swelling was all but gone, but he still had trouble moving it. Pulling the repaired pant leg over his knee, he grabbed his crutch and climbed to her feet. Hobbling to the table, he twisted and fell to his seat. "I see we're having fish again."

"Yep. And every night until we find something else." Inyalia slid her dagger behind the side fin. Twisting the blade, she drug it toward the tail. The entire side came free. Flipping it, she repeated the process and carried both pieces to the fireplace.

"What I would give to have my spice shaker. At least then we'd have some flavor."

"I'll be glad when you heal up enough to walk. All you've done for weeks is complain. You complain about the food. You complain about your pack. You complain about being stuck in here while I'm mapping the cave and gathering supplies. How about you pull your big boy pants on and find something useful to do?" Inyalia tossed the other fish at him, sticking out her tongue. She was only half serious. He needed time to heal. But he was also complaining more and more each day. Or what she guessed was days. It did little good trying to track them in the underground. They could have been trapped for weeks, or even months. She couldn't be certain. Even tracking the days through the vent in the outside hall had proven useless. It didn't seem to matter how often she checked, or if she spent an entire day watching it, it was always dark. But at least they had food, water, and shelter. And the company wasn't half bad when he wasn't complaining.

Tylor caught the fish with ease. Drawing his own dagger, he cut in, silently mimicking her nagging. His only hope was she didn't see him. She'd caught him unaware across the back of the head last time. Walking his blade, Tylor removed the fillet, though it took a bit more sawing than it had Inyalia. "Speaking of the cave. Did you find anything new?"

"Possibly. I think I found the tunnel where the air is coming from."

"That's good. I'm almost finished with my brace. Hopefully it'll let me walk without this damn crutch. Maybe we can explore it in a couple days."

"I was planning on checking it out tomorrow. There's no sense in you exhausting yourself if it turns out to be nothing. And I promise, if it leads somewhere, I'll come back to get you."

"How thoughtful." Tylor smiled sarcastically. He was grateful for everything she'd done, but he was going stir crazy. All things considered, they had a pretty decent setup once it'd been cleaned. But he was feeling trapped. He did the same things, over and over, every day for longer than he knew. The monotony was making him irrational and grumpy. Handing the fillets to Inyalia, he watched her lay them across the hot skillet.

Dipping her hands into a bucket of water, Inyalia scrubbed the slime away before drying them on a piece of cloth. Sliding both, the bucket and rag to Tylor, she returned her attention to the meat. "What do you think the world is like outside?"

"I'd imagine it's not much different from when we last saw. If I've learned anything being a wild elf, it's that most people don't care about you once you pass out of their immediate vicinity."

"That's kind of a sad worldview." Inyalia flipped the fish, listening to it sizzle.

"Sad, but true. All too often, when people claim to miss someone, it's the things that person did for them that they really miss. Once that usefulness is gone, most people no longer care." Tylor washed his hands and pushed the bucket to the center of the table. Glancing up, he caught Inyalia staring at him. She had a sorrow in her eyes that he didn't like to see. At least not in her. She was always so alive and ready to do something. Dragging her down was the last thing he intended "So, tell me again about the Guardians."

Inyalia watched him for a long moment. She could see the wheels turning in his head. His change of subject was little more than an excuse to talk about something else. "I've already told you a hundred times."

"That's an exaggeration. It's been like three times."

Inyalia sighed. "Fine. What do you want to know?"

"Well, you said they called you the child of Jorhn."

"No. Child of Jordnye. Any idea what it means?"

Tylor shook his head. "No. The historians give name to many of the ancients, but I don't recall ever hearing that name. And the armor, they just gave it to you?"

"Yep."

"I'd really like to know what the symbol on the collar means. I've studied every insignia the corps uses. Never seen that one."

"They didn't say. Just that troubling times are coming and I witnessed the beginning, so I'm the one that got a warning. Oh, and apparently the continued existence of the rangers is dependent on me. Like that's not a lot of pressure to put on anyone."

Tylor chuckled. "You'll do fine. From the moment I saw you, I knew you were destined for greatness. Besides, if the daughter of Kalen Highlor can't save the day, no one can."

"You're not helping."

"Sure I am. I'm preparing you. I thought that's what mentors were supposed to do."

Oh, so now you want to be my mentor. When I needed your assistance, you were tight lipped about everything."

"When you needed my assistance, it was my duty to see how you did without it."

"You guys really need to rethink that system." Inyalia pulled the skillet from the fire and laid it between them.

"Well, maybe when you take over you can change how things are done."

"Shut up and eat your food."

Quietly, Tylor twisted the small piece of wood he'd used to tighten the brace. It hurt, but it was the only way to ensure it would remain in place. Tucking it through the loop, he gave the apparatus a squeeze, pleased with the end result. He couldn't feel the pressure in his knee. Spinning on his hind end, he removed the bars holding it stationary and allowed his leg to bend.

To his pleasure, it did so without shooting pain through his entire body. If anything, it was only a mild pain compared to what it had been. Testing himself, he pushed off the table and put full weight on it. Teetering slightly, he found his balance and took a small step. A smile formed. It was going to work.

Tucking his daggers away, Tylor grabbed his crutch and hobbled to the foot of Inyalia's bed. She'd be up in a few hours and he didn't want to disturb her. As quiet as he could be, he approached the shelf next to her. Lifting the rolled piece of cloth, he pulled it free and carried it to the table. It sprawled out, covering nearly half of the stone top. Several blackened lines trailed the cloth, forming a huge map of the cavern structure. Each line was beset by a number. Memorizing his path, calculating the numbers in his head, Tylor grabbed the broken chunk of flint Inyalia had given him and tucked it into his pocket. Certain he knew the path, Tylor placed a small stone on the only line not capped with a heavy X and made for the back room.

Reaching the makeshift blanket, Tylor pulled it aside and opened the gate. It only took a moment to crawl through the wall, but the stiffness in his leg made it a harder task than he'd realized. Setting foot on the cavern floor for the first time, he removed the flint and struck it. The sparks landed in the oil-soaked torch and it flared to life. Tylor stood silent for a few moments, recalling the map, familiarizing himself with the change in his surroundings. It was a long walk to the new tunnel. The last thing he wanted was to get lost. That wouldn't help either of them.

But Inyalia's map was extremely detailed. He could have followed it with his eyes closed. Turning the direction toward the unexplored area, Tylor limped along the clay and stone floor. He was moving slower than ever, but at least he was moving. The new passage was just under twelve-thousand steps. At his current speed, he'd reach it about the time Inyalia woke.

Rolling, Inyalia's eyes shot open. Something wasn't right. Looking to Tylor's bed, he wasn't there. She sat up, searching the room. He was nowhere to be seen, but her map laid upon the table. Shaking her head, Inyalia kicked her legs off the bed and stood. She knew what he'd done.

A heavy sigh escaped her. He was growing restless, she knew that. But to go into the caverns in his current state was foolish. They didn't know what was beyond the immediate area. Something had to have created the hole in the first place. And the only weapons Tylor had was his daggers. He'd justified he didn't need anything else, but she didn't believe it. Even if he didn't care to use a bow, it was better to have something with some reach. Especially when an enemy had the same advantage.

Fuming, Inyalia dressed, locking her armor into place. She was relieved to see that Tylor had done the same. At least his sense hadn't fully abandoned him before undertaking such a foolish task. Inyalia rolled the map and tucked it away. Gathering the few supplies they regularly used, she heaved her quiver to her shoulder and set out. With any luck they wouldn't be returning, and it wasn't like Tylor was here to use them.

Inyalia reached the caves, running as often as she dared. His tracks suggested he wasn't more than an hour ahead. And if he was going to be here, she wanted to be with him.

Reaching the last intersection before the new passage, Inyalia scanned the floor. Easily, she found his tracks. It wasn't so much his footsteps that gave him away. They were nearly nonexistent, save for the areas where the floor was moist. It was the crutch he used that she was able to follow without much effort.

Finding the tunnel, Inyalia turned into it. The air was warmer here than it had been, but it was a subtle difference. Following the tracks, silently counting her steps to add it to the map, she continued on.

There was no denying the heat now. What had been a comfortable cool was now almost hot. More importantly, Inyalia was beginning to see further than her torch allowed. That meant she was either right behind Tylor, or there was another light source.

The latter meant she needed to proceed with caution. Snuffing her torch in the clay, she wrapped the head with a torn piece of mattress and tucked it into her pack. As expected, she could see just fine, but the flicker of flame was absent. Whatever was providing light was clearly not a torch or basin of any kind.

Drawling an arrow, Inyalia slowly advanced. She only hoped Tylor had the sense to take similar precautions. Making her way around the bend, Inyalia discovered her light source.

Glowing fungus clung to the walls of the large room. It radiated various shades of blues, yellows, greens, and orange. A deep chasm split the room, leaving a single trail to follow to the right, but there was clearly another path on the other side. If only she knew how to reach it. But the other path was irrelevant at the moment. Tylor's tracks continued on this path. He was her first priority.

Steam rose from the chasm, creating a thin layer of fog toward the ceiling. With the protruding stalactites it felt rather ominous. Inyalia could hear what sounded like boiling water down below. She was beginning to sweat with the unexpected heat. Taking a deep breath, she pushed on, hoping to find Tylor before trouble found him.

The steam continued to rise, and with it the heat. Inyalia walked for another hour, keeping her bow at the ready. She was fortunate for the glowing fungus, but she suspected it was a result of the steam. She only hoped it didn't produce toxic spores. That would have been a hell of a way to go after everything she'd been through.

Rounding the corner, the tunnel opened into a somewhat small chamber. Rock formations grew from the floor, creating a series of shallow pools. And there, leaned against the side of one of the larger puddles, Tylor rested.

He'd disrobed and was sprawled out in the steaming water. His armor and clothes were piled along the rim. A wide smile breeched his lips.

"Glad you could join me. Come on in, the water's fine."

Inyalia lowered her bow. She wanted to hit him, but she was also happy to see he was okay. "What were you thinking? You leave in the middle of the night, and now I find you—taking a bath."

"Relax. I wouldn't have left you. I got my brace finished and wanted to test it out. What better way than by doing something useful."

Inyalia smirked. "Well, you have a point there. You were becoming quite rancid."

"I was referring to finding out where this tunnel goes. But now that you mention it, finding these pools was a good thing. The heat is loosening my leg nicely. I can almost bend it completely now." Tylor splashed. "Come on. Take a break. We've both needed a bath for a long while."

Shaking her head, Inyalia dropped her pack and laid her bow across the top. She wasn't comfortable letting it out of reach. But there was only one way in and one way out. She could see both. Letting her shoulders droop slightly, she unbuckled her armor, laying it beside her pack. Turning her back to Tylor, she glanced over her shoulder. "Close your eyes."

"What? It's not like you have anything I haven't seen before."

"Well, you haven't seen me, so close your eyes."

Exhaling, Tylor closed his eyes and waited.

Quickly, Inyalia undressed and climbed into the pool. Submerging herself, she leaned against the smoothed side, watching both tunnels while keeping Tylor across from her. She'd be lying if she said she didn't care for him. But she wasn't ready to physically act upon it. "You can open your eyes now."

Tylor smiled, seeing her across from him. "See? The water feels amazing."

Inyalia smiled, though it was a false smile. He wasn't wrong, but she was somewhat uneasy about being unarmed in an unfamiliar place. Keeping her eyes locked on the entrances, she casually waved her arms through the hot water.

Studying her face, Tylor leaned between Inyalia and her focus. "Hey! It's going to be all right. I scouted ahead before coming back here. It opens into another large chamber with an old rock bridge that looks nearly collapsed. That's what brought me back here. It could be the only way out and I didn't want to risk it breaking until we both made it across.

It seemed he was using his brain after all. A genuine smile formed this time. Inyalia let herself relax slightly. Feeling the warmth, she closed her eyes and laid back.

"See what I mean? This is wonderful." Tylor stretched out, his feet breaching the surface with a splash that threw water over Inyalia's head.

"Hey!" Her eyes shot open. Seeking retribution, she splashed water back at him, ensuring he suffered far worse.

Tylor thrust his hand forward, sending a towering wave toward her. He was glad to see she was loosening up.

Inyalia gasped, feigning shock he'd do such a thing. Laughing, forgetting the severity of their circumstances for a moment, she flung her arms, sending her own waves over him. Lost in the moment, she hadn't realized the movement was carrying them closer. She paused, just out of reach, staring into his deep brown eyes.

Tylor wanted nothing more than to reach out and pull her to him. She was so beautiful and smart. Not to mention the fact that he had little doubt she could kick his ass in battle. But he was her mentor, even if in title only. And she was his friend and commander's daughter. It didn't matter that she was only a few cycles younger. He had a duty. To betray it was to dishonor himself. Frozen in the moment, he stared at her, wanting to move closer but knowing he had to pull away.

A loud click drew their attention to the edge of the tunnel. Four squat, but broad men stood there, strange looking spears pointed their direction. Only they didn't hold them like spears. And they didn't have a blade for the head. Instead, it was capped with a flared tube that resembled a horn. Each of the short men carried a long, thick beard, but they ranged in color from red to black, and their armors were of a heavy metal vaguely reminiscent of steel.

The lead man stepped forward, keeping his odd-looking spear directed at them. "Looks like we got ourselves a couple o' trespassers."

Chapter XIII
Creatures of the Dark

Inyalia studied the strange spears. They weren't shaped right to provide a clean throw. If anything, they would have been better suited for use as clubs. But the short men weren't holding them as such. Placed against their shoulders and pointed, there was no way they could get a good throw. With so many things in her favor, Inyalia lunged for her bow. She was fast enough, she could fire two, maybe three arrows before they got a good hit. And by then Tylor could be upon them with his daggers.

An ear shattering boom filled the chamber, echoing long afterward. Smoke rolled from the end of the horn-like tube, leaving a thick haze to mix with the steady supply of steam. It smelled of sulfur.

The volume of the spear made Inyalia jump. She'd never heard anything quite like it. Moreover, some kind of projectile hit the rocks in front of her bow, blocking her path. Having fired a few of her own, she knew a warning shot when she saw one.

"Don't try that again, lass." The man whose spear was smoking tipped it toward the ceiling. He grabbed a small parchment wrapped cylinder and bit the end off. Inside was filled with a black sand. He poured it into the tube before stuffing the rest of the cylinder atop it. Spitting the parchment plug, he drew a long metal rod from the underside of his spear and pack the contents of the tube, much like tamping a pipe.

One of the others stepped forward, keeping his spear trained on them while the lead man reloaded. Gesturing with the end of his weapon, he spoke. "Git out o' the pool and stand by that wall!"

The others filed around him and began rummaging through the gear piled on the floor. They collected everything except the tattered clothing, leaving them where they lay. Carrying the effects from the chamber, they fell into a defensive formation just outside.

The lead man slung his weapon over shoulder. It rested on a leather strap. "All right, ye two. Get dressed. Yer commin' with us."

Inyalia shot a wicked glare to Tylor. She was furious. But it wasn't directed solely at him. She was angry with herself as well. She knew better than to let her guard down. She knew better than to disarm. But she ignored her instincts. It really didn't matter that Tylor had told her it was safe. She should have checked for herself. Hastily, she rushed forward and snatched up her clothes. Any modesty she'd had was currently drowned in rage.

Tylor limped forward. Without the brace, his knee was weak as ever. And now, due to the water, it wasn't even stiff enough to keep him upright. Losing his balance, he crashed to the floor.

Inyalia, barely having her breeches in place, rushed to his side.

"What's wrong with ye? Git up an' get yer clothes on."

Inyalia's head whipped around, spitting venom at the short man. "He can't. His leg was damaged. He can't walk without his crutch!"

The man gestured to one of the others, holding out his hand. He held the wooden crutch a moment later, inspecting it. "I'm afraid I can't do it, lass. Wouldn't take anything ta make it a weapon." He handed the device back to the other.

"There's another way." Tylor pulled himself into a sitting position, cradling his leg. "With my things, I had a small brace made of wood and cloth. It'll allow me to walk. If you get it, I think you'll see that it can't be used as a weapon."

Though mostly hidden by his dark red facial hair, the squat man smiled ear to ear. "Anything can be used fer a weapon if yer desperate enough." He nodded to the one who had handed him the crutch.

The man dropped the bundle of armor and began digging through the loose pieces. Finding what he believed the male elf was referring to, he pulled it out and handed it to his superior.

Inspecting it, the lead man decided someone would have to be extremely desperate to use it in a lethal manner. There were far better options with rocks and sticks. He tossed it to the elf. "Put it on and let's go."

"Hurry up, lass. I won't be tellin' ya again." One of the others poked Inyalia in the ribs, urging her away from the male.

Inyalia glared her distain. Getting to her feet, she snatched her tunic off the floor and pulled it over her torso. She wanted nothing more than to put an arrow through him, all of them. But that wasn't an option. They had her bow. And with their strange weapons, she now had no doubts that they were much quicker than she.

Tylor twisted the straps and secured them into place. Removing the joint locks, he tested the motion. It was a little looser than he preferred, but he'd made it when his leg was still swollen. It seemed the water had helped in that department as well. But after a few hours of walking, he had little doubt it would revert. Covering himself, Tylor slowly got to his feet.

"Let's go!" The man who'd poked Inyalia barked, taking position behind them.

The lead man turned and marched out the tunnel, and the other two waited for them all to pass, taking position at the rear of the group.

The stone walls had transitioned flawlessly from natural cavern to carved stone. Inyalia wasn't sure when one had ended and the other began. They were led through a series of tunnels, over seemingly damaged bridges, and through holes that, upon first glance, didn't appear large enough for the smallest child to crawl through. But these odd men seemed to see things differently than Inyalia did. They traveled paths she would have believed untraversable if not being ushered by the end of a weapon. She was surprised by how bright it was. The glowing fungus had grown more dense the deeper they went. There had been the occasional lowlight, especially in the narrower tunnels, but it never lasted long, not that it bothered her sight much in the first place.

She knew Tylor was having trouble keeping up. He'd been wincing with each step for over an hour now and she didn't know how much longer he was going to be able to keep pace. Their captors seemed to recognize this, she noticed they'd slowed when he began to fall behind.

The perfectly square corridor they walked came to an abrupt end. Seeing the man ahead of them stop short of the solid wall, she did likewise. Watching, he stood there for several moments, as if waiting for something she couldn't see.

A series of rhythmic clicks began to echo in the distance. Gradually, it got louder, closer, until finally, Inyalia saw what they were waiting for. A platform lowered from the ceiling, revealing many chains, sprockets, ropes, and pulleys on the underside for the briefest moment before it settled perfectly into the floor.

The lead man signaled and marched onto the platform.

A firm but otherwise gentle impact prodded Inyalia forward. She stepped over the threshold, unable to see where the floor ended, and the platform began. Who were these creatures, whose craftsmanship surpassed even the elves? She had a decent idea, judging by the story Tylor had told her on the mountaintop. But he'd also said they disappeared long ago. If they'd been here all this time, why would they show themselves now?

Guarded on all sides, Inyalia felt the ground move as the platform started clicking again. It traveled up, caging them in a vertical tunnel. Even if they had the means to escape, there was currently nowhere else to go. Waiting for what felt like forever, the lift finally came to a stop. Inyalia was frozen by what she saw.

Stretched out before them was a grand underground city. It held many streets and buildings as most surface cities did. But it also had many that extended into the floor and ceiling of the massive chamber suggesting that it had multiple layers, each likely as grand as this one. The center most structure was dome shaped and round. It was easily taller than the cavern chamber surrounding them, but unlike the other buildings, it extended into without adjoining. It was difficult to tell from the distance, but it almost looked like the floor and ceiling was carved out around it, and a series of thick chains kept it suspended in the center.

Inyalia stood in stunned silence, taking it all in. She'd seen grand cities before, considering her own capital among the most beautiful. And while this one wasn't overly colorful, it held a beauty of its own standard, far superior to anything her people had built. Not even the craftsmanship that had forged Dragon Sanctum could compare to the underground city before her.

"Welcome ta Deeprock City. She's a beaut, ain't she?" The lead dwarf smiled, looking over his beloved home. Giving them a moment to appreciate the wonders before them, he marched forward, exiting the lift before it could begin its descent once again.

The general design of this layer reminded Inyalia of an amphitheater. They were led along the outer ring, which seemed to be the highest point. It was perfectly flat all the way around, or so it appeared. Without tools she couldn't be certain, though she suspected with the amount of skill that had gone into building this place, a level floor was probably nothing to write home about.

The descending rings got progressively wider as they neared the center. Each was adjoined in many places by stone walkways, bridges, and ramps. And each, save for the outer ring held hundreds of structures, both large and small. The outer ring held only four, set equal distance apart. A ramp protruded from the back side, seeming to be the only entrance into the city itself.

Approaching one of the outer buildings, Inyalia counted four guards awaiting their arrival. Like their captors, they stood of similar height and width. They held a stockiness she hadn't seen anywhere else. Between that and the speed of their weapons, what chance of escape did they have now? These creatures had an intimate knowledge of the underground passageways, seeing things Inyalia hadn't, even when she knew where to look. It was like the stronghold atop the mountain all over again, only this time, it didn't reveal its secrets even after going through.

Their escort came to a stop before the stationed guards. Their lead took a step forward, gripping the extended arm of one of the guards and pulled him in to a brotherly hug. The two exchanged a few words in a language Inyalia couldn't understand. Though the tone suggested it was an exchange of humor. Ending their laugh, he turned and pointed to the subdued pair, continuing his story. He gestured toward the lower half of Tylor.

The guard nodded in agreement and added his own commentary. Giving a quick salute, he turned and barked orders to the men behind him.

Inyalia watched the gate to the large house open. Their escort returned to his station, marching in a seemingly formal capacity. Doing an about-face, so he was facing the guardhouse once again, he signaled and the group marched forward as a whole, pulling Inyalia and Tylor in step with them.

As they passed, two of the stationed guards spun and fell in beside the group. The added security would ensure there were no last minute attempts to flee, not that Tylor had much chance to go anywhere with his leg. And Inyalia wasn't about to abandon him, even if she knew how to escape the underground.

In silence, they navigated the guardhouse, passing through a number of pinch points and open barriers. It seemed the house was built for a single intention of slowing large numbers in the event of an attack. Passing the final gate, they descended onto the ramp that led to the city's next ring.

Inyalia hadn't seen it before, but upon the ramp, she realized just how far of a drop it was between the outer ring and those within. A wide chasm separated the two, making it impossible for someone to simply jump, or lower themselves with a rope. And with the glowing red and heat that radiated from the chasm, the ramps appeared to be the only safe means of crossing.

Another guardhouse stood at the base of the ramp, similar in design to the one above. Only this one held an extended balcony around the upper level, which was occupied by several of the stout beings, each one armed with the loud boomsticks their captors carried. Inyalia noticed a few minor differences between her captors and the city guard. The guards wore red tabards over their armor that depicted what appeared to be a blackened stone in the center. This wasn't overly surprising, as even the elves made sure their guard were clearly affiliated in case of emergency. It was for this reason the rangers wore no such tabards. They operated away from the larger population, and tabards didn't hold up so well in the elements. But it was the change in weaponry that brought some questions.

Aside from those atop the guardhouse, none of the others seemed to carry the odd projectile weapons. Instead, large axes, heavy hammers, massive picks, and even the occasional sword made up the bulk of their assortment. Though even the swords, as simple in design as the weapon was, were much different than any she'd seen before. These were thick and made of a black metal that seemed to shine of its own accord. Inyalia had a feeling the head of her last real arrow was made of the same material. Considering where she'd found the ore, what else could it be?

The added guards fell back, taking position outside the ramp fixed gate. It served as the initial opening to the new structure, as well as the last line of defense if the ramp was overrun. Entering the second guardhouse, Inyalia saw four new guards, posted in each corner of the room. They watched in silence, refusing to give the slightest sign of life.

Unlike its counterpart atop the ramp, this room was completely open on the inside, save for a thick rope railing that barred off a square shaped hole in the floor. The outer perimeter was unobstructed, offering three doorways that led into the city proper.

The escort came to a stop just inside the gate. Their lead broke formation and approached the right-side corner post which the rope rail had been drilled through. Placing his hand atop the wooden post, a series of clicks began to echo from the hole before them. A moment later, the railing began to descend into the hole, disappearing from sight as a wooden platform filled the gap.

Their escort started forward, marching them to the center. Once in position, their lead took his place on the lift and waited. It began to descend, carrying them into darkness.

Inyalia watched the linkages in the walls around her. She could see the chains moving, carrying the lift between layers. The rope railing began to raise back to its original location once they passed. All light disappeared, sealing them in complete darkness. Inyalia could hear the movement around her, but her vision was useless down here. She was nervous, though being captured and held captive had much to do with that. And now, with the darkness of the pit, she had no idea how she was going to defend herself, if such a basic desire was even possible. Feeling Tylor's hand wrap around hers brought a mild comfort, though it did little to quell the uncertainty growing inside her.

"Step forward ten paces and turn around." The lead man's voice ordered from behind them.

Keeping their hands locked together, both Inyalia and Tylor started forward, counting off their steps. Tylor was slow to keep up, his steps being about half their usual stride. Reaching the count, they released their grip and turned.

Cries echoed in the dark. The underground void was much larger than either of them could have anticipated. It was chilly, but not cold. A slight draft traveled through the air, though it was too subtle to offer direction. The clank of iron bars being drug surrounded them.

Inyalia didn't need to see to know she was in a cell. Even the temperature around her seemed colder now.

"The magistrate will wanna speak ta ya before yer sentence is passed. I suggest ye get comfortable, ye may be here a while."

"Wait!" Tylor demanded, suddenly coming to life. It was as if every thought he'd had since their capture was escaping him at once. "What sentence? We haven't done anything wrong!" He rushed forward, slamming into the bars now entrapping him.

"Save yer breath. Ye'll get the chance ta tell yer story ta the magistrate." An audible click echoed in the dark.

Inyalia felt the ground beneath her move. Catching her balance, she realized she was moving horizontally, away from the lift that had carried them here. Hearing a heavy sigh to her left, she turned, finding a set of bars. "Tylor, is that you?" She suspected as much but wanted to be sure.

"Yeah."

Sticking her arm through the narrow gap, she spoke softly, hoping they were alone, though she knew otherwise. These short men were too cunning to simply leave them to their devices. And considering the number of guards they'd seen in the open, there were probably twice as many around them now. "Tylor?" Inyalia placed her hand on the sleeve of his tunic. She was pleased to feel his hand settle over hers.

"I'm sorry I got us into this. Had I done what you suggested and waited, we wouldn't have fallen into this trap."

Emotions swelled inside her. The anger that had initially been present had all but faded. All that was left was a deep desire for survival. Swallowing, Inyalia searched for the words. She was torn between ridicule and comfort. He deserved both. But the situation was too dire to waste it on torment. He knew he'd made a mistake. But this wasn't his fault alone. She'd been equally as guilty. Nodding, forgetting he was just as blind as her, Inyalia caressed his arm. "Your apology is accepted, though you can't have all the blame. I knew the risk when I disarmed. Just promise me one thing."

"Anything."

"If you have an opportunity to get out of here, I want you to take it. Even if that means you have to abandon me."

Tylor was silent for a long moment. He knew they weren't alone. And suggesting a prison break was likely to bring more attention than they needed at the moment. Carefully selecting his words, Tylor spoke to both Inyalia and the unseen guards surrounding them. "Inyalia, I'm sorry, but I cannot do that. I promised your father that I'd do everything within my power to see you safely returned. Besides, with my knee, I wouldn't make it to the lift before they'd fill me with holes." He closed his eyes, wishing he could speak openly. He wanted to fill her with hope, rather than submission. These men, these dwarves, he suspected they were called, knew the language of the elves. That meant there was no chance of plotting so long as they were present. Besides, if anyone needed to escape this place, it was Inyalia. And he intended to do everything within his power to make sure that happened. He hadn't been lying when he made the promise.

Inyalia retracted her arm, feeling his hand fall away from her. If he wasn't willing to fight for survival, what hope did they have? Turning away from him, she laid on the cold ground of her cell. Using her arms for support she closed her eyes and awaited judgement.

Levi Samuel

Chapter XIV
An Unexpected Ally

Inyalia's eyes shot open, unprepared for the sudden jarring of her cell. She couldn't recall how long she'd been asleep. But that wasn't saying much. There were many events over the past few months of her life she couldn't recall, most of them beginning the moment she entered the Hall of Guardians. Picking herself up, she fought gravity to stand. It was then she realized her cell was ascending. If only she could see, she'd be able to grasp exactly how these men had built the prison. There was something to be said about the security of a cell that could transport prisoners without having to remove them first.

A blinding light erupted from the ceiling overhead. Inyalia shielded her eyes, hoping they'd adjust quickly. That had said more than enough. She'd been in total darkness long enough for this sudden light to cause pain. Now, more than ever, she hoped Tylor was with her. If he'd been taken while she was asleep, or even left behind when her cage began to move, she wasn't sure how she'd react. "Are you here, Tylor?"

"Yes. I'm here. Listen, I counted the guard patrol while you were sleeping. One passes every hundred and twenty-six seconds. I wasn't able to tell if it was one, or many. But if you have the chance to escape, that's the patrol count. I'm sorry I couldn't give you more detail when we last spoke. I couldn't risk them overhearing and expecting anything other than complete obedience."

Inyalia smiled. She should have known better. He hadn't given up. He was just thinking like a tactician, something she needed to do more often. "Do you have any idea where they're taking us?"

"No. But if I had to guess, I'd say we're on our way to see the magistrate. Judging from the shouts and cries I heard in the dark, it doesn't sound like they execute their prisoners. Instead, I believe they use them for slave labor. That may work to our advantage in the long run.

We just have to stay together long enough to form a plan." Watching the opening drawing ever closer, nearly upon them, Tylor rapidly added his final words. "I don't know when we'll have the chance to speak freely again. But I promise, I'll do everything within my power to get us out of here."

They passed through the opening, light enveloping them. Inyalia blinked several times, letting her eyes adjust. She could see a combination of flame and glowing fungus around the walls of the large chamber. With the light, she noticed their cells were open along the top. That would have proven useful were it not for the glossy metal holding them. The bars were far too slick to climb.

Her eyes adjusting, Inyalia searched her surroundings. A handful of guards were posted around the outer edge of the room. It reminded her of the theater in Camruun City, the center being a large, circular platform that set closest to the ground. The further from the center they got, the higher the seats rose, eventually creating the outer walls. This was no different, except there were only two rows of seats, one at ground level, the other midway up the enclosed wall. There was a wide opening behind them, and another smaller entrance fixed with a closed door straight ahead.

One of the stout men stood at the midpoint between their cages and the closed door. Inyalia studied him from head to toe. Unlike the others, he wasn't wearing armor, though his posture suggested he wasn't unfamiliar with it. A set of elegant red robes covered his broad form, throwing great contrast to his thick black beard and long dark hair. His hands were clasped, one over the other in front of him, waiting for the cells to stop moving.

Hearing the door beneath them clank shut, Inyalia watched the man approach. His piercing blue eyes were youthful, but the wrinkles upon his flesh said otherwise.

"Greetings. I am Gailen Stoneheart, Cousin ta our emperor, Gaius Stoneheart, an' Magistrate o' Deep Rock City. It's me duty ta hear all complaints an' oversee sentencing o' crimes committed both wittingly and unwittingly, within the confines o' this fine city and her outlying regions. Ye've been charged with trespassin' in the second degree. How do ye plead?" Gailen paused, awaiting their answer.

"Not guilty!" Tylor stated defiantly, refusing Inyalia the chance to speak. The last thing he wanted was for her to say something that could potentially incriminate her.

A smile came to Gailen's face, though his beard hid most of it. Casually, he approached the cells, refusing to take his eyes off the outsiders. "Were ye, or were ye not found an' arrested in the hot pools?" Carefully he studied their faces, searching for any sign of how they'd found their way into the mountain. That was a far greater threat than a simple trespassing charge. They'd sealed every entrance in and out nearly a thousand years prior. Severing all ties to the outside world had conserved their way of life and allowed their economy to flourish. If the way had been opened, mistakes of the past were bound to repeat themselves.

"I refuse to answer that question on account of its nature. There's no answer I can provide that would be considered anything other than an admission of guilt." Tylor glared his defiance into the old dwarf. This was going to be a battle of wills. It was a long shot, but if he could twist the words to their favor, perhaps he could clear them of any charges. Though even with a clear name, it was unlikely they'd be released.

"Yer objection is noted. Allow me ta rephrase." Gailen paced in front of the cells, looking from one elf to the other. There was something familiar about the female. He simply couldn't recall where he'd seen it. "Two days ago, one o' our scout patrols responded ta the sound o' laughter. In one o' the hot pool chambers, they discovered two elves, one male, one female, engaged in allusive activity. Both were promptly taken inta custody an' provided their clothes. All other gear, weapons, armor, an' effects, with the exception o' a knee brace were gathered an' delivered fer evaluation." The dwarf gestured to a table at his left. Every item from Inyalia's pack had been laid out for inspection. Their weapons rested on one end, and both her, and Tylor's armors were hanging from a wire stand that was far too large for their slender frames.

Gailen turned his attention back to the elves and continued reciting the report. "Both prisoners were ushered ta the prison block, where they were secured fer trial." Pacing behind the cells and coming back into view, he paused in front of the male elf, careful to remain out of reach. He doubted either would be foolish enough to attack through the bars, but he wasn't going to give them the opportunity. He didn't desire their blood on his hands any more than he desired their presence in his city.

There were far greater concerns which demanded his attention. "Is this recollection o' the report I received accurate?"

Tylor glared at the ancient dwarf. Factually, everything he'd said was correct. How could he find a loophole when every detail had been accounted for?

"It is." Inyalia stated.

Gailen turned his attention to the female. He wondered when she would speak. Marching to the front of her cell, he studied her closer, hoping something would remind him why she seemed so familiar. "Then ye admit that ye were trespassin'?"

"Inyalia!" Tylor shook his head, warning her to keep quiet.

"I do."

"I see. And how did you find yer way into the caverns?" Perhaps she'd be able to give the answer he desperately sought.

Inyalia remained quiet for a moment, deciding what she was willing to say. Tylor's tactics weren't helping anything, though she knew what he'd hoped to achieve. A subtler approach was needed here. As ridiculous as it would sound, the truth was the best option. If nothing else, maybe these creatures were familiar with the guardians. Maybe they'd be sympathetic to their cause and allow them to go free. Even if they didn't, they wouldn't be in any worse position than they were now. "There's a place at the top of the mountain my people call, The Hall of Guardians. Some time ago, when my friend and I were there, rocks began to fall from the sky. We barely escaped with our lives, but we got trapped inside. We found a room that led into the caves. But we couldn't spend the rest of our lives there. We set out to find a way back to the surface. And that's when your people found us."

A smile came to Gailen. It was the way her mouth moved when she spoke that reminded him where he'd seen it before. And if her words were to be believed, which he did, that meant the way to the outside was still shut. He was familiar with the guardians. In fact, he recalled a time in his youth when the guardians had served as allies of his people. The halls had been a gift, back when their two peoples associated. "Tell me, youngling. Do ye have an ascendant named, Aeldren Soulaire?"

Inyalia stood frozen for a moment. She hadn't expected to hear that name from anyone, let alone in this place. "My grandfather is named Aeldren. Though I never knew his surname. My father doesn't like to speak of him."

"I thought so." Gailen's smile grew wider, unable to be hidden behind his black beard. Stepping forward, he got within an arm's length of the girl. "I've got some stories about yer grandpa." Shaking his head in pleasant recollection, he grabbed the corner of her cell and gave a sturdy twist. It clicked and the bars began to sink into the floor, leaving her unharmed at their center. Turning his attention to the male, he repeated the process, watching the cell disappear. "Now, don't be tryin' ta attack me first chance ye get. It won't end well fer ye."

Inyalia stood confused, watching the old creature turn away from them as if he'd served his purpose. She wasn't sure what she'd said, or even if any of this had anything to do with her. One thing was certain though, her grandfather had made a reputation with this guy. If only such pleasantries existed between her father and him. Unsure what to do, Inyalia took a step toward the man, carefully watching the guards around the room. They didn't seem to care. "Excuse me, but I'm afraid I don't understand what's going on."

Gailen reached the table where the gear had been laid out. Signaling Inyalia to join him, he looked over their belongings. "Long ago, yer grandfather served me emperor well. He was one o' the few outsiders who was offered permanent residence within the city. He declined. Said the world was too large fer him ta remain in one place fer long. I respected him, as did many o' us." Lifting the blackened arrow, Gailen inspected the material. "I knew there was something unique about ye when I saw this. It's not o' dwarven make, but it was made on dwarven forge." He handed the arrow to the young elf, casually making his way toward the armors.

Tylor stepped over the crack in the floor where the cell had disappeared moments earlier. He was just as confused as Inyalia. But apparently something had worked in their favor, even if neither knew exactly what it was. Approaching the pair, he listened intently, hoping to catch anything of importance.

"Like the arrow, this armor is made o' dwarven ore, but not by dwarven hand. However, if ye look at the sigil on the collar—," Gailen paused, giving them a moment to inspect it. "—this markin' hasn't been seen fer quite some time. Not since before me people explored beyond the mountain, during the time o' the guardians themselves."

"What's it mean?" Inyalia asked, recalling that Tylor had been unsure of its meaning as well. All other rangers wore the insignia of their rank in the same location. Why was her armor different?

"It's from a language few speak, an' even fewer can read. Simply put, it means, champion. Yer grandfather was awarded a similar sigil when he saved our emperor an' earned his place among our people."

"What's this mean for us?" Tylor asked, still uncertain as to what was happening.

"Ye're free ta stay here as long as ye like. Or if ye wish ta return ta the surface, we can dig ye a way out. But know, once ye leave, there's no comin' back."

"I understand." Inyalia laid the arrow with the others. "I appreciate the offer, but we need to reach the surface. There are things happening that we need to be a part of."

"I can admire that, lass. It'll take about a week ta make the preparations fer yer departure. Please, do me the honor o' staying at me villa while ye're here. Ye can stock on supplies and leave as soon as the way is clear."

"Thank you."

"It's the least I can do fer the granddaughter o' good ol' Aeldren. Especially one whose earned the favor o' the guardians."

Tylor leaned against the stone column, looking out over the subterranean city. Absently, he rolled the cuff of his new tunic between his fingers. The material was thick and extremely soft, gliding against itself like silk. Though this was clearly something different. The slick fibers had been dyed a vibrant blue, nearly glowing in the artificial light. His breeches were of the same material, but black in color. The dwarven clothes felt good against his skin. They provided plenty of warmth in the cool underground, while allowing enough airflow to keep him from sweating. Realizing he'd been fiddling with the sleeve again, he released it and rested his hand on the pommel of his new weapons. The dwarves had been more than accommodating. Aside from the new clothes and daggers, they'd provided him with a pack, replacing nearly everything he'd lost, including a new and improved spice shaker. This one he didn't even have to grind the herbs himself. He simply put the whole leaves into it and twisted. A grinder inside did the rest. But best of all, they'd built him a new leg brace.

Lifting his foot, Tylor began running through the exercises he'd been instructed to perform. The new brace was far superior to the one he'd made from scraps. It buckled around his knee, much the way his leather greaves had. But this provided just the right amount of pressure in exactly the right places. It aided natural movement, while prohibiting all others. While wearing it, the pain was nearly nonexistent. Though Tylor suspected that had something to do with the healer who'd come to see him twice so far.

She'd started with a paste that soaked into his skin. From there, she massaged the area, bringing full movement back to the joint. Tylor had been a bit nervous when she first arrived. These dwarves were nothing if not gruff in appearance. Even their women were broad and heavy built. But she'd had the gentlest hands he'd ever felt.

He was grateful for the comforts provided. The food, lodging, and accessories they'd received over the past week in the underground had all been wonderful. Even the city itself was beautiful. And life here was simple. But simple was another word for boring.

"Still hurting?" Inyalia approached the wall of columns overlooking the city center. Tylor had spent nearly every day since their arrival leaning against one pillar or another, silently watching the dwarves perform the tasks of their daily lives. To a degree, Inyalia could understand why. Being here and seeing it for herself, they all seemed so content. There were farmers and traders, craftsmen and scholars, nobles and peasants. In many ways, social life here was extremely similar to that of her people. Except these people lived underground.

"Not as much as you'd think." Tylor finished his exercise and returned his foot to the stone floor. He felt a comfort in watching the life of the city. It was something he'd thought about frequently, but never taken time to do. There was always something more important that demanded his attention. But here, all he could do was wait. And in waiting, he discovered he was torn between a desire for action and that of a normal life. Tylor longed for whatever semblance of normal he could find in the outside world. But he was a wild elf. A normal life was something he could never possess.

Inyalia watched her friend and mentor for a long while. She knew he was growing restless. That was what had landed them here in the first place. He hadn't been able to get it out of his system before they were captured. Even now, while they were no longer prisoners, they were restricted to the magistrate's villa without an escort. It was grand, and plenty large. But they'd explored every inch of it within their first two days. There was a small forest, closer in size to the park of Camruun City, that had been Inyalia's favorite place. She was fascinated that they'd been able to successfully grow surface trees in the undermountain. But with the right dirt, and the proper combination of glowcaps, they'd been able to replicate a suitable substitute for sunlight.

Inyalia stepped forward, taking position beside Tylor. Carefully, she bumped into his shoulder, breaking his focus on the distance.

Unprepared, Tylor stumbled, but he managed to catch himself. His gaze shifted to Inyalia, finding peace in her mischievous smirk. "What was that for?"

"I just wanted to make sure you were still mobile. You've been standing there most of the day." Inyalia found the term amusing. She had no idea if it was day or night. Not even the dwarves seemed to know, having trapped themselves underground long before even her father's birth. But they'd managed to maintain some trace of the surface world they'd left behind so long ago. A few hours after last meal, every public fire was extinguished. It didn't do much for the glowcaps or the occasional villa using magical lighting, but it created enough darkness to feel like night. "Gailen will be here soon. Do you want to see if we can go for a walk after dinner?"

Tylor nodded, reclaiming his position against the ornate pillar. "That sounds nice."

A false smile came to Inyalia's lips. She was just as ready to leave as him. But she couldn't deny that it had been nice learning about a people so different from her own. Turning away from the overlook, Inyalia made her way through the garden. The grass and manicured shrubs were a comfort she never expected to find in such a place. The dark green leaves blended perfectly with the robes she'd been given as replacement for her tattered clothing. For the first time in as long as she could remember, she felt clean. Her hair had been brushed free of all tangles and braided down the back. Were it not for the dark ceiling overhead, the undermountain held many qualities of home.

Entering the villa, Inyalia made her way past two of the house servants who were busy cleaning. She'd spoken to them a few times, but they rarely had anything to offer, save for complete agreement on all subjects, or the occasional deferment to their master. Inyalia had questioned their freedom a few times, but they insisted they were paid for their labors. Being unable to find fault, she decided it best not to press the issue.

Turning toward the guest quarters, Inyalia made her way along the wing and quickly found her room. It was a simple thing, housing a single bed, small table and chair. Gailen had had a weapon rack and armor brought in for her gear. He'd explained that having them on hand was a normal thing in dwarven society. It was a show of good faith that she had nothing to fear.

The room offered luxuries she hadn't had in so long, but it was the balcony that made it something special. Outside the sliding door, she felt like she was flying. The guest rooms faced Mountain Heart, placing each balcony alongside the huge rock suspended at the city's center. Mountain Heart was the royal district. The emperor, his family, and the royal guard resided within the core of the floating rock. Inyalia had only been inside it once. Gailen had wanted her to meet the emperor, believing he would find joy in knowing their friend yet lived. Unfortunately, the emperor refused to see anyone. But that didn't stop the rumors from circulating.

Inyalia hadn't been told anything directly. In fact, most of the dwarves, while polite to her face, seemed to object to her presence in the first place. Aside from Gailen, most hadn't given her so much as an opinion. But it seemed they were unaware just how keen an elf's hearing could be.

During her tour, she heard many of the dwarves speak in hushed voices, believing her out of ear shot. It seemed the emperor had taken to locking himself away, refusing to come out for days at a time. Some said he was ill, while others refused to comment. Inyalia suspected those few were the result of her presence. But since the emperor was unavailable, Gailen offered an alternative.

The magistrate took them into the museum, where all the cities riches were held. It took but a moment in the lower levels of the heart to discover what dwarves loved above all else. Mountains of gold, silver, and jewels were piled in the treasure room. Ancient and beautiful armors, weapons, and trinkets were on display for all to see. Boxes of jewelry covered every available surface, each piece labeled with a golden plaque that had been carved in dwarven writing. It seemed every trinket, bobble, and piece of metal within the museum had a story to tell. And Gailen was more than happy to relay them.

It was then that Inyalia realized a major difference between the dwarves and her own kind. Each family was allowed to accumulate their own wealth. And each did. But the wealth of the people as a whole was something to be treasured. That was why everything was on display, and so easily accessible. The riches belonged to everyone, and therefore, the dwarven people took great pride in their achievements.

Inyalia watched the hovering stone for a long moment. Along the sides, there were numerous openings and carved pathways that wrapped the perimeter, though they were difficult to see from a distance. Even now, she could see only the faintest lines where the guardrails protected the royals from carelessly toppling over the side, and she was just on the other side of the chasm.

Taking in the view, it was nothing compared to the void beneath the suspended heart. Far below, beyond the glow of fire, fungus, or spell, Inyalia could see the occasional flicker of light. It wasn't like the outer ring, which was protected by fire and molten rock. This was far more interesting. This was an underground river, capable of drowning the entire city.

A knock at the door pulled her from her thoughts. Stepping through the sliding glass, Inyalia closed it and approached the entrance. Pulling it open, she peered into the hall, seeing Gailen's wide smile. He always seemed pleased to see her.

"Good afternoon. Am I disturbing ye?"

Inyalia returned his smile. There was something about the old dwarf that brought her peace. "Not at all."

"Excellent. I wanted ta let ye know, the tunnel has been cleared. Ye're free ta leave whenever ye wish." For the briefest moment, a lonely frown appeared beneath his facial hair, though it was gone before anything could be said of it.

"Thank you. I appreciate everything you've done for us." Inyalia placed her hand on his arm, bending her knees just enough to look into his eyes. "It means more than you know."

Gailen's cheeks flushed. "It's been me pleasure, lass. I hope ye have a safe trip. And when ye see that ol' man, Aeldren. Tell em' I'll be seein' em' in hell." A hearty chuckle escaped the old dwarf. He grabbed his plump belly, containing his laughter. Backing away from the door, he turned to leave. "I'll let ye gather yer things."

"Thank you, Gailen." Inyalia repeated and closed the door. She felt for the old dwarf. He'd been so kind since he learned of her heritage. But it was more than that. Gailen once had a wife and daughter. Unfortunately, they'd gotten sick sometime back. That seemed to be the only thing the dwarves didn't like about sealing themselves away. With no trade to the outside world, many plant species were no longer available. And that meant their medicines were extremely limited. Gailen had lost his family within a few days of each other. Since then he'd spent his time in work. But now that he had company, he'd let his guard down slightly.

Making her way to the armor stand, Inyalia pulled each piece free, fixing it to her with relative ease. She was surprised at how easy it fell into place. The buckles nearly clasped themselves, saving her the effort. Attaching the final piece, she gave a quick series of twists and stretches, ensuring everything was where it belonged. Such comfort shouldn't have been possible in armor. Yet, had she not applied it herself, she wouldn't have known it was there.

Inyalia strung her bow, resting it over her shoulder. She didn't expect having to use it, but she decided to err on the side of caution. The dwarves were friendly, at least the ones she'd met. But some were less than enthusiastic about her presence. What if it was all a ruse, designed to gain her trust? She wasn't willing to risk it until they were safely out of the mountain.

Lifting her quiver, Inyalia studied the collection of arrows that protruded. She counted six of the training arrows, at least three of which had been spelled by Lorena. Though it was impossible to tell which three now that they'd gotten mixed up. She could see the last white feathered arrow that had saved her from Alona. And there were twelve new ones, dwarven in design, that were made of the blackened metal. Though these didn't have the crystal fragments she'd seen elsewhere. Strapping it in place, she slung her pack and made for the door.

Inyalia was nearly to the courtyard when a loud commotion erupted beyond the villa. A dull roar echoed within the cavern city. Looking around, it seemed the servants were as concerned as she was. Inyalia followed, searching for any sign of Tylor or Gailen. They had to be around here somewhere.

The servants rushed from the manor, spilling into the street. The dwarves, both civilian and soldier were scattered about, shouting to the others in their native tongue. Panic was clear on their faces. They ran into each other, toppling carts and overturning hastily packed wagons. Something wasn't right. There was a fear about the city that Inyalia hadn't noticed before.

"Inyalia!"

She heard Tylor's voice amidst the sea of frightened screams from the surrounding city. "Over here!" Inyalia raised her arm, waving it overhead.

Tylor was dressed in his armor, his daggers sheathed at his side, and his loaded pack fixed securely to his back. He searched desperately for the woman in his charge. Seeing her near the entrance, he ran toward her. "Inyalia, we have to leave right now!"

"What's wrong? What's happened?" The worry on his face was bleeding to her.

"We don't have much time. Gailen went to your room to warn you. We need to find him and flee this place."

"Tylor, tell me what's happened!" Inyalia held her ground, refusing to move until he spoke.

"Damn it, Inyalia. We don't have time!" Shaking his head, knowing he wasn't going to get anything further until he spoke, he started talking, urging her to follow. "I'll explain while we run."

Inyalia accepted his terms and began jogging back into the villa.

"Apparently the emperor went crazy and started killing his guard. A few made it out. He's on his way to the failsafe room." Tylor picked up the pace, turning a corner. Leaping up the small staircase, he turned again, entering the guest wing.

"What do you mean, failsafe room? What's that mean?"

Gailen stepped from one of the rooms. He was wrapped only in his robes, but a large axe hung across his back, supported by a thick leather strap. "It means he's gonna bury the city, lass."

Inyalia froze, comprehending the words. "He's going to bury the city? How?"

Gailen sighed, clearly wanting to make a run for it. "When ye live underground, there be certain dangers not found elsewhere. As a precaution, we dwarves build everythin' with that thought in mind. If we have ta collapse a tunnel, or level a section ta stop an enemy from reachin' us, we will. Our entire city was built this way. Gaius is headed fer the failsafe rooms. From there, he can collapse every tunnel, bridge, an' room we've ever used. It'll kill the city, lass. That's why we have ta move now. Yer tunnel isn't far. If we can reach it, just maybe, we'll get far enough away ta avoid gettin' smooshed."

"Like I said, we have to go now." Tylor reassured her.

A loud rumble echoed through the cavern. Inyalia could feel it in her feet. The walls shook, and the ceilings cracked.

"It's too late!" Gailen conceded, fear replacing his usual cheerful demeanor.

Running to the nearest window, Inyalia looked out, seeing the chains suspending Mountain Heart release. The huge rock crashed into the void, crushing everything in its path. Homes were decimated in the blink of an eye. The floor broke in many places, large chunks disappearing into the darkness below. They didn't have long before the oblong stone that made the city's core would teeter and crush the villa. In the distance, the cavern roof began to collapse, burying everything beneath in a cloud of dust.

Surveying the destruction, Tylor turned to their patron. "You said the tunnel isn't far. Is there any chance to reach it?"

Gailen shook his head in defeat. "No, lad. Even if we reached it before Mountain Heart fell, we be too close ta avoid the collapse. There's no hope."

Finding her resolve, Inyalia stood tall in defiance of her impending doom. Turning to face her companions, blocking out the death occurring at her back, she clung to her desire for life. "There's always hope! Follow me, I have an idea."

Chapter XV
Burying the Past

Inyalia ran as fast as she could, though that wasn't saying much. The ground shook vigorously, knocking her from her feet on many occasions. Reaching the door to her room, she threw it open and rushed inside. Hearing Tylor and Gailen behind her, she ran across the room and onto the balcony, overlooking the devastation. The glass door had shattered, leaving jagged bits on both sides. Searching the distance, she found her query.

The chains that had once held Mountain Heart suspended, were laying slack at the edge of the void. The massive core groaned, partially obstructing the hole it had once straddled. It wouldn't be long before it toppled over, crushing the very spot they were standing.

Drawing her bow, Inyalia took out her favorite arrow and looped her rope to the end. This was going to be far different from fishing, but it was the only chance they had. Nocking it, she took aim.

"Inyalia, this is crazy. Regardless of where you shoot, there's no way it's going to support any of our weight." Tylor observed, trying to piece together her plan. Nothing about it made any sense.

"I have ta agree with em, lass. What's on yer mind?"

"Patience." Inyaila tossed the bundle of rope over the balcony rail, keeping the loose end in her hand. Adjusting her aim to account for weight and distance, she fired, jerking at the last moment.

Her arrow launched, pulling the rope with it. The tail end kicked, growing wider with each revolution. There was no way it would sink into anything it hit, if such a feat were even possible in a city made of stone.

"Come on. Come on!" Inyalia pleaded, begging her arrow to obey her command. The rope was beginning to raise, telling her she was nearly out of room. If it went taut before it reached its destination, she had no doubt the force would rip it from her grip. Watching the arrow, it flailed about, twisting away from its mark. Just before the shaft smacked the iron mount where the chain had been fixed, it hooped the other way and slipped through the gap.

"Yes!" Inyalia nearly jumped with joy, seeing the arrow connect. Wasting no time, she whipped the rope as hard as she could, spinning it with a twist. The wave traveled down, throwing the wooden shaft over the line. It wrapped around itself a few times, locking into place. It wasn't as strong as a grappling hook, but it would work for her purposes. Moreover, it would get her close enough for the next stage of her plan.

Quickly tying the rope to the bannister, Inyalia pulled hard, ensuring it would hold. "Follow me as quick as you can." Inyalia slung her bow and jumped over the ledge, catching the rope. Swinging her weight, she hooked her feet over it and crossed her ankles. Dangling, she pulled herself toward Mountain Heart, letting the rope slide along the side of her leather boot.

"Go on, lad. I'm a bit heavier than the both o' ye combined. I'll wait fer her ta get ta the other side."

Tylor nodded his understanding and mounted the rope. It stretched quite a bit but remained solid. Within a few moments, Tylor was right behind her.

Inyalia reached the chain mount and climbed from the rope. She could feel Mountain Heart swaying beneath her. It wouldn't last much longer. She only hoped they were out of the way when it decided to fall. Reaching out, she grabbed Tylor's hand and pulled him up beside her. Looking across the gap, she was surprised Gailen hadn't started across yet. "Come on! We only have a few minutes before this thing's going to fall!"

Gailen smiled and unslung his axe. "Go on without me, lass. Ye're gonna need yer rope, and I need ta stay with me people!" Giving no room for argument, Gailen slammed the blade of his axe down, severing the knot. The rope fell free, losing little more than a few inches.

"Gailen!" Inyalia lunged forward, hoping to somehow stop him. He was doomed if he didn't come. There was no certainty her plan was even going to work, but at least they'd go out trying if it didn't.

Tylor caught Inyalia, pulling her toward him. "He's made his decision. We have to keep moving. What's next?"

Inyalia sniffed, wiping the tears from her face. Taking a deep breath, she pulled the rope toward her and removed the arrow, returning it to her quiver. Grabbing the dwarven made grappling hook, Inyalia tied it off and began swinging it in an underhand arc. She slowly let the rope out, increasing the arc until it reached maximum size. Timing it out, she released, watching it soar across the void and hook around one of the massive chain links. Pulling tight, she patted her hip, silently telling Tylor to grab hold and hang on. This was going to be the hardest part of her plan. She only hoped it worked. Stealing a final glance across the void, her eyes fell on Gailen. He hadn't been a friend for long, but she would remember him for the rest of her life. They shared a long stare, saying more in silence than they could have with words.

Taking a deep breath, Inyalia rocked backward as far as she dared, feeling Tylor move in unison with her.

Together, they charged forward and leapt, keeping the rope taut. It was a bit more of a drop than either of them had prepared for, but the rope caught soon after their feet left the iron mount. They swung through the void, unable to see what was below, while everything about began to disappear. The rumble grew louder as another section collapsed, raining dust and stone upon them.

Inyalia glanced up, seeing the city's core begin its final descent. She felt a pang of guilt when it crashed into Gailen's villa. The mansion exploded beneath the weight. They needed to get out of the way or it would treat them in a similar fashion. Reaching the lowest point of the swing, Inyalia could see the flashes clearer than ever. Her guess had been right. Silently thanking the guardians for protecting her, she released the rope.

Falling through the air, Inyalia realized Tylor was no longer holding onto her. He'd been there moments earlier. Spinning uncontrollably, she searched, but he was nowhere to be seen. Just then, she impacted the surface. It forced the air from her lungs. She felt like she'd hit solid rock, but rock wouldn't swallow her the way this had. Gasping for breath, Inyalia's mouth filled with water and she began to sink beneath the rushing liquid. She needed to control herself now more than ever. If she panicked, she'd inhale water and drown. She couldn't let that happen. She'd been through too much.

Kicking as hard as she could, trying to focus on the shimmers of burning light above the surface, she felt her lungs reach their capacity. Unable to break through, she knew she was done. After everything, she was going to drown.

A pair of hands tore through the freezing cold and latched onto her shoulder straps. They ripped her through the water, closer to the twinkling light overhead. Inyalia saw Tylor's face through the rippling liquid. Breeching the surface, she expelled the water filling her mouth and drew air in huge gouts. Panting, she felt him lay her across something solid. Coughing, desperate to expel the water she'd swallowed, Inyalia rolled to her side, seeing what it was they were laying upon.

It appeared to be a large paddlewheel that had broken from its axle and gotten wedged between the rocks.

Looking around, Inyalia saw several others, turning casually in the flowing river. She knew the city's lifts and doors were water powered. Gailen had told her that much, but she hadn't fully understood it until this moment.

Coughing the last bit of water from her, Inyalia forced herself to breathe through her nose. It was the only way to restore control. Finally, she sat up and turned to Tylor. "I thought I'd lost you."

"You nearly had. My leg got caught in the rope. I managed to cut myself free just before I crashed into the wall. You owe me a dagger by the way." Tylor smiled, though it was interrupted by a loud crash overhead.

Inyalia glanced up, seeing the stone core tear through the floor. It was coming down faster than ever. They needed to move. Inyalia jumped to her feet as quick as her body would allow. Fear and confusion placed a heavy tax, making every action twice as difficult. Running for the edge of the overturned paddlewheel, she dove into the water and swam for the distance.

Mountain Heart crashed into the massive river, filling the void. A huge wave flowed out from it, raising the level nearly fifty feet.

Arm over arm, kicking as hard as her legs would allow, Inyalia tried to outswim the coming wave. It was lifting them faster than she could move. And soon, it would throw them over the edge, crushing anything unfortunate enough to be in its path. There was only one more option, and it was likely suicide. Timing her words between strokes, Inyalia shouted to Tylor. "We—can't—outrun—it.—Have—to—take—shelter." She altered course, moving parallel to the encroaching wave.

It took Tylor a moment to see what she had in mind. The water level was rising dangerously fast. Fortunately, the dwarves had taken that into account when they built the waterwheels. Each one was fixed to a shaft that could raise or lower depending on the river's level. It was going to be close, but the chance of survival was much higher than trying to surf the wave inside a rocky canyon.

Inyalia reached the wooden wheel. It continued to spin, faster than ever with the increased flow. Grabbing hold of the spokes, Inyalia felt herself being tumbled through the water. She had no idea how many times she'd gone around, but she finally managed to climb between them. Inside the wooden device wasn't much better. Were she not holding on for dear life, she had no doubt it would beat her to death in a matter of seconds. That was provided she didn't blackout from dizziness first. Aside from that, the hardest challenge was timing her breath. It took many revolutions to realize that she had to suck in the moment the water released her. If not, she'd miss her chance to catch a breath.

Tylor treaded just outside the large wooden wheel. Seeing Inyalia make her way inside, he gave her a moment to get situated. The wave would be upon him any moment. Out of time, he latched onto the spokes and attempted to pull himself inside.

Something heavy crashed into the water beside them, breaking the wave for the briefest moment. Splintered wood showered the area, and the wheel came loose.

Both Tylor and Inyalia held on to anything they could, their wheel thrashing at the cap of the wave. It hit the wall, toppling over. Jarred loose, they collided with one another, slamming into the sides and spokes, unable to make heads or tails of anything. It flipped and spun too rapidly to grant breath, not that the rushing waters were willing to offer it in the first place. The wheel slammed into a stone causeway and began to break apart. Piece by piece, it abandoned them until there was nothing left to provide shelter. Separated and alone, the water swallowed them and the world went dark.

The low hum of rapidly beating wings echoed somewhere in the distance. Feeling something land on her face, Inyalia brushed it away. Slowly opening her eyes, a sea of dark rolling clouds greeted her. Her body ached. She was bruised and battered from the memories rapidly returning to her. Grunting, she rolled to her side and looked around.

She was lying in a shallow pool of mud. The ground had been washed out, laying over stalks of grass and trees alike. A shallow creek snaked through the earth not far from where she lay, though whatever water had once flowed through it had long stopped. It seemed the bulk had continued downstream, leaving little pockets here and there that had yet to soak in.

Wincing, Inyalia pushed herself up, her hands sinking into the soggy ground. Getting to her feet proved quite the chore. She was out of breath, feeling as if she'd just escaped a squadron of rangers. Mud clung to her armor, pressed between layers and caked to the stitching. She ran her hands over it in a desperate attempt to knock it away, though her efforts proved folly. All she managed was to smear it further.

Peering into the sky, the dense clouds blocked out any sign of the sun. It was bright enough to suggest daytime, but there was no way to determine if early dusk or dawn was nearer. Either way, there appeared to be a storm on the horizon, and if the speed of the clouds was any indicator, it was moving fast.

Unable to intuit direction, Inyalia searched her surroundings for any significant landmarks. Considering she'd washed out of the mountain, locating that would be a start. Turning, Inyalia saw the wall of rock not far in the distance. She was maybe a thirty-minute walk, which seemed quite impressive considering she didn't remember anything after the paddlewheel came apart. What surprised her further, the hole in which she guessed was her exit had been filled. It was pretty evident water had flowed from it, but now stone spouted from the hole, running in a smooth column that spilled to the earth. The surrounding trees had burnt to ash, leaving nothing but charred wood encompassed in stone.

Inyalia stared at it for a long moment, wondering how she'd survived. But the mountains were of little concern now. She'd been carried away from them, which meant Tylor had to be further down river.

Inspecting her bow, she was pleased to see it survived the tumble wheel, though she couldn't say the same for the bulk of her arrows. Two of the blunt tips, four of the dwarven arrows, one of which was broken, and her special arrow were all that remained. Moreover, her pack was nowhere to be seen. Sighing, Inyalia unslung her bow and gave it a test draw to ensure it would function properly. It'd been through a lot. She couldn't risk it failing her in a moment of crisis. But that seemed to be the story of her life recently. One crisis after another. Confident it would perform, Inyalia drew one of the dwarven arrows and set out in search of Tylor.

Inyalia walked for hours, keeping an eye on the sky. It remained a constant shade of gray, never growing darker nor brighter. She had a feeling when night came, it would happen suddenly and without warning.

Following the path of uprooted trees and drowned vegetation, the stalks all pointed one direction, serving as a guide in the wake of destruction before her. The creek was all but nonexistent here, having grown in size to a small river in places and shrunk to little more than a stream at others. This was one of those places. The ground was nearly flat, all but the winding path where the water had eroded over time. Unfortunately, that also meant the flood spread wide when it came through, requiring her to do a wider sweep.

Inyalia had found a few pieces of curved and broken wood a few miles back. It could have belonged to the paddlewheel, but there was no guarantee. Theirs hadn't been the only one to break free, so it could have been any of them. Or it could have been part of a discarded barrel that got picked up somewhere along the way. There was no telling.

Cresting a hill, Inyalia paused, seeing the remnants of a fair size village resting along the trickle of water that cascaded gently down the path. The settlement was in ruin. Most of the buildings had long since collapsed upon themselves, while others retained only their stone walls and bricked chimneys. There were a few that had thatch roofs and wooden doors still intact, but they were few and far between. The flood had hit this place pretty hard, but from the looks of it, there wasn't much left to damage.

Keeping her bow at the ready, Inyalia made for the ruined village. Tylor could have ended up at any one of them, though with the distance she'd traveled, she was beginning to fear for his wellbeing. At any case, she couldn't move on until confirming his fate one way or another.

The first row of buildings were utterly destroyed. Piles of debris were scattered from the water's impact. Inyalia had no idea if they've fallen before or after the flood, but it didn't much matter. With the condition of this place, no one had lived here for several cycles, if that soon.

Inspecting the scattered rubble, Inyalia caught a glimpse of broken wood embedded in a partial wall. Moving closer, she knocked a few of the stones aside. To her surprise, they weighed next to nothing, more like plaster than stone. Moving a few others, she uncovered what was left of the center portion of a paddlewheel. The spokes were splintered where they'd broken, but there was no mistaking its origin. That renewed her hope. If the paddlewheel had traveled this far, it was possible Tylor had as well. She only hoped he was still alive.

A faint whistle traveled through the air, seeming at peace with everything in the world.

Drawing back the string, arrow ready to fly, Inyalia cautiously stepped away from the shattered building. Rounding another, in search of the unexpected sound, she saw a man crouched before the small stream. He wore tattered robes of gray that appeared to have been elegant at one time. Though now they were coated in dirt and torn in many places. The fabric was thin from age, displaying pock-marked skin beneath.

Continuing his song, the man dipped a wooden bucket into the shallow water. Watching it fill, he slowly tilted it, collecting as much as possible without allowing debris to enter. Lifting the bucket, he quit whistling and stood. "Are you going to point that thing at me all day, or step forward and introduce yourself?"

Inyalia was taken back. How did he know she was there? He hadn't looked her direction, and she hadn't made a sound. It was possible he could smell her, but unlikely. If being carried in a flood and washed out of a mountain hadn't removed any scent she'd been carrying, nothing would. Though she had been walking for a few hours. Seeing the man turn to face her, Inyalia lowered her bow. For his age, his voice was surprisingly full of youth. She squinted, trying to identify where she'd seen him before. "I know you. I saw you in Caelum when I met the Emerald Circle. They called you the—."

"The Watcher, yes." The old man smiled and slowly approached. "My name is Kael." He extended his shaky hand. "And you're Inyalia Highlor of Trendensil, if my memory is still intact."

"I am." Inyalia shook his hand, uncertain what to say. She'd heard the stories of this man. Many said he was the founder of Caelum, creating the Emerald Circle as a means to prolong his life and share the burden. Others thought him a crazy man who enjoyed feeling involved. Among all the questions racing through her mind, a single one found its way to her lips. "What happened to you?" She recognized the face before her. There was no mistaking it. But the man she'd seen in Caelum was at least a few hundred cycles younger. This man was nearing the end of his life.

Kael gestured for her to follow. He turned and slowly made his way toward one of the few buildings that remained intact. "I assume you're referring to my rugged good looks." A weak chuckle escaped him. "I'm afraid I don't have enough time to spin that tale. But I'll answer what I can over dinner."

Inyalia paused. "Oh? I'm sorry, but I can't stay here. I'm looking for my friend. I think you know him. His name's Tyl—."

Kael held up a hand, silencing her. Reaching the wooden door, he pushed it open and pointed inside.

Inyalia stepped forward and looked into the single room hovel. In the center of the room there was a small table, set with wooden plates, mugs, and eating utensils. Two chairs were pushed under the opposing ends, though the one closest to the door sat at an angle, suggesting it had been used recently. A stone fireplace had been built into the right-side wall. From an iron rod, hung a blackened kettle that steam seeped from. A small fire burned beneath it, though there was no wood or smoke evident. Raising a questioning eyebrow, Inyalia looked upon the old man, unsure what he was attempting to show her.

"Look again. Only this time, without expectation."

Taking a deep breath, Inyalia returned her focus to the room. It was as it had been, only there were more questions than answers. She saw a broom sweeping the floor by itself. It fell still when it noticed her looking. There was a block of cheese on the table, rocking itself across a grader. Slithers fell into a bowl beneath it. A painting of an open field hung on the wall, seemingly uninteresting until the wind blew, swaying the stocks of grain inside it. And, laying upon an old wooden bed to the left, was Tylor. He appeared to be sleeping, and surprisingly in one piece, though a blood-soaked bandage was wrapped around his forehead. She watched his chest rise and fall in a steady rhythm. Returning her attention to the man, tears began to well in her eyes. "He's alive!" She smiled, throwing her arms around Kael.

"Oh!" The old man gasp, catching the sudden and unexpected weight. Unsure what to do, he gently patted her back, allowing her a moment to collect herself. "As I was saying, I'd be more than happy to answer some of your questions over dinner."

Chapter XVI
The Fractured Pieces

"I can't believe this is all that's left!" Inyalia set the mug of broth on the table, lost in the old man's words.

Kael let out a defeated sigh. "I wish it weren't so. I did everything in my power to stop it. These ruins are all that's left of my beloved Caelum." Perking up, he took a long draw, clenching the mug in both hands. "But, I'm confident I would have done no different, were I faced with the same decisions again."

Staring deep into the youthful eyes of the deteriorating body before her, Inyalia felt sorrow. Kael had devoted his life to the pursuit of knowledge, both his own and others. He'd sacrificed so much to ensure everyone made it out. And most would never even know about it. "I admire you." A smile came to Inyalia's lips. Glancing over to Tylor, for what had to have been the hundredth time, she wondered if their stories would ever be so grand. "There's one part I don't understand."

Kael brought the brim to his lips once again, awaiting her question.

"You said you sacrificed all of your power to slow the corruption. So, how do you do that?" Inyalia pointed to the dancing flame beneath the kettle.

"Ah! Well—," Kael paused, searching for a way to explain it in a manner she'd understand. "There are many types of magic. Some work together, others don't mix at all, and there are a few that seem like magic to the untrained eye, but are something else entirely. Take the Hall of Guardians for instance. It seems like magic, but it's not. The secret of the halls is held in the crystalline stone found only in those mountains. Like the arrow you carry, it acts like magic, but it's far more powerful. My people called it psionics. It's a rare and powerful force that can both create and destroy worlds. But it's far different than magic. When Caelum fell, I gave everything I had to her preservation. But it wasn't enough. My city, my youth, even my friends. All of it disappeared in a few heartbeats. All I have left is a few more hours, and the psionics I was born to. They're as much a part of me as the skin wrapped around this dying form. I expended everything to save Caelum. And when I awoke, my psionics had returned, though nothing else did." Kael fell silent, lost in thought.

"I'm sorry. I didn't mean to remind you."

A faint smile appeared, and Kael slid his chair away from the table to stand. "What's done is done. I failed them. I must accept that. My only hope is they passed easily. There's nothing more horrendous than having your body torn apart by uncontrolled magics." Making his way to the kettle, Kael scooped another ladle of broth into his mug.

"Well, I for one am happy to have met you. I wish it wasn't so close to the end, but you make it sound almost like a reward."

"Oh, it is. When you've lived as long as I, seen and done as many things, and narrowly escaped certain doom on many occasions, death is but another adventure I have yet to experience." Laughing, as if a joke had just been told that only he understood, Kael returned to his seat. "Speaking of which, it's time for me to go. I wish you the best in your travels, Inyalia Highlor. I expect you'll do many great and wonderful things." He stood, keeping his gaze locked firmly upon her. "Before I go, I wish to impart a gift. Would you be so kind as to retrieve your dark crystal arrow?"

Inyalia pulled the white feathered missile from her quiver and handed it to him.

Turning the pristine instrument in his hand, Kael thoroughly inspected every inch of the blackened bolt. The head began to glow a bright purple, ebbing under his touch. Closing his eyes, he flipped it end over end several times, walking the shaft between his bony fingers. It came to a stop, fletching side extended toward Inyalia, awaiting her to reclaim it. "Thank you. I'm afraid I really must be going now. Your friend will be ready for travel in the morning."

Inyalia wanted to call out to him. She wanted to say anything to make him stay. He'd been a welcome relief. But none of it mattered. He was gone before the words could escape her mouth. Taking a deep breath, Inyalia glanced at the firepit. The magical flame that had danced all night was gone. The broom rested against the wall, refusing to move. And everything mystical in her life was gone. Everything except the arrow in her hand.

Turning to Tylor, Inyalia lifted the crusty-red bandage. She was pleased to see the wound was nearly healed. Whatever Kael had done was clearly working. She just had to wait until morning. Ensuring the blanket was securely covering him, she approached the wicker chair at the foot of the bed and took a seat. Getting comfortable, her eyes closed, and she drifted off to sleep.

<center>~~~</center>

Tylor slowly came to. He was warm. That was a luxury he hadn't experienced in quite some time. But more than that, he was comfortable. Laying there a moment longer, wishing to somehow preserve it, he sighed and pulled the blanket off him. Opening his eyes, he sat up and looked around the small hovel, trying to remember where he was. It was no use. He'd never seen this place before. Seeing Inyalia asleep at the foot of the bed, a smile came to his lips. He wanted nothing more than to let her rest. They'd been through so much already, the least he could do was give her a while longer.

Kicking his feet to the warm floorboards, Tylor stood and made his way to the table at the center of the room. It was loaded with the remnants of a decent meal that had long since gone cold. The room was mostly empty save for a few odds and ends lying about. Near the edge of the table, Tylor found a wooden pail half full of water. He dipped his hands and began washing his face. The cold water clung to his skin, both waking him and making him feel revived. Reaching his forehead, it soaked into the wrapped bandage. He hadn't noticed it until now. Probing the area, Tylor searched for any sign of damage. There was no pain, and he couldn't feel anything out of the ordinary. Finding the end, he carefully removed the dressing. If it was covering a wound, he didn't want to risk reopening it.

The blood stains brought concern. How was he not in pain? The realization made him freeze. "I'm not in pain." He repeated aloud trying to make it make sense. His head didn't hurt, not where the bandage had been, nor anywhere else. His body didn't ache, and best of all, his knee felt as if nothing had ever happened. He felt as if every injury he'd ever suffered had somehow vanished overnight. Lost in the moment, Tylor began stripping from his clothes, wiping the cold water over his body. It was refreshing, but mostly he wanted to check for any lingering wounds whose persistence was strangely absent.

Hopping on one leg, his other foot in his hands, Tylor caught a glimpse of Inyalia still asleep in the chair. He'd completely forgotten about her presence. Cheeks flushing red, he nearly fell. Scurrying to his clothes, he pulled them on, unconcerned that he was still wet. He was embarrassed. It wasn't like they hadn't seen each other before. But that time was a bit different. And they were both conscious, and being taken prisoner. The latter probably had more to do with it.

Awkwardly, Tylor looked about the room, searching for anything worthy to be called food. Inyalia had done so much to take care of him. The least he could do was ensure there was something to eat when she awoke. And be clothed. Clothing was a must.

Between the rations the dwarves had given him, and a small box of dried oats resting on the table, Tylor believed there was just enough to make a breakfast fit for a king. A poor king, but a king none the less. Scrounging some wood, he went to work building a fire under the kettle and emptied what remained of its contents. Rinsing it out, he added all the clean water he could find and brought it to a boil. Pouring in the oats and dried boar, he gave it a quick stir and waited.

An aroma of meat and dwarven spice filled the hovel as the mixture returned to a boil.

Inyalia shifted in her chair, the scent rousing her. Looking around, she found Tylor near the fireplace, tending the kettle. She sat up, pulling the blanket she'd covered herself with away. She'd forgotten to remove her armor before bed, but it was just as well. As rapidly as things were happening lately, sleeping in it was the only way to ensure she was ready if a quick exit was required. Moreover, she was surprised it hadn't hindered her. Sleeping in armor was a surefire way to wake up sore the following morning. Its ridged nature meant it couldn't flex, which kept the body from relaxing overnight. These were all elements her new armor didn't seem to possess. Stretching, Inyalia picked herself up and approached Tylor. Wrapping her arms around him, she hugged tight, pressing the side of her face against his back. "How are you feeling this morning?"

Tylor placed his hand over her forearm, returning her hug as best he could. "I feel great. Though I'm afraid I'm going to have to stop running around with you. You're bad for my health." He laughed at his joke, drawing a spoonful of porridge to his lips. Blowing across it gently, he took a sip, savoring the smoky flavor of meat combined with the sweet dwarven spice.

Realizing she'd held onto him a little too long, Inyalia broke away and made her way to the table, hoping he didn't notice her embarrassment. "Do you remember how you got here?"

Happy with the results, Tylor scooped the food into a pair of bowls and carried them to the table. "No. I remember the paddlewheel crashing, and a few moments trying to catch my breath. But the rest of it is gone." Setting a bowl in front of the young ranger, he pulled out the other chair and dug in.

Inyalia watched him for a long moment before turning to her own bowl. "You were rescued by The Watcher."

Tylor stared over the brim of his meal. If The Watcher had been here, why were they still here? With is power, he could have seen them back to Camruun City without a second thought. "Where is he?"

"Gone." Inyalia lingered on the word for a moment. She was happy to have shared his final few hours, but now that he had departed, he was just another loss added to the ever-growing list. "Caelum was destroyed. He gave everything trying to protect it, including his own life."

Giving her his full attention, Tylor stared at her blankly. "How did he pull me from the water if he sacrificed himself?"

"It's a long story. I didn't understand most of it. When I met him, he said he only had a few hours left. He took my arrow and did something to it. And then he was—gone." Inyalia gestured, trying to relay the message better than her words could.

"That's a shame. I only spoke with him once, but he seemed like a good guy."

Nodding her agreement, Inyalia lifted her bowl and took a sip of the chunky concoction. It was sweet, with a hint of spice. "We're east of the mountains." Inyalia added, as if somehow their whereabouts was important to their situation. She wanted to get home, but it seems so far away. There was only one road that led into Trendensil, and it was nearly a month south.

"Do you know where the nearest city is? If we can barter a couple horses—."

Inyalia cut him off. "What do we have to barter? The only things I have left are on me. And seeing the treasures the dwarves value, I doubt they slipped a handful of gold into your pack." Shaking her head, wishing there was another way, Inyalia swallowed the last bit of her food. "No. We're on our own. This far outside Trendensil, the only thing our status would buy is a mediocre ransom."

Tylor smiled. He couldn't help but admire the way Inyalia's nose crinkled when she was worried. Reaching across the table, he laid his hand atop hers. "Hey, we're going to be okay. Even if we have to walk. Icefall Pass is what, south of here? If we stay near the mountains, we'll reach it soon enough. Once through, its three days to Dragon Sanctum. We can report in there. With everything that's happened, I doubt anyone would object to us taking a little longer to get home."

Inyalia smiled, though she had trouble finding comfort in his words. He meant well. And his presence was comforting. But she'd never been this far from home before. And certainly, never for so long. Adding another month to the journey felt like a lifetime.

Pulled from her thoughts, Inyalia felt a strange vibration from her quiver. It moved of its own accord, like something was trying to get out. Yanking her hand free from Tylor's, she grabbed the tail of its strap and ripped it free of the buckles that held it stationary. The quiver came free, jumping about in her grip.

Grabbing the handful of arrows, Inyalia instantly knew which one was causing the commotion. The arrow Kael had touch was glowing as bright as ever. The purple light was near blinding. Lifting it, Inyalia heard Kael's voice. It was as clear as if he'd been standing beside her.

"My gift to you."

Lightning shot from the arrowhead, crackling in the air in front of the door. Only instead of disappearing the way normal lightning did, it remained in front of them, forking in all directions, growing denser. The blinding light became more intense. Bolts of purple energy arced, contained between floor and ceiling. With nowhere else to travel, it grew wider, blocking off the doorway. The wooden barrier behind it began to distort, breaking into several pieces. Piece by piece, it fell away, revealing something else, somewhere else, within the gaps. Faster, the pieces changed, and with a loud crack, it solidified, leaving an opening wreathed in crackling bolts of energy. Inside, was the last thing either of them had expected to see. Camruun City's main gate stood a short walk away.

Inyalia stared blankly at the opening, lost for action. She didn't know what to do. She didn't know what to say. Slowly, she stared at the arrow within her grasp, realizing the head had reverted to its dormant state. Returning it to her quiver, she turned to Tylor, equally stunned. "I guess this saves us quite the trip."

"I suppose so."

Inyalia buckled the straps of her quiver and returned it to its rightful place. Grabbing her bow, she started toward the opening.

"Are you sure it's safe to go through? What if it's a trap?" Tylor couldn't take his eyes off it. He'd seen many portals before. He'd even used a few from time to time. But this was unlike any portal he'd ever seen.

"It's safe. Consider it a final parting gift from The Watcher." Inyalia smiled at him and stepped through.

Camruun City stood before them, displaying its grand majesty. Never before had the gates been closed. That was part of the city's appeal. It was a place for the people, open to any elf who sought admittance. Status was irrelevant. Nobles and commoners alike were welcome. So why were the gates closed now?

Inyalia slowly approached the guarded post. Sentinels were everywhere. Some paced the allure, other stood outside the gate, watching the newcomers. There were even a few bowmen in the turrets, though from their appearance, Inyalia wasn't sure most of them knew which way the arrow went.

Tylor stopped just before reaching the first set of guards. "What's happened? Why are the gates closed?"

The elven watchman looked the pair over. "You two must've been living under a rock. I would've imagined a pair of rangers would have more details than the rest of us." Shaking his head, the guard signaled behind him and the portcullis slowly began to rise. "There's been a few attacks at the southern border. And something's happened out west, but nothing official's been announced. The higher ups thought it best to seal the gates until further notice. I'm afraid not much else has come down the pipeline."

"Thanks for the update. I assume we're free to enter?"

The guard nodded and stepped aside.

Tylor and Inyalia passed through the fortified entrance. The usual splendor of visiting the city was gone. It had always seemed so grand and elegant. The sunlight always reflected off the golden turrets about the outer wall and citadel. There were a few other buildings that could be seen for miles, but they didn't compare when taking it in as a whole. But now, the glow was absent. Camruun City had always been a bright and lively beacon of everything that was right in the world. But now it was cold and gloomy. Everything from the rolling clouds above, to the golden streets below seemed dull.

Inyalia watched the people as they passed. Most never paid any attention beyond their immediate interest. But now, every eye in sight was set upon them, questioning their presence, asking what was happening. It was uncomfortable.

The main road traveled straight to Aceldon Citadel, passing through several gateways that, like the main gate, were always open but were now sealed. The gatehouses were little more than massive archways that served in both beauty and defense. But the citadel was not their destination. They needed to get to the Ranger's Stronghold in the Military District.

Passing several small roads, Inyalia was shocked by how barren the trade district was. It was the largest section in Camruun City, stretching from the main gate to the first archway, and extending beyond both sides of the grand wall that ran through the city's center. When she'd visited in the past, it seemed so crowded and full of excitement. The east half was always filled with traders of all kind, offering the finest wares, fresh produce, livestock, and an assortment of other goods. The west side was where all the shops were located. Inyalia recalled visiting the smithy when her father needed to replace the bellows on his fletcher's forge. She couldn't see the store fronts from the main road, but judging by the relatively small number of people, it was unlikely any were open. But it wasn't the closed shops nor the lack of tradesmen that had her concerned. It was the few people still about. She'd seen their expressions once before, but never so close to home. She recalled it when Deep Rock City fell. These people, her people, were scared.

Nearing the end of the main road, just before the first archway, they turned left, skirting the northern edge of the craftsman's square. From here it was a straight shot into the Military District.

Inyalia recalled the path from her childhood. It seemed so long ago, and so much had happened since then. But the walk was the same, save for the gloom that had settled over the city. The Military District always seemed so big. It was, but it was also spread out, which made it less intimidating.

Approaching the archway that separated the district from the rest of the city, Inyalia glanced down the road to her left. It served as a divide between the trade and military districts. Once it passed through the noble quarter, it circled around and led to the southern entrance, where the magi sector was located. There wasn't much that direction other than a bunch of manors and a few of the more expensive shops.

On more than one occasion Inyalia's father preached about the mentality of the nobles. They were more than content to spend three times as much coin on something, simply because someone claimed it was worth more. Inyalia remembered him taking her into one of the shops. They looked at a yellow dress with a hem like scrolling flowers. Inyalia desperately wanted it, but he told her to wait. They then went to the market square, where the exact same dress was on display in the tailor's shop. Only the price was less than half. *Be on the lookout for artificial inflation,* he'd say. *Just because something looks nice doesn't mean you can't find it elsewhere, for a fraction of the cost.*

Pulled from her memory, Inyalia followed Tylor through the arch and onto the road leading straight into the district. They passed a row of stocks.

Inyalia had only seen them occupied once. The guards had locked a thief in the wooden device. She wondered how anybody could handle such torture. He'd been humiliated and put on display for all to see. Aside from the uncomfortable position, there was rotten fruit smashed upon his face and littering the ground around him. Flies bit at his skin, lapping up the sweet juices and blood alike. He'd been helpless to do a thing about it. Inyalia remembered him like it was yesterday. She recalled thinking she never wanted to be a thief. It was too embarrassing.

The road continued between a few large buildings and opened into a bricked courtyard. This was the second largest section of the city, next to the trade district. It spanned nearly half a mile wide and was twice as long, divided into four sections. The magi held quarters to the south, though there was no official tower here. Straight ahead, comprising the lower west wall, the Ranger's Stronghold was the smallest section of the district. With so many other strongholds spread across Trendensil, their presence here was little more than a formality. North of the rangers and extending beyond the wall was the Navy's Hub. They had their own gate which opened to the port. And everything else was the property of the Army, encompassing the entire north and most of the east section. It connected to the royal quarter and Aceldon Citadel beyond that.

Where the rest of the city's populace had been morose, the people here were the complete opposite. Soldiers rushed from building to building. Carts were loaded with supplies. Weapons, armor, rations, even tents and bedrolls were being transported from the various supply warehouses and taken elsewhere. Inyalia had never seen the army this active before. If she didn't know any better, they were preparing for war. Lost in the sight of it all, she hadn't noticed Tylor continue on without her. Running to catch up, she dodged a unit of soldiers dressed for battle. They were marching south.

Inyalia caught up just as Tylor reached the stronghold. Compared to the other buildings in the area, it was relatively simple. The rangers rarely operated within Camruun City, though there was rumored to be a small detachment that served as the king's personal guard. Between the city guard and the army, there wasn't much room for them. It was for that reason, Inyalia was surprised to find the stronghold packed full of rangers.

Tylor fought his way through the mass. There were representatives from nearly every unit, all crowding for space. Something major had to have happened for this kind of turn out. Fortunately, most were Ranger-Sergeants or lower. That gave him some room to move, as no one wanted to get in the way of a lieutenant. Reaching the main chamber, Tylor made his way to the staircase along the left wall. It curved around to meet its twin at the upper level, but he didn't need to go that high. This was simply a means to give him a better view as to what was causing the commotion.

At the head of the chamber, upon the mezzanine, the Ranger-General stood over a large table. Several pieces of parchment were scattered before him. Desperately flipping through the pages, he looked up at the officer standing before him. "Lieutenant Sykes, I want you to take your company to Ryse. You'll rendezvous with Lieutenant Mayers. We cannot allow these animal attacks to continue. There's too much at stake elsewhere. Wipe out the bear population if you have to. Just ensure the attacks stop."

"Yes, sir!" The lieutenant gave a quick salute and turned, disappearing among the throng of rangers awaiting order.

Searching the faces around him, Kalen selected another officer. Returning his attention to the stack, he flipped through, selecting a task suited to the elf's abilities.

"Inyalia!" Tylor shouted over the chatter. Grabbing her arm, he pulled her through the masses and onto the stairs with him.

Inyalia scanned the crowd, finding her father at the head. He looked older than she remembered. He had bags under his eyes, and his skin didn't appear as golden as it once was. If anything, he appeared to be in desperate need of sleep.

"Let's get to him. I believe he'll want our report. And of course, he'll want to see his daughter." Tylor smiled, seeing her eyes light up. Taking her hand, he led her through the crowd. They were reaching the officers, which meant his rank was less likely to aid them much longer. Seeing an opening, he squeezed through and rapidly climbed the steps.

Inyalia followed as close as she dared. She was feeling trapped among all these people. But more than that, it made no sense. Why was her father dealing with the masses? He enjoyed knowing the men under his command on a personal level, but this went against everything she knew of the corps. Where was the chain of command? The Ranger-General oversaw the corps as a whole. His orders passed to the Ranger-Lords, who commanded the four battalions and served as his advisors. Each battalion was comprised of ten companies, and each company held five units of rangers. It was the lords who should have been passing orders to the captains, who in turn would carry it down the line. Where were the lords? And why were so many others here?

Inyalia searched the men surrounding her father. Only one face stood out. Ranger-Lord Traevon Duskwillow of Dragon Sanctum was present. But where were the others? More importantly, why were any of them here? Amidst all the commotion, she hadn't thought about that. The Ranger-General was expected to visit each and every post from time to time. But most of their business was handled in the sanctums. Dragon Sanctum had been the favorite simply because it was so close to the southern border, as well as home. What had happened that brought so many of them here?

Reaching the top of the mezzanine, Tylor ushered Inyalia passed the last few officers, letting her move ahead of him.

Kalen returned the salute and watched another lieutenant disappear. He was in desperate need of a break. He'd been at it all day, and the list of people needing direction wasn't getting any smaller. Searching for another face, he froze, lost in the sight of his daughter. Joy overwhelmed him. But he was on duty, he couldn't let it show. Kalen glanced behind him, making sure the Ranger-Lord was present. "Traevon, take over for me here. I need to retire to my office."

"Yes, Sir!" Traevon stepped up to the table and began sifting through the reports.

Stepping from the lingering crowd, Kalen gestured for them to follow. Approaching his office, he inserted a key and opened the door. Stepping inside, he waited for them to enter.

Inyalia stepped through, Tylor on her heels.

No sooner than they were clear, Kalen closed the door and wrapped his arms around Inyalia. "My dear girl, I feared you were dead. When word came that Caelum had been destroyed, I—," Stopping himself, Kalen released his hug, keeping his hands on her shoulders. "I'm glad you're okay." He smiled wide, inspecting her armor. "And what's this?" He fingered the insignia upon her collar. "I can't say I've seen that one before." Swollen with pride, he hugged her again. "You did it. You became a ranger. I can't tell you how proud I am."

"Thanks, dad. I missed you too." Inyalia took a deep breath and pulled away. As much as she wanted to rejoice with seeing her father again, much had happened that required his attention. She finally understood what it meant to put duty over pleasure. "Dad, I don't know how to tell you this, but something's happened."

Kalen's smile faded. Backing away, he leaned against the edge of his desk. "I know. That's part of the chaos out there. In the last month three of my four Ranger-Lords have perished. Two were killed, and the third— well, we haven't found him yet. I've never seen this kind of outbreak before. And none of the books speak of anything even close to this magnitude. I've had entire companies vanish into thin air. Captains desert or end up dead. And the steady supply of lieutenants I send to replace them rarely report for duty. Those that do, don't last long enough to gain the experience needed." Glancing at the mass confusion outside his window, Kalen continued. "Traevon and I are about all that's left to dish out orders. And don't even get me started on the Army. In a single night, a quarter of their strength evaporated. A third of the Navy along with it."

Tylor listened intently. He had trouble believing what was being said. But Kalen had no reason to lie. "Sir, if I may?"

Kalen nodded. "You should know by now, you'll always have my ear."

"These attacks. Are they isolated?"

"Sadly, no. That would give us a direction to start. The animal attacks along the southern border have become more frequent. Somethings got them riled up. I've sent three companies to Ryse to deal with it. The first never reported back. The second's been ineffective. Hopefully the third will make a difference. But those are nothing like the issues we're facing elsewhere. We've had units slain or go missing as far north as Greensborough. The army's massacre happened in Largar'Thor. Two thousand men were executed while they slept. Not a single alarm was sounded. The same night fifty ships bound for Hailsort were loaded to capacity with soldiers, sailors, and gear. Not one returned." Kalen exhaled, his shoulders drooping. "Our own numbers haven't suffered to that extend, but it's far from an acceptable loss. We've lost nearly half a battalion so far. Most of them from Dragon Sanctum. That's why Traevon is here. The sanctum—It's been destroyed." Kalen fell silent, staring at the floor.

"Who would dare?" Tylor asked, fury growing within him. Dragon Sanctum was an important piece of their heritage. "Who could have had the strength to do such a thing, especially without heavy resistance?"

"That's the thing. We don't know. It happened in the dead of night. All the torches extinguished in unison. And it was gone before we knew what happened. Traevon narrowly escaped with his life. He crawled from the rubble and reported to me directly. Had I not been home, I could have easily been crushed in the collapse."

"For all our sake, I'm glad you weren't, Sir."

Inyalia stood in shocked disbelief. How could so much have happened in her absence? Was there anything she could have done to change it? How was she expected to combat an enemy that hasn't shown itself? A million other questions flooded her mind, but they were all silenced by her father's voice.

"I'm sorry, Inyalia. But Baal was with one of the units that disappeared." Tears fell from Kalen's eyes. Speaking about it renewed the pain inside him.

Inyalia froze. She didn't know what to do. She didn't know what to say. There was a pain deep inside her that threatened to never heal. She'd been so focused on her own troubles that she'd completely forgotten that Baal was just as involved. Forcing herself to speak, she stepped closer to her father and stared into his dripping blue eyes. "He's just missing, right? You haven't found a body?"

Stealing himself, Kalen wiped his tears and answered. "At this point, yes. He's still just missing. But the King himself has forbidden me from sending any resources beyond our borders. He's under the delusion that all of this is simply going to blow over. Like things can ever go back to how they used to be. But it's not just him. His advisor, Tycondus—," Kalen wrinkled his nose in disdain. "—he's got the council and nobles alike convinced that this is all some hoax that has nothing to do with us. They cower behind their walls, expecting the problems to simply go away. Idiots!" Kalen released a heavy sigh, shaking his head. "You have no idea how many times I've tried to make them see reason." Realizing what he was saying, he stopped himself. He wanted to bask in the sight of his daughter, not point out the shortcomings of the ruling casts. "I'm sorry, Inyalia. I shouldn't be placing my political frustrations on you. You've only just returned to find your world flipped upside down."

Inyalia forced a smile. It was the last thing she wanted to do. But her father needed it. "It's okay, dad. I understand." Taking a deep breath, she prepared herself for what was to come next. It wasn't going to be easy. In fact, it was probably the hardest thing she was ever going to have to do. But she had to do it. She had to ask. There was no way around it. Swallowing hard, Inyalia opened her mouth. One way or another, her life was about to be changed forever. "Dad—Sir." Inyalia closed her eyes. She couldn't look at him right now. It would make it too hard. "Having passed my trials and ascended to the title of Ranger, I request permission to take the status of wild elf."

Kalen froze. He hadn't expected her to make such a request. Turning his attention to Tylor, he searched for the words. "How does—Did you know about this?"

Tylor's stood shocked, his gaze shifting between Kalen and Inyalia. Why did she ask that? She knew his story. She knew what being a wild elf meant. Why would she ever ask for it? "No, Sir. This is the first I'm hearing of it. Inyalia, you are aware of what you're asking, right?"

Inyalia opened her eyes. Tears fell freely down her cheeks. "I am. And yes. I know what it means. Please understand, I don't ask because I wish to be released from my family bonds. I ask because that's the only way I can do what needs to be done. A wild elf is excused from being assigned to a unit. It means I can never marry or hold political power. Being released means I can travel south, beyond our borders, without permission of the nobles or the king. It means I can find my brother and I can bring him home."

"Inyalia, you don't have to become a wild elf to go after your brother." Kalen pleaded.

"Dad, you said it yourself. They won't let you send anyone. That means if I go, with or without your permission, they'll punish you. I can't let that happen. As a wild elf, I can serve our people without playing their game. But we can't fake it. I have to be released. It's the only way they'll believe you didn't send me."

Kalen wiped a tear from his cheek. "My child, if you desire to become a wild elf, there's nothing I can say or do to stop it. I wish you would consider another option. But if this is your desire, you have my full support. Your mother and I will always love you. But I hope you know, she's going to skin me alive when she finds out."

Inyalia cracked a smile. Throwing her arms around him, she spoke into his armor. "Thank you, daddy."

Kalen held her tight. It was likely the last time he'd have the opportunity. Once her status was filed, she would legally no longer be his daughter or heir. "I have one request."

Expecting something major, Inyalia released him, staring into his tear-soaked face.

"Provided he agree, I would ask that Tylor accompany you. He's always been loyal, and I trust him completely."

Inyalia smiled. "I'd planned to ask him anyway. That is, if he doesn't still think I'm bad for his health." Inyalia turned her attention to her only friend.

"It would be my pleasure."

"Good. Now, if you gentlemen will excuse me, I need to find a few others who are willing to break all the rules."

Tylor and Kalen watched her leave.

Waiting for the door to seal, Tylor spoke. "Don't worry, Sir. I'll take care of her."

"Thank you."

Chapter XVII
Misfits Company

Putrid odor lingered in the air. It was vaguely reminiscent of rotten apples and feces. Refuse littered the street, scattered where it had been discarded. There were broken supply crates and shattered ceramic jugs lying near the towering walls.

A careless fly landed on Inyalia's face. She swatted it instinctively, feeling its innards smear. Her nose wrinkled in disgust as she wiped it away. This was the first time she'd visited the slums. Before now, she'd never had a reason. And even if she had, her father would never have allowed it. Being here, she understood why.

These people were filthy, though not just in the way they lived. It was in the way they looked. The way they talked. Even their movements repulsed her. Everything about them told her to run. But she couldn't. She was on a mission and she wouldn't be leaving until it was complete.

Every set of eyes Inyalia met looked upon her with distain. These people had their own system. Not even the city guard held presence here. And in return, they stayed to their own, avoiding the nicer parts of the city. That in itself was cause for concern. The rangers were far from city guard, but they still held authority. That was the true enemy of people like these. It didn't matter which banner you fought for, if it stood for authority, these people had a problem with it. But if anyone was capable of both entering and leaving the slums unscathed, it was a ranger.

"You're sure she's here?" Inyalia looked to Tylor. She was relieved he'd agreed to accompany her. Having backup was a necessity in such a place. Were she alone, there was little doubt the scum that ruled these streets would have brought trouble. But there were two of them. And if there were two rangers in the open, there were usually more in the shadows. That was sure to give them a little protection if someone wanted a fight. Of course, that wasn't the case. But the thieves and low lives didn't need to know that.

"That's what they said." Tylor marched beside her, scanning the maze of alleys that intersected Bloody Lane. It was an ominous name, but well deserved. Rain didn't often fall upon Camruun City, but when it did this street ran red. Some said it was the blood of the workers who'd built this section of town. They'd disappeared before completing construction, which had left it unresolved since King Aceldon's grandfather held the throne some nine-hundred cycles ago. Though Tylor thought differently. The stone beneath his feet was of a different cut than what paved the rest of the city. And being of a different quarry, he believed it more likely to have a higher iron content. But it was a theory. There was no easy way to confirm either possibility.

Watching a rather large roach scurry into one of the many sewage drains set into the road, Inyalia shook her head. "I don't get it."

"Don't get what?"

"Why anyone would want to live this way."

Meeting the eyes locked upon them, Tylor kept pace. "Many have no other choice. They have nothing but the clothes on their back. If my time as a wild elf has taught me anything, it's the general public cares for nothing, or no one but themselves. They idolize those perceived above them. And they condemn anyone considered lesser."

Inyalia was silent. There was a pain in his voice that said more than words. He didn't have to say it. The tone said it all. He'd suffered at the hands of the people he'd pledged to protect. She felt foolish. It hadn't been that long ago that she'd had everything in her life handed to her. She was the Ranger-General's daughter. It was no wonder she'd been targeted during her trials. She was just another pampered noble who'd never had to work for anything. Realizing this, she stopped. "I'm sorry."

"For what?"

"I never considered how life was for anyone other than myself."

Tylor chuckled. She was young, but she was quick. "You don't owe me an apology."

There was a mild comfort in his words, but it still bothered her. Taking a few exaggerated steps, Inyalia caught up. "Just because I don't owe it doesn't mean I won't offer it. I've had a sheltered life. Prior to meeting you, I pretty much had everything handed to me." Playfully, she shoved him with her shoulder.

Tylor veered slightly off course, correcting almost instantly. "Just think, now that you're a wild elf, you gave it all up."

"It was the right thing to do. Not because I owe anyone anything, but because I won't allow someone else to control my actions."

"Oh, I understand. Probably more than you know. But, speaking as one who walks the path you so brazenly volunteered for, it's far from easy. You'll be met with distain by nearly everyone. Every time you walk into a room, you'll be the topic of hushed whispers. Rumors and jokes will spread like wildfire. Most of the time, they won't even bother telling them in a hushed voice." A feeble smile was all he could offer. Gesturing to their surroundings, Tylor continued. "You'll be considered little better than these people that you don't understand."

Absorbing his wisdom, Inyalia approached the wooden door they sought. Pausing outside, she turned to meet his gaze. "I appreciate the warning. But there are two benefits you haven't mentioned."

"Oh?"

"All of those people, the ones who whisper and spread gossip. They'll never know the freedom we have. And each one will underestimate what we're capable of." Unbolting the door, Inyalia pushed it open and stepped inside.

Nodding to himself, Tylor smiled and followed after her.

Inside, the pub was packed to near capacity. What had been a roar of voices and chatter moments before was now dead silence. The drop of a pin could have echoed within the cramped public house. All eyes set on the pair of newcomers. From the back of the room, someone coughed, breaking the silence. With that, most of the patrons returned to their delights, occasionally glancing toward the two rangers.

Inyalia squeezed through the gap of people. Most were kind enough to move, but many held fast, forcing her to go around. Finally, she made her way to the bar. It took a few minutes for the barkeep to approach. When he did, Inyalia was surprised by his words.

"I don't want any trouble." For an elf, he wasn't much to look at. His lip was curled on one side, and his skin was wrinkled, though he was far from old age. But it was the scar that ran across his face that really stood out. His left eye was glazed over where it had passed, and while the wound was old, it appeared to have festered.

"I—We weren't planning on causing any." She shot him a confused look.

"Don't mean trouble won't find you."

"We'll try to be quick about our business then. We're looking for a girl. Blonde hair, about this tall. Her name's Lorena." Inyalia lowered her hand.

"Can't help ya. Ya might try the brothel, two blocks down. Heard they got some new girls."

"Oh, for the love of guardians!" Tylor stepped around Inyalia and slammed a small coin purse on the bar. Retracting his hand, he glared at the barkeep, awaiting a more reasonable answer.

Lifting the purse, the barkeep tossed it a few times, staring up as if lost in thought. His tongue came out of his mouth before a wicked smile replaced it. "Upstairs, third room to the left."

"Thank you." Tylor spat, turning toward the staircase on the far side of the room.

Inyalia watched Tylor storm toward the stairs. Turning back to the barkeep, she gave an apologetic smile before rushing after Tylor. There was quite a bit she had yet to learn. Fortunately, Tylor would be around to make sure she learned the ropes. She caught up and stepped into his wake, making sure no one took a cheap shot. The last thing they needed at the moment was a pub brawl.

Reaching the top of the stairs Tylor turned left and march to the intended door. Rapping his knuckles against the sturdy wood, a resounding echo filled the narrow corridor.

A crash could be heard on the other side, followed by Lorena's voice. "Ouch. Go aray!" Even through the door, it was obvious she was slurring.

Refusing to give up so easily, Tylor knocked again.

Grunting echoed and staggering footsteps approached.

Inyalia listened to the locking mechanism. It rattled and clicked, though remained stationary. It seemed almost as if the simple device had suddenly become complex.

A moment later, the door cracked open and Lorena peered out. Her eyes were sunken and red. Her usual straight hair was unkempt and dirty. And she smelled of stale liquor.

"Wat'd ew what!" Lorena staggered against the door, using it for both balance and protection. She swayed gently, groggily attempting to bring her unwanted visitors into focus.

Inyalia stepped closer. She'd never expected to find her like this. Lorena had seemed so resilient before now. But a part of her understood.

The mage had failed her trial in the vision cave. She'd allowed that failure to control her, which led to another failure. She was a talented mage. One of the best conjurors, according to her superiors. But none of that mattered anymore. She'd quit. By resigning her station, she was no longer allowed to study at any tower. And a mage without a tower was like a ranger without an arrow. It was still possible, but much harder.

Squinting to get a better look, Lorena began to recognize the face before her. "Inallea? What doo you wa—?" Before she could complete her question, she slouched against the door and began to snore.

Tylor's arms shot out, catching her before she crashed to the floor. "She's completely wasted." Pushing the door open, he carried her to the bed.

"Not completely. It could have happened to any of us. She just needs to regain her confidence." Inyalia followed them into the room, closing the door behind her.

"No, I mean, she's drunk. Three sheets to the wind, sloshed."

"Oh!" Inyalia chuckled, her cheeks flushing at her ignorance. She'd never been drunk before. "Well, I stand by all the stuff I said. Maybe by helping us, we can help her. Besides, I don't think there's anyone else who would be willing to help us."

Tylor sniffed one of the open bottles lying on the table. The fumes burned his nose. "I know of a few who might."

"Do they have her abilities?"

"No. But it wouldn't hurt to ask them anyway. We don't know what we're going to find. And having a few more sets of eyes can't hurt. Besides, we don't know she'll even agree to help."

"She'll help." Inyalia insisted.

"I hope you're right."

"No!"

"What do you mean, no?"

"N—O, no!"

Inyalia sighed. "Why not?"

"Because I said." Lorena insisted, pinching the bridge of her nose. Her head throbbed and she really didn't want to be having this conversation.

"That's not a real reason."

"It's good enough."

"I beg to differ."

Shaking her head, Lorena glared at the young ranger. "What do you want from me? I helped you get to the halls. That was our agreement. Any truce we had has since expired. I no longer need you. And you no longer need me. Just—Go away. Let me drown in my misery."

Tylor pulled the door open and stepped into the hallway. "Come on, Inyalia. We've wasted enough time here. We need to go meet the others."

Slowly, Inyalia picked herself up. She paused, reaching the threshold. Turning back, she looked upon the fallen mage with pity. "You know, I believe you have what it takes to move mountains. But it doesn't matter what I believe. If you don't believe in yourself, you'll never move a damn thing. But you're wrong. I still need you. And whether you're willing to admit it or not, you still need me. If you can find the courage to pull yourself out of this gutter, you'll find me at the Broken Arrow Inn. But if it takes you longer than two days, don't bother. We won't be there." Inyalia closed the door behind her and rushed to catch up with Tylor.

A conniving smile resonated over his hand of cards. Sliding a few coins toward the pot at the center of the table, Tylor awaited his opponents.

Vansin had never been accused of being overly intelligent. But he knew when to fold. "I'm out." Laying his cards face up, a pair of peasants, the lord of elves, the prince of thieves, and the bear squire stared at the others.

Tylor, Inyalia, and the fourth sitting at the table, a royal named Gilea, quickly scanned the revealed cards. Silently, they calculated what remained unaccounted for.

"Too rich for my blood." Gilea smiled at the intended pun. He was the King's third cousin, and had no problem reminding everyone of that fact. Tossing his cards so the others could see, he waited in anticipation, wondering which of them was going to take the pot. It hadn't grown to excessive amounts, but it was sitting just over a month of soldier's pay.

Inyalia inspected the cards. Gilea had had a pair of kings, a pair of knights, and a squire of swords. Not a bad hand, but it couldn't beat hers. Raising an eyebrow to Tylor, she studied his face for a moment. He wore a wicked smirk, suggesting he had something worth holding. But she'd spent enough time around him to know when he wasn't completely certain. And there weren't many hands more certain than the one she held. Stealing a quick glance of her cards, she forcefully held a straight face and slid another gold piece to the center of the table. "Call!"

Tylor smiled at her. "A royal family." One by one, he dropped his cards atop the pile of coin. "King of Elves. Queen of Swords. Prince of Swords. Lord of Bears. And Lady of Thieves. Read it and weep!" Reaching out, he scooped the pile, pulling his winnings toward him.

"Not so fast!" Inyalia smiled wide. His flush was impressive, but being of different suits, it didn't beat her hand. Laying them together, she displayed a Royal Assassination.

Tylor stared blankly at the pile of assassins surrounding the king of swords. He shook his head in defeat. "How the hell do you keep winning?"

Inyalia drug the coins toward her, tossing the cards into the center for the next deal. "My father taught me. We used to play almost every night."

"I should have guessed. It appears we've been hustled, boys." Tylor took a sip of his drink, watching their last companion step through the tavern door. "Raemus is here."

The others turned to look. The newcomer was dressed in ranger armor and carried a quarterstaff in addition to his satchel and pack. Making his way through the crowd of soldiers, rangers, and sailors, he was met with condescending glares.

Inyalia turned to Tylor. "I understand now."

"What's that?"

"I understand why someone of his skill would agree to help us."

"No, you don't." Tylor assured her.

"How so? Half elves are considered lower than wild elves. What else could it be?"

Vansin leaned in, joining their conversation. "That one doesn't care about title or blood." Chuckling to himself, he took a long draw of his tankard before continuing. "He once punched a Commander in the nose. Funniest thing I ever saw. They tried to throw insubordination charges at him. Didn't do any good. Army has no authority over Rangers. But even if it did, the half-blood's too valuable to swing from a rope."

Inyalia arched an eyebrow in question.

Taking pity on her, Tylor leaned close so only she could hear. "He has a bit of a complex. He doesn't know when to walk away. But that's a good thing if you need him. He's taken arrows and sword slashes trying to get to someone."

"I heard rumor that he once got hit by a catapult's shot." Vansin added.

"I'm not sure that's true. But once he sets his mind to something, he'll do everything within his power to make sure it happens." Getting to his feet, Tylor extended his hand to the half elf.

Raemus shook it gently. "Thanks for the invitation." Looking over the table of outcasts, he gave a respectful bow. "Sorry I'm late. Had to correct a Captain who thought I was his property." Standing to his full height, he continued. "Anyway, if you'll still have me, I'm ready to go when you are."

Turning to address the table, Tylor looked from one to another. "I guess this is everybody. You all know where we're headed. And you know we don't know what to expect when we get there. If you've had second thoughts, now's the time to speak up. We won't hold it against you."

"I will!" Vansin laughed. "If you can't trust them to stand and fight, you can't trust them at all."

"Okay, so, the rest of us won't hold it against you."

The others laughed.

Gesturing toward the door, Tylor looked to Inyalia. "Let's move out."

Together, they got to their feet and gathered their effects. Shuffling toward the door, Inyalia kept watch for Lorena, hoping she'd make the right choice. They passed through the opening and into the street.

The rolling clouds left a continual shadow over the city. Already, the guards were lighting the lamp posts for the coming dark. Most of the commotion in the Military District had died down. The bulk of the army was posted along the outer west wall. It was the most likely place of attack, being nearest the port. The navy's fleets were docked between Camruun City and Largar'Thor, protecting the entire coastline. If anyone wanted a fight, they were going to be in for a rude awakening. All that was left was the Rangers. They were posted throughout Trendensil. Any attack by land was sure to be reported and prepared for days in advance.

Making their way through the street, Inyalia took position next to Tylor. This was her expedition. There was no question of that. But he knew the others. And he had combat experience. She couldn't think of anyone better to serve as the unit commander.

Reaching the archway that separated the Military District from the crafts square, the band of misfits stepped onto the golden road. It wouldn't be much longer before the city would be far behind them. If everything went according to plan, they'd defy the king's orders, be labeled traitors, find and rescue some elves, and likely be exiled from their homes forever. Or it could all fall apart, and they'd walk into an ambush, only to join the ever-growing list of casualties. Either way, it was going to be the adventure of a lifetime.

"Inyalia!"

Stopping, Inyalia turned to see Lorena running toward them. She wore clean robes, and had a pack strapped to her shoulder. "I'm glad to see your head's been removed from your ass."

"I deserve that. I'm sorry. If I'm not too late, I'd like to help."

Inyalia smiled and clapped they young mage on her shoulder. "I'm happy to have you. I don't suppose you'd be willing to expedite our exodus, would you?"

Reaching into her satchel, Lorena grabbed a handful of spell components and began gathering the energies required to open a portal. "Where would you like to go?"

"As far south as you can take us."

Levi Samuel

Chapter XVIII
Storming the Keep

The air crackled with energy, collected in a single vertical line of orange light. It grew intense and began to spread wide, opening a doorway through space.

Inyalia stepped through, inspecting the overgrown field around her. Where it had once been green and luscious, the stalks were now wilting and brown. Just ahead, there appeared to be a road where the grass refused to grow. To her right, a forest of leafless trees stretched on as far as the eye could see, their limbs twisted and menacing. Beyond it, tall hills shot into the sky. They weren't nearly as tall as the mountains to the left, but traveling them would be no easy chore. Hearing the others step through behind her, Inyalia turned to greet them.

"What a charming place you've brought us. I can't wait to write home about it." Gilea glanced around, clearly unimpressed with their surroundings.

"Patience, Gilea. I doubt this is where our journey ends." Tylor took a defensive position a few steps ahead of the group, trying to identify their location. It looked vaguely familiar, but different.

The portal closed behind Lorena. Spotting the road, she trekked through the waist high grass, signaling the others to follow. "We're on the southern road. This intersection will take us to Risolde. The road over there leads to Icefall Pass."

Tylor could see it now. He'd traveled the Icefall Pass only a few times, always by caravan. But he'd never taken the time to study the roads leading out of the kingdom. Turning his attention to Inyalia, he gestured to the intersection. "Which way do you want to go?"

A rhythmic echo carried the sound of marching boots on the wind. Listening intently, it wasn't the uniform beat of an elven detachment. This was different, heavy and somewhat disorganized. Whoever it belonged to, they didn't march in step. Instead, it was the number of boots that created the familiar, yet unknown beat.

Tylor turned to Vansin. "Who would be in this area with any kind of force?"

Shaking his head, the warrior listened for any discernable identifiers. Every army had a distinct way of doing things. Often times they could be recognized simply by the way their boots hit the ground. Vansin had traveled all over Irayth. He'd met armies most had never heard of. Each of them had their own unique methods, usually a result of their physiology. The shorter races often took small strides, which sounded more like scurrying to the untrained ear. Humans were a difficult lot to identify, as they marched in nearly every way possible. But it was typically dependent on where they were trained. Their physical size kept them from being too out of the ordinary, but some kicked the ground when they stepped. Some hiked their knees, and others were stiff from head to toe. It seemed the humans used marching as a formal way of expression, rather than a means of unit travel. They were certainly an odd sort. But it was the larger races that these echoing steps belonged to. Focusing, Vansin isolated the individual beats. The collected whole made it hard to tell them apart, especially since they weren't in unison. He could hear their feet slap the ground with each step. That denoted a heavy bulk. And there were many of them. But it wasn't the steps that told him who the newcomers were. It was the disorganization that had ultimately done that. He simply had to identify the other factors first. "We need to take cover. They'll crest the hill in a moment."

"Who?"

"Orcs!"

The group reached the trees just as the band of brutes came into view. Settling into position, where they could see without being seen, they watched the orcs approach the intersection and turn toward Risolde.

Inyalia counted right at thirty strong. She'd never seen an orc before. They were certainly an ugly bunch. The shortest of them towered over the tallest elf. If she had to guess they were at least seven foot tall, some even taller than that. But it was their bulk that concerned her. It couldn't be compared to an elf. If anything, they were stocky like the dwarves, but even that was a pale comparison. These beasts were solid muscle, wrapped beneath heavy metal armors, and carrying large, vicious looking weapons. Their swords were jagged along the spine and handguard. The lower portion of the blade was serrated, while the upper part was curved and razor sharp. The tip was also unlike any she'd seen before. It had been sharpened, making it ideal for stabbing, but it was shaped more like a rock pick, suggesting massive amounts of damage on a backhand swing. There seemed to be two variants of the weapon. Most carried a single hand, comparable in size to a short sword. But there was one, the largest among them, whose sword was easily heavier than two fully grown elves.

Inyalia gulped, watching the deadly instrument pass. She was frightened. These were the scariest creatures she'd ever seen. Even Alona's attack hadn't frightened her as much. But it wasn't the thick armors, nor the jagged weapons that did the trick. It was their eyes. They marched with complete focus, their vision locked to the back of the orc ahead of them. Not a one searched the grass or looked toward the distance. It was as if they were of single mind, moving toward their destination with no other thought or concern. It was those dark eyes, set in a field of rough and scarred gray skin that told her these things enjoyed killing. If these were the creatures responsible for Baal's disappearance, how could anyone stand against them?

"Do you think they're what's been attacking us?" Gilea asked, watching from behind a wide tree trunk. His elegant armor was nearly invisible, adopting the appearance of the bark. Though the enchanted material did little to hide his head or sword.

"Hard to say. I don't know much about them. But their presence is questionable at best. We should follow to find out." Tylor gave the signal, forgetting that not all of them were rangers. Breaking from his position, he skirted the forest's edge, keeping the band within sight.

They moved through the trees at a slow pace. It didn't take much to keep up. These orcs weren't overly fast. But they seemed to march with an endurance difficult to match. Reaching the foothills, they had to move further from the road. It was the only way to continue following without being in the open. Though keeping sight on the orc patrol was of little importance now. Risolde was obviously their destination. Nothing else rested along this road. And anything beyond would have been more accessible from other routes, not that there was much beyond other than a few small villages. The tail of the Icefall Mountains extended nearly to the coast, making this chunk of land less than desirable to nearly everyone. Even Risolde itself would have settled elsewhere were it not for the mage college the city had been built around. Using magic as a primary means of transportation meant they could operate without direct access to the trade routes, while maintaining the defense the mountains offered.

Climbing the foothills, Inyalia stayed to Tylor's flank. It wasn't nearly as difficult as she remembered from their previous trek. But these were far from the mountains that rested less than a mile to the east. Reaching the top, she watched the others spread out and take position.

Raemus laid on his belly, squinting through a sight glass. He appeared to be a half-blood of few words. Inyalia only hoped his reputation was one well deserved. Not many had his abilities, and if they had to fight these orcs, they were certainly going to be needed.

Lorena lingered near the edge of the path they'd climbed. She panted heavily, wiping the sweat from her brow. It seemed the short climb had affected her most of all. But she'd also spent quite a bit of time drinking her sorrows away in recent past. That was bound to weigh on anyone. At least until it was completely purged from her system.

Tylor knelt beside Vansin. They passed a sight glass back and forth, inspecting the city far beneath them.

"I count twelve along the front entrance. And—our patrol just went inside." Vansin handed the glass back to Tylor.

"Thirteen. You missed the one standing in the gatehouse."

"What? Let me see that!"

Tylor handed it back, studying what details he could without it. "Inyalia, you're going to want to see this." He twisted, finding her not far behind him.

"Oh, I see him now. You'd think for being so big, he wouldn't be so well hidden." Vansin handed the glass back to him, expecting the girl to be the next one to use it.

Inyalia couldn't help but feel that Tylor and Vansin had known each other for quite some time. They were obviously friends of some caliber. That was a good thing. She assumed she was his only friend, which while happy to be such, she wanted Tylor to have more in life than just her. Approaching the pair, she crouched beside him. Accepting the sight glass, Inyalia brought it to her eye, squinting through the dense, transparent stone. Her vision was blurry around the edges, but the places she could see were much closer. She scanned the city walls, counting several of the creatures along both sides and the front. There was no need for a wall along the east. The mountains served that purpose.

Working her way toward the city center, she was shocked at how filthy the city was. Debris littered the streets in all directions, most of it cloth. Many of the doors were wide open or busted in. The buildings looked to be of human construction, but that was more of a guess than anything. Aside from the few times she'd been to Ryse, Inyalia hadn't seen many human buildings.

There were far more orcs than she'd imagined possible. Where had they all come from? And more importantly, what were they doing here? Inyalia's vision fell on a mass piled in the city's center. It took a moment to recognize it for what it was, but when she did, she had to look away. "Are those—bodies?" She felt sick.

"Yes. Hundreds of them."

"Did you see the spikes just south of the gate?" Vansin asked.

Taking a deep breath, Inyalia brought the sight glass back to her eye. Locking in on the area the warrior had specified, she noticed the three large wooden poles sticking from the ground. A platform had been erected behind them. But it was what remained beneath that drew her attention. Three sets of ranger armor hung loose around what had at one time been elven bodies. All that remained of them now was shrunken skin, wrapped around bone. Their arms were shackled around the large poles, keeping them trapped. But it was the shorter spikes that ultimately killed them. Each ranger remained impaled, the spikes having entered their rear and exited between their shoulders and head. Inyalia knew what she was looking at. You didn't execute rangers and leave them on display without sending a message. Handing the sight glass back to Tylor, she looked away from the gruesome scene.

Weighing in on the conversation, Raemus spoke from his own viewing point. "Are you seeing what's happening at the top of the school?"

Tylor sighted in. Finding the half-elf's interest, a sudden gasp escaped him. "They're executing people in troves."

Inyalia ripped the glass from his hands and returned it to her eye, searching fervently. She had to find Baal. Locating the college, she found the place Raemus had mentioned. Elves and humans alike stood in two massive lines that disappeared behind one of the archer turrets. They were beaten and weak. Most appeared starved. Their clothes were filthy and tattered, stripped of all but the essentials. But what Inyalia found most odd, none of them were bound. They calmly walked to their deaths, seeming unbothered by it. Inyalia didn't want to see any more death, but she couldn't look away without seeing the executioner. The rangers outside had died a most grotesque and horrible death. She hoped these were at least quick and painless.

Two sets of gallows had been erected from repurposed wood. Five bodies dangled from each one. That seemed to be the main method used. But occasionally, one of the prisoners was pulled out of line and walked to a chopping block between the hanging decks. The swift fall of an orcish sword ensured the head rolled away clean.

Inyalia felt the bile rise in her stomach. Unable to contain herself, it expelled from her, splattering before her.

Gilea erupted in applause, smiling and laughing. It wasn't every day he saw a greenhorn spill her guts at the sight of her first real world experience. "Charming! Absolutely marvelous! I can't tell you how honored I am to be traveling with one of such—fortitude, such— resilience. Truly! The bards will sing tale of your—."

"Gilea, drop it!" Tylor snapped, pulling Inyalia's hair into a tail to keep it from dangling into the mess. Helping her up, he stared deep into her eyes. "Are you all right?"

Inyalia wiped the vomit from her mouth and took a deep breath. "I will be. I'm sorry. I didn't mean—."

Tylor cut her off, pulling her close to him. Hugging her, he felt a comfort he hadn't felt in so long. "It's okay, Inyalia. If any one of these guys claims to have reacted any differently their first time, I'd say they're a damned liar." His gaze burned on Gilea's persistent smirk, daring him to argue.

Pulling away, Inyalia stared up at Tylor. She loved being in his arms, but there were more important things she had to do. "They're killing all of them. We need to free them. Before it's too late." Her head nodded in reassurance. It was the only option, the only way she was going to find her brother before he ended up in the line.

"No. We need to report our findings and come back in force." Tylor rebutted.

"We don't have time for that. With the rate they're executing them, everyone will be dead long before we can return. Not to mention, the nobles have banned anyone from crossing the border. If we return, we'll have to answer for that, which will delay us even longer. And who's to say they'll let us come with an army, if they let us return at all?"

"The kid's got a point." Raemus admitted, picking himself up. "You know how the nobles are. They'd just assume pretend everything's fine, opposed to actually doing anything about it."

"I know this is hard, but we don't have the manpower." Tylor pleaded, hoping for once, Inyalia would actually listen to him.

"We'll have to sneak in."

"And if we're discovered?"

"I'll find Baal and get out before we are."

"Inyalia, look at the facts. You said it yourself, with the rate they're killing people—," Tylor paused, trying to find the proper words. "He's been missing for a while. I'm sorry, but if he was here, he's already dead."

"No! He's in there. And I'm going to find him and get him out!" Inyalia realized she was shouting. Quieting herself, she turned toward the path. "You can come with me, or not. Either way, I'm going to find my brother." Refusing to debate it a moment longer, Inyalia made her way down the path, and disappeared between the hills.

Tylor stood, dumbfounded. Going in was suicide. How was that not obvious? Shaking his head, he watched Lorena follow after her.

"You know my stance on the matter. Those people need our help." Raemus walked past him, falling in behind Lorena.

"It was only a matter of time. Someone always has to make the stupid decisions." Gilea gestured toward the city.

"Shut up." Tylor sighed, drawing the sight glass to watch her progress. He couldn't let her go alone. But it was stupid to go in blind. "Gilea, how good's your aim?"

"You want me to put you out of your misery? I'm sure I can manage that."

"Vansin, you're better at close range. Can Gilea use your crossbow to cover us from here?"

The warrior picked himself up, unslinging the wooden device. Handing it to the wayward royal, Vansin pulled his hip quiver free. "The pointy end goes that way."

Smiling, Gilea loaded the weapon and tested the sights on a small tree. "Aim's a bit off. Pulls about three inches left, and one inch high. But I think I can manage."

Tylor and Vansin made their way down the hills, hoping to catch the others before they found trouble.

Inyalia stopped at the edge of the road. From here, she could see the gate, and the deceased rangers just past it. Taking a deep breath, she waited for the orcs patrolling the top of the wall to turn away from her. It wasn't long. Inyalia did one final check before stepping out. She had roughly fourteen seconds to find cover before they found her. Wasting no time, she scurried across the road and took position against the base of the stone wall. Silently counting down, she moved in the shadows, working her way toward the mountains. It would be a difficult climb, but she could see a path that looked just wide enough to get her over the wall. Nearly out of time, Inyalia ran for the rocks. That was her only chance. If she didn't make it, this would be over before it even began.

Movement caught her attention to the right. Midjump, Inyalia saw an orc step into sight. He'd been on ground, near the rear of the wall and out of view. How could she have been so foolish? But it was too late now. He'd seen her. Her only chance was to silence him before he could raise alarm. Inyalia reached for her bow. Twisting her wrist, she grabbed an arrow and had it nocked. But she wasn't in position to fire.

The orc raised his horn to his lips. Before he could give blow through it, a thud echoed in his mind and his body became unresponsive.

Inyalia landed, her bow drawn, ready to fire. She watched the orc topple over, a slender bolt protruding from his skull. It seemed the others were looking out. She wanted to offer thanks, but how could she without drawing attention. Giving a subtle salute to her unseen protector, she scanned the rocky terrain, pleased to find a better way into the city.

The air shimmered and Lorena came into view beside the young ranger. "I was just about to blast him when he fell over." Lorena gestured to the dead orc.

"As was I. I'm glad someone up there is keeping watch. I didn't see him until it was too late."

Raemus stepped from the shadows, joining the women. "Perhaps we should continue this conversation elsewhere? The orcs just cycled. They're going to be right above our heads in about three minutes."

Inyalia pointed where the city wall and the base of the mountain connected. A deep ravine had been mined out, allowing water to flow away from the city. The ravine would hide them easy enough. But it was the iron grate that had her attention. A grate meant sewers. And sewers meant a way into the city. "Down there should work."

"That it will." Raemus climbed into the ravine.

Tylor and Vansin skirted the wall, seeing the others drop into a ditch. Noting the dead orc, they took position on either side of the large creature. He weighed a ton. Heaving against the mass, they half carried, half drug him toward the ravine their companions had disappeared into. From here, they saw them at the entrance to the sewers.

"Clear." Tylor announced, as loud as he dared. He and Vansin rolled the orc into the ravine, where he wouldn't be noticed by the wandering guards atop the wall.

Carefully, the pair climbed down.

"I'm glad you decided to join us." Inyalia smiled at Tylor.

"Just don't make me regret it."

"I'll do my best."

A click echoed, and Raemus pulled the grate open, revealing moss covered brick on the back side. Laying it on the floor, he waited for the others to crawl inside.

It wasn't over large. In fact, there was no way one of the orcs could have fit. But an elf had a little room to move. Inyalia squirmed side to side, working her way deeper into the tube. She was glad there wasn't a whole lot of water. But the little that remained was cold and rancid. The ceiling rose slightly, allowing her to get to her hands and knees. It wasn't pleasant, but it was better. As far as she could tell, the walls were about twenty feet thick. She had to be pretty close to that by now. Sure enough, just ahead, the sewers opened wide, granting enough height to stand with ease.

Picking herself up, Inyalia looked around. Numerous iron ports in the ceiling displayed what was left of the daylight, though the constant cloud cover kept it mild at best. It wasn't much, but it was enough. Approaching the first one, Inyalia peeked through the holes, stealing a glance of the city streets. Due to the angle, her view was somewhat limited, but she could tell they were just inside the wall. She could see the back of an orc, standing not far from the drain. They'd have to be quiet. Sound was certain to travel down here, and anyone standing near one of the ports was bound to hear them.

Tylor stopped beside her. Glancing up, he signed in Ranger's Speak.

Inyalia nodded and returned sign. *Not here. Enemies present. Find new location. Go there.*

Tylor nodded. Taking lead, he marched down the corridor, occasionally scratching the sidewall with his dagger. He didn't know how big this place was, but knowing the way out was crucial to their survival.

They walked for nearly an hour, inspecting each grate they came to. Some had iron spikes driven into the wall, which made looking out much easier. But most didn't offer such luxury. The sunlight was rapidly fading, allowing even less through the vent holes. If they didn't find their query soon, it would be too dark to do so. They'd have to spend the night here and try again in the morning. It was simply too dangerous to combat an unknown enemy when they knew next to nothing about them.

Lorena approached the next port. Pausing, she tested the limits of her magic around it. This one was different. Smiling, she waved Inyalia and Tylor over. "This one radiates magic. I'm willing to bet its right outside the college."

"Why do you say that? Inyalia spoke in a whisper.

"Same reason the doors to a tower are guarded. If someone goes in or out, the proper authorities want to know about it. This being a college, can you think of a better escape than through the sewers?"

Inyalia thought for a moment. She was guilty of her own mischief on occasion. Sneaking out of a magic school seemed pretty difficult. But she wasn't a mage. If she was, such a thing was probably the equivalent of locking a door. It didn't make it impossible to bypass, just a bit more complex. "Can you get through it?"

A soft glow emitted from Lorena's hands. It didn't produce much light, which was good. Nothing said *here we are* like a glowing beacon. Carefully, she probed the area around the grate. Each time her hand made contact, the glow jumped, displaying a complex series of markings and sigils. They disappeared nearly as quick. Touching two places at the same time, Lorena drug her hands toward the center. She appeared to be struggling with some unseen force. Her fists clenched, she pulled them together, locking a single hand around the hidden barrier. Using her free hand, she shoved it to the sky and twisted.

The sigils came into view, flashing for the briefest moment. And then they were gone.

"The lock has been disabled. But I can reset it if I have to."

Inyalia looked for the iron spikes, but it seemed this one didn't have them.

Tylor crouched and interlocked his fingers.

Inyalia stepped into his hand, balancing herself against his shoulder. Standing, she peeked through the grate, pleased to see it was relatively unguarded. There were two orcs across the street, but they were facing the other direction. Holding the iron device, she signaled Tylor to turn around. She needed to make sure they were clear all directions before heading up.

Tylor waddled around, giving her a full turn.

Inyalia signaled and jumped down. "It's clear. Only guards are the two we saw four grates ago. But they're facing the other way. Lorena was right. We're right in front of the college."

"All right. This is where we're going up. We need to be quick. Once we get inside, if we encounter any orcs, take them out as silent and as fast as you can. We can't afford to let them alert the others." Seeing their understanding, Tylor reached up and lifted the grate. It came free with relative ease. Carefully, he slid it to the side and stepped aside, locking his fingers once again.

Inyalia stepped up and jumped through the hole. Pulling herself up, she rolled and took a defensive position, watching for any orcs. She had two arrows nocked and aimed. It was a complex shot, but not difficult. She'd been training herself to fire multiple arrows since she was seven. So far, she could fire three, two of which hit with complete accuracy. The third usually hit, but it was about a foot off target. With a little more practice, she had no doubt she could work her way to five at once. But that was some time off.

Lorena appeared through the hole, landing flat-footed on the street. No sooner than her feet connected, she moved into the shadow under the college's portico. Summoning her energies, she attempted to cloak herself. The spell didn't work. Moving toward Inyalia, she leaned forward and whispered in her ear. "We have a bit of a problem. My magic isn't working here."

"Why not?"

Lorena pointed to the college. "Warded." Falling back, she returned to her shadow and began working on the entrance. To her surprise, it wasn't locked.

Raemus climbed through the hole. Getting to his feet, he scanned the area. Nothing required his immediate attention. Content, he approached the college, falling in with the mage.

There was a bit of a delay, but Vansin was the next to appear. Rolling, he stuck the top half of his body back in, locking his legs around the hole. With minimal effort, he pulled himself up, Tylor in tow.

Once everyone was inside the college, Inyalia lowered her bow and followed after them.

Chapter XIX
Trading Lives

The door clicked shut, banishing the sliver of light that lit the dank corridor. A musky odor hung in the air, made tolerable only by the scent of lamp oil.

"Lorena, would you mind providing us some light?" Tylor took the lead, searching his way in the darkness. When the door was open, he could see openings to each side, and a grand staircase somewhere in the distance. But now, it was little more than a guess as to which opening led where.

"I can try. The last spell wouldn't work. I believe the college is dampening my ability somehow."

"A magic school dampening magic ability? That seems a bit silly." Raemus stated casually, feeling the edge of a doorway. Carefully, he made his way past, staying with the group.

"It's only silly out of context. A training mage isn't always in control of their abilities. Or, an exceptionally talented mage may try to show off. In the tower, there were entire wings that prohibited casting of any kind. They used them to level the playing field. If none stood above the others, they could be taught together. At least that's the line they fed us. Whether it's true or not, I have no idea." Lorena concentrated on a simple light spell. She didn't want something so large as to betray their position, but the ability to see was crucial to their survival. Sparks flickered in the palm of her hand, glowing for the briefest heartbeat before dying. She tried again to the same result. "I'm sorry, but it's simply not working."

"It's okay. I saw a few sconces mounted on the walls. I'll bet we can simply relight one." Tylor reached high, feeling around for the metal devices he'd seen upon entry. Finding one, he ran his fingers along the side, until he found the bowl. Carefully, he lifted it and brought it down.

"I've got one." Feeling for the oil inside, he set it on the floor, careful to keep it from spilling. A quick swipe with the flat of his dagger sent sparks of flint arcing down. It took a few tries, but the oil flared to life. Sight returned, he grabbed the base and carefully returned it to its mount.

Peering into one of the side rooms, Vansin closed the door. "Nothing interesting here. Not much but overturned furniture and rubble."

"Same over here." Raemus announced.

Tylor moved toward the main room, glancing up the stairs at its head. From here, he could see the balconies of at least six levels. It appeared as if each one expanded all directions, centered on this central chamber.

Tormented screams echoed from one of the upper levels, silencing all else.

Inyalia skirted the side of the room, ignoring the adjoining hallways. Stepping onto the stairs, she started up.

"Inyalia, we need to stay together." Tylor rushed across the room to keep from shouting.

"We aren't going to find anything down here. Baal will be with the prisoners." She rushed up the steps two at a time.

Sighing, Tylor signaled the others.

Scouting their surroundings as best they could, they ascended level by level, searching for the source. Another scream echoed, seeming right on top of them.

Inyalia froze, her arrow aimed, but not drawn. "It came from this way." She started down a hall on the fifth floor. Minimal light filtered into the hallway from a few of the open doors before them. Inyalia moved along the left wall, scanning the distance for any perceived threat.

Taking position opposite her, Tylor approached the first door on the right. Peeking around, he squeezed the grip of his daggers, expecting to quench their thirst at any moment. "Clear." Stepping past, he mirrored Inyalia.

Lorena trailed on the left, followed closely by Raemus. She wasn't sure how she could help. A mage was only as useful as her magic. No! that wasn't right. Which rule was that? Recalling her training, Lorena silently recited the Rules of Wizardry. There were ten of them, each taught as short quips. Some were pretty logical, while others were little more than turn of phrase, but she'd been required to memorize each and every one. There were two which applied to her current situation. Rule one, magic isn't always the answer. And rule ten, sometimes the greatest magic is no magic at all. Neither answered her question, but it did make her think of rule five. When something seems impossible, try looking from another angle. Aside from her dagger, hidden beneath her robes, she was unarmed. But she had an archer in front of her, some guy with a staff behind her, Tylor to her right, and as best she could tell, a walking meat-shield just behind him. She was plenty protected. She simply had to wait for the right moment, or somehow find a way to break the antimagic field.

Hearing the screams, Inyalia through her arm up, signaling the stop. Cautiously, she peeked around the corner seeing two orcs standing in the room. She couldn't make out much detail, but someone was strapped to a table, flailing as best the bindings would allow. Signaling Tylor in Ranger Speak, she prepared herself.

Tylor nodded his agreement and started the countdown. Balling his fist, he lunged across the hall and flung his dagger.

Inyalia leapt across the opening, releasing her bow string. Her arrow embedded itself at the base of the orc's skull just as Tylor's dagger found its mark on the other. Rushing into the room, she made sure no others were present.

The elf strapped to the table squirmed, uncertain as to what was happening.

Raemus rushed forward to inspect him. He'd suffered some muscle damage in his legs, and a few broken ribs from where the bindings had been tightened, but overall, he was in fair shape. "Calm yourself. We're going to get you out of here." Laying his hand atop the subdued elf's chest, he focused his power. A gentle glow radiated and sank into the elf.

He fell back, his struggle abandoned for the moment.

Vansin knelt to inspect the dead creatures. There wasn't much to do about them. Their armors were too large for anything but reforged steel, though the weapons were interesting. Vansin grabbed the short blade, which was nearly a longsword by comparison. It was heavy, but that just meant he needed to train with it. Strapping it to his pack, he searched for anything of value.

Raemus went to work unbuckling the straps, starting with those around his chest. No sooner than they were free, he heard the bones snap into place.

The elf's back arched in pain, but he fell still once again.

Ensuring the mended bones had set properly, Raemus addressed Tylor. "We need to get him out of here. I don't think he has the strength to continue with us."

Leaning over the suddenly calm elf, Inyalia stared into his eyes. "Where are they keeping the other prisoners?"

Weakly lifting his arm, the elf pointed the direction they were headed. "They keep the—" He winced as another pop echoed inside his chest, forming tears in his eyes. "I don't know where they keep all of them. But there are two rooms that way, right across from each other."

"Thank you." Inyalia glanced around the room. Lorena, since you're limited at the moment, would you mind staying with him until we get back?"

"I can do that. Maybe it'll give me time to explore the wards and possibly break them."

"Do what you can." Directing the group as a whole, Inyalia spoke louder than intended. "The rest of us will clear the prison rooms and send everyone here."

The wounded elf sat up. His ribs were clearly visible beneath his skin. How long had it been since he'd last eaten? "Be careful of the blackguard."

"Blackguard? What's that?" Vansin asked, standing. The dead orcs didn't have anything else he cared about. But he'd severed their heads for good measure.

"It's one of the bigger creatures. Their commander. He has this way of twisting what's in your head. That's how they captured us. I was home, asleep in my bed. Next thing I knew, we were locked up. It took a while to fill in the gaps, but quick flashes started happening about a week ago. They're doing some kind of experiments on us. Most break before they get their results. But once the blackguard comes, you don't return to the cells. You move to another room, or you go outside."

"Why were you here? Was the blackguard coming for you?" Tylor asked, curious as to what kind of trouble they'd found themselves in.

"I don't know. I couldn't understand what they were saying. They brought me here after I got caught sharing my rations with one of the others. They just strapped me down right before you came. I don't know what they were planning to do to me."

"All right. Lorena, you stay with him and see what you can do about the wards. Inyalia and I will scout ahead. Raemus, you stick to the back.

Can't have you getting hurt. And Vansin, do your thing if we encounter more than we can handle on the jump." Tylor turned and made his way out the door. He wasn't thrilled with going head on against the orcs, but they'd already gotten involved. There was no way they could leave the prisoners behind now. He only wished he knew more about these orcs. Especially the one they called Blackguard.

Inyalia made her way down the hall, silent as could be. The floors were covered in carpet, which helped tremendously. Scanning each room as she passed, she was starting to hear sounds of life. Coughing, crying, whispers, and a guttural tongue she did not recognize. Moving closer to the sounds, she signaled Tylor. He seemed to be hearing the same things.

Stepping into a shadow, Tylor readied his daggers. The door was closed, but he was certain there were at least three of the brutish creatures on the other side. Glancing at Inyalia, he was pleased to see she was ready. But it was not the time to act. They needed to alert the others first. Signaling for her to hold, he turned and crept back down the hall to where Vansin and Raemus waited. "We've found the rooms. Both doors are closed. I fear it'll be too loud to hit one at a time, so we'll need to do both together. Inyalia and I will take the left. You two take the right."

"Got it." Vansin smiled wide. His knuckles popped against the grip of his morningstar. Readying his shield, he followed Tylor to Inyalia.

Moving just past the door, Raemus prepared his quarterstaff and nodded to Vansin.

Signaling the count, Tylor threw the door open and rushed inside

Inyalia spun around the door frame, firing off three arrows in the blink of an eye. Each one sailed harmlessly past Tylor. Two of the three found their mark. The first sank into one of the brute's eye sockets. The second entered the mouth of another and exited its skull. And the third arrow hit its target, but proved ineffective. Inyalia watched her arrow, aimed straight for the final creature's mouth. Were it any other beast, she had no doubt it would have been a killing shot. As it were, the razored head was no match for its dense tusks. It struck with near perfect precision, breaking the thick ivory. But it was just enough shock to send the bolt ricocheting into the wall.

Tylor was upon the third orc before the broken tusk hit the ground. Leaping atop the creature, he drove his dwarven dagger into its neck. His second blade slipped between the buckles of its armor. Tylor twisted the blade and retracted, rolling just before the dying beast hit the ground.

Picking himself up, he watched the final moments of its life as the dark blood pooled beneath it.

In the other room, Raemus busted through the door, his staff ready to strike. He was surprised to find the room empty, save for one elf and one human. The pair sat idle in the center. Their eyes closed as if in meditation. He studied them for a moment, watching their chests expand and retract. They were clearly alive, though in some kind of trance. The commotion they'd caused would have warranted the attention of the most devoted monk. Yet these two remained unphased.

Vansin was right behind him, his morningstar raised. "What's going on here?" He lowered his weapon, searching the room for anything of interest. Seeing nothing, a look of disappointment settled upon his face.

"Clear." Tylor announced from across the hall.

Vansin sighed deeply and turned, peering at the fallen bodies. "All clear here." Shaking his head, he slung his shield and sauntered to the other side. Leaning against the doorframe, he watched Tylor cleaning his blades. "You told me I'd get some action. Thus far all I've done is follow you around and clean up. When do I get to make a mess of my own?"

Tucking his daggers away, Tylor smiled at the impatient elf, eyeing the sword strapped to his pack. "Patience, my friend. Have a look around. We're in another city, surrounded by who knows how many orcs, and most of them want to kill us. I believe the odds are heavily in your favor. Though if I had it my way, I'd never look upon another orc for the rest of my life. Besides, you already got one of those spiky swords. What more do you want?"

"I want to spray some blood. And yes, I got me a sword. But it wasn't my kill. I can't properly claim it until I've earned it!"

Inyalia approached the near dozen prisoners huddled near the far wall. Their arms and legs were bound by a thick abrasive rope that ran through iron cuffs. She searched their faces. Most were battered and underfed, but there were a few that appeared to still have some strength. They were likely new arrivals, though new or old was irrelevant. They were all frightened and confused. "Stay calm. We're going to get you out of here." Kneeling beside one of the elven women, Inyalia laid her hand upon her shoulder. "What happened here? Why were they holding you?"

The woman threw her arms around her savior. Sobbing onto Inyalia's shoulder, her words were nearly indistinguishable. "They started tes—us here and—that to us? The big one—tools he uses. My—killed my son—." A sickening pop ended her attempt.

The prisoners gasped, backing away as far as their bonds would allow.

Inyalia blinked in shock, staring at the thick piece of wood protruding from the woman's head. If it were about three times smaller, it would have resembled an arrow. Dropping the lifeless body, Inyalia's eyes fell to the doorway.

Three orcs stood at the entrance, their vicious weapons drawn and ready for blood. One carried the bow that had fired the shot. His hand was reaching for another bolt. A fourth stepped into view from around the corner.

Inyalia knew this had to be the Blackguard. He stood nearly a foot taller than the rest, and nearly as broad. How he'd been able to squeeze through the doorways was anybody's guess. Her attention shot to Tylor and Vansin, standing just inside. They were still, facing the orcs, petrified. Why hadn't they attacked? How did they not see the orcs coming? And most important, why were they just standing there now?

Desperate screams echoed inside Tylor's mind. He wanted to warn Inyalia. He wanted to do a great many things, but all attempts proved futile. He was a prisoner, trapped within his own body. How was this possible? He saw the orcs enter the hallway. He recognized the look of surprise upon their ugly pig faces. He'd tried to speak, tried to attack. But nothing happened. He couldn't move. The tether tightened around his neck, draining him of everything but life. It was a small thing, nearly invisible. But it was clearly there. The slither of green light resembled a blade of grass, but it shimmered. It extended from his neck, ending at something in the large orc's hand. If he could just find some way to cut it, perhaps that would free him.

Anger flooded Inyalia. She wanted to lash out. But even on her best day she couldn't land four killing shots in so little time, especially with the enemy so close. Granted, they'd have to rush her, which would allow at least two shots, but it wasn't enough. Their weapons would cut straight through her bow. And then she'd really be defenseless. If only she'd taken her sword training a little more serious. Perhaps then she'd have a fighting chance. Racing through her options, Inyalia was having trouble finding a way out of this.

Raemus stepped into the hall, seeing the orcs. Instinctively, he spun, extending his quarterstaff. It struck the big one in the back of the head. The shock nearly knocked the wooden weapon out of his hands. Worse yet, the orc shrugged it off, turning to face him. A sadistic smile settled upon him, and he felt something wrap around his neck.

Seeing the large orc turn, Inyalia knew this was her window. It was now or never. Leaping backward, Inyalia nocked and fired. The arrow landed in the closest orc's shoulder. It wasn't a killing blow, but it would keep him from striking Tylor. A second arrow flew, catching the archer in the chest. The dwarven arrowhead tore through the heavy breastplate, but it didn't sink as deep as she desired. The last of the three smaller orcs was nearly upon her. She was fortunate only one was able to enter at a time, but she was no match for their obvious strength. She had to end this one before he got to her.

Grabbing the last of her dwarven arrows, Inyalia nocked and fired. She watched the fletching twist as it left. The distance to its mark wasn't far, but it had to be precise. The orcish weapon swung, its razor-edge glimmering in the lowlight. Her arrow skimmed the blade. She saw the loose fibers of shaved wood and plume separate, but its path remained unchanged. The deadly weapon was nearly upon her. Just a few more inches and she'd be dead.

The bite of sharpened iron reached her. The blade impacted her left collar bone, retracting no sooner than it made contact. Not even her armor could have saved her had the arrow not struck. It hit the orc at the top lip of his breastplate, knocking him back as it tore through metal and sank deep. Inyalia picked herself up and nocked another arrow. The dying orc gasped as he took his final breath and fell still. She'd never forget the sound of his death throes as he weakly clawed at the arrow embedded in his chest.

The blackguard turned to face the puny elf. She'd wounded two of his guard and killed the third. That made her an excellent candidate for his tests. These other prisoners lacked the will to withstand his attempts. She would fare much better. Gripping the polished tool his master had given him, Ormik channeled another lasso and cast it at the young girl. He watched it sail across the room, opening just before it reached her.

Inyalia stared down her favorite arrow. The large orc was studying her. She could see the thoughts behind his eyes. That made him unique. She hadn't seen anything but the desire to kill in the others. Suddenly, the crystalline head exploded in a bright purple glow. Her arrow released as if it had a mind of its own. The glow revealed a whip-like strand headed straight for her, but it wasn't moving anymore. It was frozen, trapped within the bright light. For the briefest moment, time was still. And then, as the arrow swallowed the strand, it went after its true target.

Fear overcame Ormik. How did she destroy the lasso? How did she even know about it? Most couldn't see it until it had already taken hold. Even then it required an uncanny perception. Ormik trembled. He felt the power of his tool urging him to obey. That was the curse of using it. He was slave to it, as it allowed him to enslave others. His hand brought the tool to bare. He couldn't help himself. Shielding his face, his fear evaporated, replaced by pain. The purple headed arrow struck the crystal object, shattering it into hundreds of tiny pieces. The jagged shards tore into his arm as the arrow ripped through his hand. All his worry and pain faded as the glowing head struck him between the eyes. Ormik fell backward, unable to move. His body spasmed, but he had no control of it. He was a slave no longer. The device was gone. All those he'd tortured were free. And now, finally, so was he.

Tylor collapsed beside Vansin. Seeing the two remaining orcs, he leapt onto the closest one, embedding his daggers. It took three stabs before it finally collapsed.

Having his first opportunity for a fight, Vansin charged the wounded orc. His morningstar connected before he could unsling his shield. A spray of dark ichor spattered across the wall. Throwing all his weight into the charge, Vansin managed to knock the beast aside. It crumbled, holding the side of its head in despair. Again, Vansin struck, the spikes of his weapon destroying the creature's hand. It mashed into its head, spurting blood across the elf's face. A sadistic laughter escaped the warrior. Again, he swung, and again. There was little more than pieces of cracked skull and brain matter, but he kept swinging. Tasting the blood on his lips, Vansin spun around, finding a new target. He leapt atop the one Tylor had killed, bringing his shield down on its throat. Hammering it, the head came free, torn and gruesome. Looking around, he wanted more. He needed more. Unfortunately, none were left.

Tylor backed away from the blood sodden elf. Putting his daggers away, he raised his hands and slowly inched toward the warrior. "Easy, Vansin. You'll get your chance for more. But you have to control yourself now."

A hearty laugh escaped the warrior. "I haven't lost my mind yet. Believe me, you'll know if I do. And just a heads up. If that happens, don't come near me. Just point me at the people you want dead and let me go. I'll come back when I'm done."

"Good to know." Tylor turned toward Inyalia and entered the room. Kneeling in front of her, he inspected to make sure she wasn't hurt. "Are you okay? What the hell happened?"

Inyalia picked herself up. "Yeah, I'm fine. I guess Kael's magic is still in my arrow. I thought it was all gone when it opened the portal for us."

"I got that part. I mean, how did he control us like that? And if they have the ability to do that, how can we hope to fight it? We don't all have magic arrows that will explode at the last minute."

"I don't know, Tylor. I think it had something to do with the box he was holding. We should take the pieces just in case. Either way, we'll just have to take it a day at a time." Collecting the arrows that were worth salvaging, her favorite among them, Inyalia turned her attention to the prisoners. It was going to take a while to remove the ropes, but once she freed a few, they could free the rest.

Raemus entered the room. "You guys need to see this." He led them across the hall to the two prisoners sitting in the floor. They remained where he'd left them, but their eyes were now open, staring blankly straight ahead.

"What's wrong with them?" Tylor waved his hand in front of the elf's face. He looked somewhat familiar, but he couldn't place it.

"I don't know. Never seen anything like—"

Inyalia was the last to enter. She'd cut the two strongest free, directing them to help the others. Taking position between Tylor and Raemus, she set eyes on the pair. "Baal!" Forcing her way between the two, she threw her arms around her brother. "Oh, Baal, I knew you were still alive!"

Eyes locked on the wall, Baal didn't budge. He was clearly breathing, but he never once blinked.

"Inyalia, something's not right here." Tylor attempted to pull her away. It was no use.

"Get off me!" Inyalia snapped, locking her arms. She'd found him. And she wasn't about to let go.

"Inyalia, please."

"It's like they're in some kind of trance. I've known monks who enter similar states. But never this deep." Raemus inspected the human.

"It's kind of like that thing the big orc did to us." Vansin interjected.

"Exactly!"

"But that means—." Tylor drew his daggers and looked toward the door.

"What?" Inyalia turned her attention to Tylor, keeping hold of her brother. "What's it mean?"

Tylor crept toward the opening, stealing a glance down the hall. It was clear save for the few prisoners who started to gather. "We were released when this one died." Kneeling, he checked for a pulse. Finding none, he got back to his feet. "If these two are still enthralled, there has to be another blackguard around here somewhere."

"We should leave. Now that we know what's happening, we can come back in force and end it." Vansin approached Tylor at the door.

"I hate to admit it, but I agree. There are too many unknown variables happening here. And we've found quite a few prisoners. We can only help so many at a time." Raemus ran his hand around the frozen human, careful not to touch him. He couldn't feel any poisons, but that didn't mean they weren't suffering from other afflictions. His skills were limited to natural ailments. Magical affects and curses were beyond him.

"We've found Baal. That's all I wanted. If he can't move, we'll just have to carry him." Inyalia got to her feet, releasing him for the first time. "Let's gather the others and head back."

"Most are strong enough to walk, but a few need assistance. I'll do what I can for them." Raemus started toward the door.

"How do you expect us to carry them and fight? Vansin asked.

"Maybe some of the other prisoners can help?" Tylor glanced at the steady train gathering before them. "Okay, here's the plan. I'll see if some of the stronger prisoners will help us carry them. Raemus, collect Lorena and get the rest into the sewers. Maybe Lorena's made some progress with the wards and she can use her skills to make sure that happens without incident. They'll have to stay quiet or all of this will have been for nothing. Vansin, Inyalia, and I will take the rear, making sure no one follows us. Any questions?" Taking their nods as approval, Tylor turned his attention to the prisoners. "You, you, and you. Can you help us carry a few people?"

Inyalia ran her hand over her brother's head, patting down his unkempt hair. She'd never seen him so disheveled. His long brown hair had been hastily chopped, leaving it uneven and patchy. He'd never been plump, but his skin sagged from his boney face and arms. She had no doubt the rest of him was the same. He needed food and water. And likely, many days rest once she got him out of here. Throwing his arm over her shoulder, she pulled him up.

The moment Baal's body moved, a blood curdling scream escaped his mouth. "Intruders! Intruders are here! Summon the guard!"

"Baal, it's me! It's Inyalia!" Inyalia released him, moving so he could see her. "It's me!" Tears flowed down her cheeks. What had they done to him?

The human began to shout, repeating Baal's words. In unison, they began to echo. The words could be heard elsewhere, throughout the complex. Some resounded on the floor above, others, below. But it was always the same words, timed near perfectly after the initial outburst. The pair before them went silent for a moment. And, standing, they began anew.

Baal grabbed the dagger from Inyalia's waist, swiping wildly around him.

Wasting no time, Vansin rushed across the room. "Forgive me, girly." Bringing his fist across Baal's cheek, he collapsed into silent slumber, dropping the dagger. Instinctively, he backhanded the human, knocking him from his feet. It took another hit to knock him out.

The ceiling shook, rhythmic with the sound of rushing boots.

"Just great. They've alerted the whole damn place!" Vansin fumed, heaving the unconscious elf to his shoulder. "Come on. Get the other one. We have to leave now!" Vansin handed Baal off to one of the prisoners and drew his morningstar and shield.

The remaining two ran over and collected the human.

Inyalia sat stunned, watching it all happen. Why did Baal not recognize her?

Tylor approached and knelt beside her. "Inyalia, I know this is hard for you, but we have to move. They'll kill us if we stay."

"Come on!" Vansin shouted, following the rush of prisoners making for the exit.

Pulling her to her feet, Tylor and Inyalia took position behind the others. Passing the room where Lorena had waited, she was nowhere to be seen.

"I hope Lorena and Raemus made it out." Inyalia could hear the footsteps getting louder. They sounded like they were right above them.

"They're leading the way. Just stay close. We can't afford any more setbacks."

Reaching the stairs, thick bolts began to rain from the sky.

Inyalia stole a glance behind her. She didn't know how many orcs were present, but there were more than she could count in a split second. One of the arrows passed by her face. She could feel the wind off it. Had it not been for Tylor pulling her aside, it would have ended her right there.

They ran down the stairs as fast as they could, reaching the ground floor. Guttural curses spewed behind them, accompanied by arrows. The orcs were gaining. At this pace, they'd be upon them by the time they reached the main door.

"Look out!" Tylor twisted and sliced, knocking an arrow out of flight.

Seizing the moment, Inyalia fired, hitting her target. The orc tumbled down the stairs, tripping a few others. It wasn't much, but every little bit helped.

Light filled the corridor as the door came open. The sounds of battle could be heard outside.

Firing another arrow, Inyalia heard the crowd of people moving again. She didn't have time to look. The last thing she wanted to do was waste valuable time checking behind her, only to run into someone.

Vansin batted an arrow away from him, ready for the beasts to advance. They were doing so, but slowly. It seemed they had some tactics in them after all. They were bottlenecked in this hall. All advancing would do would interrupt the steady flow of arrows. "It's times like this, I wish I had my crossbow!"

"If it's any consolation, I wish you had it too." Tylor dodged a bolt, hearing it impact one of the prisoners behind him. Stealing a glance, one of the elven women had been unfortunate. She was already dead. "With any luck, Gilea's putting it to good use outside."

"Fall back!" Vansin shouted, seeing the hall rapidly emptying. Most of the prisoners had made it out. Though at least five had been hit, including the human he'd knocked out. There was no saving them now. If they weren't already dead, it would be a kinder mercy to make it quick.

Inyalia was down to six arrows. Backing away, she stepped over a body, narrowly tripping. It was fortunate. She released just as an orcish arrow was headed toward her. The heads collided, sending both to the floor.

Bodies littered the ground around them. All were dead but one. The human had woken up. He was shouting about the intruders. Grabbing Vansin's legs, the warrior ended his suffering with a single blow.

They reached the door, hearing combat right behind them. The orcs ahead had stopped firing and were now advancing into the hall. Filtered sunlight fell upon them as they stepped outside.

Inyalia fired a last shot through the crack. The green head impacted the metal armor of the encroaching horde and bounced harmlessly to the floor. Her face sank as the door sealed. She'd hoped it had been one of the enchanted arrows. It was the last blunt tip she had.

A large explosion shook the ground, throwing chunks of orc and rubble alike into the closed doors. Instinctively, Inyalia threw her weight against the wooden barriers, holding them shut. She could still hear movement, inside, but it would slow them a bit.

A hearty laugh echoed from Vansin. "Well done, girly! I'm glad you finally did something useful!" He clapped her on the back and stepped between her and the door. Dropping his shield, he stuffed it between the bronze handles. It was a tight fit, but that's what he'd hoped for. With any luck it would keep those inside from flanking them. Lofting the spiked mace, he spun around to see what kind of trouble they were facing at their escape.

Raemus held off two orcs. The iron port was wide open. A few of the prisoners failed to make it into the hole, but it appeared most had succeeded. Lorena was nowhere to be seen. With any luck, she was halfway to the exit by now.

Charging, the warrior swung his morningstar. It caught one of the orcs by surprise, delivering a damaging, but sadly not fatal blow.

Inyalia chose her target. More orcs were running toward the sound of battle, and likely her explosion. She really should have considered that beforehand, but it was the best option to slow their approach. Releasing the string, she watched the wooden missile sink to the fletching. The orc collapsed in the street. She was down to four arrows, including her favorite.

A loud crash echoed from the college doors. The orcs had recovered and were battering at them.

Tylor inspected the shield. The wood and iron were beginning to separate. It wouldn't hold much longer. Surveying their options, he counted five orcs across the street, running toward them. Inyalia had just felled one. The two between Vansin and Raemus would be dispatched any moment, and the horde behind the doors would be free after another hit. He had to buy them time to escape. Turning to Inyalia, he gently placed his hand upon the side of her face, drawing her attention to him. "Inyalia, this was not your fault. You followed your heart to save your brother, and you were right. He was alive. Remember that. You were right."

"Tylor, what are you saying?"

He smiled and removed his hand. Tylor turned and flung his dwarven dagger. It flipped end over end, sinking to the hilt in the side of Vansin's opponent's head. Running down the stairs, he jumped, burying his other blade in Raemus's target. Retracting both blades, he charged toward the approaching group. "Get out of here, now!"

Another crash echoed from the door. The band holding the shield together came free and a piece of wood split. It wouldn't survive another impact.

"Tylor!" Inyalia launched an arrow into the orcs. She couldn't see where it hit. Tylor was in her path. He swiped and swatted, spun and rolled. Nothing could be seen but a swath of blades and blood.

More orcs came around the corner. He was outnumbered twelve to one. Tylor ducked one of the wicked weapons, sinking both daggers into the brute. Abandoning them, he ripped the jagged sword from the creature's hand and put it to work against the others.

"Come on, girly. We have to go before they get through." Vansin pulled her toward the hole.

"No! We have to help him!" Tears spilled down her face. She fired at one of the new orcs, though it didn't do any good. His sword sliced Tylor across the chest.

"You don't want to see this." Vansin begged, trying to pull her away.

Tylor was losing strength. His reflexes were slowing. Another sword swipe spun him around. His eyes met Inyalia's.

She watched, helpless as a sword erupted from his chest. He winced, but his eyes never fell from her. Another sword impaled him, knocking him to his knees. She could see the tears in his eyes. Those tears were all that mattered. The orcs abandoning him were of no concern. The exploding doors behind her were irrelevant. Vansin and Raemus dragging her away didn't matter. She had one focus, and that was the love of a man who'd given everything to protect her. She could hear his words, though he didn't say them. It was all in his eyes. "Inyalia, I love you!" It was powerful, raw. And it meant everything. But it could never be. Not before. And not now. Her eyes locked on his, he smiled. A smile that remained when the orcish weapon severed his head from shoulder.

"No!" Inyalia screamed, struggling against her companions. Tylor disappeared from her sight. It wasn't until she landed in the fetid water that she realized they'd thrown her into the sewer. And without help, there was no climbing out on her own.

Waiting for Vansin and Raemus to drop, Lorena slid the grate closed. Hearing it click into place, she snapped her wrist, reactivating the sealing ward. "We need to go. Most of the prisoners are already through. Gilea's waiting on the other side."

They ran as fast as their legs could carry them. Inyalia ran as well, but only because they were pulling her. She was numb, her senses dulled. She couldn't even cry right now.

Loud crashes and hurried boots rushed overhead. Some of the orcs had managed to remove the iron covers, but they were too large to climb into the tunnels. Instead, they blindly fired, hoping to take out as many of the scurrying rats as they could.

Inyalia saw the exit just ahead. They were nearly there, but it didn't feel like a victory. She'd claimed her brother. But he clearly wasn't himself. And it cost her more than she'd been prepared to pay. How could she have let this happen? Inyalia crawled through the tunnel, being urged forward by Raemus.

Reaching the other side, Gilea stood a short distance away. The crossbow was aimed at the top of the wall, firing as rapidly as he could load it. He was shouting, but Inyalia couldn't hear what he said. There was a dull ringing that blocked out everything.

A flash of light caught Inyalia's attention. She turned just as Lorena's portal opened. Only a handful of prisoners remained in addition to their little band. Inyalia stared at the glowing orange ring, displaying the ranger's stronghold just beyond. She wasn't sure she wanted to go through. It would take her away from Tylor. Away from a love that could never be. Perhaps it would even take her away from herself.

Arrows planked the ground around her. Glancing back, she saw the orcs lining the parapets. Another group swarmed from the road. They were closing in. A part of her wanted them to come. At least then she wouldn't feel so empty inside.

Shouting faces were all around her. Lorena, Gilea, Vansin, Raemus, all of them were trying to get her attention, but she couldn't hear them. The ringing was too deafening.

A sudden and forceful shove launched her into the portal, solidifying her mistakes.

The story will continue in Fall of the Nightking

Be sure to stay up to date with the newest Eldarlands books at
http://www.levisamuel.com

Please leave a review at your online retailer.

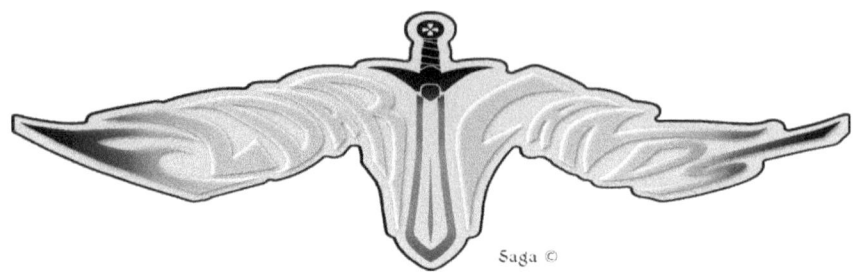

Saga ©

Continue the Adventure

Heroes of Order Trilogy

Whispered schemes of an imprisoned god call the wicked Dreualfar from their subterranean lair. Like a plague, they spread across the surface, waging war where they can find it.

But when chaos ensues, a band of mercenaries step forward to restore order. Armed with a unique collection of skills, and a deeply knotted history, the Dreuslayers dive into shadow to confront the enemies of Dalmoura head-on.

What began as a simple job quickly escalates into a battle for the ages. Will good triumph over evil? Or will the Dreualfar succeed in releasing their dark master?

Find out in the first trilogy of the Eldarlands Saga.

Author's Notes

In many ways this is both the first and last book I've written. Explaining the last is easy. It's the most recent. But explaining the first is a bit more complicated.

I didn't know it at the time, but the first book I ever wrote was never going to go anywhere. I learned a lot from it. It shaped the foundations of the writer I am today. It was the writing of that book that allowed me to connect with so many others in the entertainment industry and begin my quest down this often trying and exhilarating path of authorhood. It provided questions which I didn't know to ask. Those questions gave answers that opened the doorway to some of my most influential resources. For that, I will always cherish my first book. But it would never be published. There were far too many mistakes.

This career choice has been packed full of mistakes. Many of them I didn't recognize as such until I gained the experience to know otherwise. And while I strive to minimize them in the future, I'm sure I'll continue to make a great many more.

My original concept for this book was a rework of my first. I knew I'd have to rewrite most of it, but I'd hoped to be able to salvage a fair amount. That wasn't the case, though I'll spare you the long and complex reasons as to why. What matters is the story you hold here is entirely new, woven into my Eldarlands Saga. For me, this book is a new beginning, though not just as an entry point into the world I've created.

Throughout life we go through a number of changes. Some are physical. Our bodies age and change shape. Muscles come and go. Our sight and hearing alter for various reasons. But its our experiences that truly shape us. Sometimes a simple thought can make us question everything we know. I don't plan to get too detailed on this as it's a rather large rabbit hole to follow. But I will say that I've stumbled upon many of these questions during the writing of this book. They've shifted my mindset, allowing me to see things differently than I once did. Whether that had any impact on the story itself, I can't say. I was simply writing a story that I believe people will enjoy, while expanding upon the world I've built. But the truth is, I've experienced many firsts with this book.

I started scheming this story some time ago, though I can't remember exactly when. Some of my notes go back a few years. But I didn't start writing it until May of 2018. With the rapid release of the Heroes of Order Trilogy from September to November, I'd planned to finish this and have it ready by December. As so often happens, life had other plans.

My grandfather is currently 83 years old. His wife passed away in North Carolina a few years ago and he decided to return home to the little town in Arkansas where he grew up. I had a few memories there as a kid, visiting relatives and enjoying life as children so often do. But my experiences there later in life were somewhat limited.

Grandpa wanted to come home. So we built him a cabin. He moved in and was doing well for a while. But his time in solitude had an impact. Slowly, he began to slip away. He started spending every day between his bed and the TV. Hoping to get him active again, we build him a shop. We came to visit as often as possible and to keep him company, as well as help out around the place. But it wasn't enough. We had our own lives and responsibilities to attend. And in our absence, Grandpa continued to withdraw.

Near the middle of November, we had to make a decision. His memory was failing. He'd forget to eat. And when he did, it was little more than cookies and milk. He quit showering and using soaps altogether. And on more than one occasion, he'd endangered himself. He could no longer remain unobserved. But the options were few.

My family holds freedom among the most valuable things in this world. Being trapped is one of the worst fates imaginable. It's for that reason, among others that we knew he wouldn't survive in a nursing home. There was no way we could do that to him. Additionally, both my mother and aunt were only a few short years away from retirement. It made no sense for either of them to give that up to take care of him fulltime. Though if no other option was available, either of them would gladly have done so.

It fell to my siblings and I. My youngest sister is getting married in May, conveniently the same weekend this book will release. And the other is nearly finished with her degree and looking at a future in Florida. My brother is autistic, which ruled him out. That left only me. Of us, I was the logical choice.

I'd spent the past ten years building my platform with the intention of surviving solely on my writing profits. At the time of writing this, it still hasn't happened. But by accepting the mantle and moving to Arkansas to take care of my grandfather, I wouldn't have to worry so much about making enough money to pay the rent. There was a bit more to consider than that but, it also gave me an opportunity. By being free of regular employment, without having to worry about survival, I would have more time to write and improve my craft. These are the exact things I've been striving to do, but they came in a manner I did not expect.

The last weekend of November, my daughter and I moved. It's been a trying experience. Grandpa can be quite stubborn. But once the initial settling in happened, and a routine was established, it became much easier. My daughter's grades have improved drastically. I don't have to fight her to get up and go to school. And the freedom away from the city cannot be matched. Though I'll admit I've found it difficult to focus on my writing. There are numerous distractions to contend with when you're taking care of a ten-year-old girl. Add an 83-year-old man with dementia to the mix and you'll be on your toes, or dragging them, pretty much every hour of every day.

Since our move, I haven't pushed my career as hard as I would prefer. I need to push as hard as possible. I know I'm on borrowed time. Grandpa isn't going to last forever. As difficult as it is to consider, one day I'm going to attempt to wake him for breakfast and he isn't going to wake. I know this. I'm prepared for this. My only hope is I've made enough of an impact on enough people before that day comes to continue my existence here. If it weren't for all the damn bugs I'd say its about perfect. I've found comfort in this place. And with any luck that comfort will translate into more books written, more fans obtained, and maybe, eventually, I'll be able to get all these stories out of my head and onto paper. I look forward to seeing what new ideas appear once the old ones have blossomed.

That said, I hope you've enjoyed this book. It's the result of many months of exhaustion and dedication. I literally made myself ill trying to get it finished on time. I rewrote many chapters many times over, all to make it the best book I can currently write. I felt love for the characters. I cursed their poor decisions. And I urged them on when all hope seemed lost. And now that the dominos are arranged, prepare yourself. They're going to come crashing down in the next installment.

I ask but one favor. Whether you enjoyed this book or not, I hope you'll consider leaving a review with any online retailer. Whether you give it one star or five, reviews tell me how I can improve my craft. They help other readers to decide if a book is worth their time. And in many cases, they're one of the biggest contributing factors to any author's success or failure.

Thank you for reading my work. I hope I've made a lifelong fan.

Levi Samuel
March 2019